Rebecca hesitantly waited to discover why Bright Arrow had led her to this secluded spot so far from the Oglala camp. He stepped away from her to allow his gaze to leisurely and thoroughly study her from head to foot. She quietly submitted to this intense scrutiny, trembling at its unsettling effect upon her.

His gaze riveted to her panicked eyes. He came forward; she backed away, instinctively sensing some vital drama about to unfold. He chuckled mischievously when her back made contact with the rocks, preventing any further retreat from him and the inevitable. She gasped in surprise and swallowed loudly, fearing the bold intentions she was reading within those hypnotic black eyes which roguishly enticed her.

She held her breath as his hand came forward to stroke her silky hair and satiny skin. His touch was gentle, but disturbing. As if mesmerized, she rigidly watched as his face came toward hers. She trembled and tingled as his mouth claimed hers, tenderly plundering and deftly explorin

JANELLE TAYLOR

Tender Ecstasy

ZEBRA BOOKS
KENSINGTON PUBLISHING CORP.

ZEBRA BOOKS

are published by

Kensington Publishing Corp.
475 Park Avenue South
New York, NY 10016

Tenth printing: December, 1991

Printed in the United States of America

For Deeny A. and Joyce P., whose echoes of encouragement never fail to inspire me.

ACKNOWLEDGMENT TO:

Hiram C. Owen of Sisseton, South Dakota for all his help and understanding with the Sioux language and facts about the great and inspiring Sioux Nation.

Thank you.

ECHOES OF YESTERDAY

Hark, what strange madrigal do I hear,
Chanting loudly with messages to fear,
Spanning the distance o'er land and time,
Carrying deadly secrets—both yours and mine.

Cruelly it plays o'er the landscape of our life,
Severing our hearts with a two-sided knife,
Traipsing o'er mountains of fervent emotion,
Echoing across valleys like a golden ocean.

Its melody beginning so soft and low,
Rapidly and surely it begins to grow.
Louder and deadlier its notes begin;
Where and how will the ominous song end?

Telling of a love which began in the past;
It cries out in anguish, Too fragile to last?
Secrets to unmask, tales to unfold . . .
Destroying those lives in its rigid control.

As closer it dances, its demands shine clearer,
Deeds of our past reflected in life's mirror.
Both friend and foe sing courageously
And end the drama in tender ecstasy . . .

Janelle Taylor

"What treaty that the white man ever made with us have they kept? Not one. When I was a boy the Sioux owned the world; the sun rose and set on their land; they sent ten thousand men to battle. Where are the warriors today? Who slew them? Where are our lands? Who owns them? . . . . What law have I broken? Is it wrong for me to love my own? Is it wicked for me because my skin is red? Because I am a Sioux; because I was born where my father lived; because I would die for my people and my country?"

— Chief Sitting Bull

Prologue

In the spring of 1776, a beautiful and gentle English girl entered the rugged Dakota Territory along with a wagon train led by a white scout, Joe Kenny. The journey was long and arduous, and ended in tragedy for all but the young woman, Alisha Williams, and the daring scout.

Alisha Williams was caught and enslaved by a powerful warrior who tormented her with his kindness and his brutality. Finally, the indomitable and proud Sioux Indian, Gray Eagle, was able to confess his love to his white slave. Together, they resolved that their forbidden love would somehow overcome all the savagery of the frontier that tried to part them.

It took over a year of pain and sacrifice for the two young lovers to find happiness together, but the Great Spirit Wakantanka smiled upon the invincible Gray Eagle and his courageous white captive Alisha Williams. With the help of their friend, Joe Kenny, the two lovers were able to settle their differences. The two were able to marry according to Indian tradition and the white bride was accepted as a half-Indian princess, Shalee.

It was early June of 1777, and Joe was taking his leave of his friends. He grinned in satisfaction as he watched the two lovers embrace, smiling into each other's eyes. He listened as they told him of their expected child, a child who would embody the best of two worlds. He chuckled mirthfully as he related his own good news to Shalee, "I think you know the girl I'm going to marry as soon as I make it back to St. Louis: Mary O'Hara. She'll make a fine wife for a man like me. We've known each other for years. We talk through that sign language I taught her. Got her waiting for my return. If she wasn't mute, she'd be singing about now."

"No one deserves happiness more than you, dear Joe. You've saved my life many times and now you bring great joy and peace into our lives. I'll never forget you. I hope you and Mary are just as fortunate and happy as we are." She cast her virile husband a look of smoldering desire and deep love.

Gray Eagle returned his wife's radiant smile as he spoke to his white friend, "I also wish you much happiness, Koda Joe. I owe you much for bringing us such joy and peace. In time our love would have come to view, but only after much more sadness and pain. We endured too much suffering when Shalee lived as Alisha. But the past is dead now. Come and bring your new wife to see our child when he is born, for he will be the best from both our kinds. The blood of the Indian and the white will join within our child. My wife has spoken the truth, for not all whites are bad," he admitted with a rueful grin as he gazed at Princess Shalee and then at his friend Joe Kenny. "Truce would be easy if all whites were like you two." They all laughed.

Joe's heart sang with joy and relief as he watched the look of love and desire which passed between the English girl and the mighty Sioux warrior. The season for new beginnings had arrived. As Princess Shalee left the two men to return to their tepee, Joe faced his friend to bid him farewell. "This past year has been difficult for many people, Wanmdi Hota. At last the problems between you and Alisha—" he promptly corrected himself, "Princess Shalee have been settled. It's funny how things work out sometimes. Who would have ever imagined Alisha Williams was a Blackfoot princess who'd been kidnapped as a baby from her people? I'm glad for both of you it worked out this way. She wasn't ever meant to be a white slave, not even to the awesome Gray Eagle," he jested. "I've never seen any two people love each other more than you two do," he remarked with sincerity and warmth.

"What of you, Koda Joe? You will soon join a woman. Do you not feel these same fires of love?" Gray Eagle teased his companion, dismissing the reality of his wife's white blood for all time. No one would ever learn the truth of how Alisha was accepted. Alisha was now viewed and accepted as Princess Shalee; and from this moon forward, she would cease to be Alisha Williams.

"It's different between me and Mary," Joe confessed. He explained his hasty and unexpected marriage to the powerful warrior beside him, "Mary O'Hara's only seventeen and she can't speak, but she's a good and gentle creature, Wanmdi Hota. I've known her for years. She's had a hard life in Jamie's roadhouse; she's like a white slave to that evil uncle of hers. She's in deep trouble right now; she's pregnant. The man she loved was killed before he could marry her. Watching you and Shalee, I've learned what I've been missing all these years alone. I think it's about time I settle down."

"You could accept the child of another man as your own?" the warrior asked in surprise. "What of her remaining love for this dead man?"

"In time, I'm hoping she'll forget him. But I can't allow her and her child to suffer for a foolish mistake."

"Love is a powerful force," Gray Eagle said. "But often it does not die as easily or quickly as a man. It will be harder for you to forget his ghost if you knew him."

"Yep, I knew him all right," he admitted sullenly. "You did, too," he added before thinking.

"How is it possible I knew him?" Gray Eagle asked.

Joe hesitated and shifted apprehensively. "I don't think we should discuss him."

Gray Eagle eyed his friend pensively. "I do not understand. A koda can trust another koda with the truth and with his life."

"The girl I'm marrying carries the child of Powchutu," he reluctantly informed the stalwart man beside him. "Before you say anything, let me explain," he hastily continued at the look of rage and hostility which stormed across the handsome features of Gray Eagle. Powchutu was the half-breed who had left Gray Eagle for dead in order to keep Alisha for himself. "Mary met Powchutu while he was pretending to be Alisha's brother. When Alisha refused to marry him, he turned to Mary. Of all people, you know how cunning and persuasive he was. She's young and innocent; she honestly loved him. From what I've learned, he was actually going to marry her. But he was killed before he learned about the baby. Mary has enough troubles being in the hands of that evil O'Hara and being unable to talk; she doesn't need to add another problem with a fatherless child. As far as anyone will know, the child will be mine."

. "What about Shalee? Does she know of this unborn child of Powchutu's?" the warrior demanded, envisioning that half-breed scout who had nearly destroyed his love.

"No. And I don't think she ever should. He was like a brother to her, no matter the suffering he brought into her life with his obsessive love. Powchutu's dead; the child will be mine," Joe firmly declared.

"As you say, Koda Joe. This will remain a secret from my wife. I do not wish her to ever hear his name again. If he still lived, I would slay him myself!"

Many months passed. During February of 1778 in the domain of the Eagle, the Great Spirit delivered a son to the famed warrior Gray Eagle and Princess Shalee. As the illustrious warrior leaned over to kiss the moist brow of his beloved wife, he stated in a clear voice laced with love and pride, "We shall call him Bright Arrow, Grass Eyes. He will grow straight and fly true like his name; he will be the shining light which will lead the Oglala to greatness after I am no longer chief."

During August of that same year, far to the East in the wilderness near the central section of the Missouri Territory, Joe Kenny and Mary O'Hara Kenny delighted in the birth of their daughter Rebecca. Mary lovingly observed her rugged husband as he held his daughter for the first time, laying to rest the bittersweet memories of the half-breed scout who had once controlled her life. For one last time, she grieved over her two dead loves and for what was never meant to be. This tiny Rebecca would reveal the love and loyalty she owed this gentle man whom she had wisely married last July. It was over now; she would never visit those two graves again.

Both children grew and learned under the guidance and influence of their parents and peoples. During the next seventeen years, many changes took place in the frontier and in the lives of those two children, children from different worlds. At fifteen, Rebecca Kenny's world was torn assunder by the tragic deaths of her parents from cholera. In a near daze, she was taken to live with her great-uncle in St. Louis, helplessly following in the footsteps of her mother as a scorned free laborer to Jamie O'Hara. But far away to the west, the son of Gray Eagle and Shalee grew tall and strong, a vital and happy child. Chief Running Wolf died, making Gray Eagle chief of the mighty Oglala Sioux, placing Bright Arrow next in line for that powerful rank.

Over this span of years, a massive surge of white settlers and soldiers flooded the Indian territories. Atrocities and hatred increased; the racial war seemed endless. Great Britain, Alisha

Williams's motherland, had been defeated by the American Colonies and had granted them independence. This truce opened the path for numerous white settlers to spread westward. The hard journey created a new type of American settler: one who was as daring and defiant as the intrepid Sioux whom he boldly and recklessly confronted. A bitter clash resulted from the head-on confrontation between these two powerful forces. Tragic defeat was inevitable for one side or the other.

In the spring of 1796, Princess Shalee is thirty-seven years old. Even so, her beauty seems to increase with the passage of time. At forty-three, Gray Eagle is still an indomitable warrior. He is on constant guard against those evil white forces which could take his lands and slay those he loves. How he wishes the days were as peaceful as they were before this heavy influx of whites and Bluecoats. But he knows times will never be that way again. But neither can there be truce and safety. He longs for other children which Shalee has been unable to give him. Each time his only son Bright Arrow faces grave danger, he fears what life would be without him; and fear is a repulsive sign of weakness in a brave.

Bright Arrow has gradually and inevitably become a noted warrior whose courage almost matches that of his legendary father. At eighteen, he is very much a man: virile, handsome, powerful, and self-assured. At his father's side, they fiercely struggle to withhold their lands from the rapidly advancing white man. Unaware of his mother's real identity, he believes his beloved mother is the half-breed daughter of Chief Black Cloud. He has never questioned the fluent English which his father and mother have taught him, a cunning weapon to be used against his white enemies.

In May of this portentous year, another wagon train heads westward toward the Dakota Territory from St. Louis. The seventeen-year-old Rebecca Kenny is forced to accompany her cruel and deceitful great uncle on this fated journey to establish a new roadhouse and trading post at Pierre. The golden-skinned, auburn-haired, tawny-eyed beauty finds herself at the mercy of her cruel kinsman. Orphaned and penniless, she plots to escape his evil plans for her as their perilous trek into the wilderness continues.

As if foreseeing the deadly fate in store for both the white man and the Indian, an ominous song imperceptibly sings above the cries of pain and the shouts of hostility, a mesmeric chant which calls both friend and foe into a new and fatal drama. Spanning time and distance, the mystic melody begins its ominous notes, ever increasing its volume. Its sound reverberates across the savage frontier. Its echoes of hatred and revenge are heard throughout the forests and prairies, threatening this new generation of forbidden lovers and challenging the two hearts whose love has surpassed all difficulties these past eighteen years. . . .

Chapter One

"Weren't you warned not to stray so far from camp?" Captain Jake Selby's voice cut into Rebecca's thoughts. "If you can't obey orders, then I'll confine you to camp!"

She whirled to face him, anger and resentment sparkling vividly in her eyes. "Then order your men to stop gaping at me!" she protested in annoyance, the soldiers' offensive behavior pushing her beyond control.

Amused chuckles greeted her ears and grated upon her already frayed nerves. "You can hardly blame them for admiring a beautiful woman," he playfully chided her, his own eyes branded with undisguised lust as they surveyed her from auburn head to dainty foot. "It gets mighty lonesome out here," he murmured in a suggestive tone, a lecherous grin tugging at the corners of his wide mouth.

She glared at him, then asserted contemptuously, "I was told that was the reason for bringing along those other two ladies," a definite tone of scorn placed upon the last word.

Rebecca grew rosy just recalling the lewdness she had witnessed along this tormenting journey from St. Louis to Fort Dakota. She was not a fool; she knew this man—as well as many others—had made loathsome offers to her despicable great-uncle for her so-called "services." She hated them all! She raged against the fate which had taken her parents' lives, leaving her defenseless and penniless and heartbroken, placing her in the guileful hands of her insidious kinsman.

"Come now, Miss Kenny; you're the only real lady hereabouts," he rebuked her. A lazy half-grin ensnared his full lips as he submitted his repugnant solution to her dilemma, "You know my generous offer of protection stands clear anytime you wish to claim it. You caught my eye the first time I saw you. You wouldn't have any worries at all with me," he promised, allowing his reprehensible gaze to rove over her tempting body and beautiful face once more.

Rebecca stared at him, barely containing her disdain. She studied him for a short time. Not that Jake wasn't nice-looking or doubtlessly the best choice of the entire troop, but he was too brash and coarse. A streak of savage ruthlessness and deadly over-confidence exuded from him. He was detestable, dangerous.

Jake had previously made it indelicately clear that she could not long elude him and his amorous plans for her. Dread seized her innocent heart until she felt she could hardly breathe. Only her lucid eyes exhibited these emotions which the defiant, proud tilt of her dainty chin sought to conceal.

"If your dear uncle has his way, you'll end up far worse than you would with me," he taunted her.

Admittedly Jake was correct, but she puffed up indignantly and bravely refuted his tactless words, "Don't be ridiculous, Captain Selby! Uncle Jamie would never treat me in such a crude and offensive manner. Besides, I find such nasty talk as repulsive as such vulgar conduct. You forget your rank and manners, sir," she boldly rebuked him with the hope he would drop this line of conversation. When mocking laughter filled her ears, she tartly added, "If it's female companionship you seek, I suggest you return to camp and visit the wagon of Lucy and Kate."

His jovial laughter died instantly. He scanned her taut body and pink face. "You strike me as a smart girl, Rebecca; so don't pretend you believe what you just said," he acidly scolded her. "As for that mealy-mouthed uncle of yours, he would sell his own mother to my men if a good offer was made! When the time comes, which it will, I doubt you will find me as 'repulsive' then as you think you do now," he smugly gloated, a knowing leer playing ominously upon his full lips and wickedly shining in his green eyes. "I desire much more from you than your charming body and eager responses in my bunk. I want my own private stock who has more to offer than a tasty body and a lusty appetite. I want a female who is just as valuable out of the bedroll as in it. I want a female who knows nothing of men, one who can be trained to pleasure me in the ways I choose," he brazenly listed his demands to an open-mouthed, wide-eyed, stunned girl of seventeen.

"How dare you speak to me in this disgusting manner! Uncle Jamie will severely reprimand you for this unforgivable conduct!" she nearly shrieked at him as her voice returned and her senses cleared. What a horrid man he was!

Jake threw back his head and chortled in sinister amusement. Gluing his eyes on her alluring face, he informed the girl, "I dare because it will soon be too late to fulfill my wishes, my vixen. Jamie's getting old and his greedy palm is getting mighty itchy to collect on the countless offers from my men. You know there's only one man in this camp who can prevent his naughty plans for you," he asserted. "If I were you, Rebecca, I would make my own choice known as quickly as possible. Private stock doesn't include used goods," he crudely threatened the frightened girl. "But either way, I will eventually sample and enjoy your . . . many charms," he vowed, chilling her soul with his determination.

When he reached out to boldly caress her flawless complexion, she shrank from his offensive touch. She made the mistake of voicing her decision, "I would die first! No man will ever treat me like a Kate or Lucy." Her eyes were hard with aversion.

"We'll soon see, won't we?" he sardonically debated, relishing his eventual triumph.

"You filthy animal!" she spat without thinking. "You'll never touch me!"

At her stinging insult and adamant rejection, Jake's face grew livid with anger. Seething fury was displayed by the tic which quivered along his stubbled jawline. His green eyes squinted to slits of virulent resolve. His tone was glacial when he finally spoke between clenched teeth, "I swear you'll be mine, one way or another. If you hinder my private ownership, you'll regret the day you were born a female. You've spurned me too long as it is. I know all about skittish, young virgins; I told you I would break you in gently," he sneered, as if she were some wild filly to be bridled and mastered. "Your fate is as plain as these gold stripes on my shirt, so stop fooling yourself! If you give in right now, I'll forget your past insults. If a man has a mind to, he can inflict a lot of pain upon a woman. If I'm not the first with you, I just might forget to be gentle and loving. As for Jamie O'Hara, I'll kill that old coot if he tries to stop me from having you," he growled.

She mutely stared at Jake in abhorrence and alarm, for she knew he meant every single word. She trembled and shook, even though this lovely May afternoon was sunny and warm. She was helplessly trapped like a fatigued animal in peril of survival. Her strength was no match for her predator's. If only her father were here to protect and to comfort her . . .

Rebecca closed her eyes tightly against this monstrous evil which was invading her heart and life, thick lashes lying like tiny black feathers upon a snowbank. A tear eased down her cheek, for she honestly did not know which choice to make. How could she safely refuse Jake's crude demands? By that same token, how could she ever relent to them?

Assuming her admission of defeat to him, Jake leaned forward to claim his beautiful prize. Terrified by his intimidating proximity, she protested in a tremulous tone, "I can't . . ." Her heart thudded heavily in her chest like an exhausted rabbit's as the talons of a mighty eagle closed over him.

He leaned back to gaze down into the face of exquisite beauty, soft innocence, and utter panic which had haunted his dreams for many weeks. He smiled and casually stated, "You can, and you will, because you have no other choice for honorable survival. It's either me alone . . . or life in the wagon with Kate and Lucy. Since we both know you can't endure a whore's life, the choice is clearly me. In that light, why stall the inevitable?''

Honorable survival! Rebecca's brain shrieked. Was survival worth such a degrading price? A harlot was a harlot whether it was for one man or twenty!

Jake's mouth hastily came down rough and insistent upon her tender lips, parted for another brave refusal. His lips were bruising; they demanded a pleasing response which she could never grant. She instinctively struggled against his massive weight, his brute strength, and his dangerous and unruly lust, just as he vainly tried to enflame her with his fiery passion. She unknowingly kneed him in his taut groin as she attempted to stomp his booted foot to gain her freedom. He instantly doubled over in pain. A groan tore from his tight lips.

Seeing her chance for escape, she shoved him backwards and headed off into the dense cover of the woods. Blind fury overruled his agony; he was quickly upon his feet and hotly pursuing her. He rapidly diminished the scant distance between them. Keenly aware of what would take place when he caught up with her, she desperately ran as fast as she could. Her lungs burned and her side ached from her futile exertions. Her respiration came in quick, sharp pants. Her face was as white as a fluffy cloud upon an indigo horizon. Sheer terror flowed in her veins, for she knew her flight was as fruitless as it was vital.

When a strong hand snaked out to abruptly halt her flight with a painful grip upon her flowing auburn tresses, she was jerked backwards and imprisoned within his powerful arms. Jake yanked her around to face him, throwing her against the rough, sticky bark of a spruce tree. He pinned her to it with his robust frame, glaring down into her ashen face with its crimson cheeks. Her chest heaved; she shuddered in unmasked terror.

"That was a dumb mistake, Rebecca. You shouldn't have done that," he icily stated.

"Please, Captain Selby. Don't do this wicked thing. I can't! Please," she begged and reasoned to no avail.

"You owe me, woman! And I've had enough of your silly refusals! I'm taking you here and now!" he thundered at the quivering girl.

"My uncle will kill you for this!" she screamed at him. "You're all a bunch of savage animals! I hate you! I'll never let you touch me!" she cried out, inwardly knowing there was no way to prevent his inevitable assault.

"Before this hour's past, you'll be the sole property of Captain Jake Selby. Accept it, Rebecca; you're mine," he vowed.

Before Jake could carry out his threat, a look of shock and pain stamped his obdurate features as he lurched forward against her. A loud exhalation of air rushed over her curly head and she realized she'd heard a curious thud. He did not cry out or even speak. He simply gaped at her in horror, then collapsed to the ground, revealing the reason for his strange actions and anguished look: a tomahawk was buried between his shoulder blades near his evil heart and a stalwart Indian warrior was now facing her!

Too stunned to react, she merely stared at the incredibly masculine vision before her watchful eyes. Uncontrollably her eyes roamed his towering, virile frame; his shiny black eyes that revealed nothing but her mirrored image; his bronzed, handsome face that had a small, solid yellow circle painted upon each cheek and on his forehead; and the silver arrow which was suspended from a leather thong around his neck. Without even trying, he evoked tremendous strength, dauntless courage, and total masculinity. Never had she viewed such a perfect and compelling specimen of manhood and mettle. She marvelled at his arresting visage of undeniable prowess. It seemed he was a potent magnet, and even her iron will could not resist him.

Gradually returning to her senses, Rebecca glanced at the dead man at her feet, then settled her wide eyes upon the intrepid brave. He had neither moved nor spoken, and confusion flooded her murky eyes. It seemed absurd to thank this Indian for his timely intervention; assuredly his motive was neither chivalrous nor amicable. Nor did she know what to do. She was at his mercy; yet, he made no attempt to harm her. To flee was impossible, so she remained where she was. She glanced in the direction toward camp, but did not call out for help. She would later contemplate and regret her inaction. . . . And the Indian wondered why the girl he had been furtively watching for two days didn't utter a sound.

Assailed by this perilous situation and perplexed by the brave's distracting effect upon her, she attempted to conceal her apprehension and inexplicable enchantment by kneeling down to roll Jake's limp body away from her feet and legs. If the opportunity to escape presented itself, she wanted to be ready to flee. A rip in her paisley dress ensnared itself upon one of the shiny brass buttons on Jake's navy blue shirt. Unnerved, she anxiously yanked upon her full skirt to free herself, not wanting to touch Jake's bloody body again. The stubborn fabric refused to yield, trapping her there upon her shaky knees.

As she reached out a quivering hand to untangle her torn dress, a bronze one pushed hers away to perform the task. Then the brave nonchalantly removed the crimson-stained tomahawk with its decorative feathers wavering in the breeze from the back of the man who had been about to brutally ravish her. She fearfully waited·for the bloody weapon to also end her life; it did not. Instead, the deadly weapon was indifferently wiped clean upon its victim's shirt and returned to its owner's sheath. They both stood up.

Her puzzled gaze came up to study this copper-skinned creature with bold onyx eyes, compelling features, and a sleek midnight mane. He was so close that she could feel the warmth of his breath upon her face. His oblique gaze drilled into hers, mystifying Rebecca. Unknown emotions washed over her. She froze in curiosity and indecision. Her amber eyes scanned his striking face and upper torso once more. For some reason, she did not feel frightened or endangered.

Who was this god-like man, and why was he here? Why had he killed Captain Selby, then obviously spared her life? Why was he captivating her wayward senses in this manner? What was the magical light which glowed within his dark gaze? What should she do or say? her spinning mind asked.

Her answers came almost instantly. Shrieks of surprise, screams of pain, terrified shouts of alarm, and ominous gunfire reached them. Her head jerked toward the direction to camp. Her face went ashen; her brown eyes grew wide and luminous. She visibly shuddered. No one needed to explain what was happening over there.

The wintry tone of another Indian brave asserted his dauntless claim on the vulnerable white girl to the appealing warrior who was before her, "Ska winyan de mitawa!"

Both Rebecca and Bright Arrow hastily turned to confront this new hazard. There was insufficient time to make any assessments about this Indian's intentions or about her precarious position between them. The second brave surged forward and seized her wrist in a cruel grip, snatching her to him and painfully crushing her against his sweaty body which was as immovable and as sturdy as a massive oak tree.

Thoughts of her own survival and safety blotted out the pandemonium from camp. A cry of intermingled pain and terror was torn from her dry lips at the new brave's savage treatment. A chilling aura of enmity and aggression exuded from him. In panic, her free arm reached out to the first brave and her entreating expression pleaded for his assistance, and she tremulously cried out, "Help me!" She didn't know why she begged him to come to her aid, unless she unconsciously sensed a greater strength in him and an irresistible attraction to him.

Her cries and pleas were unnecessary, for

Bright Arrow had previously determined to have Rebecca for himself. There was a deadly, deceptive calm to his puissant mien when he faced his antagonist, drawing himself up to his towering height of well over six feet, and assuming an arrogant stance of vivid challenge and portentous warning. He forcefully vowed, "Hiya! Akicita Itancan!" He lightly pounded upon his firm chest as he declared that he was the chosen band leader for this raid, denying Standing Bear's brash claim upon Rebecca. "Ska wincinyanna de mitawa," he confidently announced his prior claim upon the startled girl. Bright Arrow held out his hand to the girl, mutely beckoning her to come to his side.

She instantly reached out to accept his terse command, but was brutally thrown to the hard ground behind the opposing warrior. Bright Arrow gingerly withheld a sudden furious outburst in defense of her. The two braves glowered at each other, each waiting for the other to make the first move in this duel of wills. In rising alarm, she watched as they simultaneously lunged at each other to begin a fierce battle for her possession. Suddenly aware of her freedom and their busy contest, she leaped up and ran toward camp, oblivious to the danger there.

Bright Arrow shouted a warning to her, but she did not understand his language. He then issued one to Standing Bear, for he knew she

31

might be slain or captured by another warrior, creating more dispute over her eventual ownership. The struggle for her instantly halted as both men hastily pursued the fleeing girl. As she reached the outskirts of the large clearing, she stopped so quickly at the appalling sight which greeted her numbed senses that she nearly toppled over. Her hand flew to her mouth to stifle a scream. Fear such as she had never known before stormed the very core of her being.

Tom Dinkle and Bill Raines were battling two warriors in hand-to-hand combat and were certain to lose. Jamie O'Hara, her traitorous kinsman, was lying dead in a pool of scarlet liquid which was greedily absorbed by the dry earth. The Shosshoni scout Two Feathers was desperately attempting to withdraw a blue-feathered arrow from his left arm before he was assailed again. Two of the wagons were smoking, while others were already being plundered; the outcome of the raid was a foregone conclusion.

A woman's scream of terror and anguish rent the still air like a clap of thunder. Bill Raines, a private in the cavalry, suddenly noticed Rebecca's presence and frozen expression when the warrior he had been battling was slain by Two Feathers. He shouted at Tom Dinkle to shoot her, not to spare her from multiple ravishments, but to selfishly deny these Indian braves what he himself could never enjoy . . .

"Shoot 'er, Tom! If we can't have 'er, I'll be hogswaggled if they will! She ain't gonna pleasure them after refusing us!"

When Bill attacked the warrior who was claiming the upper hand with his friend, Tom whirled and aimed directly at her heart. Paralyzed by fear and disbelief, she mutely stared at him. Tom squeezed the trigger just as a lethal arrow imbedded itself between his eyes. He fell backwards, dead.

Burning pain seared Rebecca's bosom as a stunning impact struck her. The air rushed from her lungs, her vision blackened; then, merciful nothingness imprisoned her.

Bright Arrow anxiously looked down into the colorless face of the lovely creature whose life he had just saved for the second time in one day. Just after he had thrown himself into her chest to knock her down, Tom's bullet whizzed over them, barely missing its target. He studied her intently, trying to reason out her inexplicable and overwhelming appeal to him.

Was it her beauty, her compelling aura, or something else which had constantly pulled his attention to her for the past two days while he had been tracking this wagon train of Bluecoats and supplies? Was it the defiantly proud way she had behaved to the other whites or the harsh manner in which they had treated her? What was this new and strange emotion which coerced him to desire her beyond all reason? He did not know.

He smiled to himself, pleased by his secret knowledge of the white man's tongue, delighted that his cunning father had taught him to learn this useful weapon. His father . . . Bright Arrow knew he could never successfully compete with the living legend which ruled the Oglala people and his family's tepee. There would never be another warrior such as the proud, invincible, powerful Gray Eagle of the awesome Oglala Sioux, he proudly concluded. He reasoned he would be satisfied only to match his father's skills, reputation, and power. No man could be more fortunate than to be born the son of Wanmdi Hota of the fierce, dauntless, indomitable Sioux.

He chuckled softly as he deliberated upon his good fortune, for it was also his good luck to be born the son of Princess Shalee: wife to the greatest warrior to ever ride the open plains and daughter to the chief of the famed Blackfoot tribe, a member of their great nation which was comprised of seven Sioux tribes. Bright Arrow wondered if Rebecca was anything like the white girl Jenny whom his grandfather Chief Mahpiya Sapa had enslaved and loved, who had given birth to his mother Shalee thirty-seven winters ago. This strange girl with her amber eyes looked more like an Indian than his mother did with her entrancing eyes the color of newborn leaves in the time when Mother Earth renewed her face. How could he so despise the blood of the whites when a small amount of it ran within the beautiful body of his beloved mother? Shalee was the wife of Chief Gray Eagle; she was the half-blooded daughter of Chief Black Cloud; she was loved and respected by all seven Sioux tribes. Love and pride suffused his stalwart frame.

Yet, Bright Arrow knew, times had changed since his grandfather had taken a white girl to his heart. In moons long past, the first white men had come in peace, fleeing the evil of their own kind, living in harmony with the Indians and Mother Earth.

But the moon had come when more white-eyes arrived, white-eyes with evil hearts and greedy hands. Then, the aggressive Bluecoats had joined them, determined to rule and to steal all Indian lands. Many winters had passed as the hostilities and hatred steadily increased. An unending war had resulted. Neither the Indian nor the white man would yield defeat or withdraw. The war would continue until one side lost. Bright Arrow could not imagine either side conceding. The day had come when only a few whites could be regarded as friends. He hastily dismissed the tuggings of foolish guilt which briefly entered his mind. What did it matter that women and children were not white warriors?

He was proud he was not a white-eyes and was fortunate to live under the shadow of Gray Eagle and Shalee. Their guidance and influence had been vital to his happiness and growth. As was the Indian custom, until he married or became chief, he would remain in the tepee of his father. Still, he was growing restless for independence and power. He hungered to make his own decisions and to live as he chose. But without a wife, he could not seek his own tepee. And as long as he lived with his parents, he fell under their rule and wishes. He wondered if this was the reason why so many braves and warriors married so young. Even so, to take any female as wife just to gain his own tepee was repulsive. When he took a mate, it would be a unique female who could share his heart.

As to the white girl Rebecca, he fumed inwardly at the reality that he could keep her only if his parents, especially his father, agreed. To be a man and a noted warrior and to be forced to let another rule his life and manhood tore at his pride and contentment.

Bright Arrow rolled off of the diminutive body of Rebecca, annoyed by the uncontrollable stirrings of passion and tenderness which her smell and touch inspired within his traitorous body. What was wrong with him? He was a renowned warrior with countless coups! He was the only son of Gray Eagle and Shalee! This white girl was his avowed enemy! How dare she spark such forbidden emotions and unspeakable thoughts within him! If she were awake, he would punish her for such an offense! He raged against these novel feelings of guilt, self-betrayal, and carnal weakness. Was he so charmed by her that he could not resist the magic of a girl who was not even attempting to enchant him! To suddenly realize that he could not fault her with his emotional defeat only infuriated him more. What was this powerful attraction to a stranger, an enemy?

Defeating the white man, who had rashly attacked him, Standing Bear came forward to restate his claim upon the unconscious girl. ''The girl is mine, Bright Arrow! I will take her now! Does the noble son of the Sioux chief lower himself to take a skinny white girl to his body and Gray Eagle's tepee? Will your father permit a despised white eyes to lay upon your mat and enjoy your touch? Surely you would not exalt an enemy to such a high place?'' he taunted the formidable young brave, determined to have her himself.

The Sioux warrior frowned at the nefarious Cheyenne brave. This was not the first time Standing Bear had mocked or belittled him before others. Until today, Bright Arrow had found some crafty way to discourage confrontation between them. Now Standing Bear was boldly and willfully using this innocent girl to entrap him. Could he allow this childish game to continue? Could he permit Standing Bear to humiliate him, to make him appear a coward? Already several of the other warriors questioned his tolerance for this spiteful brave. Still, he would unselfishly seek another truce by reasoning with him. A great warrior did not lightly take the life of another noted warrior.

"I have spoken, Standing Bear. Do not continue to defy me. I was chosen the band leader for this raid. It is my right to say who takes the white girl. I say she is mine. Twice I have spared her life. I claimed her first. Do you protest the laws of our society? Did you not also lift your hand to vote me leader? Did you not willingly agree to follow me and my commands?" he rebuked the seething Cheyenne brave.

The flinty look in Bright Arrow's eyes and the unrelenting tone of his voice should have enlightened Standing Bear to his determination to have this unique white girl, but Standing Bear foolishly and recklessly chose to ignore them. This was one time when he would not and could not cower before Bright Arrow, not with the others aware of the conflict brewing between them. Once and for all, he must assert himself; he must best Bright Arrow in battle, or forever ride in the dazzling shadow of the famed son of Wanmdi Hota! Being one of three warriors in line for the rank of next chief of the Cheyenne, he would gain many coups if he conquered the illustrious Bright Arrow. A satanic gleam filled his jet-black eyes as he envisioned the defeat of the supposedly invincible Gray Eagle himself, too weakened by grief at the death of his only son to adequately defend himself. Once he removed both warriors, he could not only capture this lovely white girl but could also ensnare the breathtaking Princess Shalee. Even at thirty-odd winters, she was still the most beautiful, desirable woman alive! In addition, he could forcibly overtake the Oglala tribe and join them to his own. With two deadly blows, he could rule this entire region . . .

Bright Arrow astutely observed the ominous light which glowed in Standing Bear's eyes and the cruel sneer which curled his lips. Without a doubt, Standing Bear was up to some mischief. Standing Bear's next words alerted him to his treachery. Astonished, he listened carefully.

"No, Bright Arrow; she is mine. I lay claim to her here and now. The raid is past; you are no longer band leader. You speak from the shadow of a mighty eagle, but I speak for myself. If you take her, it will be after I am dead. A powerful bear does not listen to the childish whisperings of a slender arrow who quivers before a worthy target. I stand brave and tall as my brother the forest warrior. It is past time for me to pluck the offending arrow from my side, one which clouds my eyes and steals my glory. If you desire this white girl upon your sleeping mat, then you may take her after me. After I have taken my fill of her, she is yours," he voiced his brazen ultimatum, one he knew Bright Arrow must refuse.

Bright Arrow considered his situation. Was there more to this infuriating challenge than met the eye? Bright Arrow did not wish to slay his Cheyenne brother, but neither did he wish to appear a coward nor to give up the white girl. Standing Bear's treatment of captive women was no secret; this girl would never survive his brutal assaults. Somehow Bright Arrow could not bring himself to permit Rebecca's enslavement to another, especially one such as Standing Bear.

What would his father do in this same predicament? The truth was that his father rarely found himself in such a precarious position. His name alone could drive fear into the hearts of his boldest enemies! How he wished Standing Bear had not openly dared him to protect his name and honor; now, more was at stake than the mere possession of this defenseless white girl . . . All that he was or ever could be was controlled by his imminent decision.

He inwardly raged at being forced to defend himself simply because he was the son of Gray Eagle, to prove himself worthy to be the next leader of the mighty Oglala, to prove he was even half the man and warrior his father was! Why couldn't the others accept him for himself? Why was he continually called upon to prove the indomitable blood of Wanmdi Hota also flowed within his veins? Why did younger braves rashly believe that to defeat him would in some magical way also defeat the unconquerable, fearless Gray Eagle? Didn't each man stand upon his own merits and skills?

Being cornered, Bright Arrow saw no way to handle this matter other than to fight for his honor and for the possession of the white girl. He reluctantly agreed, "If it must be this way, Standing Bear, I accept your challenge with great sadness. I do not wish to battle my Cheyenne brother, but you leave me no other choice. May the Great Spirit protect the life of the brave He chooses. Come, the others must view this contest between us."

They left the still unconscious Rebecca where she was and walked into the clearing, now cluttered with discarded plunder and lifeless bodies. Bright Arrow signalled for the others to gather around them. He related Standing Bear's challenge and his reluctant acceptance to the astonished group of braves. While the others cleared an area for their battle, Bright Arrow and Standing Bear each conversed with his closest friends, expressing their motives and feelings.

Lucy and Kate were bound securely to a lofty

birch tree at the far side of the clearing, each female knowing their existence had been altered in only two ways: only the race of their villainous masters and the currency for their carnal services had changed. Their payments would now consist of only survival and sustenance. Yet, necessary whoredom among their own people could not compare with enforced harlotry at the hands of merciless enemies in the Cheyenne camp.

Presently, the others formed an unbroken circle around the two braves to witness this significant contest of iron wills which was long overdue. Red Cloud and Deer-Stalker stepped into the human enclosure to perform their duties. In turn, Bright Arrow and Standing Bear each had his adapted hand secured behind his waist with a strip of leather. Each man's sheathed knife was placed on the opposite side to his habitually used hand. This handicap was intended to force each warrior to use his cunning, agility, and strength to get himself free to attack his opposer while defending himself and hindering his rival.

Standing Bear and Red Cloud exchanged sly grins as they mutually recalled how many times Standing Bear had practiced this dangerous impediment for just such an occasion. But the self-assured, ambidextrous Bright Arrow wasn't the least concerned with this seeming detriment. In preparation of an unforeseen injury to his left hand, he had wisely and diligently worked on the strength and quickness of the right one.

The circle shifted to accept the entrance of the other two warriors as they left their friends' sides to witness this ominous battle. Bright Arrow and Standing Bear faced each other, awaiting the signal to begin their duel. The moment Deer-Stalker shouted "Ya!" Standing Bear fell backwards and delivered a stunning kick into Bright Arrow's groin. The forceful and painful blow sent him stumbling backwards to hit the hard ground with a heavy thud and a loud exhalation of air.

Standing Bear quickly came to his knees and snatched his knife from its sheath. As he struggled awkwardly to sever his bond without cutting himself, Bright Arrow quelled his agony and nausea to hurriedly defend himself. With lightning speed and hopes of stalling his foe's progress, he came to his knees and hurled his head into Standing Bear's chest, toppling him just as a small nick was made in his restraining thong.

Shoving with powerful shoulders, kicking with nimble feet, and hitting with hard fists ensued. Dust and stones flew as the two determined warriors battled for victory. During the fierce scuffle, Bright Arrow was gradually sapping his energy and chafing his wrist as he attempted to forcefully overcome or to weaken his confining thong.

Standing Bear seized his enemy's knife and tossed it aside. As Bright Arrow whirled to retrieve it, Standing Bear claimed his own weapon from the ground and nearly freed his right hand. Yet, Bright Arrow's quick reflexes promptly restored his own weapon to his grip. Standing Bear jerked on his hand to complete its freedom. He grinned in sardonic pleasure as he rushed at Bright Arrow, slashing upwards in his desperate attempt to open the warrior's lithe frame from navel to throat. Bright Arrow artfully stepped aside to avoid that shiny blade and to kick his deadly challenger in the buttocks, sending him face down to the dry earth.

Instantly Bright Arrow's right hand sought to sever his rawhide tie. But he only managed to sunder it halfway as his malevolent adversary charged him. Standing Bear halted his attack and assumed a crouched position as he fearfully viewed the blade held so confidently and skillfully in his rival's supposedly weaker hand. The steadiness and easy control of the perilous knife told the vexed combatant he had misjudged his competitor's skills and cunning. He cautioned himself to patience; after all, Bright Arrow's better hand was still securely bound behind him.

A satanic gleam sparkled in Standing Bear's black eyes and a taunting sneer curled up his lips. He contemptuously stated, "If you yield to defeat, my quivering Arrow, I will spare your life in exchange for your horse and wanapin."

Bright Arrow laughed in amusement. He confidently vowed, "The victory will be mine, Standing Bear. But I will spare your life and your honor if you call a halt to this treachery."

"Then you will die this sun, for I will never yield to you," his foe asserted.

Sweat glistened on both men as their ragged breathing belied their exertions. Their eyes locked in battle as they sized up each other. Yet, this battle was far from over. Both possessed the stamina, cunning, and brute strength to become the winner if the right moment presented itself. The major difference between the two warriors was obvious: Bright Arrow was too soft-hearted and idealistic; Standing Bear was obsessed with revenge and hatred. Such warring emotions claimed much of their energy, causing the battle to continue longer than necessary.

"Cheyenne and Oglala, hear me well," Standing Bear called out. "I have offered Bright Arrow his life, but he refuses my generosity." With his knife at readiness, he turned slightly as he spoke, "His eyes have been blinded by a white . . ." With all eyes and attentions on him, Standing Bear abruptly halted his verbal distraction to whirl and slash out at Bright Arrow.

Astute and watchful, Bright Arrow avoided

the wild lunge. He ducked just as the knife swished overhead. He rammed Standing Bear in the side and knocked him off balance. Before Standing Bear could take advantage of his foe's handicap, Bright Arrow had his left hand free.

Bright Arrow flexed his left hand to restore its circulation and dexterity. To unsettle his self-appointed rival, he agilely and casually tossed his knife back and forth between his deft hands. The two men began to gingerly and slowly move in a circular pattern, eyes and senses alert as each anticipated a moment for successful attack.

"Is a white whore's body worth the life and honor of an Oglala brother?" Standing Bear mocked him.

"Is your death worth the foolish dream of taking my place?" Bright Arrow retorted.

"Keep your necklace and horse, but give me the white girl in exchange for your life," he altered his offer of truce.

Knowing his foe was only trying to disarm him, Bright Arrow parried, "My loins would rebel at her needless sacrifice. Once you used her and slayed her, you would seek another excuse to challenge me. The brightness of the Arrow blinds you, Standing Bear," he rebuked, then laughed heartily.

"Will you still laugh when the Bear's claws have severed your throat and torn her body to pieces?" he smugly challenged.

Before Bright Arrow could reply, Standing Bear gave the Cheyenne war-cry and recklessly rushed at him, hoping to catch him off guard, failing to do so. Careful to avoid contact with his adversary's weapon, each man struggled for triumph and self-protection.

It was obvious to the other braves and to Bright Arrow that Standing Bear was out to slay him. Bright Arrow knew what was at stake; he hastily pressed his advantage in order to end this affair. With just a few more swift and cunning moves, Standing Bear lay mercifully dead in his own blood. It was Bright Arrow who sang the Death Chant for the fallen warrior. He then gave the command to search the wagons for anything of value to them, to prepare Standing Bear's body to be carried home, and to make ready to head out.

When Bright Arrow went to retrieve his costly prize of war, she was missing. During the fight she must have regained her senses and fled while everyone was deeply engrossed in the battle between the two warriors. Noting her shallow tracks upon the face of Mother Earth, he knew it would take but minutes to trace and to seize her. He grinned mischievously at a new idea which came to mind, his annoyance giving way to pleasant intrigue.

He went to his warriors and related his coming sport with the audacious white girl. He told of how he would stealthily trail her until

47

she was utterly exhausted, overly confident, and halted for rest. He laughed as he confidently told of how he would pounce upon her and take his pleasure upon her terrified, weakened body. He spoke of how he would taunt and intimidate her until she pleaded for mercy. He said he would take his ease in punishing her for instilling disloyalty and dangerous desire within the heart and body of Standing Bear. Her mind and body would discover the same pains and humiliation which the fallen warrior's had! But he secretly hoped her inevitable suffering would lessen the guilt and anguish which he now felt at being forced to kill for her.

Pleased with Bright Arrow's crafty plans, the others cheered him on as he set out in pursuit of the bewitching girl who had cast her evil spell upon Standing Bear, a spell which had forced Bright Arrow into a deadly duel in order to break it. The Cheyenne warrior Red Cloud silently and bitterly observed this action before setting off upon a course of his own to alert his tribe and White Elk to the untimely death of Standing Bear, a man who might have become their next chief if not for the Oglala warrior Bright Arrow . . .

Rebecca had been frantically running along the lush riverbank in her haste to flee the hostile Indians who had attacked them. Her racing heart had not slowed from its terrified pace since she had awakened to discover those same two braves doing fierce battle again, no doubt to decide her fate. She feared for the life of the one with bold yellow markings upon his handsome face, for he had saved her life twice in one day. She didn't have to deliberate her fate in the brutal hands of that other brave, the one with jagged red lines streaked fiendishly across his harsh features in a menacing pattern.

Suddenly realizing that she must be leaving a trail which even a child could follow, she gingerly stepped into the stream and hurried along as quickly as the cool, swirling water would permit. She halted just long enough to lift her soaked skirt and petticoat, hoping the removal of this tanging heaviness from around her legs would increase the distance between her and that ghastly sight behind. She was positive her enemies would come after her when her absence was discovered. Hopefully she could elude them until they either gave up their search or she happened upon some other whites.

As time passed and she remained free, her hopes for escape and survival climbed and soared. Dusk was near; the spring air and the clear water had become chilly. Soon she would be forced to leave the stream and to halt for rest. Perhaps she would make it after all. Perhaps they didn't care if she got away. What would they want with a scrawny girl who wasn't even a woman yet? Perhaps they were too busy with the two buxom doxies and the goods in the wagons to . . .

She froze in consternation, her gaze naked with fright and disbelief.

No! It couldn't be! But, it was . . .

Chapter Two

About twenty feet beyond Rebecca, the tenacious warrior with the yellow markings upon his impervious face soundlessly eased from the woods and gently prodded his magnificent stallion into the stream to block her path of escape! Claiming a position in the midst of the swirling water, he seemed to be calmly awaiting her approach. He majestically posed upon the broad back of the splendidly mottled horse against the diminishing light of the day. His stoic expression and impenetrable gaze disguised his intentions, revealing nothing more than that he was obviously the winner of the battle which she had fled hours ago. But hadn't she known all along this robust warrior would be the victor . . . ?

She honestly didn't know if she wanted to cry or to laugh, to flee his magnetism or to yield to his power. At least he was the one to come after her and not that odious brave. But that didn't surprise her; her crazy elation did. Yet, she perceived something vaguely different about him this time. His carriage was commanding and arrogant. She tensed as she gradually comprehended what was disquieting her: a cold and forbidding air flowed from the Indian and chilled her heart more than the rippling waters did her feet. She could almost tangibly feel the resentment and leashed antagonism in his wintry mien. His intense stare and haughty manner were nothing like they had been that afternoon. Why did he seem so changed in only a few hours? Or had she been too enraptured by her first view of him to assess him accurately?

The truth glared at her. He had slain the other brave who had boldly challenged for her. Now, he evidently blamed her for that battle and for his death! The night breeze blew his sooty hair; his jet eyes drilled into her frightened tawny ones. He kneed his huge beast and slowly came toward her. Paralyzed by fear and hypnotized by his gaze, she could not move or speak. She waited for her fate. . . .

He reined in his mount within two feet of her. Rebecca realized the horse did not seem winded. So, the Indian must have been dogging and watching her all afternoon, waiting for the right moment to confront her! She looked up at the man who was towering above her. Why didn't he strike her dead? He nonchalantly positioned himself sideways upon the animal's broad back and lazily rested his ankle upon his thigh. He placed his elbow upon his knee and propped his chin upon his balled fist. He stared down at her.

What was he doing? Why was he just sitting there watching her? Why didn't he kill her where she stood? Why didn't he say anything?

Time passed and still nothing happened. Whatever he was doing, it was getting darker and chillier. She turned away from him to head toward the bank, resigning herself to defeat. Her wet feet and legs and the soggy dress caused her to shiver. He nudged his horse around her, positioning them between her and the inviting bank, preventing her weary progress. She looked up at him in confusion. Nothing. There was no change in his expression or mood at all!

She shrugged, reasoning he must want her to exit upon the other side. But when she attempted to do so, he again blocked her departure path. "What do you want with me?" she cried out in exasperation. "Which way do you want me to go? I know I cannot escape you now," she wretchedly admitted to both of them.

Still, nothing. She made several more attempts to leave the steadily cooling water, but he hindered each one. She was utterly baffled by his silence. The next time, she pretended to head one way until he moved in that direction, then she tried to quickly bolt in the other one. The weight of her soggy dress and the numbness of her feet denied Rebecca any agility and speed. She prayed she could clear the grassy bank and conceal herself amidst the trees and thick underbrush. But he was too quick and alert for her ploy.

His horse hastily backed up and reared into the air. Startled, she slipped and fell forward into the water. She floundered and coughed as the water surrounded her. By the time she regained her balance, she was soaked from the chest down and her lengthy curls were dripping. She brushed the water from her face and gaped at him in fearful astonishment. He was not concerned at all! Was he trying to intimidate her or to torment her? He had certainly not been hostile or cruel that afternoon! Why should he blame her because that other brave had carelessly challenged his rank?

Rebecca hugged her icy hands and wet arms around herself, trembling noticeably in fear and from cold. "Why are you doing this to me? If you wish to punish me or kill me, then why do you hesitate? Surely you have slain many whites in your time. What do you want from me?" she shouted at the silent, intrepid Indian who refused to answer her.

More time passed. Her teeth began to chatter; tremors swept her slender body. A blue cast tinged her lips. Her feet and ankles ached from the numbing, biting chill of the stream. How she longed for her woolen cloak to keep out the night air.

At last, tears glistened upon her thick, dark lashes and eased down her ashen cheeks. Did this Indian intend for her to remain thus all night? Why? Did he want her to grovel and beg? Did he wish to drive her insane from fear? This waiting was intolerable!

When her fatigued mind and troubled body could take no more, she foolishly shoved upon the flank of his horse to move him aside. That was a reckless mistake, for Tasia instantly tried to bite her shoulder. Both Rebecca and Bright Arrow reacted immediately: She stumbled backwards to avoid those strong teeth, and he yanked upon the animal's reins and commanded him to halt his intended attack.

Rebecca helplessly toppled into the freezing water again. This time, she made no attempt to get up. She simply sat there and wept from mental and physical exhaustion. She ignored his quick reflexes and the fact he had prevented his horse from biting her. All she knew was how very tired, cold, and frightened she was.

What did it matter anymore? Everyone was dead; she was alone, a prisoner. He was only torturing her before killing her. Why prolong the inevitable? Why not just end it swiftly?

Yet, he did nothing! He just sat there watching her wallow in her misery and helplessness. An idea came to her mind to force him into either ending it now or revealing his intentions. She would pretend to faint and fall into the water, face down. If he quickly came to her aid, she would know he meant to spare her life after her appropriate punishment for some unknown and innocent crime against him. If he did not, she would still have her answer . . . Either way, the truth would be out!

She ceased her crying and stood up. She slowly took several steps toward the bank. When his horse moved before her line of vision, hysteria seized her. Instead of a pretentious swoon, she grabbed the brave's dangling leg and yanked upon it with all of her might. Taken by surprise, the end result was natural.

She fell backwards into the water with the astonished man upon her. She thrashed wildly until he was also soaked. Then, she audaciously yelled up at him, "Now you can see how the night air feels upon wet skin and clothes! You're mean and curel; and I despise you!" she panted at him, brash courage dancing brightly within her lucid gaze. "Why did you seem so different this afternoon? I thought you so brave. I did not think you so cruel."

Bright Arrow's first thought was to drown her that moment, a deadly idea which flashed vividly upon his scowling face and within his obsidian eyes. Yet, her tormented words changed his mind. Reading his initial reaction clearly, she shouted at him, "Go on and kill me! Do you think I care anymore? My family is dead. I have nothing and no one to live for. I would rather die than be your captive! I hate you! I hate you all!" she cried out in utter hopelessness and anguish. The countless months of bitterness and loneliness churned violently within her youthful body. This new torment was too much to add upon the stack of cruelties from the past two years. Dejected and heartbroken, she sobbed openly, subtly aware of his rigid control and curious change of mood.

Her pain was like an open cut which stung him deeply. Her eyes betrayed that she had known great suffering and abuse many times. Perhaps she was too young and innocent to vent his ire and power upon. She was broken; what purpose would more punishment serve? Still, how could he show her kindness and leniency? How would she view them? How would she respond? As he reasoned upon this predicament and her bold act, he had the time to see the courage of her action. Without her knowledge, she had won a small measure of respect and fondness from him.

He grinned. There were many ways to tame a wildcat with the claws of a she-bear, the cunning of a vixen, the daring of a she-wolf, and the antics of an otter!

The area in which they had landed was shallow and did not completely cover Rebecca's body. He was resting half-on her. His right knee was tightly wedged between her thighs, making movement impossible. As she struggled with him, he captured her flailing wrists and pinned them above her head against the stream bed. To keep the water from her ears and splashing over her face, she held her head up until her neck grew stiff and tired from the constant strain. When she tried to rest it upon her upper arms, he pulled them outward to prevent her comfort.

Unable to hold her head up any longer, she lay back and relaxed her entire body upon the sandy bottom. What else could she do? The water filled her ears and blotted out all other sounds except the swift drumming of her heart—but at least her face remained above the surface.

They remained this way for another spell. She was chilled to the bone, but he didn't seem to be fazed at all by their surroundings! She was utterly mystified since he wasn't even wearing a buckskin shirt! Unable to stop herself, she finally pleaded with him, "Please . . . it's so cold. I'm sorry for what I did to you. I'm sorry we're enemies. I'm sorry you killed the other brave," she miserably confessed. "But I'm not sorry you won that fight with him!" she unwittingly added, then wished she hadn't— until she assumed from his lack of response that he could not understand English.

Rebecca frantically searched her memory for

any word he might comprehend. "Lakota," she finally murmured, hoping it truly meant friend.

It drew a spontaneous reaction from Bright Arrow. He stared down at her in visible curiosity and surprise. "Lakota?" he skeptically questioned in a deep voice which stirred her heart.

"Yes!" she quickly agreed in excitement. "Lakota . . ."

His mocking laughter caused her radiant smile to instantly fade. Annoyed by the warming effect of her dazzling smile, he defensively sneered, "Hiya lakota. Wasichu! Hiya koda," he calmly disclaimed any friendship, shaking his head to make certain she understood his rejection.

Tears sparkled in her eyes. What now? she sadly wondered. With her hands imprisoned, she could not give the sign for peace which her father Joe Kenny had taught her. What did it matter? He probably wouldn't understand her signing anyway. Even if he did, he would doubtlessly respond in a similar manner. It was hopeless, futile.

Abruptly Bright Arrow stood up, then leaned over to gently pull her to her feet. He took her hand and led her over to the bank. He agilely stepped out of the stream and extended his hand to her. She warily glanced at it, up to his impassive face, and back at his beckoning hand. Her cold, trembling hand hesitantly slipped into his strong, warm one. With one powerful move, she was standing beside him upon the dewy grass. She could not imagine his next move . . .

She uncontrollably shuddered as the night breeze played through her drenched hair, lightly caressed her wet flesh, and filtered through her saturated clothes. Her teeth chattered with cold. Water dripped from her auburn curls and tattered dress to puddle in her soaking shoes. She leaned over and removed them, then sat down to rub her feet to restore the circulation in them.

Sighting some fallen branches, Rebecca jumped up to collect them. She approached Bright Arrow and softly entreated, "Could we make a fire to warm and dry us?" She anxiously awaited his reply. When he did not move, she piled the wood into the shape of a fire and pointed to it. "Fire?" she implored again. Her golden brown eyes were alluring and soft. Her gaze passed over his brawny physique which was smooth, hard, and lithe. His well-developed frame which bespoke energy, quickness, brute force, and excellent health.

"Hiya," came the concise answer she had dreaded. She assumed he was either unaffected by the damp chill or he was maliciously pretending he wasn't.

She was cold, frightened, and utterly miserable. Unbidden tears came forth again. She scolded her feminine weakness. She studied him just as intently as he was scrutinizing her. Unable to stop herself, she reached out to test his flesh for a chill. Puzzlement flooded her eyes. She exclaimed in enlightenment, "No wonder you don't want a fire; you aren't even cold! Naturally you don't want me to be warm and dry. Why should you consider the feelings and comfort of your dangerous enemy?" she sarcastically sneered. "You certainly don't want me to regain any strength. I just might overpower a fierce warrior, and we certainly can't permit such an insult!"

Frustrated and vexed, she shouted at him, "My God, you savage! What possible threat could I be to you? I'm no match for your strength! I can't compete with your cunning and skills! I can't even match your hatred and hostility! Kill me or leave me alone!" she stormed in anguish.

She presented her back to him. How long could this deadly farce continue? She was totally exhausted and terrified. But fear and dread were exactly what he wanted! If he would only do or say something!

Her father's words of long ago sounded and resounded within her mind like echoes in a deep, dark canyon. She reflected upon his past advice; he had often spoken of the Indian's contempt and pleasure derived from the pleas and fears of a white captive. Her father had known and befriended many Indians during his life. He had scouted for several wagon trains until he viewed the result of the animosities between the settlers, soldiers, and Indians. He had related many gruesome tales of his past adventures to her. He had halted that well-paying job to settle down to his trapping and trading. He had met and married Mary O'Hara and had taken her to his beloved wilderness to share a life of serenity and hardships.

As Rebecca was growing, he had taught her many things about this demanding wilderness, about its creatures, and about Indians. Yet, he had died from cholera when she was only fifteen: long before he could complete her education for surviving in this rugged and perilous land. That same illness had also taken her mother's life as Mary had lovingly cared for her father. Rebecca's life had been spared through the insight and stubbornness of her parents. She had been forced to live in a lean-to under the watchful eye and strict hand of Moses, her father's best friend. After their deaths, she had not even been allowed to enter their cabin. Following her father's strict orders, the cabin and all inside had been burned to prevent any further spread of that dreaded disease. Moses had then spirited her away to her mother's uncle in St. Louis . . . only to endure a hellish existence as Jamie O'Hara's slave, a harsh life for which the gentle and naive Rebecca Kenny was totally unprepared and ignorant.

Mary O'Hara Kenny . . . her mother had been such a pure and vivacious soul. Mary's untimely death had come when she was only fifteen years older than Rebecca was now. How very cruel life could be! A racking sadness gripped her heart as she recalled her mother's muteness. Rebecca had often wondered what life would be like without words and songs. Yet, her mother's handicap had consequently taught Rebecca sign language. Rebecca asked herself if she could have been as cheerful as her mother was under those same conditions. Would she have been withdrawn and embittered? For certain, her mother had been a very special woman . . .

Weighing the possibility that this brave might comprehend her, she turned to face him again. Even after all this time, he had not moved or spoken. He just stood there watching her, unnerving her! He was utterly fearless and infuriatingly patient! Was there some point to his odd behavior? Was there something he expected of her?

She hesitantly made the sign for truce and friendship. He keenly observed her expressions and movements, intrigued and astonished. His puzzled expression falsely told her that he did not understand. She fretted and probed her memory once more. She placed two fingers to her lips and made the sign for talk as she whispered, "Talk wasichu?" She repeated her first two signs and stated firmly, "Rebecca lakota. Peace. Friendship."

A contemptuous scoff and truculent laughter were her answers. Still, she persistently tried to bridge the communication gap between them. Pointing to herself, she stated "Rebecca."

Touching his golden chest, he announced his Oglala name, "Wanhinkpe Wiyakpa." Pride and self-assurance emanated from him; yet, he had responded.

Elated and relieved she smiled, hesitantly repeating his difficult name. "Lakota?" she ventured in wishful anticipation. Her soft smile tugging irritably at his warring heart.

He shook his dark head. "Rebecca wasichu. Rebecca kaskapi." He observed her closely to see if she comprehended the words "white" and "captive."

"Hiya understand," she replied, touching her forehead with the sign of confusion. She was certain by now that "hiya" meant no!

He pointed to the coppery skin upon his arm and declared, "Wanhinkpe Wiyakpa Oglala. Rebecca kaskapi, wasichu," he explained their differences, stroking her arm to indicate its color.

He gently seized her wrists and bound them with a leather thong. Pointing to her bonds, he stated, "Rebecca kaskapi."

She stared at the bonds, then up at him. The confining thong made his word quite clear:

prisoner. Naturally she, like all other whites, had heard of the mightly Oglala; they were accurately rumored to be the most powerful tribe in the Sioux Nation. She feared to ask her next question, but could not resist knowing the truth. "Gray Eagle Oglala? Wanmdi Hota?" she unnecessarily clarified the name which could strike terror into the heart of even the bravest white man or Indian foe.

He inhaled sharply, then glared at her in stunned silence. Who was this girl who knew signing and who called his father by both his English and Oglala names? How did she know which tribe he belonged to; for most whites collectively called them Sioux, no matter which of the seven different tribes they spoke of!

"Wanmdi Hota Oglala. Wanmdi Hota a'ta. Wanhinkpe Wiyakpa Oglala," he insolently declared he was the son of the infamous Gray Eagle just to terrify her.

She echoed his new word in confusion, "A'ta?"

At her coaxing look and vivid interest in him and his words, he impulsively devulged part of the valuable secret which his father had cautioned him against recklessly or foolishly giving away. He pointed to the shiny arrow which was suspended from the thong around his neck. He spoke his name in Oglala, then said it in English, "Bright Arrow." He inwardly hoped this delicate girl had heard many colorful tales about him.

"Your name is Bright Arrow?" she hastily seized upon this narrow path of verbal exchange, his name unknown to her.

Instantly aware of his boastful slip, he skillfully covered his annoyance with himself. He presented her with a puzzled look. He pointed to her and said, "Rebecca," then to himself and declared, "Bright Arrow," as if that was all the English he knew! His white name was all this dainty and compelling girl was going to cleverly pull from him!

He squatted and picked up a pointed stick. He began to scratch upon the smooth surface of the damp ground. When he pointed to the marks, she knelt down beside him to study them in the rays of the full moon. He tapped the limn of a female stick figure and stated, "Shalee." In turn, he tapped the rough sketch of a smaller masculine figure and cheerfully declared, "Bright Arrow." He touched the larger figure of a man who was wearing a chief's flowing bonnet and beamed with love and pride as he disclosed, "Wanmdi Hota! Gray Eagle, a'ta." He then enclosed the three figures within a single tepee, repeating their names together. He firmly stressed, "A'ta!"

Whether his word meant chief or father, his limn was as clear to her as a spring morning upon the open plains. She stared at him in utter astonishment and panicky comprehension. She trembled. "You're . . . Gray Eagle's son . . ." She swallowed loudly and with great difficulty. She was a captive to the son of the most notorious chief of the Sioux!

Her incredulous gaze slowly and anxiously passed over his striking face and virile frame. She was as quick witted and alert as he was. "Without a doubt, you could be no one else," she apprehensively agreed with her own mental conclusion. "Of all the warriors out here, why you?" she murmured in dread, calling to mind the countless tales of Gray Eagle's hatred and warfare with the whites. From what she had heard, the Sioux battled the encroaching whites more fiercely and successfully than any other tribe. Their chief was feared and respected by all who entered this territory.

She nervously glanced at her bound hands. "Bright Arrow's kaskapi?" she inquisitively whispered to test his motives and control. Discovering his identity only increased her confusion about him and his odd conduct. What would such a great warrior want with a lowly enemy?

She nearly swooned when he insensibly expounded upon her precarious position. She openly stared at him as he uttered his decision about her destiny.

Angered by his previous error in judgment and caution, his tone was belligerent and smug as he vowed, "Rebecca Bright Arrow winyan."

"Winyan?" she uncontrollably echoed, fearing to learn the meaning of that portentous word.

He seemed to search his own mind and memory for a word which she might comprehend. But in reality, he merely sought a word or sign which would not give away any more hints to his vast knowledge of her tongue. He pointed to her and exclaimed, "Winyan." When her eyes still revealed cloudiness, he drew a female figure upon the ground. "Winyan," he snapped impatiently, tapping the sketch. "Rebecca winyan! Rebecca Bright Arrow winyan. Squaw!" he tersely sneered to clarify any remaining doubts. Surely she had heard that repulsive word!

"Squaw?" she repeated in disbelief. Her stunned look said she indeed knew about that scornful rank. "I'm to become your woman? But I'm white, and you're Oglala!" she absurdly argued, as if that difference had anything to do with her new role. Fear gripped her heart. "Rebecca wasichu! Bright Arrow Oglala! Bright Arrow Gray Eagle's . . ." Not knowing how to say son, she altered to, ". . . A'ta. Hiya squaw! It's impossible . . ."

His expression waxed cold, revealing total indifference. He was usually cool-headed, stoic, and patient. But this girl had a curious way of destroying each of those vital traits! Nettled he growled, "Hiya Winyan! Rebecca wasichu squaw!" he voiced the contemptuous difference between her conclusions.

Consumed with panic, she shouted, "I can't be your squaw! I've never known any man! We can't . . ." The full reality of her perilous situation rapidly sank in. He was going to make her his slave to serve him in any and every way! No! her mind screamed. This could not be happening . . . "Koda," she foolishly and futilely pleaded.

He impassively shook his head. "Hiya koda. Squaw."

Her heart was beating so heavily and rapidly that he could see its forceful movements in the vein in her throat. To him, she appeared more frightened of him as a man than as an Indian foe! "Rebecca squaw," he devilishly repeated again just to frighten and annoy her.

"No! Hiya!" she screamed at him. "I won't let any man treat me that way! I'll die first!" she bravely claimed.

Bright Arrow withdrew his deadly blade from its leather sheath. She guessed he had comprehended her words and was about to comply with her challenge. Instead, the knife performed a much different task; he seized the front of her tattered dress and nonchalantly slashed the flimsy material from neck to hem. She gasped in shock and embarrassment. She struggled to move away from him and his probing gaze.

His taunting laughter filled the ominous

silence which was broken only by her ragged breathing and the soft murmuring of the brook. Careful not to nick her arms, he steadily worked until the soggy dress was held high within his grasp like a trophy of battle. He grinned roguishly at her, watching the crimson look which exposed her shame and terror. He casually tossed the demolished dress aside and reached for her again.

She vainly attempted to roll free of his seeking hands, but found herself pinned to the hard ground with his right knee pressing into her abdomen. She struck out at him with her bound hands. He easily captured them and pinned them above her head with only one of his powerful hands. Her face whitened as the knife headed for the shoulder straps of her white camisole. She squirmed, but could not prevent his determined intention. Within moments, the camisole and petticoat and bloomers were lying with the dress.

Her face flamed a brighter red. She closed her eyes against his scrutiny of her naked body. The only thing she could deny him was the pleasure of her pleas. They would accomplish nothing more than to draw hearty laughter and taunts from him. She wondered how she could ever endure this agonizing, degrading treatment.

Something strange was taking place! He was gently drying her off with his blanket! He pulled her to a sitting position and began to dry her long hair as much as possible. When he handed her the damp blanket from his hand and indicated for her to complete this task, she seized the blanket from his grasp and placed her back to him. She wrapped it around her chilled frame and snuggled into its warmth and protection.

Lusty chuckles reached her ears. When she turned to glare at him, she froze in disbelief and panic at the vision of masculine virility standing there: naked, resolved, and very obviously aroused! She had never viewed a nude male before; yet, she realized here was a magnificent, perfect specimen. She cringed in horror as alarm travelled her features and settled within her wide gaze, knowing his intentions. She tore her luminous eyes from the sight before them. She covered her face to hide this vision of brawny manhood from her mind and to conceal her modesty.

He placed another blanket upon the ground beside her and lay down. He reached for her. She flinched from his touch. She acutely felt and smelled his proximity. Danger invaded her mind and body. She did what she had promised herself she would not do; she pleaded for release and for mercy.

Following a brief and fierce struggle, she was imprisoned beneath him upon his blanket. He stared down at her. She was like a timid, frightened doe. Their gazes met and fused as she softly beseeched, "Please, Bright Arrow, Hiya . . ."

She was breathtaking and fragile in the soft moonlight. Her amber eyes were gentle and compelling. Her voice was like a flower, silky and inviting. She was defenseless and vulnerable. A novel feeling of tenderness and potent desire flooded his taut body. If he wanted to experience the many delights she had to offer, then he could not be brutal with her. He smiled, thinking what a joke it would be on her if he could trick her into yielding to him: her enemy and treacherous captor.

His sensual smile was beguiling, disarming. She stared at it, speculating upon its meaning. Her watchful gaze returned to his alluring, igneous eyes. His hand tenderly pushed some straying locks of damp auburn hair from her face, then lovingly caressed her golden cheek. She tensed as his finger ever-so-lightly moved over her quivering lips. She watched him intently as his hand and gaze lazily explored her face. If she didn't know any better, she might think he was trying to tenderly seduce her rather than to brutally rape her! Fear mingled with another, unknown emotion.

When his mouth came down to claim her lips, he had to hold her head still between his hands. His pervasive kiss told him it was her first real one. Pleased, he deepened his next one, knowing she was too inexperienced to resist him long. His romantic onslaught was calculated and utterly intoxicating. She quivered apprehensively as he placed feathery kisses upon her eyes, face, neck, and mouth. He skillfully nibbled at her ears and lips. Helpless, she had no choice but to allow his seeking, stirring assault.

He shifted to lie half on her prone body, allowing him the freedom to discover her entire frame. Having visited the "wokasketipi" where the female slaves—Indian and white—were held until sold or traded, he was very experienced with the female body. He had often joined other braves in a game to test their sexual prowess by seeing who could extract an uncontrollable response from a female who was selected for her beauty, appeal, or hefty appetite upon the mats. That enjoyable, educational sport had taught him many things about female ways. Too, there was the added knowledge learned from captured whores who tried to use their talents to win favor or mercy from the braves.

Having been raised in a tepee with his parents, he also knew the vast difference between carnal sex and love; for no two people loved as deeply, strongly, or passionately as Gray Eagle and Shalee. Of innocent mind and virginal body, this girl would be no match for his sexual prowess! Besides, he had already recognized the unwitting look in her eyes which declared her thoughts about him as a man! The others would certainly enjoy hearing about his success when he related it to them tomorrow, and that delightful deceit strengthened his purpose.

As his eager mouth worked upon her lips and ears, his deft hands stroked and fondled her renegade body. His blissful game was measured. As fiercely as Rebecca tried to prevent any response of pleasure from his actions, she could not. When his warm and moist lips travelled down to tease at her full breasts, she trembled and moaned in irrepressible hunger. She pleaded again until his mouth silenced her words. He stormed her virginal castle until it lay conquered, totally within his powerful control.

The pain and shock of his initial entry brought on another brief struggle. Yet, he patiently continued his enticing caresses and fiery kisses until the hurt faded. She was now his; this truth gave him a heady sense of power over her—and it also inspired a deep emotional bond which he failed to notice. She was his . . .

With the pain gone and his gentle assault intensified, she could no longer resist the callings of her own fiery body to extinguish this consuming fire which gnawed hungrily at her womanhood and attacked her youthful, romantic heart. Her will and reason were swept away in the violent surge of passion which flooded her body and mind. She denied all reality but him. Soon, she was like a rough, white stone which was ready and willing to be artistically shaped into a valuable arrowhead which would bravely attack the unknown. He calmly chiselled, chipped, smoothed, and honed her. The moment of completion of his task came . . .

Her slender arms went up to encircle his neck. Her still-bound hands pulled his head closer to hers; her graceful fingers played in his ebony hair. She pressed her eager body tightly to his; her lips hungrily accepted his kisses. Her body and mind craved some new and forbidden hunger which it instinctively knew he could feed and sate.

He briefly questioned her powerful attraction to him, for no other female had ever responded or yielded to him in this stimulating manner. Never had he experienced such pleasure and such intense hunger. When sheer ecstasy exploded within him, he discovered a stunning satisfaction and a rapturous aftermath which were both new and frightening. He had made this girl a woman, a woman whom he already desired as he had no other. Why was this union so unlike the many others he had experienced? he asked himself, disturbed and angered by the powerful magic which she had cast upon him. She had reached and shaken the very center of his being, and that troubled him deeply.

When his labored breathing slowed and eventually returned to normal, he lifted his head and stared down at her. She, too, was gazing up at him. Her eyes were filled with this same mixture of turbulent emotions: confusion, serenity, alarm, surprise, and fierce desire. Desire? he questioned his own perception. Her next words increased his confusion and worry . . . Her eyes and voice revealed an intense honesty that haunted him. She was just as troubled and distressed as he was!

"I don't understand what happened between us, Bright Arrow, and you can't explain it to me. I've never known or felt anything like that before. So strange . . . and so powerful . . . If love is like this, then why do so many women fear and despise it?" she absently reasoned aloud, totally mystified by this bold contradiction and the unfamiliar emotions which were still racing through her. "There was some pain, but it was brief. How could such a thing feel so wonderful and be . . ." She flushed a deep crimson as she suddenly became aware of her own voice and wanton words. She quickly and defensively hushed.

If he had not comprehended her misuse of the word love for sex, he would have laughed at her childish notions. So, he deduced from her naive confession, he had given her great pleasure with little discomfort. He smiled down at her and confidently announced, "Rebecca Bright Arrow squaw." Unprepared to sacrifice this intoxicating closeness of spirits and bodies too quickly, he relished his pretense of gentleness and affection.

His stirring tone and disarming expression denied any insult in his claim. Enamored and enchanted, she smiled and demurely admitted, "It would appear that way . . ." She eased her bound hands over his head, puzzled by how they got there. She pondered her lack of restraint and abandonment of will and reality. Curious about these unknown feelings and wildly wonderful sensations, she boldly ran her forefinger over his sensual lips as he had done to her earlier.

"Are kisses always like that?" she asked, forgetting their language barrier. She touched her own lips to see if they felt any differently now that he had deftly plundered them. "No man has ever kissed me like that before. It causes such strange reactions. I do not understand such feelings, Bright Arrow," she artlessly confessed, wishing he could explain them to her. Evidently he knew a great deal about love and women! she surmised, irrational jealousy flooding her romantic heart.

Another time flashed vividly across her dazed memory: her struggle with Jake Selby. "No," she murmured softly as if absently thinking aloud. "All kisses aren't like that. Captain Selby was mean and rough; his kisses were disgusting and painful." Those conclusions brought new mysteries to the hazy surface, ones which she couldn't explain or comprehend.

She abruptly questioned, "Why didn't you hurt me like he did? Why were your kisses so unlike his?" Consternation filled her as she refused to face the truth which was boldly staring her in the face with piercing, laughing jet eyes. In horror, she recalled something her father had once told her. He had said that a special man evoked inexplicable, wonderful emotions within a woman who was in love with him. Was this what he had been referring to? Was this how she was to judge who was to become that special, unforgettable man of her heart?

"No!" she cried out in panic. "It cannot be true! How could I possibly love you? We're strangers! We're different! We're enemies!" Distressed deeply by such thoughts, she attacked him, "Why did you kiss me like that! Why did you force me to feel such wicked things! You are evil and cruel, Bright Arrow! No!" she cried out as if in physical pain. "It cannot be true! I won't allow it!"

She glared up at him, holding him totally responsible for the betrayal of her own body and mind. He had surely tricked her! "This is all your fault! I know nothing of such things!" she angrily shouted at him. "Hiya squaw!" she forcefully denied his terrifying and masterful hold upon her and her wanton attraction to him.

Amused, he laughed genially. "Ni-ye mitawa, Rebecca," he reiterated his claim upon her, totally confident in his enthralling power over her life and her body. He smiled tenderly and caressed her cheek. If she so stubbornly demanded, he would unselfishly prove these things to her again . . .

She shoved his hand away from her face. "No! Hiya!"

Challenged and obsessed, he leaned forward and kissed her thoroughly. When one kiss failed to halt her struggles, he assailed her senses with many more. She fought against him and her aching need for him. She lost the battle to him even before he made his first move. Within moments, the raging passion which consumed her could not be bridled; it raced through her like a wild stallion across the open plains, reveling in its freedom and joyful existence.

If possible, their possession of each other was more satisfying than the first time. He shuddered from the stunning impact of their union. When she lay exhausted and snuggled into the protective, inviting embrace of his arms, he savored this unique tranquility and this previously unknown feeling of completeness and supreme joy. At that precise moment, he knew he would never give her up until she failed to make him feel such powerful and wonderful feelings. He would take her time and time again until her magic was dispelled forever. He would seek out her secret allure which could drive a man wild with desire, could shake his body with such fierce unions, could grant him such total peace and relaxation, and set her apart from all other women. He would take and enjoy all she had to offer before he could part with her. When that day came, he would share her with his best friends and allow them to discover why he had kept her for so long and to instill envy within them for his having possessed her first.

It never occurred to Bright Arrow that he would never wish to part with his gratifying white captive. It never entered the brave's mind that Rebecca's magic was so strong and compelling or that it would increase to the bittersweet point where he would battle anyone and anything to keep her forever! Yet, those times and days were destined to come . . .

Weary in body and relaxed in spirit, Rebecca was quickly asleep within her lover's arms. Suddenly vexed by this portentous magic which came in the form of white skin, he was briefly tempted to tie her to a nearby tree for the remainder of the night just to prove she meant nothing to him. Guilt gnawed at him.

Before he could push her out of his arms and off of his blanket, a night chill passed between them. She shivered and nestled closer to his warm frame. She smiled in her deep slumber and murmured his name. Such was the undoing of his cruel intent. He studied the lovely white creature who was now his captive.

Rebecca was his! If he so desired to sleep with her body touching his, then who could stop him! Besides, she fit nicely and perfectly against him; she was soft and enticing. She was small and helpless. A delicate girl was no threat to a powerful warrior! She filled him with heady power and excitement. She was also his responsibility. It was up to him to safeguard her health and life. If she caught a chill and took sick, she could die. That horrible thought distressed him more than he cared to admit. She was a fragile flower which could too easily and carelessly be destroyed.

He enfolded her within his warm arms and held her possessively. The rest of the night passed without either of them moving from their entwined position.

Chapter Three

Rebecca stirred and stretched, yawning and sighing contentedly. Her arm touched something dreadfully unfamiliar: another person was resting beside her! Her panicked gaze flew open wide and she hastily sat up to see who dared this brazen insult.

Her alarmed eyes fused with the calm, ebony ones of the Indian brave who was casually propped upon his right elbow, watching her closely. Last night's events flooded her mind, breaking through the defensive barrier of her mind like a rain-swollen river assaulting a weak dam. The handsome brave smiled up at her, remaining in his reclining position. Deceived and charmed by his continued amicable behavior, her brownish gold eyes softened as she returned his gesture.

She hesitantly confessed, "I was afraid. I . . .

thought you were . . . someone else." Her look of relief pleased him, mystified him.

Without words, he reached up and gently pulled her down beside him. His hand playfully traced the exquisite features of her lovely face and stroked the softness of her tousled curls. When he leaned over to kiss her, she caught her breath in eager anticipation. New flames leaped within her body, as within his. Any logical reason to resist her new-found love deserted her spinning mind.

He expertly fanned those igneous coals of smoldering passion until a raging fire blazed within them, encompassing them in an emotional furnace which refined and purified their unity, forging and joining them together in spirit and heart. Neither would be satisfied until this feverish wildfire was extinguished in the only way possible, which it was. In the contented, relaxing afterglow of their third union, he bored his obsidian eyes into her amber ones and huskily vowed, "Rebecca, Bright Arrow . . . winyan."

He noted the startled look of surprise and uncertainty which captured and brightened her serene expression at his second choice of words. She dauntlessly and lovingly caressed his chest as she smiled and whispered, "Yes . . . Bright Arrow's winyan . . ."

He kissed her lightly upon her forehead before he left her side to bathe off in the stream.

As he washed and then dressed, she lay there daydreaming about him and all they had shared. Who was this intoxicating interloper who had trespassed upon her body, demanding she become his willing property? Yesterday she had been a supple, green bush; today she was in full bloom like a delicate Yucca plant, one which was beautiful and pure white, one which could be plucked or destroyed by a careless hand.

She tranquilly concluded, life is so very strange and unpredictable. How is it possible for such feelings to be so all-consuming and sudden?

He came back to where she was. He pointed to the stream and softly commanded, "Yuzaza, Rebecca." He gallantly assisted her to her feet as she timidly held the blanket up before her. He glanced at her tight grip upon it, then studied her rosy face. He chuckled mirthfully, then repeated his order for her to bathe.

His back was to the stream as she followed his command. He rolled up the blankets and secured them to his horse. He turned to find her anxiously staring down at her torn clothing which was totally unusable now. He came to her side and led her over to his splotched Appaloosa. He mounted with graceful agility. He leaned over to lift her up to sit before him. Once again she held on to the blanket to keep it from slipping away from her naked body. She timidly refused to meet his humorous gaze.

He grinned mischievously as he playfully tugged upon a curl which rested upon her creamy breast. He pulled her trembling body close to his before he prodded his animal to move out. Knowing she had many surprises in store for her today and for many days to come, a frown lined his forehead and knit his brow in deep thought. He was irritated to discover his sadness and anger at the reality it would never be this way between them again. He was helpless to prevent the loss of something very special. He hadn't even returned to his people yet and already he was feeling the pains and misery of her sacrifice. He was infuriated by the fact that duty and honor controlled his life more than he himself did! It would be impossible and even dishonorable to keep her, and yet he wanted her so much that it frustrated and angered him. Why did the laws and customs of his people overrule his wishes?

As he became aware of his brooding line of thought, he chided himself for his weakness and foolishness. He was a warrior! The loss of this scrawny slave should mean nothing to him! He must harden his heart against her; he must control his forbidden desire for her. He must remember at all times who and what they both were . . .

If this was only a cruel joke upon her, then why wasn't he laughing or relishing it? He could easily envision the amused looks upon the faces of his war party when he rode into camp with her nestled against him. Surely he could count many coups for this feat of great prowess. Then why wasn't he pleased with his accomplishment? Why wasn't he looking forward to revealing it to his warriors and to her? He knew why; whatever this mysterious attraction was between them, it would brutally end the moment he exposed his treacherous betrayal.

He ordered his mind upon another, less weighty, subject. How many warriors could wipe out a white woman's people, enslave her, ravish her, and then have her eagerly cling to him in open love and acceptance? No one could deny the naked passion which flickered brightly and uncontrollably in her doelike eyes. To extract all he could from her before their closeness was ended, he would willingly deceive her with this loving treatment which was so clearly disarming and enslaving her, which would appear only a cruel ploy once the truth was out. By the time they came to his braves' camp, she would be so enthralled by him that she would artlessly reveal his powerful hold upon her spirit and body. Hopefully, she would be so ensnared in his lover's trap that she would be unable to resist him even after he proved unworthy of her love, acceptance, and trust. Hopefully, she would be wise enough to follow his future commands without forcing him to punish her. He refused to dwell upon the pain his deceit would bring to her and upon their fragile, forbidden union. There was no hope for a relationship between a white girl of seventeen and a Sioux warrior of eighteen.

Bright Arrow decided to treat Rebecca as what she was: his captured foe, his white slave and whore. He would not reveal his gentle treatment to her. He would allow his people to believe she had helplessly fallen under the awesome spell of Bright Arrow, invincible son of Gray Eagle. That was a logical tale since he was desired by countless women, white and Indian, younger and older.

Just as Rebecca anxiously questioned their destination, Bright Arrow reined in his horse and pointed to her plundered wagon. To prevent a forest fire, the wagons had not been set ablaze. They had been left to display a grisly warning to other white settlers who might pass this way in their greedy encroachment upon Indian lands.

The sight which greeted her eyes was ghastly. She buried her face upon his firm, smooth chest. Tears burned his muscled flesh. "Why did you bring me here, Bright Arrow? Do you wish to hurt me or to torment me? We must go," she pleaded sadly. "There is so much death and pain here."

He kneed his horse and moved closer to Jamie

O'Hara's wagon, one he knew from his previous scouting. He grasped her chin and lifted it. He read the agony which was lucidly engraved in her somber eyes. He smiled, then touched the blanket around her. "Rebecca heyake. Waya-keto," he stated, telling her to look inside the wagon for her clothes. After all, he couldn't take her home stark naked.

He lifted her as easily as a feather and placed her bare feet upon the tailgate of the wagon. "Ya. Rebecca heyake. Bright Arrow o'winza," he stated as he tugged the blanket free from her nude body.

She shrieked in dismay and hastily attempted to shield her shapely frame from his smoldering gaze. He laughed, enjoying the sight she made. He held up the blanket and mischievously shook it, saying, "Bright Arrow o'winza." He pointed into the wagon and declared. "Rebecca heyake. Ya," he said, motioning for her to enter it.

Enlightenment dawned on her. She slipped inside and rummaged through her trunk. It was obvious she couldn't take very much with her, so she settled upon a cotton skirt and blouse. She pulled out another similar outfit, both of blue chambray, her normal serving attire from Jamie's roadhouse back in St. Louis. She sat down to pull on a pair of lowcut mocassins from the bottom of her trunk. Her father had made them for her, but her hostile uncle had refused to permit her to wear them. Surely this brave would not object to them! She savored their soft comfort, pushing aside thoughts of her deceased parents.

She folded the other skirt and blouse and placed them upon a square of green material. She quickly brushed and braided her hair, then put the comb and brush in the same bundle. She gingerly lifted out the small, tanned skin which had a picture upon its inner surface: a miniature oil drawing of her parents which had been done by a travelling artist who had passed by their cabin while journeying through the rugged wilderness. He painted unknown wildlife, dauntless settlers, stirring landscapes, and wild Indians. It had been a treasured gift to her for her assistance and great interest in his work.

"Rebecca, ku-wa," Bright Arrow called out for her to return, wondering at her delay.

She hurriedly placed the precious painting within her small bundle and secured it tightly. She made her way past the boxes of gear and crates of goods which were of no use to Jamie O'Hara now. "I'm ready," she softly replied, extending her arms to him.

He hesitated momentarily as his appreciative gaze scanned her appearance. She was softly innocent and naively trusting. She exuded youthful vitality. He astutely noted the braids and the mocassins. He wondered if she were trying to make some point with them or if there was some importance to her possession of them. He smiled and reached out to take her. Once more she buried her face against his muscled chest as they traversed the full length of the ravaged camp. In the midst of her new love and confusing experience, she had totally forgotten about the Indian raid! Now, she had to blot it out of her mind again.

She placed one arm around his narrow waist and held onto her prized bundle with the other. They rode away from the nightmare which had begun her trek to destiny. The wind tore her words of gratitude from her lips, but he still heard them. How he dreaded to hurt this gentle creature . . .

As she rested her head against his brawny shoulder, Rebecca's thoughts were playing hide-and-seek with her logic. Her new life seemed a puzzle which she could not piece together. She concluded that if it was her destiny to be an Indian slave, then she could not have selected a better man if she had been allowed to do the choosing herself! From the corner of her eye, she studied him.

Bright Arrow seemed kind, thoughtful, gentle, and understanding. He was unlike the wild savages that populated the tales she had heard along her journey West. In fact, he was more of a real man than any white one she had ever met. He was definitely strong, brave, alert, and cunning. He was so very handsome and virile.

He was the most beautiful and magnetic creature she had ever seen or known. He was being so patient and friendly with her, even though she was his captive enemy. He was indeed a rare man. Yet, she ignored one vital fact: Bright Arrow was the son of Gray Eagle himself . . .

Admittedly, her feelings and thoughts were colored and controlled by his friendly conduct. She sighed peacefully and snuggled up to him. His embrace tightened around her. Her trusting, naive nature did not warn her of the inevitable deception. To Rebecca, her submission to Bright Arrow seemed right, natural.

It had been two lonely, unhappy years since her parents had died so suddenly and unexpectedly. Her eager, empty heart yearned for the love, joy, and acceptance which Bright Arrow was guilefully showing her. She had not felt this safe and happy in two years; it was delightful and irresistible; it was stimulating and exhilarating. Her youthful heart had never known such fulfillment and she failed to question it.

They rode for hours, only halting briefly to rest his horse. Rebecca's shyness gradually departed as he offered her some dried strips of meat and bread pones; things prepared by his mother for his raid. They ate, then drank from a nearby stream. Later, they remounted and headed out again—she mistakenly assuming he was happily taking her home to his village.

About mid-afternoon, Bright Arrow abruptly reined in his horse. She glanced up at him. He seemed to be listening for something. His gaze fused with her inquisitive one. Before she could ask if something was wrong, his mouth came down upon hers. His kiss was brief, but pervasive. It ended almost before she could respond to it. He scrutinized her startled expression, as if it held some special meaning for him. She was confused by his fathomless, intense gaze. As she stared into those obsidian depths, she felt adrift in an endless black ocean. She smiled. He glanced over her auburn head as if willing his keen eyes to see through the verdant copse before them. When his gaze returned to hers, it was stormy and dismal. Something was troubling him. Did his acute senses detect danger?

When he spoke in his tongue, she could not comprehend his words or intentions. "I wish it did not have to be so, Rebecca. But I am bound to my laws and ways, just as you are to yours. This game between us was unwise. It will cause you much sadness and pain. I cannot spare you what is to come. Had I but known of what was to grow between us, I would not have come after you yesterday. I should have yielded you to Standing Bear. My loss of face could not have pained me more than your loss of will. It would have been better not to have known you this way than to lose you now. You are white, and I am Oglala; our destinies cannot be joined. For what I must do, you will hate me. Still, I cannot change the hatred between our peoples. If I but had the courage and strength, I would draw my knife and end this magic, forbidden thing between us here and now. Hate me if you must, but you are mine . . . for a while longer."

He kissed her again, slowly and hungrily. She was baffled by his mercurial moods and the turbulent mixture of emotions which made his voice tremble. She could sense some turmoil within him, some reluctance and desperation which bewildered her. He picked her up and placed her behind him. He pulled her arms around his waist, binding her wrists before she guessed his intention. He inhaled deeply, then slowly released his breath.

She innocently said, "This isn't necessary, Bright Arrow. I can hold on without falling off. The thong hurts. I did not understand your words," she declared to this quicksilver creature. "I would never escape from you."

As if she had not spoken at all, he kneed his horse into a fast gallop. She told herself he hadn't understood her words either. She decided he must have done this for her safety at his currently swift pace. No doubt he was eager to reach camp or there was peril in the wind.

But within the hour, she comprehended the meaning of her bonds. Even so, she still did not realize the full implication in his change of mood and behavior. It would be hours before her ravaged heart and mind would accept the obvious truth.

As he called out to the band of braves who were just ahead of them, she could sense his growing excitement and pride. The group halted its steady progress to await them. Her conduct played right into his wily scheme, for as they approached the group, she pressed close to him for solace and protection.

He slightly calmed her fears by whispering over his left shoulder, "Rebecca Bright Arrow winyan." Slyly deluding her, she relaxed against him.

The warriors joked and talked in their tongue, jesting about the lowliness of Rebecca's position. He laughed heartily as he related the highlights of their night together. He shrewdly weaved a colorful, intriguing picture of punishment and pleasure. No one doubted his words as they witnessed the way the white girl clung to him and acted toward him. They applauded his great prowess and trickery. His companions openly admired Rebecca's beauty and courage. Confused and unnerved by their scrutiny of her, Rebecca snuggled even closer to Bright Arrow and innocently rested her satiny cheek against his hard back. How she wished she were sitting before him, enjoying his protective embrace!

"She must be very wise, Bright Arrow, for she

bows to your power and skill . . . both in battle and upon your sleeping mat," one brave gleefully quipped. The other warriors chuckled and ribbed each other, delighting in this stimulating sport.

"What female could find the will to deny the prowess of our noble chief's son?" another jested, bringing more hearty laughter and genial agreement. "Have we not witnessed his great magic and prowess many times?" he roguishly asserted.

"Perhaps she was only afraid to resist you, or perhaps too empty-headed to know how," yet another brave taunted. "She clings to you as a feather to a greasy hand. How will you pry her free, oh noble warrior who is as true and straight as an arrow in flight?" Several pairs of midnight eyes brazenly scrutinized her comely face and provocative figure.

Bright Arrow laughed heartily. He joshed, "Look at her, Sitting Elk. Who would wish to free himself of such beauty and pleasure? Perhaps one day I will permit you to see where her real value lies. The women we have taken to the Tipi Sa cannot even compare with the one who . . . slept upon my mat last night," he jauntily ventured in a suggestive tone which clearly indicated his real meaning.

Howling laughter filled the warm air. An innocent Rebecca never suspected the intimate topic of this conversation which they were so obviously enjoying. Generous offers were made to him for sharing this special prize. "It is too soon to share what I tasted only last night, my friends. When I have taken my fill of her, I will trade her for the best offer," he smugly announced to prove his interest in her was superficial.

"But what if there is nothing left when your greedy appetite is sated?" the first warrior asked.

"She is like the snows upon the sacred mountains; each time she melts and feeds water to the thirsty land, there is always more snow to come and to replace what has gone away forever. She is like the mighty river to the west; she has more to offer than any of us could ever take," he boasted dramatically, then threw back his head and laughed.

They eyed her closely, observing things in her which caused envy in their minds and lust in their bodies. Rebecca warily watched this jocular band of warriors, pressing as closely to Bright Arrow as she could. What were they saying? Why were they inspecting her like stolen booty? Even though she could not understand their Oglala words, she certainly comprehended their lustful looks and desirous moods.

It was that precise moment when the tense Rebecca astutely surmised she was being discussed in some assessable manner. Her face grew red and hot guessing these men knew what had taken place the night before. Noting the absence of Kate and Lucy, she assumed them to be with the other half of the war party. Perhaps the women were a gift meant to soften the blow of killing that insidious warrior who had challenged Bright Arrow?

She fearfully recognized the same desirous expressions and sensuous attitudes which had characterized the lewd men at Jamie's road-house and upon the wagon-train. Yet, her protector and lover Bright Arrow was not a Captain Jake Selby nor truculent Jamie O'Hara. He was nothing like them, or so she naively thought . . .

"It is just as well, my friend, for her eyes are only for you at this time," Deer-Stalker solemnly commented. "See how she clings to him, how she looks at him, how she touches him? Does your flesh burn like the fire, Bright Arrow? For my eyes and loins do from just watching her. Can you not share her for only one night to ease these pains and curiosity within me?" he teased his best friend.

"It would be unwise, my friend. She is new to a man and to the sleeping mat," he announced seriously. "To lend her to others would cause rebellion. I prefer to spend my time and energy enjoying her, not punishing her for defiance," he stated, a roguish grin tugging at his sensual mouth.

"She has known no man but you!" Sitting Elk exclaimed, jealousy and fiery passion sparkling brightly within his walnut eyes. The others eyed her with new covetousness. She quivered at the bold stares which devoured her.

"I was the first to take her," Bright Arrow haughtily confessed. "Yet, she reaches out as one who has known many men and many fiery nights as we shared. She possesses a powerful magic which I must keep a watchful eye upon. It would be cruel and unwise to tempt my friends to be placed under her spell as Standing Bear was. I have touched this magic and it is for me alone to enjoy. Once it has dulled, then others can take her. Come, Wi soon sleeps for the night. We must make camp," he suggested, ending this conversation which ultimately made him feel ashamed of himself.

They headed for a suitable area within an hour's ride. Rebecca was suspicious of the way Bright Arrow forced her to gather firewood and to prepare a cheery fire for him and his men to enjoy. She was then bound to a sturdy ash tree, too far away to profit from its warmth and light. As if she were suddenly invisible, the men totally ignored her! They sat around the blaze, talking and laughing and eating. She pondered and feared this drastic change within Bright Arrow. He was suddenly as forbidding and cold as a blizzard in the midst of winter. He behaved as if nothing extraordinary had ever passed between them!

At last, he left the others to come over to her, acting as if she should be grateful that he was recalling her presence! He casually untied her bond, which encircled the tree, but only long enough to allow her to eat and to drink the food he nonchalantly tossed into her lap. The aura which now surrounded him was unfamiliar and frightening, for it was potent and undeniably foreboding. The moment after she asked herself why he was so different around his men, she knew the dreadful answers: She was white, his enemy; he was a warrior, Gray Eagle's son. Before his band of warriors, he must show only the expected conduct, that of a captor's. She knew she must adjust herself to the intrepid man who was now standing before her, for they would never be alone again . . .

Hurt and disillusioned, she lowered her head and nibbled at the strips of dried meat and cakes of bread. Tears blurred her vision, several dropping upon her hands and lap. Heartache clutched at her chest; anguish constricted her throat. She angrily and proudly brushed away her tears with her bound hands. She dared not look up at him, for to do so would only reveal the torment she was experiencing. Too full of conflicting emotions to be hungry, she set the food aside after the first few bites.

Her suffering instilled the irritating response of remorse within Bright Arrow. He caught himself wishing he did not have to treat her this cold way. Her withdrawal from him somehow haunted him. He scolded himself for wanting to comfort her. Yet, she looked so fragile and so vulnerable sitting there with her head bowed, her heart full of pain and her eyes full of tears. It was clear that she had trusted him completely. He almost wished this wasn't a game to humiliate her, to prove his superiority over her. He actually missed the warmth of her body and the glow of her radiant smile! These feelings and thoughts were dangerous and shameful. The sooner he learned to ignore her, the better it would be for both of them! But willing such an act and doing it were as different as the Indian and the white man.

"Wota. Mni," he offered in a voice cautiously devoid of all emotion. When she did not seem to understand, he placed the food and water back in her lap, stressing, "Wota. Mni."

For a second time, she put them aside. "I'm not hungry. Hiya," she softly refused them. "I was a fool to trust you," she sadly confessed.

"Wonahbe?" he inquired, pointing into a thicket, ignoring her charge of betrayal. His inquiry about her need for privacy was clear, for she recognized that familiar word from earlier.

Mortified, she still nodded yes. He pulled her to her feet and led her off into a thicket not far away. "Ya," he said, indicating for her to go on alone.

Both knew she could not escape and to try would only prove dangerous for her. After she returned to his side, she thanked him in a strained whisper. Even so, she did not look up at him. She kept her eyes upon his fringed buckskins and beaded mocassins.

"Ku-wa," he commanded, motioning for her to follow him.

Bright Arrow permitted Rebecca's bound hands to rest in her lap as he wound a rope around her chest and the tree twice before tying it securely. To ward off the night chill, he tucked a blanket around her shoulders and another one around her legs and feet. This time, she did not argue against the needless bonds. Even though he knew she would not attempt to escape, she must surely know that his pride prevented him from revealing his trust in her or his respect for her intelligence. From now on, Bright Arrow decided, he would treat her as was expected of an Indian brave.

He wondered what it was about this girl that made it impossible to keep his thoughts from her. "Istinma," he murmured softly, closing her lids with their tear-soaked lashes. His finger gently trailed down her cheek to remove the salty streaks there, then softly traced across her quivering lips. "Kokipa ikopa," he whispered, knowing she was indeed afraid.

Rebecca flinched at his tormenting touch; pain knifed her broken heart at the tenderness

102

which permeated his incomprehensible words of comfort. "Do not touch me, Bright Arrow. Do not even speak to me. I shall never forgive this betrayal. I will forget all that has passed between us before tonight. Your punishment was cunning, my beloved enemy, for even brutality could not have hurt me more. Enjoy your savage joke. I hate you . . ." she vowed in a hoarse tone . . . but both knew it was a lie.

Bright Arrow vowed he would ask his father to explain the many wasichu words which she had spoken that were still unknown to him. On second thought, he concluded it might be best to ask his mother to translate this girl's words. Shalee also secretly knew this enemy's language. Perhaps Rebecca had said things to him which were better left unknown to his father! For this reason, Bright Arrow paid close attention to the English words which he did not know. Each time she spoke one, he would mentally repeat it to himself until he was sure to recall it later when he could talk privately with Shalee.

He stood up and left Rebecca to bear her anguish alone. Soon, the entire camp was asleep, all except the captive girl, who wept silently far into the chilly night, and Bright Arrow, who was all too aware of her pain and all too troubled by guilt.

Rebecca did not know which betrayal hurt more, his treachery or her own body's weakness.

Either way, the damage was done and had to be dealt with before he attempted to trick her again . . . He had vividly shown her that his actions and words were dishonest. She concluded this love was a terrible thing, for it was cruel and painful.

Rebecca gradually awakened to the dawning of a new day. The sky was clear and intensely blue in the vast Dakota Territory. The May air was crisp and fresh, promising a warm sunny day. Several birds vainly tried to outsing each other. The braves had begun to stir. It was but an hour before they were riding for the Oglala camp.

Rebecca had no choice but to lean against Bright Arrow's solid frame because of her bonds around his waist. His warmth and smell filled her nostrils and cruelly attacked her traitorous emotions. How she wished she was not riding with him, touching him, inhaling his manly scent.

When they rode into the Oglala camp, many of Bright Arrow's people gathered around them, jubilant and curious. The raiding party was congratulated, cheered, and questioned. Few paid any attention to the girl tightly secured to Bright Arrow's body. They saw she was clearly the personal captive of their leader's son. As female captives were a common sight, they did not deserve any special attention. Since she was already claimed, she would not be offered for trade or sale—today.

The excess of goods and treasures were generously shared with those in need or were traded to the highest bidder. Boastful stories about the cunning, daring attack upon the Bluecoats' wagon train were bandied about.

When things settled down, Bright Arrow walked his horse over to his family's tepee. It was one of the largest and most colorful in the camp, highly decorated with the numerous coups of his father. Bright Arrow cut Rebecca's bonds free, then slid off the animal's back. He reached up, seized the girl by her tiny waist, and lifted her down beside him. She was a treasure so small and yet so valuable! He handed the reins to a boy who led the splendid mount away to be watered and rubbed down.

Bright Arrow grasped Rebecca's forearm and pulled her inside the tepee. His parents were not there. He assumed them to be walking in the nearby forest for it was their custom about this time of day. He released his grip upon her arm, walked over to a mat, tossed her small bundle upon it, then turned to face her.

She had not moved from the spot where he had released her after entering this private abode. She stood watching him, her eyes large and sad. He studied her a few moments, pondering what he was supposed to do or say now. This situation was as new and trying for him as it was for her.

"Ku-wa, Rebecca," he called out, signalling for her to come to him.

She tensed and paled, also ignorant of what was expected of a captive white girl. She quaked; her legs refused to obey his command. When he repeated it more sternly, she was compelled to move forward by the sheer force of his commanding tone. She slowly and reluctantly walked over to stand before him. She stared straight ahead at the bronze flesh of his chest. She glued her eyes to the silver arrow he wore as if entranced.

When Bright Arrow reached out and touched her cheek, she jumped and inhaled sharply. He lifted a heavy chestnut braid and tossed it over her shoulder. With one hand behind her neck and the other around her waist, he pulled her rigid body up to his. His eager mouth came down on hers, determined to instill the same hunger in her which gnawed at him. But Rebecca remained rigid and unresponsive.

Another savory kiss followed, then another. His lips nibbled at her ear, then pressed feathery kisses upon her tightly closed eyes. She quivered in uncertainty and desire for he gradually shattered her resistance. By the time his mouth returned to hers, she no longer wanted to remain cold and stiff within his imprisoning embrace. With a soft moan of defeat, she surrendered her will to him. She feverishly returned both his kisses and embraces, matching his ardor and desire. God, how she needed this loving contact and acceptance!

Without warning, his loving assault ceased. He held her possessively against his taut body, commanding his overheated passions to cool. He could not permit his parents to unwittingly walk in upon such an explosive situation. He, son of Chief Gray Eagle and Princess Shalee, could not be discovered in the throes of unbridled passion with a white captive. He must seek out his parents and explain why he had brought home his captive. In dread, he speculated upon their mixed reactions. He could not determine how they would respond to this unusual deed, for no warrior fought the encroachment of the white-eyes as fiercely as his own father.

He pulled away from her and huskily commanded, "Yanka, Rebecca." Craving her almost beyond any measure of control, he knew he needed some fresh air and a definite change of scenery. He did not realize his voice was laced with softness, sadness, and reluctance.

Rebecca looked up at him in confusion and open desire. He gently pushed her to a sitting position upon his mat and said, "Yanka, Rebecca. Bright Arrow ya Gray Eagle, ya

Shalee." He motioned he would leave to find his parents. He touched his lips and gave the sign for talk. "Ia a'ta, Shalee. Rebecca yanka."

Dread also consuming her, she nodded her comprehension. She, too, could not imagine what they would say or do about her sudden presence in their tepee. She had heard plenty about the illustrious Gray Eagle. Tragically most of it had not been from her father, his friend from times long past.

Bright Arrow smiled encouragingly and left. He walked into the edge of the woods and called out their names. It was not long before an answer came. When he joined them, his parents were standing beside the river, arms about each other as two young lovers who could not touch enough. The brave wondered at this magic which still passed between a woman who was nearly thirty-eight summers and a man almost forty-four. Yet, theirs was an ageless and powerful love: one he craved to experience and to enjoy himself. This romantic sight warmed his racing heart. In turn, they each embraced Bright Arrow, relieved to have their only son home safe.

Shalee's forest-green eyes lovingly caressed her beloved son, a warrior whose towering size and nearly matchless prowess belied his eighteen years. He was so much like his father in appearance and character. She wondered why her heart did not burst when filled with so much love, pride, and happiness.

"A'ta . . . ," he hesitantly began, alerting Gray Eagle to his problem. He smiled at his lovely mother. She affectionately returned it. He slowly began to relate his incredible tale which would rapidly alter each of their lives . . .

Chapter Four

Bright Arrow proudly disclosed how his band of mighty warriors had easily overcome the Bluecoats and destroyed them, conquering them with only two minor injuries to his own men. Although she said nothing and her expression remained calm, he perceived that his mother did not agree with the necessity of his actions, for she disliked the raids and their bloody outcomes. She was definitely concerned with more than his personal safety and survival.

When Bright Arrow had fully recounted the events of his raid, he gingerly spoke of the challenge and death of the Cheyenne brave. He hastily explained his reasoning and motives. Gray Eagle and Shalee listened to the tale about the white girl who was now in their tepee. Most noticeably, Gray Eagle's expression grew wary and glacial, while Shalee's revealed astonishment and inexplicable anguish. When Bright Arrow finished his narration, he silently waited for their response, which seemed too slow in coming . . .

After taking a moment to absorb this incredible event, his father questioned, "You killed a Cheyenne brother to possess a white girl?"

The choice of Gray Eagle's words proclaimed his opinion. Even the challenge for a mere white girl was reprehensible! Bright Arrow carefully selected his words of explanation, "There was more at stake than who would claim the white girl, Father. Standing Bear openly taunted me. He tried to shame the son of Wanmdi Hota. He wished to torture and kill this innocent girl. His treatment of white slaves is no secret. I saw no reason for her pain and death. I did as I thought my father would have done; I reasoned with him first. When he refused a truce and continued to mock me, I was forced to fight and slay him. I could not dishonor myself or my name. The other warriors agree with what I had to do. Was this not right, my Father?" he asked.

"What of the white girl? Now that you have shed Indian blood to possess her, do you plan to keep her in our tepee? Is she still as desirable as she was before the blood of Standing Bear was upon her hands?" he asked, a strange look upon his face.

Bright Arrow was alarmed and perplexed by the odd tone in Gray Eagle's voice. He slowly answered the question, "The girl still pleases me, Father. I will keep her for a time. She is different from the other whites. She does not see me through the eyes of an enemy. Hatred for me does not live in her heart."

Gray Eagle stiffened; his jet eyes narrowed. "Why is this girl unlike the many others you have seen and taken?" Something about his father disturbed Bright Arrow, but he did not know why.

"I do not know, Father," he replied honestly. "There is something about her spirit which calls out to mine. She does not behave or speak as other white-eyes. She is gentle and fragile. I feel responsible for her life and safety. I spared and protected her. Why, I do not know," he confessed.

An unknown light shone brightly within Gray Eagle's gaze. "You are saying this girl is special?" he queried in a deceptively calm voice; yet, his displeasure was obvious in his stormy eyes and tense frame.

"Yes, Father. I wish to keep her until I can understand what great magic she possesses. I must know why my spirit is warmed by hers." He stood proud and respectful before his parents. He answered candidly, even though he secretly wished he could deny them the whole truth.

113

"What did the others say when you took this girl for yourself?" his father pressed, alert to any change in his son's expression and tone.

"They, too, wanted her. They made many offers to buy her, but I refused them . . . for now." He smugly boasted, "When you see her, you will understand why they did not mock me for desiring her."

"What does this girl say about her enslavement to you?" he asked. "Does she know your secret?"

"As always, I pretended not to understand her tongue. I spoke only my English name. This girl knows many Indian words and signing. She has wisely accepted her captivity."

"She knows signing?" Gray Eagle pressed, intrigued.

"It is a strange kind, but I could understand most of it. The whites she travelled with were bad to her. It seemed she was their prisoner in some unknown way. One called her uncle was going to sell her to many Bluecoats for their pleasure. Another white-eyes with many yellow stripes upon his garment was trying to force her onto his mat when I killed him and took her. She was unhappy with them; she was much afraid. She is very beautiful and young. But with me, it was not the same. She accepted me and trusted me. She clung to me as a small child for protection and in open desire as a woman. It pleased the other braves to view such prowess in their leader."

"She does not resist your power over her?" Gray Eagle's eyes probed those of Bright Arrow. He was alarmed by the sincerity and warmth in them.

"She is wise and obedient. I could read the pain in her eyes when she learned of my hold upon her. She no longer trusts me, but she does not defy me," he announced, unwittingly hinting at his prior gentleness and leniency with her.

Gray Eagle then asked the question he most dreaded, "Had she known another man before you, my son?" He knew from experience the undeniable magic of first possessing a special woman.

"No, Father; I was the first to take her. I tricked her into responding to me. I thought it a cunning punishment," he murmured ruefully.

"How did you take her?" That odd tone again laced Gray Eagle's voice.

As feared, Bright Arrow lowered his gaze in guilt and shame. "I was not rough with her, my father. Her mind and body were pure; she did not guess my trick. She came to me as no other female ever has. I could not find it in my heart to hurt her body, only her heart," he reluctantly admitted.

"Tell me all that passed between you," Gray Eagle sternly demanded, his irritation and anxiety steadily mounting as more vexing facts came to light.

After Bright Arrow had related his tale, Gray Eagle murmured to himself, "I see . . ."

Bright Arrow assumed it was best to withhold his strong emotional feelings for this girl, for he did not understand them himself. "Unless you forbid it, Father, I will keep her for a time," he stated, knowing he would comply with his father's wishes. "She is called Rebecca."

To conceal her modesty during their intimate discussion, Shalee had been standing with her back to them. Finally, she could no longer be silent and a cry escaped her lips. She whirled to stare at her son. Bright Arrow's attention was instantly drawn to his mother. Her face was very pale; her green eyes were wide and filled with a haunted look. She seemed oblivious to his presence. Her trembling hand went to her parted lips as if she were preventing some torrent of words from coming forth.

"Mother? Why do you look so pale and distressed?" he questioned, puzzled by this curious and highly emotional reaction to his having taken a white captive.

Shalee swooned; Gray Eagle rushed forward to catch her limp body. He embraced her tightly and tenderly until she recovered her wits. Panic flooded her sea-green eyes, as she looked up at Gray Eagle. Something in his expression hastily silenced whatever she was about to say or to ask. Their eyes met and spoke without words. Bright

Arrow witnessed this mysterious communication and wondered at its meaning.

"Are you ill, Mother?" he anxiously probed.

She smiled sadly and shook her head. "No, my son. Tell me more about this girl. What does she look like?"

Bright Arrow smiled and stated, "She is small; I could hold her up with one hand. Her hair is the color of yours. Her eyes are those of the she-wolf's; but they can soften to the ones of a doe. Her skin is darker than yours. She almost appears an Indian. Even for a white-eyes, she is beautiful. Her spirit is what makes her stand out against other whites. She is gentle and speaks softly like the singing of the stream. She is like a newborn fawn or a fragile desert flower."

Shalee watched the glow which filled her son's eyes as he talked of this special girl. Somehow this girl had touched him in some powerful, unique way. Shalee wondered if this was how Gray Eagle had felt about her all those many years ago when he had captured and enslaved her as his white enemy. The girl which her son had just described could have easily been her, nineteen years ago! A paralyzing feeling of *dèjá vu* washed over Shalee, and she trembled noticeably.

Shalee knew how very strange and unpredictable fate could be. Was it possible that her Bright Arrow had discovered a captive white girl of his own? Was it possible for him to love

117

and desire this woman just as his own father had done long ago. The signs were the same; their actions were the same. Yet, somehow this disturbed her greatly. What would happen if the circumstances of the past and the present fused into one inseparable predicament?

"Tell me, my son; how long will you keep this white girl?" she asked, unable to stop herself. Mystic fingers played an eerie tune upon her nerves and thoughts, its ominous melody echoing intense warnings within her troubled mind.

"I do not know, Mother." Their eyes met and spoke without words, telling her many things.

Shalee read these tender messages within his gaze, messages which disquieted her, messages of more than physical interest. Who was this girl? How would she alter their lives? Shalee dreaded the answers to those plaguing questions, for she clearly remembered the harsh demands and bitter anguish of Indian enslavement.

Bright Arrow glanced over at his father, then down at his mother. "Does it displease you that I have taken a white captive to my mat?" he anxiously queried, hoping his father would not utter the words of sacrifice which he dreaded to hear and be compelled to obey.

Gray Eagle looked deeply into Shalee's eyes, knowing his answer was not only for his son's ears and heart. "What of this girl when the time comes for taking a female of your own kind?" he cautiously began.

"There are many winters between now and then, my father. Could I not enjoy her until I must obey the laws of my people?" he parried his father's reasoning.

"You say this girl possesses great magic and beauty. What if you cannot part with her when that time comes?" Gray Eagle wisely ventured into the unknown dangers of this matter.

"In time, both will fade. Then, I will send her away," Bright Arrow nonchalantly voiced the promise he thought he would be able to keep.

"Look at your mother, Bright Arrow. Some women never lose their magic and beauty. Your mother grows more beautiful each moon. Her magic increases with the passing of time. If it is the same with this white slave of yours, you would be unable to give her up . . . as I could never part with my Shalee," he reasoned, tenderly eying his lovely wife and her radiant smile.

"But mother is an Indian; Rebecca is white," Bright Arrow argued, ignorant his claims were untrue.

"In the dark of night upon your mat, do you know and accept this difference? Or does Rebecca become only a woman, your woman?" his father boldly challenged, sending his point hurling home.

A stunned look flickered upon Bright Arrow's face. He indignantly replied, "I did not forget she is white. Hunwi glowed upon her face, reminding me she was not Indian." Yet, his hasty statement only entrapped him.

"Hunwi warned you she was our enemy; yet you took her with great gentleness and fiery passion?" Gray Eagle twisted the knife.

Bright Arrow lowered his head, unable to meet the discerning stare of his father's ebony eyes. "Yes, Father," he shamefully admitted. "Words say she is my enemy, but her spirit does not," he added in his defense.

"And this does not prove to you that her skin color means nothing to you?" his trenchant reply came forth.

"Not so!" his son rashly disagreed. "She is my captive, nothing more! This I swear to you, my father. I see and know she is white. I will never forget it," he vowed fervently, assured he would be true to his laws when the time came.

"You are the son of Gray Eagle, chief of the Oglala. You will be the next leader of our people. I fear this girl causes you to think with your loins, not with your head. The fact you have taken her and still keep her alarms me. I do not wish my son to be taunted and mocked for his kindness to his enemy. I do not wish my son to fall under the magic of a white girl whom he can never fully possess. To keep her invites danger, my son, for you and for this girl."

"But I cannot hand her over to the Tipi Sa!" he blurted out, exposing his deep feelings without meaning to do so.

"Then you should trade her to another warrior who does not need to stand straight and true like Bright Arrow," he advised.

Bright Arrow's eyes darted about in panic as he mentally envisioned Rebecca struggling upon a mat with another brave. Anger and jealousy flamed brightly and deadly within him. "I cannot! She is mine! When I have removed her powerful magic, then I will follow your advice. I will send her away only if you command it, my father," he declared, his eyes and voice obstinate. He was Gray Eagle's son, but he was also a grown man and a noted warrior in his own rank!

How could a frightened white girl be a threat to a powerful warrior? All he had to do was turn his head to dismiss her from sight and mind! What better way to punish one of the enemy than to humiliate her with enslavement, to force her to bend her will to any wish or command? He would find this sport enjoyable and stimulating if his father permitted him to keep her.

"Then I must go to our tepee and view this girl whose spirit has ensnared that of my only son. I will return and speak the words of my decision about her fate. Remain here with your mother."

"I must come with you, Father. She will be afraid. She has heard of Gray Eagle and the mighty Oglala." When the noble chief questioned that information, Bright Arrow related the story of his sketches upon the ground which had revealed their identities. Gray Eagle thought it odd this white girl knew so much about him.

"No, Bright Arrow. I go alone. I will test her wisdom and courage. I will see if she is worthy to be your slave. I will learn why you have chosen her over one of your own kind." Gray Eagle looked at Shalee; some unreadable message passed between them. Gray Eagle smiled at her, then lovingly caressed her cheek.

Bright Arrow reluctantly sat down beside his mother as they both intently watched Gray Eagle's departure. When he was out of hearing range, Shalee studied her son closely. "You desire this girl very much, do you not?" she inquired.

Her soft approach relaxed his tension. "Yes, Mother. She is unlike all other women. I wish she were not white. If she were Indian, I would marry her this very day. If Father says I must give her up, it will sadden my heart. I fear her loss will dull my keen senses; and fear is not good in a warrior. I do not understand these strange feelings," he mumbled sadly.

Shalee tenderly stroked his cheek, smiling into his brooding eyes. "It is not fear you feel, my son; it is concern for the white girl. It is like she would take a special part of your spirit with her if she is forced to leave your side. Desire and worry are not signs of weakness or fear, Bright Arrow," she calmly assuaged his anguish and guilt. "It is your desire for her which troubles you, not fear."

He stared at his mother, absorbing her words and perception. "You are a woman, Mother. Warriors do not see things that way. But is it so wrong to . . ." He could not complete his traitorous statement. He glanced away from her discerning gaze.

". . . feel this way about your enemy?" she finished it for him. She smiled as their gazes met and sighed. "Perhaps in the eyes of our people, but not in my heart. Must Indian laws and hatred apply to all whites, even one so young and innocent as Rebecca? What has she done to make her our enemy? Nothing! She was born white; you were born Indian. Only the Great Spirit knows why. Evil and hatred come from the heart, Bright Arrow, not from skin color. If her skin became red, would her heart or spirit be changed? If your skin became white, would your heart and spirit? No."

When he started to argue her points, she silenced him, "Hear me out, my son. If Rebecca were not special, she would not have caught the eye of my son. Yet, there are many matters to consider. There are problems which even love and desire cannot conquer. These are what concern your father. He fears the magic hold she might cast over you, a hold which is forbidden in the eyes and laws of our people. Perhaps it is unjust and unfair, but it has always been this way. I wish it were not so, for my heart yearns for peace and safety. When you are young, the heart often speaks louder than the head. But love does not easily or painlessly yield to hostility and warfare. How does this girl look at you and treat you?'' she asked.

Sensing his mother's sympathy and concern, Bright Arrow slowly confessed the truth. He was pleased and relieved when she did not gasp in surprise or speak of dishonor. She cautiously related the unknown English words which Rebecca had spoken to him, binding him more tightly to this cherished captive. Instead, a haunting sadness was revealed within his mother's forest green eyes. When she spoke, her voice contained echoes of emotions which he could not understand.

Shalee chose her words carefully, for her beloved son did not know that his own mother was a white woman. He did not know of how his father had captured, enslaved, ravished, tormented, and loved a white girl the year before he was born. He did not know of the anguish, sacrifice, and problems which they had faced and overcome long ago. He had not been told of how a desperate old woman named Matu had altered a scar upon Alisha Williams's left buttock to match the akito—an identifying tattoo—upon the hand of the chief of the Blackfoot tribe, leading all to believe she was his half-breed daughter Shalee who had been kidnapped by whites at the tender age of two and who had been miraculously returned to her people at nineteen. He did not know of how his father had challenged Brave Bear, the chosen son of Chief Mahpiya Sapa, for Shalee's hand in marriage. Their underlying secrets too deadly to reveal, these past triumphs and tragedies had long since been buried.

Naturally Bright Arrow knew his mother was the half-breed daughter of Chief Black Cloud and his white squaw Jenny who had been slain during a Bluecoat raid upon the Blackfoot village when his mother was two winters old. He also knew his mother had met and joined with his father nineteen winters ago. He knew of the potent love which they shared; he had witnessed the closeness between them. Yet, he did not know that his uncontrollable action had abruptly refreshed his parents' painful memories. He did not know how deeply they feared to watch their past life relived by their son.

Shalee observed her son as he spoke of this girl called Rebecca, this girl who resembled her, this girl who sounded so much like her . . .

Shalee dreaded to think about this girl's new existence, one which could eventually rival her own horrible past as a white captive to a formidable warrior who was the son of a chief! How could she bear to witness her past reborn in another's present life? How could she prevent such a travesty without telling her son why? How could she encourage such a forbidden union which could only lead to anguish and heartache for both the girl and her son? Yet, how could she wisely counsel him without betraying her own deadly secrets? The truth had to remain hidden for all time in order to protect the lives of those she loved.

Shalee shuddered to speculate upon the circumstances which would surround the naked truth about her: her husband's deception in presenting her as Princess Shalee, her own eager and willing acceptance of the Oglala's love and trust and that of the Blackfoot's, and her son's half-breed lineage. Even after living with the Indians for these years, their resentment would be limitless if they somehow learned of these numerous deceptions . . . Her beloved son, how could she possibly condemn him to the lowly rank of half-breed: a position lower than the white man or the Indian held in either's eyes?

Who was this girl who had been cruelly thrust into their peaceful lives? How would Rebecca change their tranquil existence and Bright Arrow? Yet, how could Shalee meekly stand aside and watch Bright Arrow treat this innocent, defenseless girl in the same unyielding manner in which Gray Eagle had originally done to her? How could Shalee forestall these warnings of portentous doom which savagely rent at her heart and mind?

Shalee's mind was plagued by too many echoes of her own yesterdays. Her own mental cries and pleas for mercy, acceptance, and love of long ago reverberated over and over within her distressed mind. All of her yesterdays were in the past; why couldn't they remain concealed there? Yet, she somehow knew they would not. The dangerous echoes would continue to come closer and to grow louder until . . . until what? She apprehensively fretted.

"Mother? What troubles you so?" Bright Arrow inquired, love and worry in his tone and curious gaze.

"Rebecca, Bright Arrow. I am a woman; I know the feelings within her. I feel great sorrow in knowing what she might endure. It will be hard for her, my son. She has already lost and suffered so much. Yet, there is more anguish to come for her. I, too, cannot bear the idea of you sending her to another brave who might use her badly. If she is as you say, her pain and fear are great. You not only control her life, but also her heart. How I wish there was no war between us."

Shalee looked deeply into his eyes as she said, "Remember these things, my son: she cannot be blamed for her white skin; she cannot be blamed for being a woman, one who has fallen prey to the strength and control of a strong man. She does not have the power to fight you or her destiny. Do not punish her for what she cannot change or control. If you wish it so, I will try to teach her respect and obedience. I would not want my son to be forced to brutally punish or to slay an innocent girl because of her natural defiance. There is much she must learn and accept. If you keep her, I will do this for both of you."

Bright Arrow could hardly trust his ears. "You would help me train this white girl?" he asked incredulously, oblivious to her real motives.

"If you must keep her, my son, then let our tepee be a happy one. This girl could change many things there if we refuse to teach her what she must know and do. Does she not deserve our help and kindness? Reckless defiance could cost her life and the peace within our home."

"I do not understand, Mother. Rebecca is white! She is my slave and must obey me! She is

128

our enemy!" he irrationally debated her confusing words. Their laws were clear: captives obeyed the commands of their masters or they were punished; that had always been the way of his kind. Was his own mother actually suggesting leniency and friendship? "Rebecca will not defy me; she is afraid, but she is smart!"

"You are far wiser and braver than you claim she is, my son. But would you silently and meekly accept captivity by your white enemy? Rebellion against enslavement and hatred is a natural thing, Bright Arrow. Yes, she might be smart and frightened. But how long can she timidly accept a life of coldness, cruelty, and loneliness? Her ravaged heart will soon cry out for freedom, honor, and happiness. She must find them within your life-circle or she will helplessly seek them in another place. Kindness will gain you far more from her than mighty power ever can. I cannot permit the war between our peoples to steal into my own tepee," she softly informed him.

"But the others will call me coward and betrayer!" he protested her assertions.

"Not if you only behave this way in our tepee. Be the Indian and warrior in the village, but only a man in our tepee. This small amount of truce will be enough for her. You will see," she promised confidently, recalling how it had once been between the English girl Alisha Williams and the formidable Sioux warrior Gray Eagle.

"What if Rebecca will not allow this trick? What will my father say when he learns of it?" he speculated as irrepressible excitement sang within his veins. Was such a ruse possible? The temptation was great.

"As for your father, I do not know. I can only hope he will permit our kindness to her. It is you, not Rebecca, who shouts of this hostility between you two. It is also my beloved son the Sioux Warrior, not his white captive, who is unwilling to deny or to prevent this emotional warfare. From all you say, you are but a man to her. But to you, she is only a white captive. You already possess her life and purity. Wherein does the justice lie for her continued punishment and rejection? She belongs to you. She desires you and accepts you as a man. Do you wish to drive these special feelings from her heart and body with coldness and torment? If she withdraws her love from you, is that not the same as losing her? What do you truly want from her?" she challenged.

When he failed to answer her question, she continued, "Have you forgotten that you own mother carries the blood of a white squaw? Does that fact make me a despised enemy? If not for Wi, my skin would be as white as snow. My grass eyes declare my wasichu blood. Does this not tell you that all whites are not evil? Because of the love and desire my father felt for a white squaw, I was born. Am I any less than I am because of their forbidden love and union, for the wasichu blood which flows within me? When your lance brings forth the blood of a white, is it not the same color as an Indian's? The real difference between the white-eyes and the Indians is in spirit. The colors of our skins are only an excuse to reveal this difference."

Bright Arrow reasoned upon her words. He decided, "You are indeed wise and gentle, Mother. But my father and the others do not feel and think this way," he apprehensively reminded her. Once again that strange and haunting look came into her emerald eyes.

"Your father is a warrior and a chief, Bright Arrow. As leader of our tribe, he must view things differently. I cannot speak of the secret matters which are in his heart and mind, for only he sees and understands them. I have loved him since the first moment our eyes met. I must obey his wishes. Yet, sometimes the good of our people must shine brighter than his love for me. This has been hard to accept and to understand, but it must be so. I would not wish to cause him pain or dishonor. Yet, sometimes we do such things because we cannot help ourselves. Too, there are times when the Great Spirit has plans for us which we do not comprehend and often resist."

"How so, Mother?" he curiously inquired, his brow lifting inquisitively.

She silently reasoned for a time, trying to find some way to make her points without revealing too much. She smiled sadly and whispered softly, "Speak of this to no one, not even your father. It would bring back much pain in both our hearts, but there are matters which might help you understand things more clearly. He would not wish me to tell you of our past days, but there is one thing you must hear. Then you will comprehend his decision and our sadness. When your father and I first met, we were both promised to others. But our love could not be halted. It quickly grew until it was an overpowering force which we could not resist. When Gray Eagle first saw me, it was much like your meeting with Rebecca. He desired me greatly, but he saw my green eyes and believed me a white captive. For this, he fiercely resisted the bond of love which stretched between us. Even when he learned I was the daughter of Chief Mahpiya Sapa, he still struggled against my white blood. Knowing your father's feelings about the whites and their evil, you can comprehend the terrible battle which raged within him. Even so, he could not forget me. His hunger for me became so great that he challenged my promised mate to win me. After we were joined, he came to love me even more.

For all these years, he chose to deny my white blood. But today, you have reminded him of this truth which he had buried within his heart. Your challenge of an Indian brother for a white woman's possession reminded him of his past challenge for the half-breed daughter of Black Cloud. Yet, he spared the life of his rival; you could not. Your words reminded him of the same turmoil which he had endured. Others also thought me white; they mocked and taunted him for his weakness and dishonor.

"Do you not see, my son? You have innocently reminded him that he also loves a girl with wasichu blood. You now show him what would have passed between us had I not been proven Si-ha Sapa. As with you and Rebecca, he feared losing me; he feared taking me. As you said, fear is not good in a warrior. For a time we tasted the pain and hopelessness of forbidden love and powerful desire; he wishes to spare you from that same anguish and humiliation, for you and Rebecca cannot find the happy solution we now enjoy. It took great love and courage for him to accept a half-breed girl. It was also difficult for the Oglalas to learn to accept a half-breed girl in the sacred life circle of their beloved Gray Eagle. Now, Gray Eagle's son also chooses a white girl over one of his own kind. Such an action might cast dark shadows over both of you; it might remind the Oglalas that I am also half white."

"But how could my father challenge for you when both of you were promised to others?" he seized upon a conflicting point which she had overlooked, forcing her to divulge more facts.

"As with Rebecca, he took me thinking I was a white girl. My love for him was so great that I openly declared my choice of him. But the laws of our peoples had to be obeyed. He was forced to win me by the right of ki-ci-e-conape, for he had possessed me first. But the outcome was unlike your fight with the Cheyenne warrior; your father spared the life of Brave Bear and gave him the hand of his chosen one in joining. There is truce between us."

"Brave Bear and Chela were your chosen mates!" he exclaimed.

"It was so, but our love could not be denied. It was the will of the Great Spirit. Since that day, there has been truce and happiness for all. We have been at peace with the Si-ha Sapa. Will our Cheyenne brothers feel the same good spirit at the news of your deadly challenge with Standing Bear? Your father is very proud and stubborn, my son. Even now, it is hard for him to remember my white blood. Your magic is much like his; Rebecca cannot resist it, as I could not resist his. You say she is much like me, and he fears you will come to love and desire her as he did me. Love me or hurt me, he will reject

134

this girl's place within your life."

"I will speak to him of these things! He must know of my feelings. I will tell him . . ."

She hastily interrupted him, "No, Bright Arrow! You must never speak of the past to him. It would only re-open many old wounds which are not completely healed; it might cause new ones which will hurt us all deeply. I beg you; do not speak of this to him. I only told you these things to help you understand what must be. He knows of your feelings, but he also knows of the price it will take for you to keep Rebecca."

"But things are good between you," he argued.

"Only because he has been able to conceal my wasichu blood from everyone, including himself. Many things were said and done between us while we resisted our love, things which even now I cannot bear to recall or to speak of to even you. Do not call our past back to life; it would be tormenting and costly for us," she entreated him. "Every day more whites come to our lands to forcefully steal them. Deeper hostility breeds with each new moon."

"What did my father do to you, Mother?" he asked, sensing some terrible agony within that haunted expression.

"Call to mind how you viewed and treated Rebecca. You did so because she is white and your captive. When I first met Gray Eagle, he thought I was white and he tried to capture me. Put the two times together and compare them. Therein lies the answer you seek, Bright Arrow . . ."

His eyes grew wide with disbelief and alarm. "But why did he not listen to your words and pleas? He took you as I took her!" he remarked in alarming distress.

She smiled through dewy eyes. "Just as you took her. With magic, gentleness, desire, and confusion. Did you heed Rebecca's words and signs? No. Does she not look more Indian than I do, than I did? Could she speak while your mouth was upon hers? Perhaps her fear, confusion, and suffering stole her speech. Did she not fall prey to your great prowess and magic: things you share with your father?"

He grinned mischievously. "Afterwards you did not hate him? You joined to him?" he teased her.

She laughed merrily, a light blush covering her face. "I fear his magic was too powerful to refuse. I loved him even at that first moment. For a time, there was rebellion and resentment within my mind. But his touch and love dispelled them. I would not want such bitter memories to return and to cast a dark shadow upon our love. You told him of your night with Rebecca, a night which compared to one with me long ago."

"Still, it is different between me and Rebecca."

"Perhaps for now, but who can tell what the new moon holds for any of us? You are the son of the Oglala chief. As with us, you will also face decisions and sacrifices which other warriors will not. Your people will come before your needs and wishes many times. Often this will be painful, haunting, and difficult for you. But as with your father and others chiefs, you will do what you must. You will bend and yield to your destiny and the will of your people, for this is deeply ingrained within your heart and mind. Rebecca will innocently suffer for what she is and for who you are; this cannot be avoided or changed. Accept it now, my son, or both of you could know great anguish. I wish I could tell you to give her up this moment, but I cannot. I know what it is like to desire someone beyond will or reason. What do laws and skin colors matter when your spirit cries out for hers? There are two things you must promise me: first, do not punish her for her tragic destiny, for she has no choice but to obey it. Second, you must keep all these words between us secret."

"I must think much upon them, but I will conceal them from everyone. You are wise and brave, my beautiful mother. Now, I can understand my father's coming decision. When he speaks it, I will abide by it," he wretchedly agreed, fearing the worst.

She hugged him tightly. "I am very proud of you, Bright Arrow. I could ask for no better son. You are indeed like your father, a man who stands far above others. We will speak again after I have met your Rebecca."

For a time they spoke of other things as they nervously awaited Gray Eagle's return. As time crept along, both Shalee and Bright Arrow became concerned. Bright Arrow was the first to give voice to their rising panic. "Why does he take so long, Mother? Would he send her away before telling me his decision?"

"I honestly do not know. He will do what he thinks is best for all concerned." A look of alarm suddenly crossed her features. What if the girl was so terrified of him that she rebelled against him and her captivity? Her own scars upon her back from a past lashing for defiance tingled a warning within her. "Perhaps we should return to our tepee. Something might be wrong. Surely he has finished his inspection of her by now. She does not know our ways; she might make a terrible mistake and defy him . . ."

Bright Arrow was instantly upon his feet. He helped his mother up and took her small hand within his larger one. They quickly walked back to camp. Shalee entered their tepee first. The white girl was in tears; she was shaking violently. Gray Eagle was towering over her like

138

some giant bird of prey about to attack her and tear her to pieces. At Shalee's voice from the entry, he whirled to face her and her seeming intrusion, eyes glacial and angry. His lofty, muscular frame was taut and intimidating.

Her curious eyes went from her husband to the weeping girl, then back to him again. "Wamndi Hota?" she asked.

When he spoke to her in his tongue, his voice was harsh and strained. "I said to wait by the stream for my return. I have not decided her fate. Go! Leave this matter to me," he sternly commanded in a tone which she had not heard in many, many years from the man she loved. The look which filled his jet eyes caused fingers of dread to seize her tender heart. She was stunned into silence. She had witnessed many confrontations with white foes, but none as tempestuous as this one appeared.

"What has happened here, Father?" Bright Arrow asked, confounded by his father's unleashed temper and tense body.

At the sound of Bright Arrow's voice, Rebecca looked up. She cried out in relief and rushed toward him. Her arms encircled his waist and she buried her tear-streaked face against his bare chest. She sobbed uncontrollably, clinging tightly to him.

Both Shalee and Bright Arrow stared at Gray Eagle in confusion. Gray Eagle's eyes narrowed, hardened, and chilled as he observed the tender way his son's arms instinctively embraced the white girl and held her possessively and comfortingly.

"Release her, Bright Arrow! It is wrong to show her such warmth and leniency. Such friendly actions breed defiance and arrogance within white slaves. She is but a white captive; treat her as such." To see this particular girl snuggled against his only son's body and drawing solace from him was too much to bear!

"But she is so young and frightened, Father," he rashly argued, unaware of the vicious war raging within his father.

"It is only natural to fear your enemy! To show kindness and to offer comfort would be an open show of acceptance and friendship to her. I cannot permit it. She has cunningly captured your eyes and your loins; I will not allow her to add your heart and your honor to her wicked collection. She is evil. She is weak and crafty. She seeks to win your heart with her false tears and pretense of desire. No white woman could truly love her Indian captor! The only magic she possesses is her cunning mind; no doubt she laughs at your weakness for her," he snarled.

In the heat of his vengeful anger, Gray Eagle's concentration was upon Bright Arrow and the despicable white girl. He failed to note the shocking impact of his cutting words and actions upon his wife, who was also white and had once stood where this terrified and helpless girl was standing now. Shalee watched this tragic scene in utter disbelief. After all these years, was his past resentment surfacing and venting?

The secrets which Gray Eagle had just uncovered about this white girl raged viciously and bitterly within him like a violent storm mercilessly attacking everything in its path. He could not believe the Great Spirit would punish and torture him in this cruel and inexplicable. manner. In Gray Eagle's attempts to extract information about her, Rebecca had innocently given away several clues to her identity. In her desperation to convince Gray Eagle that she and her father had been friendly to the Indians, she had spoken Joe Kenny's name: a name which he had instantly recognized, a name which had told him her true identity, a perilous fact which even she did not know!

Gray Eagle could barely contain the resentment and enmity which flamed like destructive wildfire throughout his virile body. Of all white females alive, he could never permit this particular girl to have his only son! He had not permitted her real father to steal his wife, and he would never allow his lowly daughter to entrap his only son. He bitterly recalled that day years ago when not Joe Kenny, but her real father, a treacherous half-breed, had shot him and had left him for dead. He remembered how her father had tragically interfered in their lives many times in the distant past. He would never forget or forgive her father for kidnapping Shalee the day after their joining, for using his own past treatment of Shalee to convince her that her new husband had left her to die in the desert while all along he lay bleeding to death from that treacherous scout's wound! If that wasn't enough evil, her father had taken his beloved wife into great peril, danger which claimed the life of his unborn child, danger which placed her under the wicked control of a yellow-haired Bluecoat from the fort which he had bravely destroyed, danger which had caused him to think his guiltless wife had betrayed him, danger which had blindly compelled him to seek her life in brutal revenge for traitorous crimes which she had not committed!

He could never forget or forgive the pain and troubles which Rebecca's father had caused. It did not matter that Rebecca had been raised as the child of his old friend Joe Kenny. It did not matter that Joe had been the man to help his wife, to later come here to explain the scout's treachery and her innocence, to be the one who brought about their present happiness and acceptance. The blood of her real father ran within her body: the blood of Powchutu, the half-breed scout from Fort Pierre . . .

Never imagining that their paths would ever cross again, Joe had carelessly confessed the truth about his wife Mary, about how she had loved Powchutu, about how she had become pregnant with his child, about how he had been murdered before they could marry, about how Shalee must never know the truth about the man who had more than once saved her life at the risk of his own and a man who had once been like a brother to her, about the man whom Shalee would have married if things had worked out differently at the fort: something Powchutu had been unable and unwilling to accept. Powchutu had craved Shalee for his own wife; he had done all within his power and skill to win her love. Now, Powchutu's daughter was standing here in his tepee, threatening to destroy them all!

The emotional battle raged on and on within Gray Eagle, creating a mixture of volatile expressions upon his normally impassive face. The floodgates upon the dam of his memory had been shattered; waves and waves of tormenting thoughts returned from the past to storm against his taut body and to carry it along in its violent surges. He struggled to escape this swirling tide, as past events reached out to engulf him. He could not fathom a guess as to Shalee's reaction to Rebecca's identity. He could not risk telling her the truth. Rebecca must leave before many secrets were revealed. Never would his only son be ensnared by the daughter of his worst enemy!

Shalee could not believe the fierce hostility and contempt which she vividly read within Gray Eagle's eyes and upon his handsome face.

"She is white! She is unworthy of your touch! Her mind and blood are evil. Send her to the Tipi Sa!" he sneered, outrage shuddering his stalwart body.

Watching her husband and listening to him, Shalee was brutally thrown backwards in time to a day when she had occupied Rebecca's place. Without warning or knowing, she shrieked, "Hiya!"

Both Bright Arrow and Gray Eagle were astonished by the vehemence in her tone and the gleam of anger which filled her turbulent green eyes. In Oglala, she murmured almost inaudibly, "Kill her or send her away, but never put an innocent girl in that vile place. I will never forgive you, my husband, if you do this terrible thing! Rebecca is not to blame for the hatred between the white man and the Indian. Why must a white girl pay for the warfare which men instigate? It is cruel and unjust! To condemn a child like this to such a brutal fate would make us appear the savages we are alleged to be! Such spitefulness is beneath you, my husband . . ."

Gray Eagle stared at her in disbelief. She had not spoken to him in this rebellious tone in eighteen years! Neither had she coldly glared at him as she did this minute, not since . . . His fury and bitterness mounted as he incredulously gazed into the beautiful and defiant expression of Alisha Williams. . . .

Chapter Five

Rebecca Kenny's head jerked around and she stared inquisitively at the Indian beauty. She anxiously wondered what was going on. Why did Shalee and Bright Arrow appear to rebel against Gray Eagle's harsh words and actions? It seemed as if they wished to protect her and he would not permit it. Indian wives and children never defied a warrior, especially not a chief! She did not understand . . .

It was clear to the frightened white girl that these unpredictable Indians were disagreeing upon some vital matter which concerned her. Before these two had returned, Gray Eagle had been trying to find some way to communicate with her. He was an intrepid, imposing man. Somehow she had innocently angered him, and she did not know why. No doubt he was furious with his stalwart son for bringing a white captive to his tepee! He was definitely enraged by Bright Arrow's comforting embrace. She was tempted to move away from her love, but could not summon the strength to do so.

Whatever the chief had said, Bright Arrow's mother was against it. Numerous questions plagued Rebecca's distressed mind. Why did her impending fate matter to Shalee? Why was Bright Arrow treating her this gentle way before his powerful father when he had treated her so coldly and indifferently before his band of warriors? This whole situation was perplexing and dangerous. She wondered if it was possible for Shalee and Bright Arrow to overrule the reprehensible fate which Gray Eagle must have suggested to them.

With two graceful catlike strides, Gray Eagle was standing before his rebellious wife. She shamefully lowered her head. She could not gaze into his naked expression of intermingled anguish, disappointment, and anger. Yet, she did not apologize for her outburst, a sign which troubled him.

"Come, Shalee. We must talk," he tersely stated, a scowl upon his handsome features. He grasped her arm to lead her outside.

"What about the girl, Gray Eagle?" she anxiously asked, resisting his command.

"We will speak first, then decide her fate. Come, there are things which must be said between us." He released her arm and headed outside.

Shalee glanced over at Bright Arrow and Rebecca. They both looked so young, so vulnerable, so confused, and so deeply attracted to each other. This was not going to be easy for any of them. What was the correct decision? She did not know.

She mutely followed her husband out of their tepee to seek privacy. They walked along in strained silence; they did not even touch. When they came to a grove of cottonwood trees, Gray Eagle halted. He turned to face her. He studied her for a time, unable to find the right words to begin their conversation.

She took the initiative. "I am sorry for my rude behavior, but I could not stop myself. I know what it's like to be in her place. She's so young and innocent, Gray Eagle. Must she suffer for the hatred between the Indian and the white man? Must it always be this way?" she entreated, her eyes sad.

"We are enemies at war, Shalee. A line must be drawn somewhere. If you do remember what it is like, then you must also remember how futile and painful such a forbidden union is," he reasoned, his temper under control. "Do you wish our son to know the same agony which we endured so long ago? If not for Black Cloud and Matu . . ." He did not complete his thought; it was unnecessary. "There is no Matu to help them. It will only cause trouble and anguish for all concerned. She must be sent away."

"It is too late, my husband. Did you not see the way they touched and looked at each other? I accepted you, and Rebecca has accepted Bright Arrow. Why is it so difficult or impossible for the two of you to accept us?"

"You are my wife. I have accepted you, even knowing you are white. But with Bright Arrow and Rebecca, it is different."

Her gaze fused with his. "If not for Matu's ruse, it would be the same between us; would it not?" she asked in a sorrowful tone, but he did not answer.

When he looked away in brooding silence, she reasoned, "Why does secrecy change things. I am still white."

"Because my honor remains unstained. Much as I love you, Shalee, I could not live in dishonor. A man is nothing without his honor. Wife or white slave, I could never part with you. But our son must join with one of his own kind. For a man to carry white blood at birth and then to mate with a girl of white blood would give his son more white blood than Oglala. Do you wish that despised fate for the son of our son? The Oglala would never accept a half-breed as their chief, nor a white girl in his life. No one knows this deadly truth better than I!"

"But our son is . . ."

He sharply cut off the remainder of her tormenting words, "No! If he joins to an Oglala, the Indian blood will be stronger. This white girl will only blind him to his rank and people. She could become as important to him as you are to me. The quicker she is removed from his life, the better. My people will question his loyalty and wisdom if he keeps this white girl. He must have no stain upon his name. What if this girl reminds my people that you also carry white blood? Dissension in my tribe would be unwise and dangerous. I must think of my people."

Shalee chose to ignore his constant use of "my people."

"What of our son?" she asked. "What of his wants and wishes? What of this innocent girl?"

"For a chief, the good of his people must come before his own desires and dreams. I know this only too well! In time, after she is gone, Bright Arrow will forget her. He will know I have done what is best for all concerned," he concluded, bitterness lacing his tone.

"If I had been traded to another warrior years ago, would you have forgotten me? Would you have thanked your father for doing what was best for everyone, including you?" she artfully challenged. "The words you spoke in our tepee hurt me deeply. After all these years, I heard how you felt so long ago."

Annoyed, he snapped, "It was different then!

You are the daughter of Black Cloud; she is white!"

"Only in the eyes of your people," she parried softly, stung by his glacial rebuke.

"But that is all which matters," he snarled, wishing she were not so cunning and persistent. Just as he dreaded, Rebecca's evil was already at work!

"That is my point, Gray Eagle. In many Indian hearts, this difference does not matter. But no one will prevent the damage such beliefs make. Each one refuses to speak out for the same reasons which you will not. So, the hatred and separation continues. Many unions between our two peoples have suffered because no one will attempt to halt this cruel injustice. You accepted me because others do not know I am white. Others warriors take and keep white squaws. Yet, acceptance is denied because each man is unwilling to take a stand against this foolishness. When will this brutal contradiction end? If a white woman is unworthy of a warrior's acceptance, then she should also be unworthy of his touch, and of bearing his children who will suffer for their mixed bloods. It is wrong," she said with dismay, unable to comprehend this vicious paradox.

"But it is our way! If I tried to speak out for white slaves, no man would follow me into battle. I cannot show weakness and friendship to those who seek to take away our lands and destroy us!" he shouted his disagreement.

"We are not speaking of greedy, evil men! We are speaking of helpless women. There is a vast difference, my husband. Why do you close your eyes to this truth?" she implored him.

"One man cannot change the minds and hearts of many people, people who have been wronged, people who have battled and hated for years. I would be a fool to do so."

"If what one man thinks and does cannot influence the minds and hearts of others, then why would Bright Arrow's taking of this girl matter?" she craftily ensnared him in his own verbal trap.

"He is the son of a chief! He is the son of Gray Eagle! He will be our next leader. It matters greatly what he says and does. To fight the enemy with cunning and bravery is one thing, but to make a foolish truce with him is another," he snapped.

"For men, this is true. But for women, it is not. A man thinks and feels first with his mind; a woman, with her heart. If a white woman can love and accept her Indian captor and his people, why can they not accept her? She has not fought against you. To punish her for the evil of other whites is not just. Would it be so degrading to point this out to the others? They know the words of Gray Eagle are wise and just. Would they not heed you? Could it not change things for many white women who have been helplessly caught in the middle of this conflict? Could it not ease the heartache and remove the guilt of warriors who wish to publicly proclaim their love and trust in their white squaws?"

"To do as you ask would openly condone these forbidden unions. They would flourish. Soon, the blood of the Oglala would be half white. In time the Oglala would cease to exist. I cannot bring such a despicable death to my people. I am no longer a young warrior, Shalee. Each day I must prove I retain the strength and cunning to lead my people."

Shalee walked off a short distance to consider his disquieting words. The problem was that they were both partially right. To solve one trouble would only inspire new ones. Would there ever be a solution to this trying situation? She feared not, for neither side would ever relent. Wisps of auburn hair wavered in the gentle breeze and danced upon her forehead and cheeks. Her emerald green eyes gazed upward at the white clouds which were drifting aimlessly upon a rich sapphire backdrop. The whisper of green leaves was nearly inaudible. Yet, none of the peacefulness or vitality of this setting relaxed her.

She turned to look at her husband. He was staring off into the forest, lost in moody reflections. Her heart relented as she viewed the weight of this burden upon his shoulders. Her gaze softened as she looked at his virile, towering frame. Time had been generous to him! His robust physique favorably compared to that of a young warrior's. He was vital, alive with strength and valor. No muscle had lost its tone; no sign of aging made its presence known. Her heart swelled with love, respect, and desire. She had not realized he feared to lose his power as time passed and gradually sapped his vitality and youth.

Shalee had ceased to think upon her English heritage long ago. From white captives she had learned of Great Britain's defeat to the American Colonies and their joint treaty. It had seemed that after the Americans won their independence from her homeland, they had turned their covetous eyes and insatiable greed upon the opulent lands of the Indians. More and more, the white settlers spread westward.

With each passing year, a noticeable change was apparent within these new Americans who attempted the arduous and dangerous trek into this promising and rapidly expanding territory. This new breed of American was as daring and defiant as the intrepid Sioux. These pioneering whites had become courageous, self-reliant, and aggressive.

Tragically, many whites were good and honest people, seeking new hope and freedom. Yet, they were too frequently overshadowed by those consumed with greed, evil, and animosity. A bitter and costly clash had resulted from the head-on confrontation between these two powerful, determined, and desperate forces. Tragic defeat appeared inevitable for one side or the other. Shalee feared to surmise the victor or the loser.

The seven tribes of the Sioux Nation had gradually spread out over much of South Dakota, lower North Dakota, upper Nebraska, and eastern Wyoming: a fact which had noticeably weakened their staunch control of this particular area. Yet, the fierce Oglala tribe remained steadfast, intrepid, and indomitable.

As the white influx had increased, her husband had resisted with all his might, cunning, and skill. He was constantly on the alert to protect his people. He often spoke of how peaceful life was before the whites had trespassed on his beautiful lands. To her dread and dismay, he was right; they were enemies at war.

"I see your points, my husband. Still, what of the girl Rebecca? She has no people. She is alone and afraid. It would be wrong to send her back to the whites who would despise her for her life with us. But it would also be wrong to give her to another warrior. She has known no man except our son. Let her remain in our tepee for a time. Perhaps the bond between them will fade. Then, you could find a good man for her. Do this for me and our son," she pleaded.

The love and gentleness which flowed from

her rolled upon him like a soothing wave of warm, inviting water. His anger was mastered. Enthralled, he wondered how he could possibly refuse her without telling her the real reason for his intense dislike for this girl. He could not even trust himself to utter the name of Powchutu. His tender-hearted wife would surely feel responsible for this girl if she learned Rebecca was the daughter of Mary and Joe. If only she were the daughter of Joe! If so, he would permit his son to keep her . . .

"What troubles you so deeply, my husband?" she softly inquired, coming over to him and gazing up into his turbulent eyes.

"I fear you see yourself in this white girl. I also fear you see me in our son. The past is gone, Shalee. Do not call it back to life. There is danger blowing in the wind with this girl's coming. I feel its warnings gusting about me. We must not tempt our son to become overly attached to her. Do not go against my wishes in this matter." There was a hint of urgent petition in his tone of voice.

Shalee voiced a deep concern of hers which Gray Eagle had not reflected upon. "What if this girl already carries the child of our son? If you send her away and the child is born to another warrior, it would also be a slave. Do you wish the son of our son to endure such an existence?"

At the thought of Powchutu's daughter

bearing his first grandchild, Gray Eagle's rage knew no limits. "It cannot be! She is unworthy to bear his son! Her blood must not flow within his child!"

"Why do you hate this girl so, my husband? What wrong has she done to you, to us? What deeds of hers do you hold deep within your mind?" she asked, perceiving something odd and cruel in his vehemence.

Cautioning himself, he merely growled, "She is white! There can be no more white blood to weaken the line of Gray Eagle. Bright Arrow must join with an Oglala," he stated fiercely.

Hurt, she felt her eyes sting with unshed tears. "Even now, you cannot forget or forgive my white blood. Tell me, my beloved husband, do you also see me in this girl? Do you fear for your son to follow your footsteps?"

"I fear nothing and no one, Shalee. I must protect those I love. To me, you are Indian," he declared softly, unwittingly answering her question in the way she had hoped he would not. She allowed this slip to pass unquestioned and unchallenged.

"Let her remain with us for seven moons. If you still feel these stirrings of danger, then send her away. I only ask that you do not place her in the Tipi Sa. She is not a whore to be taken by any brave who desires her."

"You have never forgiven me or forgotten the cruelty I once subjected you to," Gray Eagle said. "For a long time, you did not think upon it. Have you forgotten no man touched you in the Tipi Sa? But this girl's coming has called that evil moon back to your mind. I did nothing but shame and punish you for defiance. You take her side because it is Alisha Williams you see, not this white girl."

"If you do not wish me to feel this way," Shalee answered, "then do not allow her present life to mirror my past one. So much seems just as it was between us. I do not wish to recall such pain, but I cannot seem to stop these thoughts from entering my mind. It is too late to prevent the return of such memories. To send her away would bring more pain to my heart, for then I cannot alter her fate as I could not my own. If you allow me to spare her similar torment and humiliation, it will lessen my own from the past. It will be as if I am changing my own past. It will dull the bitter memories; it will seem as if the cruelty never existed. This will become reality, and the past will fade as a bad dream. Do this for me, Gray Eagle. Allow me to put the past to sleep forever." Their eyes met as she caressed his brawny arms.

"You wish to play with this girl's life just to rub out your own past? It cannot be done, my wife. When Wi has travelled the heavens many winters, the past is gone forever," he exclaimed in exasperation, trying to tame the ferocious beast of revenge which clawed at his heart.

"If that is so, my husband, then why does it haunt and control us this day?" she softly argued.

For the first time since Shalee had told him she was carrying their son Bright Arrow, Gray Eagle lied to her. "It is you the past haunts, my lovely Shalee. I am only concerned with how this white girl could endanger our son's future. It is his life we should protect and control, not hers. If we accept her, Bright Arrow will be unable to reject her. It is wrong; it is dangerous," he concluded sternly.

"But must she suffer for her cruel destiny? You do not know what it is like to be hated and rejected by both the whites and Indians. She is too young and vulnerable," she retorted, her tempestuous emotions flowing like molten lava within her veins.

"Her fate was sealed long ago when she was born to . . . whites," he caught his nearly traitorous tongue. "It is not for us to change it; it lies within the hands of the Great Spirit."

"Long ago, you thought the same of me, my husband. But the Great Spirit saw it in His heart to change my destiny. What if it is the same with this girl? What if the Great Spirit has sent her to our son, as He once sent me to you? Do you not think it strange that the events which surround them are so like our past? I feel there is some message in these similarities. We must wait until we learn these secrets," she beseeched him.

"There is evil as well as good at work in our land, Shalee. What if it is an evil spirit which brought her here to destroy us? What if Rebecca has come to reveal the deadly secrets of my beloved Alisha? She has already caused the death of an Indian brother. I say she is evil." His ebony eyes glittered.

"She did not take the life of Standing Bear. It was his lust for her and for our son's rank which brought on the challenge. Place the blame for that vile deed where it truly belongs," she reprimanded him.

"Still, she was in the middle of that battle!" he irrationally charged.

"I once stood between you and Brave Bear. Was I to blame for being caught in the middle? No! Neither is this girl. Men place helpless women in positions which they cannot control, then blame us for the results of their reckless decisions."

Gray Eagle sighed wearily. He fretted over the mysterious, powerful pull which this girl was having over his wife and son. Shalee was too smart and cunning; she could find logic to use against each of his arguments. What now? he anxiously pondered, determined to have this girl out of their lives. Perhaps he should permit this girl to remain with them for seven moons as Shalee had suggested. In that time, Shalee would learn how impossible and perilous the whole situation was. Hopefully she would find it too painful to watch her past relived in this girl's daily existence . . . Too, his son was proud; the warriors' tauntings would surely have an effect upon him . . . Within seven moons, they would both wish this troublesome white captive gone!

A sly grin eased over his bold features. He replied, "The girl can remain for seven moons. In that time, you can teach her what she must know and do to protect her life and safety when she leaves us. Then, she must leave our tepee. I could bear her presence no longer. Will you agree to this?"

A seven-day reprieve . . . That was certainly better than nothing. She smiled up into his eyes. "Yes, my husband; I will do as you say. I will prepare her to leave in seven moons. You are wise and generous. I love you with all my heart and soul. Your kindness will lay the past to rest forever," she promised, tracing a finger over his sensual lips.

He pulled her into his arms and embraced her tenderly and possessively. He could only hope and pray he had not made the wrong decision . . . At least, this way both he and his wife could have their wishes.

Back in their tepee, another agonizing scene was taking place. Her weeping spent, Rebecca sat upon a sleeping skin while Bright Arrow nervously paced the tanned confines of his home. Never had he experienced such impatience, worry, and confusion. Every so often, he would halt his aimless roamings to stare at her in a strange way. It was obvious to Rebecca that many conflicting emotions were coursing through his keen mind and virile body, none of which she could read or understand. Helpless, all she could do was return his piercing stare and await her fate.

Would the infamous Gray Eagle demand her life or just her absence? Either way, she instinctively knew that Shalee and Bright Arrow would not resist his commands, for such was the Indian way. Gray Eagle's influence was twofold: he was a warrior, and he was the chief. Yet, if she were not mistaken, Shalee and Bright Arrow were trying to persuade him to allow her to remain here. Why, she could not even imagine. Then again, she could be wrong; perhaps they argued against her prolonged suffering. Either way, the final decision would be Gray Eagle's.

She mused upon the mercurial nature of the robust warrior before her. Even though she had promised herself to resist him, she had broken that vow the first moment he had reached out for her. What was this powerful, novel emotion which could not be dismissed or denied? She feared it; yet, she also eagerly and hungrily pursued it. Love him? She could not say, for she did not know about such an emotion.

Please, God, she prayed. Make him let me

stay here . . .

Bright Arrow contemplated his mother's and father's words. There was so much to consider. Doubtlessly, there were many things which Shalee had not revealed to him. What had actually taken place between his parents so long ago? Why was this strange girl a threat to them, particularly to him? What horrors of the past did she refresh in their minds? What ominous warnings echoed across such a vast distance of time? Indeed, something troubled them deeply; yet, the fears of each varied in some imperceptible way. Would his mother ever confess the entire truth to him? What had his father done to his mother that she so deeply feared he might also do to this girl, that had forced her to reveal such long-buried secrets?

Evidently his mother's white blood meant more to her than anyone realized. Perhaps that was the reason why the raids upon whites instilled that strange glow within her green eyes. Was his father truly bothered by Shalee's half-white blood? Had he denied that fact to himself all these years? Had Rebecca reminded him of Shalee's mixed blood and of their troubled past? Did his father resent the guilt, shame, and pain which Rebecca might renew within his mother? Was it only Shalee and their love which his father hoped to protect by sending this girl away? Or did the chief fear his son might fall into the same loving trap which he had? How he longed for Gray Eagle to confide in him, to unselfishly share what he had learned and endured in his taking of Shalee . . . the turmoil in Bright Arrow's mind found no surcease.

The flap of the tepee was thrown aside as his parents returned. Bright Arrow's gaze flew to his mother's serene smile first, then to his father's stoic expression. Both Bright Arrow and Rebecca tensed in anticipation of Gray Eagle's decision.

Gray Eagle nonchalantly approached his son. He placed his hands upon Bright Arrow's bare shoulders and gazed deeply into his expectant eyes as he related his decision. Bright Arrow's astonished gaze shifted to his mother's radiant face, knowing she had somehow gained him time with Rebecca. Gray Eagle noted his look of gratitude, and he wondered at it. He should question Shalee about this curious reaction. Assuredly, Bright Arrow knew she had influenced him. But how and why? he questioned himself, feeling uneasy about it.

In his elated state, Bright Arrow affectionately hugged his father and his mother. He thanked them for permitting him to keep Rebecca for even a short time. He refused to think about what the eighth day would bring. For now, Rebecca was his.

Yet, Gray Eagle insisted upon driving a crucial point home. "It is only for seven moons,

Bright Arrow. Then, she must leave. I will take her to another village far away. It will be best if you do not know where she is . . . or which warrior takes her. Do you agree to such conditions?" he pressed, intentionally subduing the blissful joy and lack of restraint in his son.

Bright Arrow sighed heavily, proudly drew himself up to his full height, then nodded understanding and agreement. "Then, it is settled," Gray Eagle calmly announced. "But I must caution you, my son. Do not be overly gentle or friendly to her; it will only make leaving harder for her," he remarked.

"I will do as you command, my father. I will tell her this to halt any hope in her heart of staying here beyond seven moons," he stated, hesitating to see if Gray Eagle would advise against it. He did not. In fact, he seemed pleased and eager for her to know of her fate!

Bright Arrow went to kneel before the wary, frightened girl. Gray Eagle intently observed this communication. But Shalee watched her husband's eyes and expressions closely, trying to discover some hint to his true motives and feelings. He was surely hiding something from her. What and why, she dreaded to explore. Yet, with every fiber of instinct and perception within her, she knew this to be true, true and alarming.

"Rebecca, Bright Arrow kaskapi," he informed her, holding up seven fingers to indicate her length of stay with him. "Kaskapi . . . hunwi," he stressed the seven moons. When she did not seem to understand, he drew a circle upon the ground. He pointed to it, toward the heavens, then stated, "Hunwi!" He then repeated his words.

Her face paled and she trembled slightly as she comprehended Gray Eagle's decision: she could be Bright Arrow's prisoner for only seven short days. After that . . . what would it matter after she lost Bright Arrow? At least she could share that many days with the man she loved and desired, for God only knew what reason! She bravely and proudly lifted her head. She glanced at Gray Eagle's intrepid glare, wishing he did not despise and resent her so deeply and strongly. She managed to prevent the flood of tears which constricted her throat and ravaged her broken heart. She inhaled a ragged breath of air to still her racing heart and to quell her torment. She would not grovel before them; she would not plead or weep.

She touched her forehead to give the sign of comprehension, saying softly, "Rebecca understands. Bright Arrow's captive for seven days. A'ta ia Rebecca ya. Rebecca hiya cry." She used a mixture of signs, English, and Sioux which she had learned from Bright Arrow to make her feelings and thoughts known. But she could not resist asserting she knew his father had demanded her departure. She had made the sign for tears, vowing she would not weep at his cruel decision. "Rebecca ya in seven hunwi," she wisely accepted her delayed fate.

Gray Eagle placed Rebecca's welfare in the capable hands of his wife. He called for Bright Arrow to come and join him in the Ceremonial Tepee for a meeting of the tribe's warriors. A new problem had arisen while Bright Arrow had been away, a problem which demanded their prompt attention.

Bright Arrow followed his father from their tepee, neither noticing the way in which Shalee was observing them and the white girl. The two warriors—the noble one of yesterday who was fearlessly attempting to retain his prowess and powerful rank and the younger one who was fiercely trying to match his father's indomitable legend—slowly covered the short distance to the gathering of the Warriors' Society to discuss how they could withhold their lands and push back this new advance of white settlers and hostile soldiers.

The two women silently studied each other for a time. The beauty of Gray Eagle's wife was obvious. As Rebecca's curious gaze eased over the lovely female before her, it came to rest upon Shalee's eyes: eyes the shade of newborn pine needles! In disbelief and confusion, she openly gaped at this incredible fact.

It did not take Rebecca's startled outcry, "Your eyes are green!" to reveal to Shalee why the girl was staring at her. Guessing at Rebecca's astonishment and having had many years to practice the concealment of her knowledge of English, she wisely and cautiously prevented any visible reaction to Rebecca's outburst.

Rebecca uncontrollably bounded forward to stand only inches from Shalee. She stared into the emerald green eyes which were intriguing and lively. She pointed to Shalee's eyes and asked, "Why do you have green eyes?"

Shalee merely watched the girl, waiting for her to attempt some form of communication to which she could respond without hinting at her secret. Rebecca innocently complied when she quizzed, "Shalee wasichu? Green eyes," she declared, pointing to them once more.

Shalee permitted a look of enlightenment to fill those pools of sea-green which baffled Rebecca. "Hanke-wasicun. A'ta Mahpiya Sapa. Shalee hanke-wasicun. Wasichu . . . Si-ha Sapa," she explained that she was half-white and half-Blackfoot, that she was proclaimed the daughter of Chief Black Cloud.

Rebecca digested these words, then comprehended them. To test her conclusions, she entreated, "Shalee Oglala?"

Unexpectedly, Shalee smiled genially. She softly replied, "Shalee hiya Oglala. Shalee Si-ha Sapa, wasichu."

Rebecca could not conceal her astonishment. She shrieked aloud, "Gray Eagle married a half-breed? This is unbelievable!" Upon further thought and observation, she shook her head and denied her own deductions, "No, I guess not. You are the most beautiful woman I've seen. And the daughter of a chief, for I have heard the name of your father many times. I wonder if you also hate the whites as much as Gray Eagle . . ." she murmured sadly. "How I wish you could speak English and tell me what is happening, what is expected of me here. I doubt you've ever known what fear, shame, and loneliness are. I would gladly exchange places with you this very minute if it were possible. How will I ever give up Bright Arrow in only seven days?" she dejectedly whispered her anguish and doubts.

Misty, amber eyes sought solace in the gentle green ones of Shalee. "I have heard many tales of how Indian women treat their slaves. Yet, you do not seem hostile or cruel. I know I should never show fear before my enemies, but how can I hide it when my insides quiver like the leaves upon an elm tree in a violent wind? I wonder if you know how irresistible your son is, if you've ever experienced the powerful emotions which he unleashed within me. How will I ever endure the touch of another man?" At that ominous thought, she began to weep. She covered her face, naked with deep and conflicting emotions, betraying herself to the Indian princess.

Her torment and tears savagely gnawed upon

Shalee's defensive restraint. So many agonizing memories returned to haunt her. She mutely replied to Rebecca, you are terribly wrong, Rebecca; for no one knows better than I what it is to endure degradation, and overwhelming terror. How I wish I could help you, but I cannot risk exposing myself. I cannot risk the discovery of my own white blood and deceptions. I cannot endanger the lives and honor of Gray Eagle and my son. God help you, Rebecca, for I cannot . . .

The more Shalee attempted to block out the pain and fear and tears of this innocent girl, the more Rebecca's torment called out to her. She reached out and lifted Rebecca's quivering chin and smiled encouragingly into her sad eyes. "Kokipi sni, Rebecca," she softly coaxed, then smiled again.

"I do not understand, Shalee," she stated in despondency.

"Shalee koda," she ventured, hoping this perceptive, intelligent girl could recognize her offer of friendship and truce.

Astounded by this turn in events, Rebecca blurted out, "Friend! Rebecca koda?" she questioned this startling enigma.

Shalee nodded. To forestall any future problems, she quietly continued, "Shalee koda. Wanmdi Hota hiya koda. Wanhinkpe Wiyakpa hiya koda. Rebecca kaskapi."

Tears filled Rebecca's eyes, but this time they

171

were tears of joy and relief. She smiled and said, "Thank you, Shalee. I know you cannot understand me, but your kindness has removed much of my fear and sadness. Rebecca koda," she repeated happily .

"Ku-wa, Rebecca. Mni. Can. Ku-wa Shalee," she called for the young girl to assist her with the chores.

Shalee lifted the water skins from a side pole and handed them to Rebecca. She picked up the wood sling and called for the slightly relaxed captive to follow after her. Meekly, Rebecca did as she was commanded.

Soon, the chores were completed. Wood was neatly stacked into a pile; the water skins were filled. An aromatic stew of deer chunks and wild vegetables was simmering over their fire. Although they had spoken little since early afternoon, a tranquil atmosphere surrounded them.

Rebecca was confused about her role in these Indians' lives. She easily understood she was a slave to this particular family and was expected to work hard for them. But how far beyond slavery did her new position go? Would they ever accept her?

She wasn't blind or ignorant. She could witness and perceive the contempt in the warriors; far more unsettling, she could clearly read the fierce hatred and resentment in the women, especially those around her age. Not a single girl had given any indication of eventual friendship as they worked nearby. Their hostility was so strong that it felt like a tangible force. Even Bright Arrow was distant and cool in his camp. She was alone and vulnerable in this world of powerful enemies. Thank God for Shalee, for she was the only ray of hope in this dark situation.

Rebecca was overjoyed by the way in which Shalee had affably issued her commands and briskly worked beside her. Now she knew where the gentle streak in Bright Arrow came from— and also the ruthless one . . .

Shalee, too, was cheerful and serene. Things had gone extremely well between her and this charming white girl. Not once had Rebecca refused or bucked any order. Not once had she become resentful, insolent, or hostile. Starving for love and acceptance, Rebecca had obeyed her. She appeared such a gentle, loving, vivacious creature. Rebecca reminded Shalee of the girl she had once been long, long ago: that naive, trusting English lass who had come to this arduous territory at the tender age of nineteen, that innocent girl who had helplessly watched her existence torn asunder by the hatred between the Indian and the white man, that bonny youth who had miraculously discovered a powerful love and an incredible life in the arms of a warrior who had once viewed and treated her just as her own son was presently treating this white girl. How strange life could be . . .

Shalee had been powerless to control her own fate; yet, the Great Spirit was allowing her to prevent her same tragic existence from being repeated in the life of this new white girl. She prayed that Rebecca would eventually become acceptable to her husband; she prayed he would not force her to leave their tepee in seven days . . .

It was nearly dark when the two men returned to their tepee. The air was heavy with mystery and bitterness, but Shalee somehow knew it had to do with something more pressing than this white girl who had been rudely thrust into their lives. When she softly questioned her husband as she dished up his dinner, he seemed reluctant to discuss the new trouble with her. He grinned and caressed her cheek, telling her he would speak of it later.

The smile which she sent him was radiant; it bespoke a love which surpassed time and racial differences. It spoke of respect, desire, and unselfishness. Her green eyes glowed with these forceful emotions. Gray Eagle read them and lost himself within their power. As now, words were often unnecessary between them, for they could communicate with only tender expressions.

Rebecca curiously observed this unity of love and passion which existed between Gray Eagle and Shalee, which encircled them tightly within its bonds. The fact Gray Eagle could love so fully, boldly, and strongly had a mysterious effect upon her. How could this majestic, moody man be all bad? It was clear to her that his love for Shalee had been the deciding factor of her own fate. Unquestionably, Shalee had spoken up on her behalf, and he had relented in his fury in order to please her. Was it possible to become so close to Shalee that she would take her side once more in seven days? Shalee could accept her here; Bright Arrow could accept her here. Somehow she must convince Gray Eagle to permit her to stay! But how?

Bright Arrow had forbidden himself to acknowledge Rebecca's presence. It was imperative that his father remain ignorant of his private feelings for her. He laughed and chatted with his parents. The two men ate first, as was the Indian custom. He furtively studied his mother's glowing expression. He was pleased to hear that Rebecca had been helpful and obedient. He was surprised and elated to see how much his mother was enjoying Rebecca's presence. Could it be that she was intrigued by this white girl, mystically attached to her? Perhaps Shalee's white blood responded to his Rebecca? He instantly fretted, for it was unwise for his own mother to dwell on that part of herself. He admitted that his father had been right to worry . . .

Shalee served the two men, then talked with them while they ate. She fervently prayed that Rebecca would remain silent and respectful for the next six days. If she recklessly rebelled against her or either of the two men, she would be gone that very moment. Shalee would do all within her means to help and to protect Rebecca, but it was up to the girl to behave correctly. No matter how she felt inside, if Rebecca became defiant, she would not take her part.

Neither Shalee nor the two men had anything to worry about. Rebecca had heard many grisly tales of Indian captivity. She also knew many things about the Indians' customs and ways. She knew how very fortunate she was to be with Shalee and Bright Arrow; she would do nothing to shame or to anger them. She would also try her best to stay out of Gray Eagle's sight!

Nearly all Indian slaves lived under the brutality of their owners. Most existed under the daily threat of being sold, killed, or traded. Most labored hard and without reward. Most were despised and abused. Many often died, were maimed, or went insane. It was a dire life of torture, shame, and hardship. Yet, in the tepee of Shalee, there was hope; there was a marked difference to enslavement here, one she fiercely vowed to guard and to savor for as long as possible. She would do anything necessary to stay here, anything . . .

As her softened gaze observed Shalee and Bright Arrow in jovial conversation, Rebecca's eyes filled with loneliness and longing. How she wished she were sitting with them instead of being ignored in the shadows upon a buffalo skin. The silvery laughter of Shalee brought a wistful smile to her lips. She hungrily devoured their profiles in the firelight, craving their acceptance and affection. Her eyes lingered upon the powerful muscles in Bright Arrow's back as they rippled with each movement or hearty laughter. How she wished his back was not to her; how she longed to gaze into those jet eyes which stripped away her will and reason. How she wished she knew their language and could talk with them.

Her reflective gaze moved over to the virile physique of Gray Eagle. He was sitting with his left side to her, offering her a profile of masculinity which was frightening and appealing. Surely he was in his early forties. He was a pinnacle of manhood—just like his son. No doubt both men were desired by numerous women! Jealousy and envy battled common sense before she could quell her traitorous thoughts. Shalee was lucky beyond measure to have won his love. If not for Bright Arrow, Rebecca knew . . .

Rebecca's roving eyes which mutely bespoke her innermost opinions fused with the discerning ones of Gray Eagle. His obsidian stare was so penetrating and captivating that she could not look away. She shivered, unable to thwart his probe. It seemed as if he had pierced her most secret thoughts! An odd light flickered within his ebony eyes, but was quickly extinguished before she could comprehend it. Her face flushed with guilt and shame. Still, he would not release her from that potent, all-knowing stare. As if utterly hypnotized, she helplessly submitted to his intense scrutiny.

Gray Eagle's face was impassive; his eyes fathomless. As his sharp gaze slowly travelled the full length of her body several times, she felt totally naked; she felt as emotionally ravished by his magnetic eyes as she had by Bright Arrow's physical touch! She felt strangely touched and curiously punished. She feared she was more his prisoner than Bright Arrow's! What satanic power did this obdurate warrior possess?

Gray Eagle shifted his gaze to the fire, his thoughts spinning in a violent maelstrom. There was no doubt within his mind that Rebecca found him desirable. Had her bold, unwavering stare been inviting, pleading? Was it he she inwardly wanted to ensnare and not his son? Did the evil spirit of her dead father dominate her life and mind? Had Powchutu's restless spirit guided her here to tempt him, to enchant and bewitch him, to cause a rift between him and Shalee or between him and

Bright Arrow? Was the malevolent spirit of Powchutu trying to destroy them all with his beautiful, enticing daughter? The trouble was that Rebecca was so much like his Shalee eighteen winters ago . . . beautiful, desirable, vulnerable, eager, and seductive . . . What would happen if Rebecca made this lust for him known to Shalee or to his son? What would happen if he weakened his resolve and hatred for only a moment? He was to take her away in six moons. What would occur once they were alone? Were her evil and magic so great that she could . . . No! he angrily exploded. Never! It was only her resemblance to Shalee which attracted him.

Chapter Six

Gray Eagle was lying upon his back, staring up into the darkness of his tepee, catching glimpses of the full moon through the ventilation opening, noting the even respiration of his wife at his side, and listening to the muffled sounds of lovemaking from his son's distant mat: such had been the pattern of his nights for the past four moons.

Rebecca's constant presence in his tepee had taken a toll upon his peace of mind. His normally calm nature had suffered because of this girl and the danger which she could represent to them. Each day he feared some terrible secret would come to light. He had become restless and edgy. He could not bring himself to make love to Shalee while Powchutu's daughter was in sight and sound of such a precious and private union. He could not speak freely and easily with his son while Bright Arrow's eyes lingered upon his captive and his attention was upon her rather than on his father's words. Eating was difficult, for he sensed her eyes upon him. How could he ignore her presence when she stood in his line of vision, when her voice touched his alert ears, when she "accidentally" brushed against him while serving him meals, when she was obviously working her way into the hearts of his son and wife? It had been a mistake to let her stay for even one moon! Yet, he could not go back on his word. He was trapped in this distasteful, perilous situation for three more moons.

In his moody and guarded state, his words were often abrupt and evasive. He seemed wary and remote. Yet, he could not explain these unnatural fears and apprehensions to his wife. Already she admired and respected this white girl. Shalee would never permit him to send Rebecca away if she learned the truth . . . At least he could be grateful for the timely raid tomorrow which would take him and Bright Arrow away from camp for two suns. He frowned as he recalled how his son had vainly argued against going with him this time; he mentally raged at the undeniable reality of Bright Arrow's brazen attachment to Rebecca.

Yet, he could hardly fault him. Rebecca possessed a beauty and feminine mystique which could almost match Shalee's. It was tragic that she carried the blood of the man who had been his worst enemy. He reluctantly admitted that she was a valuable slave, accepting of her captivity. Indeed she was clever, strong, and resilient. It was abundantly clear she was doing everything she could to coax his acceptance! She did nothing intentionally to insult or annoy. She was too good to be real or to be trusted!

Gray Eagle wondered: Was she cunningly preventing any visible reason to justify her departure? Was she craftily portraying the perfect woman and slave, knowing how it would look if he traded such a rare and valuable captive? Who would sell such seeming perfection?

His deductions alarmed him. Only a man who feared her allure! Only a man who was frantically attempting to protect himself from such dangerous traits! Only a father who wanted a deluding creature out of his son's life to prevent his dishonor—or a father who secretly held powerful feelings for that girl himself! Yet, those feelings were not love or desire; they were foreboding and embittering. Even his loyal warriors failed to aid his cause, for they favorably remarked upon her beauty, obedience, and great value!

But if he dared to speak the name of her real father, many of his warriors would recall the dauntless half-breed scout who had almost challenged him before five thousand warriors just to protect Shalee from his capture! They would recall the vivid affection revealed between his wife and Rebecca Kenny's father. They would recall how Rebecca's real father had tried to kill him and to steal his Shalee, how the murderous scout had delivered his one and only defeat at any man's hands! Powchutu's demeaning and unforgivable deeds were abundant.

Only once had Gray Eagle carelessly allowed an enemy to take him unaware; he had recklessly allowed Powchutu to sneak up on him and to shoot him, to leave him for dead, then to run off with his wife! He would never forget or pardon the shame and anguish which Rebecca's real father had brought into his life. It had been many torturous months before the sullen Eagle had accidentally found his wife again. Then, he had nearly killed Shalee with his bare hands, led to think her traitorous to him from the past words and taunts of Powchutu when the defeated warrior had lain bleeding at the scout's feet!

If those foul deeds had not been great enough, in his turbulent distress, Gray Eagle had almost innocently destroyed his own son Bright Arrow as he had rested within Shalee's body. He would never forgive how Powchutu had cunningly and wickedly led him to believe that Gray Eagle's first child was his own! If not for Joe

Kenny—the man Rebecca honestly believed to be her father—Gray Eagle knew that both Shalee and Bright Arrow would have died by the Eagle's vengeful talons, a product of Powchutu's treacherous betrayal and overpowering jealousy. In truth, Rebecca's relationship to his old friend Joe was the only reason she was still alive. Otherwise, Gray Eagle would have sent her to her death on the first day!

Silence now reached his alert ears and keen senses. He assumed his son and the white captive were finally asleep. He wondered if the same feelings of self-betrayal and shame which he had known long ago presently tormented his son. Surely it was impossible to avoid such unrelenting emotions when a warrior weakly clung to his avowed enemy. He could recall his own agony and ecstasy: agony in public, ecstasy in private. Gray Eagle frowned in bitterness, for he knew Shalee and Bright Arrow would rebel against sending her away even though they had both promised they would not. Only three more days . . . they could not pass quickly enough!

Gray Eagle was mistaken in his assumption, for each of the three people who lived in his tepee were awake. Each was ensnared by thoughts of varying kinds; each was caught up in this drama which demanded to be played out. Weary, soon Gray Eagle was the only one asleep.

Bright Arrow lay still and silent, trying not to

disturb the white girl at his side. Gray Eagle was indeed accurate in his conclusions about his son's feelings. Bright Arrow felt and knew that same agony and ecstasy which his father had discovered and endured. Everything within Bright Arrow resisted Rebecca's loss; yet, he knew he must obey his father's dictates. If only this girl wasn't everything he wanted and desired in a female. If only she wasn't white. Sadly, she was . . .

He had observed her for many days now. She appeared happy and tranquil here. She seemed to belong with him. She had been respectful and submissive, much to his relief. His mother had taken an instant liking to Rebecca; yet, his father often made his resentment lucidly clear to all of them. No matter how much Rebecca tried to please his father and to lessen his dislike of her, she failed. This futile ploy to win his father's acceptance made her leaving an unyielding reality. Bright Arrow had no choice but to believe Gray Eagle simply could not tolerate a white girl in his life.

He sought to resign himself to their impending separation. Perhaps her departure was for the best. In truth, he could no longer deny that his hunger and affection for her grew with each passing day. As a noted warrior he could not permit himself to fall in love with his white captive. Anguish knifed his heart, for he realized it was too late to prevent such a reprehensible act . . .

Bright Arrow was plagued by the emotional battle which fiercely raged within his body. On one side was an entrancing white girl whom he craved beyond reason or control. But her skin proclaimed her as his avowed enemy. Already he had been too lenient and friendly toward her. On the opposing side were his people, his father, his friends, his undeniable destiny and duty: all scorned his attraction to this unique girl. They would never accept her, no matter how lowly her position.

He was savagely torn between these two conflicting forces, for he knew which side he must inevitably take. He cursed her magic which had compelled him to refute Standing Bear's claim upon her. Their fatal challenge should not have been over a mere white captive. He could not quell the rage which assailed him as he recalled the playful teasings and humiliating ridicule by his friends and other braves. They would never grant Rebecca any chance to earn their respect.

Dread washed over him, for he recognized the signs of unrelenting hatred and jealousy in females. Agony joined that dread, for he resisted the belief that Rebecca deserved such cruel treatment. If only Rebecca wasn't so special and submissive. If only she wasn't white . . .

Rebecca was lying upon her left side with her

slender back to Bright Arrow. She could just barely restrain the tremors of her body which would alert him to her wakefulness and tears. She did not want him to learn how deeply she loved and wanted him. She did not want him to know how much torture it would bring her to leave him in only three more days. It was clear to even her innocent mind that Bright Arrow wanted her, perhaps felt deep affection toward her. But it was also clear that he would follow his father's wishes. Unless Gray Eagle changed his mind about sending her away, she would be out of Bright Arrow's life in just a few days. Change his mind . . . She quelled her bitter laughter before it shattered the silence around her. She could not imagine that puissant warrior ever altering any decision he had made!

Why did Gray Eagle hate and resent her so much? Warriors took white slaves and squaws all the time. Why was her captivity to his son so disturbing? There was something about the way he looked at her; there was something about the way his aura emitted deep-rooted hostility. He despised her, but she realized it was not wholly because of her white skin or her enslavement to his son. Those things played a major part in his behavior, but his animosity was for a much deeper reason. What unspeakable horror did she remind him of each time he glared at her with those igneous, coal-black eyes?

She had tried in every way possible to dispel

his resentment. She had obeyed every order and command. She had forced herself to be pleasant, meek, and industrious. She had helped Shalee with anything and everything. Yet, nothing seemed to please him; nothing seemed to lessen his inexplicable hatred.

Every time Rebecca accidentally touched Gray Eagle, he jerked away as if she had burned him! He contemptuously glared at her each time she demurely smiled at him, trying to let him know she did not feel that same hostility and repulsion. He seemed offended by everything she did. Why? her ravaged heart cried.

Then, there were those strange stares of his. Every so often she would find his piercing eyes upon her. He possessed a powerful gaze which could strip a female naked. She trembled at the way his eyes leisurely travelled her entire body. Could it be possible that he desired her as a woman? Could that be the source of his resentment? Could he hate her for stirring unwanted lust within his body? Surely not, Rebecca thought, for he already possessed the most beautiful, desirable woman alive!

Didn't Gray Eagle realize it was his striking resemblance to his son which caused her to stare at him? Rebecca pondered. She often wondered if this was how Bright Arrow would look in twenty years. They were so much alike! Without a doubt, Bright Arrow could easily be a youthful Gray Eagle. Thankfully, Bright Arrow also possessed many of his mother's traits and qualities . . .

Having been raised in the wilderness, there had been little for Rebecca to learn after coming to the Sioux camp. She knew how to gather wood and to make a competent fire. She knew how to tan hides and skins and how to sew. She knew how to wash clothes in a river and how to cook over an open campfire. She knew how to prepare meat and to gather vegetables and fruits which were edible. She knew and did such chores every day at the side of Shalee.

Shalee . . . Rebecca knew how lucky she was to be in the Indian princess's gentle hands. It had not taken long for Rebecca to note her good fortune. She would do nothing to dishonor or to displease this special creature who was so patient and cordial. In fact, Shalee's acceptance encouraged Rebecca to work even harder. During these past few days, they had become friends of a sort. They clearly respected each other. They got along well. They even enjoyed each other's company and assistance. Shalee was tolerant and instructive. She was satisfied with Rebecca's skills and knowledge. Very few times did she give orders, for it was unnecessary. Rebecca was quick to anticipate her wishes and to perform them. Rebecca's lack of rebellion and insolence had inspired a truce between them.

Much to Rebecca's surprise and joy, Shalee was trying to teach her Oglala. With her knowledge of signing and her astute mind, these lessons were stimulating and helpful. Frequently the two women would burst into laughter as Rebecca attempted to repeat some word which was extremely difficult to say, for Sioux was a guttural language. How she longed to remain here with Shalee and Bright Arrow, for she knew she could easily fit into their life. But Gray Eagle was the unmovable barrier in her road to happiness.

Rebecca's troubled thoughts darted down a different path. She suspected those Indian girls had placed that snake in the leather bag she had been using the day before. It was doubtful that squirming snake had crawled inside a closed parfleche. She could close her eyes and clearly envision that scene. She could almost hear the girls' malicious laughter as she had opened the bag to place some buffalo berries inside.

Why were they being so cruel to her? She wasn't responsible for the conflict between the white man and the Indian. Neither was she to blame for being Bright Arrow's personal captive: the real motive for their spitefulness. Yet, she had suffered her fears and anguish in silence. To tell Bright Arrow or Shalee about their spitefulness would be futile. She knew she had to learn to ignore such vindictiveness.

Somehow she needed to prove to them she was not their enemy, not a rival for their beloved warrior!

Shalee lay awake hours after the other three people were fast asleep, her troubled mind reflecting upon many contradictions in the past few days. She retraced them to discover what was alarming and plaguing her so deeply that she could not lose herself in restful slumber. Bright Arrow was behaving just as she had predicted, but Rebecca and Gray Eagle were not! At first, things had unexpectedly gone smoothly and peacefully for everyone. She had even come to like this vulnerable white girl. Rebecca had gradually become a perfect slave. Perhaps too obliging and perfect?

Shalee analyzed her turmoil. Rebecca was smart for a girl of her tender years. She had quickly and easily obeyed each of their orders. Desperately wanting peace and naturally feeling a kinship to this white girl, Shalee realized she had naively drawn many erroneous conclusions. Rebecca had not revealed any defensive rebellion at all! She had not resisted her intimate place upon Bright Arrow's mat. She had presented friendship and demure acceptance. How was this possible so quickly and easily? Was she too willing and eager to accept her captivity? Was she really guileful and devious? Was Rebecca only pretending with her and Bright Arrow?

Having once been in a similar situation, Shalee could not comprehend Rebecca's agreeable conduct. It was only natural to experience some amount of resentment and defiance. Yet, Rebecca had not. Shalee involuntarily recalled how she had futilely resisted her enslavement to her intrepid warrior, now her husband. How was it possible for Rebecca not to experience those same types of instinctive emotions? How was it possible for Rebecca not to defy them in some small way? How could Rebecca simply behave as if she felt no hatred, humiliation, anguish, or bitterness? Was it all a charade until she could win their trust and somehow escape? Was she eagerly and desperately attempting to remain here forever with them? Surely she realized how lucky she was to be enslaved by her son! Perhaps she was only feigning the perfect slave in order to say with them . . . how could she blame Rebecca for such a ploy?

Yet, Shalee finally admitted what was truly bothering her. It was those subtle, powerful, confusing undercurrents which passed between Rebecca and her masterful husband! In the beginning, she had assumed Rebecca was only trying to win his friendship and acceptance. But after today, Shalee's opinions had altered drastically.

Out hunting with other braves, Bright Arrow had not been present for the midday meal. While she had been putting away the wild vegetables which she and Rebecca had just gathered for use at the evening meal, Rebecca had been commanded to serve Gray Eagle's food. Shalee had glanced over at them just as the young girl had handed the dish to Gray Eagle. Shalee had frozen in shock at the look which passed between her son's captive and her virile husband.

As Rebecca's and Gray Eagle's gazes had met and joined, the brazen girl had not released her hold upon the dish, nor had her husband pulled it from her tight grasp! He had simply drilled his ebony gaze into her tawny ones, seeming to forget his surroundings and even reality—just as the stunning captive did! For what had seemed an endless lapse of time, they had stared at each other. Then to Shalee's disbelief, Gray Eagle's eyes had calmly roved over the girl from auburn head to slender ankle. Simultaneously, the girl's gaze had boldly surveyed her husband's virile torso and handsome features with the slowness of a snail! Then, their eyes had locked once more, this time glowing with a mysterious gleam which Shalee had witnessed and still raged against.

In fury and anguish, Shalee had torn her panicked gaze from the treacherous sight before her. It had required some minutes before she could control her volatile emotions. She could not trust herself to speak or to look at either of them until she could regain her poise. Traitorous suspicions screamed accusations against both of them. She felt betrayed.

Was there some irresistible force drawing them to each other? Was this mysterious magnetism the evil which Gray Eagle had sensed and wanted to prevent? Did he secretly desire this white girl for himself? Was he envious of his son's possession of her? Was his resentment based upon sweltering lust for Rebecca? It couldn't be true!

Shalee envisioned that dramatic scene once more. She recalled how Rebecca had looked at her husband, how she had been unable or unwilling to look away from his probing and appreciative gaze. Shalee scolded herself. Had she been blind? Was this girl encouraging her husband to lust after her? Was she cunningly attempting to seduce Gray Eagle? Did she honestly believe she could steal him away from his wife, could entice him into keeping her here? What vile and wicked mischief was Rebecca practicing upon the man she loved!

After lunch, Shalee had made it a point to watch them closely yet furtively. She had no way of knowing that her husband was testing Shalee's theory for himself. She had no way of knowing that Gray Eagle was covertly trying to trick the girl into exposing her true feelings for all of them. She had no way of knowing that he suspected Rebecca of crafty seduction upon him. All Shalee noticed was the intense way in which her traitorous husband kept observing the slave girl who belonged to their son! She also witnessed the way in which Rebecca warmly responded to Gray Eagle's guile.

Tragically, all were misled and mistaken. For Rebecca only reacted with naive attempts to win Gray Eagle's friendship and acceptance; she responded to the similarity in looks to his son. As the day had progressed, Rebecca had become disquieted by the smoldering way in which that indomitable warrior kept staring at her. Each time she had uncontrollably glanced in his direction to see if he was still watching her, her artless looks were misread by both Shalee and Gray Eagle . . .

Lying there for the fourth night without the solace and affection from her husband's arms, Shalee mistakenly assumed Gray Eagle was gradually losing interest in her and was steadily desiring this younger female who rested upon Bright Arrow's mat. Indignation and jealousy chewed viciously at her. She should have allowed Gray Eagle to send Rebecca away that first day! She had been a fool to speak out for her! Rebecca was nothing like her! Shalee fiercely admonished herself. She had been a sentimental romantic and a wide-eyed idealist to help this girl who was obviously making a brazen play for her husband! She had befriended Rebecca; she had helped and comforted her. And this was to be her payment! Now she comprehended why Rebecca was portraying the perfect slave: she wanted to catch Gray Eagle's eye and heart! How dare she! If Rebecca initiated a battle for Gray Eagle, then she would most assuredly find one: a very bloody and costly one!

Shalee fretted over a previous action of Rebecca's which took place two days past. Had it truly been an accident or a simple error in judgment? Rebecca was intelligent; surely she realized certain berries were poisonous! Perhaps she had excused Rebecca's mistake too quickly. Had Rebecca secretly and vengefully tried to kill them? Or had Rebecca only desired to remove her presence, to find some way to have both men to herself? Or perhaps to have Gray Eagle to herself?

When Shalee had noted the dull red berries in Rebecca's bowl, she had instantly jerked it from the startled girl's grip just before she added them to the wasna mix. But when she managed to get her alarmed message across to the wide-eyed girl, she had appeared shocked and distressed by Shalee's reaction.

Since Shalee knew English, Rebecca's anxious response had dispelled her suspicions. She had shrieked, "I've never seen these kinds of berries before, Shalee! I thought you put them in the bowl. Who would do such a wicked and dangerous thing? We could all have died! I'm sorry. I'll be more careful," she had promised.

But now, Shalee wondered at this suspicious mistake! What better way to get a man's wife out of the picture? Perhaps his wife and his son? Did Rebecca wish all their deaths or only hers? If only she knew if this was an honest mistake . . .

Each of the three was caught up in an emotional triangle which existed only within their troubled minds . . .

Fear, sadness, and anguish weighed heavily upon Shalee's frightened mind and tormented heart. Tears eased down her cheeks, for she remembered how she had once fascinated, bewitched, and ensnared Gray Eagle. Long ago, she had been in a similar state of youthful innocence. Her vulnerability, sensual appeal, and artlessness had inspired him to boldly capture her. Irresistibly drawn to him and powerless to refuse him anything, he had enchanted her beyond reason. Even while rebelling against his enslavement and cruelty, she had fallen in love with him, coming to desire him as she had no other man.

In those first days, she had been like a stimulating and intoxicating drug to him, an aphrodisiac which plagued and enflamed his virile body. Her helpless condition had filled him with a heady sense of power. She had unknowingly compelled and enticed him to possess her, body and soul. Her inevitable submission to him had assuaged his arrogance, determination, and prowess. With her final capitulation, he had proven his power. He had easily won their battle.

She bitterly recalled how he had defensively concealed his love for her until she had been accepted as Black Cloud's daughter. But ever since the day of their first meeting, he had never looked upon another female with carnal desire. After becoming his wife, she had satisfied each of his desires and needs. Now her confidence and appeal were being threatened by this ivory-skinned girl who was a striking replica of the female who had once bravely and boldly invaded the indomitable Eagle's domain . . .

Was Rebecca becoming a similar challenge to his ego and prowess? Was she evoking those same feelings of excitement, and daring? Was he at that vulnerable age where a man wanted and needed such enlivenment, to be shown he was still virile and irresistible, to prove himself as sensually potent and magnetic as ever?

Gray Eagle's pensive mood and reserved conduct had increased Shalee's fears and worries. Caught up in his own emotional conflict, he was totally unaware of his wife's inner turmoil.

Shalee craved Gray Eagle's touch and comfort. But each time she had made a romantic overture toward him, he had smiled regretfully and pleaded with her to wait until this annoying intruder was out of their tepee. If that refusal of lovemaking wasn't distressing enough, he had even avoided her kisses, her caresses, even her gaze. This was unlike him. Before Rebecca had come to stay with them, he had been unable to have enough of her. Now, he didn't seem to want or to need her at all! His unconscious withdrawal hurt Shalee deeply, for she misunderstood the reasons behind it. She wanted and needed her lover, and he was not there for her . . .

Shalee could not help remembering something she had said to Gray Eagle eighteen years ago: "One day you will recall I am all white, and you will turn against me. I would rather lose you now than later. I could not bear it, Wanmdi Hota, for I love you more than life itself."

He had laughed heartily and hugged her fiercely, telling her, "It does not matter to me now, and it never will. From this day on, you are Shalee; you will be mine forever." But the enormous lie had always been there between them. It had coiled in hiding like a venomous snake waiting for the right moment to strike out and destroy her. It had hibernated for years; now, it had awakened in an irascible mood, wanting to attack whatever or whoever had disturbed its lengthy slumber. Enslaving her had been a huge and costly blow to Gray Eagle's pride, one he had never truly forgotten or forgiven; surely this explained the look of guilt and resentment which filled his eyes before he could conceal it.

There was only one way to test her terrifying conclusions. Tomorrow she would seek him out in private. If he rejected her touch when no eyes were upon them, she would know the truth. If he was finally turning away from her, she needed to know immediately. Then, if this girl was excessively appealing to him, she had to find a way to get rid of her; she had to find some way to restore the happiness and tranquility which Rebecca had vanquished. Tomorrow . . .

Gray Eagle gazed down into the pale face of his sleeping wife. The telltale signs of salty tears were still visible upon her cheeks and in the dampness of her hair. The blue smudges beneath her eyes told of a restless night. He fretted anxiously. Was she becoming aware of his deception? Did she sense he was withholding critical facts about Rebecca from her? Or was she simply caught up in this drama from the past which haunted him too? He should not have relented to her pleas to keep Rebecca here. In time she would have forgiven and forgotten his blatant refusal. Now, he feared she was becoming too involved with this girl. Was she hurt by his inability to make love to her while Rebecca watched and listened, just as he saw and heard Rebecca's lusty bouts with his virile son? It was even difficult to look Shalee in the eye for fear she might read his deception there. He hoped this awful distance would cease once Rebecca was gone.

Gray Eagle arose, careful not to disturb Shalee who needed to sleep a while longer. He would join his son who had left only moments ago. As he stood up, he absently glanced over at Bright Arrow's mat. Rebecca was sitting up, watching him. He glared at her, then left his tepee.

Rebecca lay down upon her back, wondering how she could ever win the approval of that valiant man who held her destiny in his callous hands and heart. She had not noticed the alert eyes of Shalee upon her, nor the annoyed scowl which lined her lovely face. She did not realize that she spoke aloud and Shalee heard her agonized prayer, "Please make him accept me. I could not bear to leave here. Melt that icy heart of his. Do not permit him to send me away . . ."

Shalee waited a while before she left her mat. Ignoring Rebecca completely, she headed for the stream to freshen up. Afterwards, she returned to her tepee to face the witch whose evil eyes were focused upon Gray Eagle.

Rebecca was patiently waiting for her daily orders. She wondered at the abrupt change in Shalee; it struck terror and sadness into her heart. Shalee's eyes revealed scorn and mistrust when they lingered upon her. Shalee did not smile at her, nor did she speak to her unless it was to give a command.

She wondered if Shalee was still angry about

the berry incident. Rebecca instantly decided she should be very careful in the future. Someone had placed those berries in her bowl, someone who wanted it to appear she had done it intentionally. But who? If Shalee hadn't caught that vicious mistake, they could all be sick or dead.

Mistake? Joke? She scoffed to herself. It hadn't been a simple mistake or a playful jest. Someone had cunningly planned to entrap her. She resolved to be alert and cautious from now on. She had enough problems without others spitefully handing her more! Apprehension filled her, for she speculated that Shalee doubted her innocence.

The silence and tension became apparent to both men by midday. When Bright Arrow questioned his mother about her aloof behavior, she smiled wanly and said she was just overly tired that day. She curiously reminded him that Rebecca was a slave, a slave who would leave them in two more days. Strange, but she now seemed to want that departure.

After his mother left them, Bright Arrow turned to study Rebecca with inquisitive eyes. But Rebecca's misty eyes were observing the steady retreat of his mother.

He approached Rebecca and questioned, "Shalee, Rebecca hiya kodas?"

Tears flowed down Rebecca's cheeks. She shrugged her slumped shoulders and sorrowfully said, "I do not understand why she has turned against me. I have done all she asked. I have tried to be obedient and helpful. Have I caused some breach between them? Perhaps your father commanded it," she suggested, then sighed dejectedly. "I forget you cannot understand me. Kodas?" She echoed sadly and shrugged confusion.

Bright Arrow smiled into the luminous eyes which pleaded for comfort and love. He caressed her cheek and kissed her lightly.

She returned the kiss and the smile. At least he had not changed. Perhaps Shalee was ill. The best thing she could do was behave in the manner which had previously been pleasing to Shalee . . .

Bright Arrow seized her cold hands and pulled her to her feet. "Ku-wa," he called to her, swaggering out of the tepee into the fresh air and warm sunshine. Without a thought to refusal, she meekly followed the self-assured warrior with a lowered head and listless spirit.

Neither attempted to make conversation as they headed to a secluded formation of rust-colored boulders which arose from the dirt, pitted and scarred by the forces of nature. They gingerly avoided the prickly cacti which grew sparingly in this arid location. Gentle winds raced through the slender blades of bunch and buffalo grasses. The terrain steadily became rocky and hard. Only an occasional tree offered shade to the warm earth beneath it.

Rebecca became aware of their ever-increasing distance from the Oglala camp and the dreamy solitude of their picturesque surroundings. Yet, Bright Arrow silently continued his trek toward the lofty boulders. The moment they stepped into a small clearing which was enclosed on three sides by towering rock formations, he halted and turned to face her. He stopped so abruptly that she almost ran into him. Her hands went against his muscled chest to catch her balance. For some unknown reason, she noticed his smooth, firm body lacked the beads of moisture which the dazzling sun and her exertions had quickly brought to her shapely body. But then, he was accustomed to this arid climate and to strenuous exercise.

She hesitantly waited to discover why he had led her to this secluded spot. He stepped away from her to allow his gaze the unhindered ability to leisurely and thoroughly study her from head to foot. She quietly submitted to this intense scrutiny, trembling at its unsettling effect upon her.

Bright Arrow's hungry gaze devoured the beauty and softness before him. She would belong to him for only one more day, for his father had insisted upon his presence away from camp for nearly two suns: two precious days which would be lost forever. He had vainly argued against going on this scouting mission.

He had been left without an honorable refusal. But for the next few hours, Rebecca would be his.

Although she was new to a man's mat and to the sweet joinings of two bodies, she had forced herself to withhold a special part from him and to deny both of them the exquisite pleasure of total surrender. Before she was lost to him, he desperately needed to have her completely. He must become as unforgettable to her as she was to him! He had felt the fierce restraint within her each night as he had possessed her body. In this private place, he would use all of his knowledge and prowess to destroy her remaining resistance . . .

His probing gaze started its journey at her auburn head which captured the afternoon sunlight and shimmered like a smoldering fire. It moved past her tawny eyes to linger briefly upon her pert nose, slightly parted lips and dainty chin. It engulfed her flawless complexion which was beginning to lose its tawny glow to become a deep bronze shade.

His igneous eyes roamed over her inviting frame with its gently rounded curves, clad in a doeskin dress which outlined her body in an appealing manner. Her graceful hands were tightly clasped together, revealing her apprehension. She unknowingly shifted from one moccasined foot to the other, bringing an engaging grin to his lips, softening his eyes and expression.

His gaze riveted to her panicked eyes. He came forward; she backed away, instinctively sensing some vital drama about to unfold. He chuckled mischievously when her back made contact with the rocks, preventing any further retreat from him and the inevitable. She gasped in surprise and swallowed loudly, fearing the bold intentions she was reading within those hypnotic black eyes which roguishly enticed her.

She held her breath as his hand came forward to stroke her silky hair and satiny skin. His touch was gentle, but disturbing. As if mesmerized, she rigidly watched as his face came toward hers. She trembled and tingled as his mouth claimed hers, tenderly plundering and deftly exploring it as never before.

She felt she should muster her strength and will to resist him, but she did not want to staunch the liquid fire which flowed over her and within her. There were no parental eyes or ears and no hostile warriors to remind her of her lowly rank as slave. As his kisses dispelled all previous reasons for denial, her arms encircled his narrow waist. Giving herself over to instinctive responses, her lips extracted the sweetness of his sensual mouth. A moan of desire escaped her parted lips as his mouth tantalized her ears with seeking, demanding nibbles.

His deft hands unlaced the ties at her neck and swiftly divested her of her garment. Before she could demurely react to her nakedness, he had imprisoned her swollen breasts against his compelling body and had fastened his intoxicating mouth to hers. When his devastating kisses had once again claimed her will, his hands began to explore and to caress her pliant body.

Helpless to extinguish the wild fire which enflamed her weakened senses, she yielded to him and his masterful onslaught. His mouth and hands steadily and deliberately quieted her last hints of resistance.

Soon, they were lying upon the earth, totally oblivious to its hard and rocky surface. She cried out in exquisite pleasure as his teeth gently teased at her taut breasts. Never had she felt such an urgent desire for him.

Time had deserted her. Reality had quickly receded with it. When he finally entered her, she arched upwards to willingly accept his full length. As he moved within her, blissful sensations increased. Her body demanded a fulfillment not yet shared or experienced. This time, there would be no desperate struggle to contain her rampant emotions and fiery passion; for once, she could allow them to run free and wild.

The intensity built to an almost unbearable peak before he carried them to the mountaintop of sublime ecstasy and mind-staggering release. He skillfully carried her over the heights of total satisfaction and into a beautiful valley of peacefulness and relaxation. She went limp in his embrace, sighing in contentment.

He rolled to her side, continuing his loving caresses and gentle kisses until every wave of passion had ceased to carry her. He propped on his elbow and stared down into her gaze. He tenderly wiped the glistening beads of moisture from her lovely face. He smiled at her, his eyes carrying a glow she had not seen before. He did want her! Could it be love she viewed in those onyx depths?

She returned the sensual smile, her hand coming up to trace the finely chiselled lines in his face. As her fingers moved over his lips, she whispered, "I never knew it could be like this, Bright Arrow. We have so little time to share these feelings." The moment those words left her lips, she began to cry, her shoulders quivering as she pulled him down to her. She clung to him, sobbing as if her heart was shattering.

He gathered her shaking body into his powerful, protective embrace. A possessive feeling he had never known before swept over him. New fires and needs coursed through him and quickly spread to her as she fervently vowed, "I love you, Bright Arrow. How can I bear to lose you?"

They joined again in a savage and demanding union which devoured their energies. As he exploded within her, he vowed to never part with her. She loved him, wanted him, and needed him. How could he sacrifice such emotions which she also shared? Yet, undeniable reality soon returned. Would he obey his father's orders? The answer, as always, was yes.

This time, he did not release her afterwards. Instead, he held her tightly and securely. She made no movement to leave his arms; she drew solace and courage from them. "I will never forget you. I can never love another," she wretchedly vowed in a voice of intense anguish.

Dusk was approaching when he sat up, observing Wi as he made his way into the waiting arms of Mother Earth. It was time to return to reality. He glanced over his shoulder, his eyes savoring the creamy body of the white girl who had unknowingly stolen his heart and innocently endangered his honor. He had discovered a beautiful dream, only to be cruelly awakened to the demanding laws of reality and to his duties. He could not even confess or reveal his love or his torment to anyone, except his cherished mother who now appeared resigned to Rebecca's savage fate.

Rebecca remained serene and still beneath his

astute gaze. For the first time, she did not feel any shame or guilt about her love and desire for him. Deep and wonderful emotions washed over her, cleansing and vitalizing her. This previously unknown emotion called love was lucidly clear to her, for it filled her heart and consumed her body.

Their eyes fused in understanding and acceptance. Even if he didn't love her, she knew he desired her beyond all reason. "Ku-wa, Rebecca," he quietly commanded, wishing Wi would tarry for many hours, knowing he would not.

They pulled on their garments and made their way back to camp, taking a roundabout path in order to bathe in the stream. He left her at the tepee entrance, heading for his horse and some much needed diversion and solitude. Rebecca returned to her menial chores as Bright Arrow galloped out of camp to race with the wind and search his soul. Rebecca was to leave him soon. Did he dare to keep her within sight of his hungry eyes and ravenous body, to enable himself to furtively watch over her safety, to accept Broken Spirit's offer for her?

Broken Spirit was growing old; his heart still suffered over the losses of his wife and only son. After his broken foot refused to heal properly, he had changed his name to reflect his troubles. In his tepee, Rebecca would be free of sexual abuse and she would be of great service to the aging warrior whose tepee and lance boasted of many brave and daring coups.

Bright Arrow's hesitation came from two directions: Rebecca would be too tempting within his daily reach and sight, and Rebecca would be at the mercy of his heartless daughter Desert Flower. Her hatred of Rebecca was no secret. Bright Arrow was well aware of how Desert Flower used every opportunity to subtly harass Rebecca and to humiliate him with mockery and veiled insults. Bright Arrow wished he could cut out her baneful tongue, for too many of his friends listened and agreed with her opinions. It would be cruel and dangerous to sell his precious Rebecca to Broken Spirit. If he couldn't keep her, it was best she be sent far away. His painful decision made, he headed back toward camp.

Things remained the same between the women for the remainder of the afternoon. Shortly after the evening meal, Shalee abruptly left the tepee without saying a word to any of them. She walked down to the stream, waiting to see if Gray Eagle would follow her. Time passed. Still, she remained there, mindlessly staring at the moon's opalescent reflection upon the darkened water. When it seemed that Gray Eagle would not join her, she sadly turned to head back to their tepee. She inhaled sharply in surprise.

He was standing only a few feet behind her,

watching her intently. Their eyes met and fused. Neither moved nor spoke. When her need became overwhelming, she rushed into his arms and frantically clung to him. "Send her away tonight, Wanmdi Hota," she tearfully pleaded. "I cannot bear your loss any longer. I need you so much."

Chapter Seven

Gray Eagle leaned back to scan her entreating expression. "But you begged me to let her remain for seven moons," he confusedly reminded her. "Why do you wish her to leave early?" he probed.

"Because you will not touch me while Rebecca lives in our tepee! I love you. I do not wish to help her if it pushes us apart. She is nothing to me. But you are my husband, my true love. I was wrong to ask you to keep her here. I do not trust her! She seeks to worm her way into our lives and hearts. This cannot be! She is white, our avowed enemy," she emotionally declared, startling him with the pitiless words and heated anger which were novel within his gentle wife.

"You did not feel and think this way a few moons past. What has Rebecca done to cause you such fear and pain?" Did he even need to ask . . .

Pride would not allow her to relate her jealousy and suspicions to him. She retorted peevishly, "She has behaved perfectly, too perfectly, Wanmdi Hota! This is strange; it is dangerous. It is not natural to . . ." She halted the rest of her traitorous statement.

"It is unnatural to love your enemy," he humorously finished for her in a curiously disturbing tone. "Did we not meet and love as enemies?"

She gazed deeply into his mocking eyes. Her tremulous voice softly asserted, "This quickly and easily, yes, Wanmdi Hota," she unwillingly confessed, knowing he would perceive her dishonesty if she denied his candid explanation. "There is something about Rebecca which frightens and alarms me. I do not understand her; nor do I trust her," she spoke just enough truth to disarm him and to conceal her motives.

"Did I not tell you these same things a few moons past? I also sensed something evil and dangerous within her. I have observed her closely, but her secrets remain hidden from me. Do you think she lies about her desire for our son?" he asked, with an odd inflection in his tone.

She promptly wondered why such a similar thought would come to his mind. "Is that what you think, my husband?"

"I do not know, Shalee. At times this love and passion seem real. Other times . . ." He did not finish, but drifted in deep thought.

Unable to stop herself, she blurted out, "Other times she openly desires you more than your son!"

Stunned by her jealous revelation and the vehemence in her tone, he stared at her, seeking what to say in response. Tears filled her eyes at his apprehensive silence. His shock was increased as she warily inquired, "Do you also desire her, Gray Eagle? Do you envy your son's possession of her?"

"What madness is this!" he snarled at such a shocking accusation. "You dare to accuse me of desiring a white whore! I would never lower my pride to take a lowly white girl to . . ." The look of anguish which filled Shalee's eyes and paled her face halted his volatile outburst. Nettled, he tried to explain, "My anger steals my tongue. I did not mean to speak so sharply or cruelly. Why would you think I desire this girl?" he asked, his tone filled with contempt.

Cornered, she was compelled to clear the air between them. "I have seen the way you stare at her. I have also seen the way she looks at you. I am not blind or naive, my husband. Do you grow tired of me? Does your age demand you prove your great prowess? Do you also fall prey to her magic as our son does?" she voiced her fears and doubts aloud.

217

"Your eyes play tricks upon you, my wife. I do no more than study her. I only wished to discover what magic she uses upon our son. I do not crave Rebecca upon my sleeping mat. I have desired no other woman since I first took you. Each time I give you great pleasure, my prowess is proven to me. I need no other female. Upon my life and honor, I have not and never will grow weary of you," he stated, smiling into her dewy eyes.

"Then why have you not touched me since her arrival?" she cried out to him, her pain vividly etched upon her lovely face. "You say you cannot do so when she is around. But what of all the moments when she is not? Do you not need me as I need you?" she implored.

"I was not aware of such feelings and pain within you. I have many things upon my mind. Once these problems are settled and the girl is gone, it will be as it was before she came," he reasoned, unwittingly acknowledging that Rebecca was the crux of their trouble.

"If Rebecca is not the problem, then how will her departure settle everything? Will your love and desire for me return only then?" she pressed, dreading his answer.

"You speak words which confuse me, Shalee. How can I pretend nothing is wrong when this white whore seeks to entrap our only son? How can I act as before when you move closer to her each day and further away from me?" he accused tersely.

"That isn't true, Wanmdi Hota!" she argued. "I have not refused your touch; you have resisted mine. I said I was sorry; I said I was wrong. She must leave our tepee."

"I gave my word to our son she could remain seven moons. I cannot go back on it. The girl is nothing to me, Shalee. When the time comes, I will take her away."

"No! Send her away, but do not take her yourself."

"You do not trust me? You think I will take her to my mat after I leave camp!" he furiously exploded in disbelief.

"It is Rebecca I do not trust . . . not you," she faltered in distress.

Incensed, he snapped, "Am I not strong enough to resist a mere white whore?"

Shalee began to weep. This conversation was going crazy. What was happening between them? Why was she so tense and frightened? Why were they at each other's throats? "I do not know what has come over me, Wanmdi Hota. Strange things are happening around me and within me. I am afraid. I cannot seem to master my mind or my actions. I feel stranded upon a mountain which is rapidly crumbling beneath my feet. I do not know how to save myself or how to stop the landslide. Help me, Wanmdi Hota, for terror rules my heart and soul," she sobbed in rising panic.

Gray Eagle's arms enclosed her within their warm and protective vise. His lips covered her face with kisses. She clung to him. "I need you, Wanmdi Hota. Please make love to me. Please tell me that all will be right soon . . ."

"It will, my love. I promise you this." His mouth claimed hers as they eased down to the grass, oblivious to all except their urgent need for each other. They made love passionately and desperately, needing to erase all painful realities.

He murmured words of endearment and comfort into her ears, his warm breath causing her to quiver with unsuppressed longing. He took her with intensity and unleashed passion, ravenous from many days of denial. She feverishly responded to smoldering fires which burst into colorful, torrid flames. Eyes of igneous black coal fused with molten, emerald ones. Each ached for the pleasure and serenity of a total union in spirit and body. His insistent tongue probed the inviting recess of her warm mouth. His hands fondled her breasts, teasing the taut nipples until she moaned in urgent need of him.

His stimulating manhood plunged into her receptive body until she was lost in a daze of mindless frenzy. His thrusts varied from hasty, savage lunges to agonizingly sweet explorations to deliberately slow piercings. When his stamina and restraint could no longer resist the pleas of their bodies, he moved rapidly and purposely to bring them to an intoxicating finality. Without a thought to being overheard, she cried out in pleasure as her body mingled the fiery liquids of her stormy release with his. Spent, they clung to each other until their ragged respirations returned to normal and placid relaxation settled in.

In the blissful aftermath of their unrestrained joining, he gazed down at her and playfully teased, "Does that take away your jealousy and doubt, my love? I need and crave no woman but you. If ever I did desire another female, it would never be Rebecca. I only desire her out of our lives and tepee. This I swear to you. She is evil. She cannot remain here."

"Wanmdi Hota? Why do you hate this particular girl so much?" she unexpectedly inquired, catching him completely off guard in this stirring moment.

In spite of his self-control, he noticeably tensed. "Once more your eyes deceive you, Shalee. She is only a white slave, nothing more," he alleged, his reaction and tone belying his claim.

Not wishing to disturb this new and fragile bond, she painfully allowed this obvious lie to pass. Later, she would demand the truth. Perhaps Rebecca held the solution to this mystery, a missing key Shalee resolved to find in order to release the green monster which intimidated her.

They lingered in that romantic setting until the moon was above their heads, suggesting they retire for much needed rest.

Gray Eagle and Bright Arrow departed early that next morning to seek vital information concerning the new fort and a rumor of white settlers who had pushed their way into the Sioux's sacred grounds to the west. It would be late the next afternoon before they returned. After which, only one day remained before Rebecca's planned departure . . .

The following day passed in moody silence between the two women: females who were visibly similar, yet, vastly different. Much of the time, Rebecca was left alone in the quiet tepee while Shalee visited other Indian wives, a gracious duty of a chief's wife. When the last chore was completed and the evening meal was over, each retired to her own mat.

"Shalee?" Rebecca called out softly across the distance which separated them in many ways. She would be leaving here soon and she yearned to depart in peace after all this Indian woman and her son had done for her.

Shalee sat up and looked over at this girl who was tearing her world and her heart asunder. "Sha?" she replied frostily, her gaze guarded.

"Shalee hiya koda?" Rebecca began, not

knowing how else to breach their language barriers. Her frightened, sad heart with its heavy burden of a dismal future craved any measure of appeasement and acceptance.

"Shalee Oglala. Rebecca wasichu. Rebecca kaskapi," the Indian princess responded. "Hiya koda," she added to bluntly send her point home, hoping to punish Rebecca's treachery, hoping to return some of the pain this girl had brought into their lives and tepee.

"But why?" Rebecca pleaded, coming to kneel before her. "God, how I wish we could communicate! How can I make you understand how important you are to me?"

In desperation and despair, Rebecca poured out her soul with all its torment, guilt, and fears, "I thought you liked me and had accepted me. I've never met any woman as kind or as unselfish as you. You're so beautiful and special. I love your son, Shalee. It will hurt deeply to give him up. I've tried to make you and Gray Eagle like me. I don't know what else to do! His fierce hatred of me is clear, but I don't know how to win his truce. I've tried to obey you. I've tried to prove I want to stay here."

In a note hinting of hysteria, her voice plunged forward in search of the answer to this agonizing mystery, "Don't you think I know how lucky I am to be in this tepee? My God, haven't I lost and suffered enough! Your people have left me with little pride or honor. What more can I do to earn your friendship? Must I grovel and beg upon my knees for what I have earned? How can I reach your husband when he petrifies me every time I look at him? I see such hatred and resentment in his eyes. I do not understand! I have done nothing to him, to any of you! After all your people have taken from me, is Bright Arrow's love and acceptance too much to expect in return? I need him! I love him! I've seen the love and closeness you share with Gray Eagle. Soon, my love and I will be cruelly parted forever. Please don't take this short time away from us."

Distressed and in despair, the words came tumbling out without control. In desperate need of inner peace, she denied herself all pride with this much needed emotional release, for so much had been tightly controlled within her for many days. She jumped up to nervously pace the stuffy confines of the tepee. She rambled on and on, telling Shalee countless things. "You don't know what it's like to be so frightened that you want to faint or to scream hysterically. You know nothing of shame, of torment without reason. If there was any place to go, I would flee this hellish life! But there is none, for the whites would scorn me more than the Indians do. There is no freedom when you no longer have a home or family." Her voice became hollow and strained as she continued.

"Do you know what it takes to force yourself

to endure such wicked things just to prevent far worse torment? It has taken all of my strength and will to hide my resentment and anger from all of you. But I needed and wanted your acceptance and friendship. I must have this time with Bright Arrow! I have cast aside all pride and blindly ignored my shame and torment. For what? For a truce which you all deny. It was only possible because you reached out to me, you helped me! Now, you've turned against me and I do not understand why. I have lost my only friend, and soon I will lose my only love. How much pain and loss can I bear?"

She pleaded with the silent, astonished woman before her, "Tell me what I do wrong! I will prevent it! I have tried to help you. I have been respectful when my heart cried out against your cruelties to me. I have been obedient when my mind screamed for me to rebel and resist this savage enslavement. But such actions only would have hurt me more. Rebellion and curses would have denied the little peace and great love which I found here. What more can I do?" she asked breathlessly.

She came to sit before Shalee. "I want to be your friend, Shalee. Must I endure such loneliness and despair? I have nothing and no one. I love Bright Arrow. Is that so wrong? I know we're different, but my heart and body cry out for him. I do not know how or why. I have tried to be friendly to your husband. If he did not look so much like Bright Arrow, then I could hate him as much in return!" she vowed, tormented by this injustice. "If my fate was not in his cruel hands, then I would cease these futile attempts to please him! I would claw that look of fierce hatred and scorn from his face!" she voiced her suppressed feelings aloud.

"What ghost am I to him? Why is his hatred of me so great? The way he looks at me . . ." She shuddered violently, "I feel as if he's probing my very soul. How could a gentle woman like you ever love such a vicious savage? How he terrifies me with those evil black eyes which seem to pierce my very soul."

Shalee listened to the enlightening words from this dejected girl, wishing she dared to question her in English. She did not. Rebecca returned to her mat and fell upon it, weeping openly and bitterly. "God help me endure the savage existence your hatred condemns me to. God forgive me, for I cannot allow it. I will die first. I hate you all! I hate you for pretending to accept me. It was only a cruel joke, just like your son's. The others laughed at the foolish way I fell into his cunning trap. I might be naive and stupid, but I know he wants me. It is your hatred which will not permit our love to grow. You will brutally kill it as you do your enemies. It isn't fair! I cannot help being white! Do you think I care if he is Indian! No! I will die before another man touches me!" She angrily wiped away her tears. Rebecca's tone became soft and entreating as she pleaded, "You're a woman; you should understand what I feel and have endured."

Bitter laughter came forth with Rebecca's self-recriminations, "I was wrong. I was so stupid and gullible. There is no happiness for me anymore, only hatred and whoredom. But I can never meekly submit to such evil. I will force your husband to kill me first. He's brutal and wicked. If I but defied or attacked him once, he would instantly end this hell for me. Oh, Bright Arrow, if only I had never met you!" she wretchedly wailed.

Shalee had heard enough, too much. Her heart was stormed with guilt and shame for what this girl was enduring. She had misjudged her and her actions. Of course Rebecca was unlike she had been at this same age! Rebecca was wiser, stronger, and more resilient. Rebecca had been born of this demanding wilderness, not to an English estate as she herself had been. The vivid reality of her erroneous judgment stunned her. Rebecca was bravely dealing with this staggering situation in the way she felt safest. She had not been an innocent in the same ways Alisha Williams, now Princess Shalee, had once been so long ago. At seventeen, Rebecca was more of a wise and strong woman than she had been at twenty!

Shalee walked over to Rebecca's mat. She

knelt beside her and tenderly stroked her coppery hair. "Hiya ceya, Rebecca," she coaxed the girl to stop crying. "Shalee koda."

Rebecca lifted tear-filled eyes to Shalee. "Shalee koda?" she doubtfully questioned her hearing.

Shalee smiled and replied, "Shalee koda. Wookiye," she offered, making the sign for peace. It pained Shalee's heart and tore at her conscience to suddenly realize she was brutally tormenting this vulnerable child as she had once been tormented by the relentless Oglala.

Rebecca flung her arms around Shalee and hugged her tightly. "Thank you, Shalee. You're the only one who gives me the courage to go on with this pretense of meekness and obedience. I cannot fight you all. Yet, it would be fatal and foolish to resist you."

"Rebecca istimna. Rebecca washtay. Shalee, Rebecca koda." Shalee pushed her down to the mat and smiled once more. What could a little kindness and friendship cost? If only there had been a Shalee for her all those years ago . . .

Both women spent a restful, peaceful night. That next day, their truce was again in full bloom. They shared a deeper bond of trust which only they comprehended. The chores went quickly and cheerfully. They behaved more like mother and daughter than Indian princess and white captive. Many noticed the way in which Rebecca warmly responded to

Shalee and the glow of affection and respect within her lovely eyes. But it seemed only natural for even an enemy to love and to respect the beautiful and gentle Indian princess who was joined to their chief.

Rebecca could not explain this new change in the Indian princess, but she readily accepted it. Still, she inwardly knew it would not alter the chief's adamant decision concerning her imminent departure.

With Shalee, it was much the same. There was no peaceful way to change her husband's mind and to attempt to do so would only cause resentment. If Rebecca was permitted to remain here with them, the decision had to come from her husband. Although she wished she could converse with this charming creature, she dared not do so.

Rebecca picked up the water skins and headed to the stream. She knelt near an area where the water was flowing steadily and placed the skin below the clear, bubbly surface. When the first skin was full, she hung it on one of the Y-shaped branches which were situated at intervals along the grassy bank to assist this particular chore. As she leaned forward to fill the second one, she was forcefully shoved into the waist-deep water.

Caught by complete surprise, her nose and mouth took in enough water to strangle her. She came up coughing and gasping for air. Drenched and shaken, she stared at the five

Indian girls giggling and ribbing each other. She retreated several steps as they ominously came forward to squat by the edge of the stream.

As if by some pre-arranged signal and devilish plan, they scooped up handfuls of mud and began to throw them at the befuddled and defenseless Rebecca. Struck rigid and speechless by this unprovoked attack, the white girl anxiously submitted to this cruel joke. She couldn't very well rush at them and defend herself; they would no doubt claim she had assailed them! They had chosen their time well, for no adults or braves were in view.

When she was completely covered with clingy mud, the girls calmly washed their hands and strolled off as they snickered and whispered, pleased by her fear and filthy condition. Rebecca glanced down at her clothes and arms, viewing the results of their mischief. Her hands went up to brush the moist clumps from her auburn hair and tawny face. She leaned forward to rinse out her mouth, nose, and eyes.

Tears of dejection pooled in her sad eyes. Sinking to her knees, she wept in despair and anguish. Would it always be this way? How much longer could she accept their cruelties and suffer in silence before she was instinctively compelled to defy these hateful girls and their people?

Pride and rebellion stormed her mind. She gritted her teeth as she suppressed her outrage and humiliation. She sat upon the stream bed as she washed her arms and legs. She ducked beneath the surface to cleanse herself as best she could without soap or a cloth. She scrubbed her dress without removing it. She would simply tell Shalee she had slipped in the mud and fallen into the water. It would be futile and absurd to run back to camp crying and ranting about her vile treatment. The Indians would laugh in her face, maybe even punish her for accusations against their daughters. Someday . . .

A much different story was taking place far from the tranquil Oglala camp. Gray Eagle and his brooding son had ridden for hours toward Paha Sapa, the Sioux's sacred grounds, to discover if careless trappers were indeed violating the grounds of sacred spirits and dead warriors. Many times in the past, the brazen whites had trespassed upon such places, and had stolen the possessions of dead warriors. Of all enemy offenses, this was the most unforgivable.

The two warriors had travelled in silence. Shortly after high noon, they left their horses in a concealed place and soundlessly made their way to the reported area of desecration. The sight which greeted their eyes filled each man with fury. They mutely studied the scene for a brief time before confronting these reckless white foes.

There were three white trappers near the river

which ran within the sacred grounds. Gray Eagle raged at this affront to Wakantanka, Makakin, the Thunder Spirits, and their dead brothers. The warning signs of death to any man who dared to enter here had been foolishly ignored. The reasons were ghastly clear: souvenirs from the scaffolds of fallen warriors littered the ground near the water's edge.

The discovery of another treasure had prevented the white-eyes' hasty departure: gold, that shiny rock which the white man lusted and killed for, and faced any danger to obtain. The two warriors listened to the argument between these bold invaders who would soon die for this evil deed.

"I'm telling ya, Pete; this is crazy! If you'd told me whatcha had in mind, I'd never have come witcha," a tall, ruggedly dressed man was shouting at the one kneeling in the shallows of the water, his pants soaked and his boots sloshing with water.

"You're the crazy one! Gold, man! We'll be rich!" Pete shouted back at the cautious man who was shaking his dark, shaggy head. Pete's eyes were glazed with greed and his mouth drooled in lustful anticipation. He held up several large nuggets as he growled, "Ya think I kin leave this here for them savages! It's mine!"

Colley added his opinion, "He's right, Dan. We'll all be rich!"

"We'll all be dead!" Dan yelled back at the

two men who had tricked him into this disastrous trip. "This is sacred ground to the Sioux. It's death just to step a foot on it. I was a fool to throw in with the likes of you two. Count me out from now on. I don't collect Indian scalps, or steal from their graves, or risk my neck for a little gold! Suit yourself, but I'm leaving. I'm not fool enough to challenge the mighty Sioux, especially that Gray Eagle."

As Dan turned to leave, Colley called out to him, "Ya got bugs eating your brain! Gray Eagle was around when I was born; he must be an old man by now. I don't fear no old chief who lives by his legend!"

Dan sighed heavily in disgust. "May God help you, Colley, when you meet the Eagle face to face. I can promise you, he ain't no made-up story. He's more real than that gold in your greedy hands. I ain't afraid to die, but I ain't no fool either. Men like you two are the reason he's hell-bent on destroying the whites. Can't say as I blame him either. Who wouldn't fight to protect his lands and his people! Keep the gold and them bloody treasures; it ain't my way of earning a living."

With that advice and those remarks, Dan made his way to his horse. He mounted up and walked the huge roan over to them. Gazing down, he suggested, "Say your prayers soon; you won't be alive at sunrise." With that, Dan Clardy slowly rode off, heading eastward.

Bright Arrow glanced at his father and signed the question of pursuit of the man who was leaving. Gray Eagle shook his head, signing in return that the man had earned the right to survival with his words and actions. Bright Arrow nodded agreement, learning more and more about his father and leadership every day. It took a great man to watch one of the whites ride away, for each knew that on another day, this same man might be facing them in battle.

The two warriors returned their attention to the men at the river's edge. Gray Eagle chose the larger and stronger man for himself and silently signalled for his powerful son to conquer the other one. Bright Arrow made his way around the men without a sound. When he was positioned on the other side of them, his father gave the sign for their surprise attack.

With the Sioux war-cry splitting the heavy silence like a roar of ominous thunder, the two warriors charged their enemies. Accustomed to perilous life in the wilderness, the two trappers reacted with drawn hunting knives, but still they were too slow.

Gray Eagle leaped upon Pete without a care to the deadly blade within his dirty, wet hand. They scuffled and struggled for a brief time, as the warrior's stamina and strength could not be matched. With Pete pinned to the hard ground, the knife in the chief's hand hesitated in midair before forcefully coming down and hastily ending this man's life. His ebony eyes had seen the golden rocks which had spilled from the white man's pockets and hands.

His jet eyes gleamed with revenge and satisfaction. Securing the white man's arms to the ground beneath his powerful legs, his bronzed hand gathered the nuggets and piled them upon Pete's drumming heart. Pete watched this curious action with terrified eyes. The fearless chief glared down at him when this odd task was complete.

Gathering a large handful, Gray Eagle sneered, "Now that Gray Eagle has easily defeated you, White Dog, do you still believe him a weak old man who is only a dream?"

Horrified by the revelation of this warrior's identity, Pete's mouth flew open as he inhaled sharply in sheer terror. Like the swift strike of a rattlesnake, the gold nuggets were jammed inside Pete's mouth and the warrior's hand clamped over it. Unable to prevent it, several had been helplessly sucked into his windpipe at his startled inhalation. He gagged and struggled to dislodge them and breathe. He could not. His eyes began to bulge in fear and his face grew livid from the lack of air to his burning lungs. The puissant warrior did not move or take his black eyes from the white man's face until his body was limp and lifeless. As Gray Eagle stood up, the dead man's head rolled to one side, the golden death returning to the

Earth from which it was carelessly stolen.

Gray Eagle turned to witness the battle which still raged furiously between his son and the man called Colley. As he observed this duel of death, distress filled him. Bright Arrow's mind was consumed by such turmoil that he was battling like a warrior in training! Fearing for his son's life, Gray Eagle did a humiliating and punishing thing: as Bright Arrow helplessly tumbled backwards from a heavy blow, Gray Eagle moved forward as if to join the assault upon this second man. As Colley whirled to confront the greater danger of the moment, Bright Arrow shamefully comprehended his weakness and the vivid reason for it. If other warriors had been present, Gray Eagle could not have intervened for even his own beloved son. Any warrior would prefer death to such a disgrace.

Tormented by this truth, Bright Arrow yelled out, "No, father! He is mine!" With that declaration, the younger warrior attacked his foe with a new determination and strength. Without delay, Colley was slain. Bright Arrow angrily withdrew his knife from the white man's heart and coldly wiped the blade upon his clothing. It was several minutes before he could slow his ragged respiration and face his father.

Gray Eagle waited silently and patiently, knowing the shame and truth which flowed within his son's taut body and turbulent mind. Finally, the younger warrior slowly turned to meet his father's probing gaze. "Your words were wise and true, my father. This battle within my heart dulls my eyes and senses. Much as I love her and desire her, I must send her away. A warrior is nothing without his honor, and I fear this white girl steals mine. Such fear and weakness must be destroyed this very day."

Gray Eagle studied his son closely and intensely. If only he did not know the great pain which filled his son's heart. If only he had not once endured this same agony and weakness for the woman he loved. Had it been so long ago that he could not vividly recall how nothing and no one could strip his forbidden love from his side? But Rebecca was not Shalee. She was white, the child of an enemy, an enemy whose hands were stained red with the blood and pain of his wife, his unborn son, and himself. Much as he wished to ease this torment within his son, he could not.

"The truth now grows in your heart, my son. Her magic has lost its power over you. In time, a worthy mate will take her place and fill the emptiness you now endure. Come, we must ride for camp."

"But what of the Bluecoat fort?" his son reminded him of their twofold mission.

"The white girl must leave your side on the new sun. There are things you must resolve within your heart before she goes. The fort will stand even after that sun. But only until the Great Spirit reveals to us how to destroy it.''

The two warriors returned the possessions of their Indian brothers to their scaffolds and chanted prayers to the Great Spirit. The golden rocks were cast into the gently flowing water. The bodies of the two whites were taken to the edge of the sacred grounds and secured to the warning posts to enlighten others who dared this offense. The sun was low on the horizon so the two warriors camped there for the night. With the rising sun, they would head home: one to his endless love and one to his lost love.

When Bright Arrow and Gray Eagle returned, they were again befuddled by the abrupt changes in both women. The aura in the tepee was jovial and light. The two women constantly exchanged smiles. When questioned about this puzzling turn, Shalee revealed the stirring words which Rebecca had spoken aloud.

Bright Arrow beamed in open satisfaction and pride, yet his already ravaged heart was newly rent by this discovery which changed nothing. It was Gray Eagle's tense mood which perplexed Shalee. He instantly demanded if Shalee had carelessly given away her secret, if she had spoken to the girl in English, if she had questioned her about anything at all. He seemed only slightly relieved when she claimed total innocence of any misdeed or error. Yet, a curious aura surrounded her husband. He suggested a walk to the stream for some privacy and fresh air. Gray Eagle and Shalee left. They headed to the stream, then strolled a lengthy distance along its lush banks.

Gray Eagle immediately hinted at suspicion of a wily trick in Rebecca's "innocent and uncontrollable" outburst. "Perhaps she suspects our secret. Perhaps she seeks to regain your affection with this trick of tears. She said nothing more?" he inquired, failing to meet her gaze. Gray Eagle mistakenly thought his voice and expression were under his control.

"I tell you, my husband; I did not give away our secret. She was consumed with anguish and sadness. Confusion filled her mind. Her pain cried out for release as mine once did many times. Do you not recall the many times I behaved in this same wild manner? Yet, it was truly without deceit or control. Just as you remained silent with me, I said nothing to her."

Shalee teased him merrily, "She does not desire my handsome husband after all. She only fears you greatly as I once did. Do not be so fierce with your stares, for they are powerful and intimidating. She does not deserve more pain from us."

"Once more you blindly reach out to her and deny the dangerous evil she presents. Do not allow her troubles to cloud your vision, Shalee.

She must leave us. This past sun, troubled thoughts of her nearly claimed the life of our son. He cannot battle fierce enemies while she haunts his mind and saps his strength. She said nothing else?" he absently questioned, again an odd gleam flickering briefly in his obscure gaze and a mysterious tone lacing his voice.

"What do you fear she might say to me?" Shalee perceptively challenged. "Do you think she will give away dark secrets to me as I once did to you? Even so, what would this matter? She is a stranger to us."

"There is nothing she can say to you," he replied, his eyes narrowing in anger at her words. Their guarded gazes fused, leaf green with sooty black, to search for hidden truths.

"Then why do I sense you worry about what she might tell me? She is a stranger to us," Shalee emphatically stressed. "What is there for her to say?"

"Forget this matter, Wife. There is nothing left to say," he firmly closed the subject. His jet eyes were as hard and shiny as highly polished flint. His frosty sternness baffled and hurt her.

Needing to comprehend this enigma, she debated, "But . . ."

He icily cut off her protest, "Silence, Shalee. I will hear no more of this daughter of . . . our white enemies. She will leave before Wi sits high in the heavens on the new day. I have spoken. Do not fight her battles for her. She has caused enough strife between us. There is pain and rebellion in both my tender-hearted wife and my love-blinded son. She will leave. I am chief and warrior; my words are law. Speak no more of her or the past!" he sullenly commanded.

"Your sharp tongue and biting words are unnecessary, my husband. I would not plead for her to remain here when her presence so needlessly divides us. But I must understand this hatred and bitterness which she brings to your heart and eyes. Why must it be this way, Wanmdi Hota? What has she done to us, to you?" she insisted.

"She steals the heart and honor of our only son!" He irrationally snapped at her. "She strips away his guard and endangers his face and life!"

"Can she be blamed for loving him? Can I be blamed that we only have one son? Your unspoken words whisper it is my fault. But it requires two people to make a child," she asserted.

His temper sorely strained, he snapped at her, "There was once another child. A child who died because of . . ." He whirled and presented his back to her, scolding himself for nearly revealing the secret which Rebecca's name held, the fact which he feared Rebecca might accidentally give away during her frenzied ravings. His seemingly cool facade was being steadily melted by destructive flames from the past which burned within his taut body.

"Because of who or what, my husband?" she demanded in unsuppressed agony when her initial shock had lessened and her speech returned. They had not spoken of her tragic miscarriage in eighteen years. "Why do you mention that treacherous, painful time now?" she asked in a small voice which quavered with anguish.

"I did not mean to remind you of such days and such pain. I merely rebel against losing the only child we have to the hatred and evil of the whites. Their numbers and strength grow as the grasses upon the plains. This girl is white. She is our enemy. In her own way, she prevents his love for a woman of his own kind. She cunningly slays his honor. This cannot be!"

"Look at me, Wanmdi Hota," she softly commanded. "Look at me and swear there is no more to this matter than you speak of. What do you hide from me?"

He turned and glared down at her, "Twice you have questioned my honor and words. Why does this girl breed mistrust and defiance within you? You twist my words and charge that I deceive you. Why, Shalee?" he cunningly put her on the offensive, looking and sounding as if she was wrongfully accusing him of some treachery. "What could Rebecca possibly say to you that I would fear? I only wish for her to not refresh your past to you. I do not wish for you to hear and to suffer with her. I wish to spare you such hurt.''

"I'm sorry, Wanmdi Hota,'' she replied sadly, feeling compelled to accept his logical explanation and to wisely halt this raging conflict. "I seem to be saying that too often these days, don't I? But you are right. Rebecca has caused trouble here, but it isn't her fault. It's just I can see her side as well as ours. This makes it hard for me to view her as you do. Soon, all will be right again,'' she vowed optimistically, lovingly caressing his taut jawline.

A lazy smile tugged at the corners of his lips. "If I did not love you so much, I would beat you for this constant doubting of me,'' he joked mirthfully, seizing her offer of a truce.

"You speak wise and true, my husband. I am ashamed to say I truly deserve such punishment. But it will be over tomorrow,'' she murmured in a tone of intermingled relief and sadness.

"Tomorrow,'' he echoed. Could it come swiftly enough?

Shalee mentally debated if this was the perfect time to relate her other suspicions to him. Immediately her mind cautioned her to wait until she was absolutely certain of them. They had both prayed and longed for another child; it would be cruel to speak of such a precious gift if she were wrong. It would be best to wait until peace and trust returned to their tepee. If her suspicion turned out to be correct, there would be much joy in their lives and hearts.

Alertly witnessing her softened gaze and provocative smile, Gray Eagle teased, "What cunning fox walks within your mind, my love?"

She looked up at him, her eyes devouring his arresting features and beguiling smile. "I was just envisioning how wonderful it will be to have peace within our lives again. I was thinking how very lucky I was to find you, and how very much I love you."

His finger reached out to trace the softness of her lips. "Each day I thank the Great Spirit for sending you to me. My heart refuses to imagine what my life would be without you. Your eyes shine as bright as Wi. Surely Mother Earth must envy your beauty and glow. You are mine forever."

His mouth came down upon hers in a tantalizing, probing kiss. He savored the sweetness of her mouth and the heated response of her lithe body. No matter what happened, it would always be this way between them. Nothing and no one could ever extinguish the fires which burned within them. "Perhaps I will allow Bright Arrow to take Rebecca away. Then, we could be alone for two moons . . ." he huskily murmured in a suggestive tone which enflamed her senses.

Alluring green eyes fused with smoldering ebony ones. "As you wish, my husband," she cheerfully agreed. "Alone . . ." How blissfully marvelous that sounded.

"You have spoiled me, my love. Your touch and nearness are like food for my hungry heart. I find I cannot live without them. I starve for you each day. Not having you on every moon makes me ravenous and greedy. Dare we make love upon the face of Mother Earth?" he hinted in a deep and stirring voice.

"If we do not, I fear I shall die of starvation. For you are also the food of my heart," she seductively replied, caressing the firm muscles upon his chest, tracing her hands over his robust shoulders and down his firm arms.

He took her hand in his and found a place where they would not be sighted or disturbed. It was impossible to return to their tepee where this same scene was taking place between his son and that damnable scout's daughter! Yet, he needed her too much to deny his body the ecstasy which only she could give.

Their lovemaking was deliberate and intoxicating. They touched and joined with fierce longing. They came together in sensuous leisure. They explored and conquered the heights and depths of passion and pleasure.

It was very late when they returned to their tepee to find both Rebecca and Bright Arrow fast asleep in the blissful aftermath of a like union of minds and bodies. So deep was their peaceful slumber that neither awoke as they went to their mat.

Shalee awakened to soft weeping that next morning. She sat up and looked around, rubbing her sleepy eyes. She briefly wondered why Rebecca was sobbing as if heartbroken until she realized what day this was. She forcefully ordered herself not to interfere in what must be done for all their sakes. Unable to tolerate the anguish which filled the young girl, Shalee left the tepee for some fresh air. Sighting Bright Arrow not far away, she went to speak with him before he left.

"When will you take her away, Bright Arrow?" she softly inquired, knowing this parting was hurting him deeply.

"I have told her goodby. I must not see her again. I will leave until father has taken her away forever. To watch them ride away would be unwise. I fear my eyes will reveal my feelings to others. I must be alone for a time."

She stared at him in confusion. "I do not understand. Gray Eagle said you would take her away."

His flinty eyes focused upon her quizzical ones. "He makes ready now. He fears I might be too weak to leave her with another," he informed her in a scornful tone which alarmed her. "For him, she cannot be gone quickly enough! He has once walked in these same steps. Why does he refuse to see how I feel? Why does he hate Rebecca so deeply? I have given you my word of honor not to speak of such matters to him. Yet, there is a dark secret why he wishes her gone, a powerful reason which I cannot uncover or understand. Do you know the reason for this hatred of her within him?" he questioned, stunning her.

"If there is another reason to consider, I do not know of it, Bright Arrow," she replied candidly. But how could her suspicions be so groundless when both her son and his captive also discerned a haunting mystery?

"I have seen the way he looks at her. There is a ghost within her which hardens his heart against her. Some unknown spirit challenges him. Who is she, Mother? What enemy does she recall to life?" he blatantly offered his solution.

Startled and baffled, she digested his questions. "Why do you say such things, Bright Arrow? Rebecca is a stranger to us."

"Then why does my father often speak of her evil blood as if he knows from where it comes? There is something strange about the way he speaks of her and stares at her which betrays a haunting memory," he argued, frowning in anger and frustration.

"This cannot be, my son. Your torment confuses you and clouds your vision. Unless she reminds him of me, of the past which I told to you in secret," she reasoned skeptically. Yet tremors of apprehension attacked her wary heart.

"No, Mother. It is not you he sees in Rebecca; it is another, an enemy. It is some past foe which he cannot forget. I am a warrior; my senses are keen. I know that look; for I have seen it many times upon the face of a man confronting an old enemy, one who has eluded and plagued him. In some unknown way, Rebecca is my father's enemy, but I do not know how or why." His brow knit in deep, moody speculation.

Fearing to relate his gnawing suspicion, he shifted nervously from one foot to the other. Did he dare to seek a truth which could deeply hurt his parents? Shalee tensed, for she also suspected some other motive behind this weighty situation. "What troubles you so deeply, Bright Arrow?" she forced herself to ask.

He summoned the courage to speak aloud his suspicions, "Has my father known another white woman? Does Rebecca favor that woman? Is she . . . perhaps my half-blooded sister?" he hesitantly voiced the only rational conclusions to this mystery.

"Never! Surely my ears do not hear such shameful words from our own son! You dishonor both your father and yourself with such vile thoughts. Gray Eagle is right; she is evil, for she makes you doubt the honor of your own father. Gray Eagle has never taken another white woman, not even in the Tipi Sa! This I swear to you. How can your heart betray him in this cruel manner? How can your lips utter such

248

wicked, traitorous words?" Appalled by his comments, she stared at him as if looking at a total stranger. As her husband had warned, Rebecca was creating rifts among them all.

Compelled to explain his wild speculations, he quietly disputed, "Have you not looked at her closely, Mother? Without a shadow of doubt, she carries more Indian blood than you do. Would that I dared to question her about this in her tongue . . ."

Exasperated, she exclaimed, "You must not! If she possesses Indian blood, it is not your father's! It would be dangerous to question her in English."

"Why, Mother? What do you fear she might say to me?" he bluntly challenged her with the identical words which she had recently spoken to her husband. "Look into my eyes, Mother, and swear to me there is no deadly secret which she can reveal."

Icy fingers of some obscure evil seized her racing heart and crushed it in its deadly talons. In horror, she trembled in fear and dread. "You think I lie to you? I swear I know nothing of this girl but for the words you spoke. All she has revealed to me, I have related to you," she tensely added.

"Do you also swear my father knows nothing of her?" he brutally refused to let this ominous matter drop. "Who is Rebecca, Mother?"

"He has said nothing to me. If Rebecca were

known to him, he would surely reveal this to me." Yet her frightened, wary look belied her confidence.

"Would he, Mother?" he defied her desperate attempt to end this conversation. "Who is her father?"

"Her father?" she echoed, trembling noticeably. "I do not know, my son."

"Go, look at her. Return and tell me who her father is. *He* is my father's enemy, not Rebecca. Perhaps you do not see yourself in her; perhaps you also see the image of her father and it hides from even you. Before she leaves, I want to know," he stubbornly persisted.

"If I study her closely and cannot answer your suspicions, will you let this matter go?" she pressed firmly.

He weighed her request, then replied, "If you see no ghost within her, then I will forget this mystery. But if you do, you must tell me who she is and why she must leave my side."

"I will search out this doubt which burns within you. Do not come to our tepee until I send for you." With that, she slowly walked toward the conical dwelling which suddenly seemed to permeate evil. Her leaden heart and legs rebelled against this ominous confrontation.

Rebecca was no longer crying. She was mechanically folding her garments and placing them upon a square of green material. Caught up in a world of hopeless despair, she did not hear Shalee's entrance or gradual approach. Shalee halted just behind her to listen to her hopefully enlightening murmurings . . .

"Why, Papa? Why must life be so cruel? If only you had taught me more about Indians . . . If only mama had taught me more signing . . . If she could have talked, she would have told me of such feelings. What do I know of love and hate? What do I know of the passions which consume men and women? If you hadn't taken mama from St. Louis, both of you would be alive now. Why did such terrible pain and death visit our cabin? Now, perhaps Rebecca Kenny will soon join you both . . ."

Rebecca . . . Kenny . . . St. Louis? Cabin? A mute mother? Kenny? Rebecca Kenny? Chills tingled upon Shalee's body. Why did this girl's words sound so familiar? So meaningful? So terrifying?

Rebecca lovingly gazed at the oil painting upon the scrap of deerskin. "You were very handsome, Papa. So strong and brave. How I wish I favored either you or mama. I certainly don't look anything like that wicked Uncle Jamie. But if I don't take after the Kennys or O'Haras, then who do I favor?" Rebecca vainly attempted to focus her mind upon anything except Bright Arrow and her impending departure.

Joe Kenny! Mary O'Hara! This was their

daughter? But how could that be? Jamie O'Hara? He was the lecherous, greedy uncle which Bright Arrow had mentioned? Shalee remembered him. When she had fled from Gray Eagle's bittersweet torment long ago, Jamie O'Hara had been the man who had forced her into the evil clutches of Jeffery Gordon when she could not pay her rent at his roadhouse! Evidently this innocent child had also been thrown into his wicked clutches just as her mother Mary had been before her marriage to Joe.

Joe and Mary were dead? But how? When? She furtively peeked over Rebecca's shoulder and stared down at the small oil painting which confirmed her suspicions. The truth which greeted her supposedly denied another one: if Gray Eagle knew who Rebecca was, he would never send her away! He and Joe Kenny had been friends many, many years ago. Joe had saved her life more than once; he had destroyed their dark past and had brought about their blissful life.

Rebecca's hand was covering her weeping eyes; she failed to see the shadow of Shalee upon her lap. Her innocent words of grief exposed Gray Eagle's heartless treachery to his shocked wife. "Why did you have to die, Papa? Who was the man you spoke of in your delirium? Will I ever understand your strange words? Why did you rave of days long past before you married

Mama? Why did you keep saying if only the
child was yours? Who was this other man in
Mama's life before you met? Why did he haunt
you so in death? She must have loved you more,
for she married you not him. Who was this
Powchutu? What is he to me?''

Chapter Eight

Shalee nearly fainted from this great shock. Her mind reeled at the misleading implications in Rebecca's troubled, rambling words. Within her spinning mind, time was racing backwards at a perilous and furious speed to a collision course with the past. Mary O'Hara had been in love with Powchutu; they had been sleeping together before his brutal murder. Of course! Mary had been pregnant! That was why Joe had married a vulnerable mute girl so quickly and unexpectedly! Rebecca Kenny's father was Powchutu!

My God, she cried silently in heart-rending agony; he knows who she is! Joe must have told him why he was marrying Mary so hastily! He lied to me! I felt he was hiding something. The evil blood which he fears is Powchutu's ... Bright Arrow was right! The ghost of her father

255

is the real enemy. Even after all these years, my husband would mercilessly punish an innocent girl for her father's crimes! He knew! He knew and lied!

Resentment, anger, and bitterness assailed her. No wonder he was so eager to have her gone! He had astutely surmised Rebecca might drop a clue to her real identity. Over and over the words echoed loudly and ominously within her head, he lied! He lied! He lied! But this wasn't the first time her love had cruelly deceived her. Powchutu had been around all those other times; now, his restless spirit was surely witnessing this new betrayal.

Was her husband so selfish and mistrustful that he would keep this critical fact a secret? Even Rebecca had not discerned the deadly truth! For all purposes, she was the daughter of Mary and Joe. Send their defenseless child to endure a hellish existence? Never! Shalee owed her old and dear friends this much; she owed them more!

Shalee touched Rebecca's shoulder and she faintly called her name in a strained voice, "Rebecca . . ."

The young girl lifted a tear-streaked face to Shalee. Bright Arrow was right; she did offer a veiled threat to her proud husband. He would never permit Powchutu's daughter to have his only son! Shalee's eyes slipped to the skin within Rebecca's hand. She knelt beside the dejected girl. She pointed to Joe's likeness and tremulously inquired, "A'ta?" She forced a smile in order to calm Rebecca.

Rebecca glanced at the skin and nodded. Shalee reached out to touch it, her finger gently tracing the tiny image of the stalwart scout who had led her wagon train to the Sioux land from the Pennsylvania Colony when she was barely nineteen. Memories of Joe's protection, instructions, and friendship crowded into her mind. She recalled how Joe had saved her life following her miscarriage after her tormenting flight to civilization with Powchutu. She remembered how Joe had persistently tracked her here after Gray Eagle's recapture. She knew it had been Joe's enlightening words which had returned the bond of love and trust between her and her intrepid husband. Dear Joe dead?

"A'ta ya?" she asked, pointing to the unseen heavens above the tepee.

"Sha. He and Mama died of a fever two years ago," she went on, not caring that Shalee supposedly could not grasp her tongue.

Shalee held out her quivering hand in askance. Rebecca hesitantly placed the precious skin there, hoping she would not damage it, knowing Shalee could take it from her if she wished to do so. Shalee gazed at the two familiar images. Shalee clearly remembered the mute girl whom she had met and befriended long ago. She had not seen Mary in eighteen years, not since her terrifying sojourn in St. Louis where they had met. Unbidden tears came to her eyes. Shalee pointed to Rebecca, saying, "Rebecca," then to herself, saying, "Shalee." She then glanced in askance at the pictures and inquired, "A'ta?"

"Joe Kenny," Rebecca replied, comprehending her query. "Mary Kenny," she added, touching her mother's likeness.

Shalee dared to venture, "Rebecca Kenny?"

Rebecca smiled and nodded. A gleam of suspenseful excitement suddenly filled her eyes. "I wonder . . ." she mused aloud. "If there is such an Indian, perhaps you've heard of him . . . Do I dare to learn such a secret?" she fearfully questioned herself. She resolved to see if Shalee would react to the name which her father had uttered countless times during his last two days. "Powchutu?" she said, nervously watching for any unusual reaction to that name.

In spite of Shalee's rigid control, she paled and inhaled sharply.

"You have heard his name! Who is he, Shalee? Powchutu!" Rebecca demanded in suspense.

"Hiya!" the forbidding, wintry word was forcefully issued like a gust of arctic air from behind Shalee. His stance was imposing, intimidating.

Both women jumped and stared up into the

withering, volatile scowl of Gray Eagle. He exuded fury and hostility. His frigid gaze went from one female to the other, daring either of them to speak. He came forward and savagely jerked Shalee to her feet. His towering body was taut with rage. He forcefully held a tight leash upon his words and outrage. "Hiya wohdake! Ku-wa!" he sternly commanded Shalee to silence and to follow him outside. He mistakenly assumed they had been conversing in English; he was furious.

Shalee held up the skin before his glacial eyes. In Oglala, she accused, "You knew, didn't you? You spoke false words to me. You know who she is. Joe was your friend! How can you do this terrible thing to his daughter? I had not believed you this cruel, my husband. How can we send his child to such a dangerous life?" she miserably demanded, wanting to discover if he knew the entire truth.

Unprepared for the discovery of his treachery, he lost control of his temper. "She is not his daughter! She carries the blood of . . ." At the horrified look which filled Shalee's eyes, he halted. His ebony eyes narrowed to slits of stormy warning. His grip became so tight and painful that she cried out. Still, he glowered at her tormented eyes of sea green.

He sarcastically accused, "It is you who knows the truth, Wife. I should not have let her remain here for even one moon. Yes, I know who she is," he confessed. "I did not permit her father to steal you from my side, and I will never allow his cunning daughter to steal our son. She still lives. After all he did to us, is that not enough kindness from me?" he asked, wondering how long she had known the truth.

"It is wrong, Gray Eagle. She does not know the truth. What harm can it do for her to remain here with us?" she pleaded.

"I know the truth!" A satanic smirk captured his striking features.

"You wish an innocent girl to pay for the sins of her father? I cannot permit it," she exclaimed, defying him and taking Rebecca's side.

"You cannot permit it?" he mocked her, his eyes and voice as sharp and deadly as finely honed steel. "You permitted her father to dishonor me! You permitted him to steal you from me! You permitted him to kill our first child! You permitted him to endanger your life and honor! You will permit his restless spirit nothing! She is evil. His roaming spirit sent her here for revenge upon me. Even in death he comes between us. He could never have you in life, and he will not have you in death. You are mine! Mine, Shalee!" he snarled.

"He never had me in any way! It was your cruelty which divided us! I have always belonged to only you. A dead man cannot control our lives. It is your endless hatred of him which does so! Have you forgotten how he saved my life many times? Once, he was like my own brother. He was obsessed by love and concern for me. Have you forgotten that he died trying to protect me?" she truthfully stated Powchutu's favorable deeds to her infuriated husband.

"He died because he stole you from my side! He murdered our unborn child! Can you forgive him that evil?" he chastised her. "I should have been the one to slay him! Vengeance was denied me!"

"It is self-destructive to hate for so long, Gray Eagle. Powchutu is dead! We cannot change what happened years ago. You accuse me falsely; I did not permit any of his evil. He honestly believed you cruel and wicked. He was only trying to protect me, to free me from your control. Must his evil blot out his good? Even so, you must share the guilt with me! He deceived you just as he deceived me. Did you permit him to shoot you? Did you protect me from him and his treachery? Did you permit the many reasons why his evil worked upon us?" she hotly attacked him in the same uncontrollable manner in which he had unjustly assailed her. "If not for your brutality and silence, his evil tricks would never have worked on either of us!" she charged. "How can you hate your . . ."

Shalee was thrown backwards by a stunning slap across her cheek. Gray Eagle shuddered with the seething rage which boiled within him. How dare she accuse him of dishonor, weakness, and cowardice! How dare his own wife excuse Powchutu's evil! Shalee stumbled and fell to the hard ground.

Rebecca was instantly between them, bravely and recklessly shielding Shalee from Gray Eagle's mindless attack. She astutely sensed the savage battle was over her and her fate. Somehow the name of her father and this unknown Powchutu had enraged the invincible chief. Who was this Powchutu? What had he and her father done to these Indians? She actually feared for Shalee's safety. She screamed at him, "Hiya! Kill me if you wish, but do not harm her for helping me!"

Rebecca dauntlessly and unknowingly stood between them just as Powchutu had once done. Deadly glimmers of violence sparked within those obsidian eyes which raked over her. Before he could charge Rebecca, Bright Arrow's powerful grip halted him. Gray Eagle whirled to confront the person who dared to interfere in his affairs. Igneous coal eyes fused and locked with guarded ebony ones.

"Do not strike her again, Father. Do not force me to battle my own father to protect my mother. Your anger and hatred have stripped away your control and reason. Think before you bring harm and sadness to the woman you love above life itself," he sternly advised, praying his father would listen and settle down.

Gray Eagle frowned at his defiant son whose prowess matched his own. "You have no place here, Bright Arrow. I must settle this trouble once and for all time."

"You are wrong, my father. The white girl is my captive. Shalee is my mother. Tell me what trouble causes you to strike her down so cruelly," he insisted boldly.

"The white girl must leave now. Shalee does not wish this. She defies me. Is this not so, Shalee?" he arrogantly demanded, knowing she would never confess the devastating truth to their son. How could she admit to being totally white herself? How could she tell her son the truth which would alter him to a lowly, despicable half-breed? How could she tell her son who and what Powchutu was? She would keep silent, for their lives depended upon it!

Bright Arrow released his firm grip upon his father's arm. He crossed the short distance to where his mother sat staring at Gray Eagle with a look of alarm and disbelief which he had never before seen upon her lovely, now bruised, face. He dropped to his knees before her. He gently captured her flawless face between his hands and turned it to him. Her wide eyes remained upon the puissant warrior who stared insolently back into her gaze.

"Mother? Are you injured?" he asked in deep

concern and affection. "Did he speak the truth? Did you defy him?" he helplessly sought the truth.

With sarcasm dripping from his words, Gray Eagle scoffed, "Our only son wishes to know if his father lies to him, Shalee. Our only son asks if my honor is stained with deceit. Did I punish you for rebellion and disrespect? I said the girl must leave here. You rebelled against my words and orders, did you not?" he contended, knowing she would be compelled to agree with his words.

Infused with pride, Shalee got to her feet and brushed the dust from herself. She lifted her chin with dignity. Her mood was strangely calm. Her green eyes were inscrutable and her expression impassive. Her voice was steady and soft, concealing the maelstrom of emotions which stormed her mind and body. Tormented, shamed, and disillusioned, she replied to his challenge with the most unexpected and shocking words he could ever imagine.

"Only you know what is in your heart and mind, my husband. To this day, I have been given no reason to doubt either your honor or your words. Why should I do so now? I did not mean to anger or to shame you with my foolish outburst and unforgivable defiance. You said Rebecca must leave. I wished her to remain. Your boundless anger did not permit me the time to tell you why I wished and needed for her to stay here. I will do so now.''

Gray Eagle tensed, not daring to speculate upon her alleged confession. Shalee noted his reaction, but ignored it. "I wanted the white slave to remain here with us because I will soon require help and strength with the chores. Many times you have spoken of other children. I have often prayed to the Great Spirit to permit me to give you another son. I wished to be sure of my suspicions before I told you the Great Spirit has finally answered my prayers. I wished to wait until there was peace within our hearts again before I shared this precious news with you and our only son. As your patience and temper have grown short and fiery with age, I must now pray we are not too old to raise another child.''

Each time Shalee used words such as "permit,'' "only son,'' "defiance,'' and "honor,'' her tone of voice held a special inflection which said much more to her stunned husband. Touching her lower abdomen, she stated, "Once more I carry the child of Gray Eagle within me. He should be born before the winter snows cover the sacred mountains. I will guard his life with my own. I will not lose this child. I will permit nothing and no one to endanger his life and safety. I was about to tell you this wonderful news when Rebecca arrived and all went wrong. Since I have not been myself lately and have been overly tired and tense, I enjoyed Rebecca's company and help. If you wish her gone, then find me another slave to ease the burden of work which could take away this gift from the Great Spirit. You are the warrior and our chief; you must decide what is safe and best for your unborn child. I will do as you command. I grow weary of these battles which steal my strength and joy."

"Another child?" he murmured in astonishment. This news was staggering, totally unforeseen. For years they had wanted another child. And now, it was to be? At their ages? He stiffened in suspicion and studied her intently. Revenge? Was this a spiteful trick to keep Rebecca here? Could his love be so cruel and vindictive? "You are sure?" he questioned.

Shalee sighed woefully, guessing his reasons. She shook her head in sadness. Was this where their destiny was heading: to lies, deceit, and betrayal? "Unless the Great Spirit plays a cruel joke upon me, then I carry your child. It has been so long since Bright Arrow's birth that I hesitated until I was certain. Yet, all the signs are present. If you do not wish Rebecca to remain here to help me, then find another captive who meets with your approval before I have need of her strength. I do not want to risk injury to this new child with hard work or an accident. I am no longer a young woman; to carry a child at my age will demand much from my body and my energy.

"I only ask you give Rebecca to a worthy man

who will treat her as she deserves. My love and loyalty belong to my family, not to Rebecca. Perhaps it would be safer and wiser for all of us if she left this very moment. My love and protection belong to my children, not someone else's. If your keen mind were free of such troubles, you would have noticed a change within me. If you doubt my words and honor, the truth will soon be visible for all to see," she declared, caressing her stomach. "I am weary in mind and body. This day has been too long and too demanding. Do as you will with the white girl. I must be alone."

She attempted to brush past him on her way out. He gently caught her forearm and stopped her steady progress. "You swear you carry my child," he pressed for the words which would make his final decision about Rebecca for him.

Without meeting his piercing gaze, she emphasized, "Before the vengeful echoes of yesterday called out to you, there was no need for such promises. I will not resist the fate you select for Rebecca. I could not alter your decision even if I tried. Her coming has caused enough trouble. I am not responsible for her or her tragic fate. I am more concerned with Bright Arrow and this new child I now carry."

She looked up at him, gluing her blank eyes to his. "No, Gray Eagle; I will swear nothing to you. You have no reason to doubt my words and honor. I say it is so; that is sufficient, or would have been seven moons past. In a short time, the truth will stand clear; it always does. I shall pray for truth and patience to come before our child does or before we are cruelly divided forever by this black shadow which threatens us. Do not *ever* strike me again or unleash your temper upon me. To do so shows dishonor to me; it might endanger this new child. If you unleash it again, I will return to my father's tepee in the camp of the Si-ha Sapa. Do not force me to seek safety for me and our unborn child with my people. There is nothing more to say. I wish to be alone now. I have many things to think upon . . ." She knew her husband could not prevent her protective flight to her alleged father; to do so would reveal deadly and shameful secrets.

"Shalee . . ." he began in a rueful tone, feeling shamed. "My anger has cooled; my reason has returned. I did not understand why you behaved so strangely or why you wished her to stay. You should have told me about our new child. We must talk," he cautiously stated, his tone contrite and entreating. But he had over-reacted, and she was not ready or willing to forgive him yet. The hurt from his incisive words was too fresh and painful to encourage her to hear him out.

"We can speak later. I wish to be alone for a time. Speak to your only son; he has many questions and doubts which you need to answer. Do what you must with Rebecca before I return. I will not allow myself to interfere again. I had forgotten the savage price for rebellion. Stay, Wanmdi Hota; I wish this torturous matter ended while I walk and think. Too much has happened this day.''

Gray Eagle knew if he left her side for two days that things would never be the same when he returned. He could perceive her withdrawal from him. He had hurt her deeply. He had humiliated her. He had struck out at her in a blind rage. He could have injured her and their unborn child. He followed her outside, out of Bright Arrow's hearing range. "She cannot stay with us, Shalee. Do you not understand this? Already she speaks the name of her real father, just as I feared. It is dangerous. Deadly secrets from our past could return to battle and defeat us. I tried to withhold the truth, knowing how it would affect you.''

"As before, you chose to remain silent. If you had told me the truth seven moons ago, I would have insisted upon her leaving that very day. Now there are lies between us once more. Even your son suspects some ominous reason for your hatred of her. What can you tell him? He is cunning and bright. He knows something is terribly wrong. How could Rebecca have revealed a deadly truth which only you possessed? Once more, your hatred and revenge carry a big price, Gray Eagle. Your words to me were cruel and untrue. Perhaps your love and faith in me are not as great as we both believed. Perhaps this is why the Great Spirit chose this moment to give us another child. Perhaps He seeks to show you the past is dead. Perhaps He hopes this child will remove the hatred which still dwells within your heart against all whites,'' she declared meaningfully.

"I love you and trust you, Shalee," he instantly protested.

"Then why did you lie to me? Many times I questioned you about the truth behind your hatred of her. You did not trust me enough to tell me who she is. Knowing your feelings for Powchutu, I would not have pleaded for her to remain for even one moon in your tepee and sight! Powchutu's ghost can come between us only if you allow it, which you did. In all that matters, she is the daughter of Mary and Joe. Can you repay our old friends by sending their innocent, defenseless child into shame and torment? There are many good warriors; choose one of them. Please . . .''

He lowered his head in deliberation of her words. As he comprehended the truth behind his actions and feelings, she softly reasoned, "There is no need for you to fear the past. I have loved and desired no man but you. Powchutu came between us while we were still enemies, while we were seeking each other. Our love is strong now; his ghost can do it no harm unless you allow it. Rebecca was raised by Joe; she has never known Powchutu. Joe's love and influence rules her head and heart. The past is dead, my love. No person should claim another's glory or submit to his punishment. I am here with you and will always be at your side for as long as you desire it or until you cruelly drive me away. I beg you, my love: do not destroy our love and happiness with deeds long buried."

He sighed heavily as he rubbed his smooth face. "You are right, Shalee. I permitted myself to forget such things. When I heard how our son had slain an Indian brother to possess her, a strange feeling washed over me. Then to hear her speak of words which gave away her true name, a warning sang within my head. The deeds of the past came rushing back to live again. Over and over Powchutu's face appeared before me. The pain he caused us was vent upon her. It was as if his daughter had come to avenge him, to take you and Bright Arrow from me. I have not been wise or just. I want nothing of the past or of him to ever touch our lives again. There is danger in my continued hatred of him. I must dispel or conquer it for all time. You must forgive me and help me," he earnestly entreated.

"How so? You must remove the barrier which you placed between us. You have revealed inner thoughts and feelings which I never knew existed; this frightens and saddens me, my husband. Do I truly know you?"

Before he could respond to her words, several warriors rode into camp. Dust flew about them. Lathered horses wheezed and neighed. The warriors halted before Gray Eagle himself. Their leader was dressed in sienna-colored buckskins and lowcut mocassins. He wore a breastplate of linked bones from the wings of many giant birds of prey. Several black feathers were situated in his stygian hair which settled wildly about his powerful shoulders when he reined in his horse. Bold slashes of red and black marked his stoic features.

In Cheyenne, he stated dramatically, "I have come for the life of the white whore who caused the death of Standing Bear. I call Bright Arrow coward and betrayer for slaying his Indian brother for a while slave. I must return to my village with this girl and with three pieces of Bright Arrow's scalp or there will be war between our tribes. White Elk has spoken. Standing Bear must be avenged before his spirit climbs the ghost trail in search of the Great Spirit. Call Bright Arrow out to face the punishment of his evil deed! Or does the aimless arrow quiver in the shadow of a noble eagle? Does the Eagle's fledgling also desire the beautiful body of a white-eyes?" he brazenly taunted the intrepid warrior whose eyes blazed in unleashed fury at this daring affrontery. Shalee inhaled sharply, then flushed crimson.

She glared at him, daring him to insult her again. His response was a roguish grin.

"Do you foolishly seek your death as Standing Bear did?" Gray Eagle thundered. "He challenged Bright Arrow to battle. Many saw and heard this. Dishonor and betrayal do not demand vengeance! My son is a man. He speaks and fights for himself. Does White Elk?" Gray Eagle mocked the arrogant warrior who was observing Shalee more closely than he was watching him! Gray Eagle was sorely tempted to yank him down and beat him. It was perilously clear that Bright Arrow had accurately and wisely sized up this matter . . .

Chapter Nine

Bright Arrow stepped outside their tepee into the warm sunshine. He gently grasped his mother's forearm and sent her back inside with Rebecca. He took his place at his father's side, his stance aggressive and confident, his eyes and expression alert and fathomless.

White Elk's gaze flickered from one fiercely proud and intrepid warrior to the other. Although his expression never changed, a wave of uneasiness and dread washed over his brawny frame. If he followed Standing Bear's wily plan, he could win the same valuable prizes that reckless brave had forfeited. If he failed . . .

The key to his success lay in disarming and irritating the Oglala warriors. Impatience and anger took a heavy toll upon a brave's concentration and accuracy in battle. He smiled satanically, for the fresh injury upon the beautiful face of Shalee revealed that there already was no peace in the tepee of Wanmdi Hota. He could easily imagine that gentle beauty taking the side of a vulnerable girl, white or Indian.

"We have ridden together many times, White Elk," the younger brave began. "Why do you call me to challenge over Standing Bear's loss of face? Red Cloud stood at his side that day. Surely he told you his words of treachery and betrayal. This new challenge does not speak well of a great warrior such as you. You bring sadness to my heart."

"The death of Standing Bear brought sadness to many Cheyenne hearts. He claimed the white whore first. You left him no choice but to battle you for her possession and his honor," he lied boldly.

Bright Arrow stiffened. "You speak falsely, White Elk! I saw and touched the white girl first. Standing Bear mocked and taunted me before our warriors. Your vision is clouded with envy and grief. Have you not heard how I tried to reason with him, how I did not wish to fight him, how I sang the Death Chant for him? What dark reason makes you deny such acts?"

"If you speak the truth, the Great Spirit will guard your life. If I speak the truth, He will guard mine," White Elk stated his purpose.

"You call me to a death challenge!" Bright Arrow exclaimed in disbelief.

White Elk glared down at the handsome brave who had captured the hearts and eyes of countless women, at the mettlesome man who would feel obligated to accept this fight. "Yes," he said coldly. "Say the time and place." An insulting grin mocked Bright Arrow.

Bright Arrow glanced over at his father who had been witnessing this display. "Father?" he began.

White Elk harshly cut into his words, "Are you a child who must ask his father's permission to save face? Does the bright arrow dull and waver when it faces a real warrior, one not under the dangerous spell of a white slave?" he ridiculed him.

Bright Arrow's truculent gaze shifted back to White Elk. "I speak to Wanmdi Hota as chief of the Oglala, not as my father," he sneered contemptuously. "When I am leader, I will need no one to speak for me or to counsel me, White Elk. In our camp, Wanmdi Hota is the law and the speaker for all warriors. Is this not so in the camp of the Cheyenne?" he craftily parried the brave's insult.

"I speak for White Elk. Does Wanmdi Hota speak for you?" he insisted, knowing he must defeat Bright Arrow first, hoping his brutal death would grieve Wanmdi Hota to the point of carelessness and defeat. Then, he could take both women! Without question, the mighty Oglala would naturally follow the valiant warrior who had vanquished two powerful legends! Still, the planning of this daring deed was far easier and braver than carrying it out!

"As chief, I must try to prevent this shameful action, White Elk. As his father, I grant him the right to choose his own fate. My son has spoken the truth," Gray Eagle implied the Cheyenne brave was a liar. "The Great Spirit will protect him as He did at Standing Bear's shameful challenge. Go. Prepare yourself to die the death of a betrayer. When Wi sits overhead, return to walk the Ghost Trail with Standing Bear," Gray Eagle declared.

White Elk laughed sardonically. He signalled to his small band and they rode a short way from camp.

"Why did you not hand Rebecca over to him and prevent this battle? You say she must leave. Why did you not use her to keep peace?" Bright Arrow asked his father.

"Rebecca is not the center of this conflict, Bright Arrow. She is only an excuse for White Elk to use for a challenge. The evil within his heart is clear. He wishes to slay us both. He wants to rule the Oglala. He also desires to possess your mother."

"My mother!" he echoed in astonishment.

"Many times I have seen the way both Standing Bear and White Elk have watched her. Their eyes glowed with manly desire. But

278

moments ago, he studied her more closely than the man he was about to challenge! This is not good. Greed and lust make a man a deadly enemy. He also seeks power and fame. This, too, is dangerous. If I had turned Rebecca over to him, it would not have ended there. He would have taunted you until you were forced to battle him. He is cunning, my son. He knows what your death would do to my spirit and senses. To melt before him and to give Rebecca to him would appear cowardly. Both you and your mother like this girl. Soon, Shalee will have need of her. To send her away now would make others think we fear to keep her. This cannot be. Rebecca remains in our tepee," he calmly announced.

"I can keep her?" he exclaimed in surprise, brows lifted inquisitively.

"I will not reveal weakness by sending her away. She must remain here to prove we buckle to no man! We must prepare ourselves for this battle."

The two men entered their tepee. Gray Eagle's eyes fused with those of his wife, while Bright Arrow's happily engulfed those of the baffled Rebecca. As Bright Arrow went to Rebecca to communicate this second reprieve to her, Gray Eagle gingerly approached his quiescent wife.

"You heard?" he asked in a strained tone.

"Yes," she quietly replied. "Can our son beat

him?'' she softly inquired, anxiety written in her eyes, past troubles dulled in the light of newer and deadlier ones.

Gray Eagle sighed heavily and looked away from her gaze. "White Elk is strong and crafty. But he is consumed by envy and evil. Such will take some of his strength and cunning. Bright Arrow must keep his head clear and calm. He fights for his honor and the girl. I said she could remain here. I thought it best to remove any shadow upon his mind.''

"Is that wise, my husband? Your hatred of her will deny peace and laughter in our tepee. Her presence hinders your love and touch. I do not wish to live this way,'' she cautiously whispered.

"Would that I did not know the truth about her, Shalee. Perhaps in time my mind will learn to ignore it,'' he stated in a tight voice, for her ears alone. "You were right. I cannot make her suffer for the deeds of her father. Still, I cannot help but see him within her. I can no more change my warring heart or the past than she can change her skin color. Your forgiveness of my anger and cruelty will help me accept her here. It was wrong to vent my anger upon you. My honor is stained by my loss of temper.''

Tears glimmered within her softened eyes, for she knew how much love and strength it took for him to say and do this. She reached up to caress his taut jawline with the back of her hand. "I love you with all my heart, Wanmdi Hota. Nothing and no one can ever change that. We both spoke in anger. We have both been bruised and punished. We must encourage our first son. I could not bear to lose him. But if the Great Spirit . . ."

He silenced her with a finger to her lips. "Do not speak or think such thoughts, my love. He cannot die . . ."

She gently seized his hand and moved it away from her mouth. "I must speak what is in my heart. If he loses and you must battle White Elk next, remember how much I need and love you. Remember I now carry another child who will also need his father's love and protection. I could not live without you."

He pulled her into his arms and hugged her possessively. "You are my very heart, Shalee. I will do all within my power to walk the face of Mother Earth once this evil has passed. I must live to see the face of our new child. I love you, Grass Eyes," he huskily murmured.

She sighed contentedly. It felt so good to feel his unbound love and warmth once more. The gusts of hatred and revenge had wreaked havoc within the man she loved. But now, the maelstrom was over; those perilous winds had calmed. Once more, he was hers. She raised her lips to his. Neither cared who saw them this time. The kiss was lengthy and deep. He covered her face with many others, then embraced her fiercely.

Bright Arrow called out to his parents, "The time has come. I must speak words you will not wish to hear."

Arms around each other, they turned to face their son. He must be allowed to speak his tormenting words. "If I do not survive this challenge, you must end this evil which Standing Bear began, my father. I am honored to be the son of Wanmdi Hota and Shalee. Soon, you will have another child. Remember him when you avenge me. I also ask for you to take care of Rebecca. Do not blame her for this battle or my death. Perhaps I have dishonored and displeased the Great Spirit by taking her to my mat and heart. Even so, the happiness she has given me makes this challenge endurable. If Wi and Hunwi could call back their paths across the sky seven times, I would still take her. If this deed must claim my life, then I mourn for what I could not help or change. Forgive me, for I love her."

His news was heart-rending, but not unexpected. Shalee squeezed Gray Eagle's hand to offer her sympathy and encouragement. She looked up at him. A look of sad resignation and disappointment filled his midnight eyes. Pride and joy filled her as she listened to his words.

"Many times we do not understand the ways and thoughts of the Great Spirit. If He has placed love for this white girl within your heart and body, I cannot remove it. It grieves me to hear and see such a deed, but I must accept it. If you wish to know her touch again, my son, then you must use every skill and instinct you possess. You must think of nothing and no one but victory and honor. If it must be, I will avenge your death. There is Shalee and another child to think upon. Yet, my first son owns my life and honor this day. Come, the time is near."

Disregarding their eyes and presence, Bright Arrow pulled Rebecca to her feet. He embraced her and kissed her. He looked deeply and longingly into her entreating eyes, perhaps saying farewell for all time. He smiled, then went to his parents. He hugged his mother and kissed her cheek.

"Pray for all of us, Mother. I love you. I am proud to be your son. Forgive what I must do and have done."

"I do not worry, Bright Arrow. You have the shadows of both Wanmdi Hota and the Great Spirit over you. You are your father's son. You cannot be defeated by evil. Know this as I do. The blood and courage of Wanmdi Hota flows within you. This will aid your victory. I will remain with Rebecca until you return for her," she stated confidently. "You will live long and happily. You will lead the Oglala after your father. You will one day become the great leader he is now. You will profit from his courage. He is all a man and a warrior should be. You will follow in his steps. This I know with all my heart. The Great Spirit sees and knows all. He will guide your hand this day. When the moment comes, He will divinely resolve this deed. He will reveal the truth for all to see."

Bright Arrow beamed. She had said the things which he needed to hear. He was ready to meet this new challenge. He hugged her once more, then turned to his father. "I will use all I have learned from you, my father. Evil must not triumph over good. Yet, the Great Spirit might have some unknown purpose for my sacrifice. I do not fear death, only dishonor. I will accept what must be." He stood proud before them, exuding confidence.

"All your mother said is true and wise, my son. It is not the time for your feet to travel the path to the Great Spirit. Be alert and quick. Do not drop your guard for a single moment. Beware of any crafty tricks. White Elk might seek to disarm you with taunts and mockery. Close your ears to such deceit. Your skill, courage and resolve will diminish his own. You not only fight for your life and honor, but also those of your family and people. You are destined to lead the Oglala. Let nothing prevent this. I will watch my son prove he is guarded by Wakantanka."

They embraced. The drumming began. Bright Arrow's gaze sought his mother's first, then Rebecca's. The significance of what was taking place transcended their language barrier. Rebecca ran into his arms. What did she care who saw her display of love and worry?

"Be careful, Bright Arrow. I love you and I could not bear to see you die. May God forgive me if I am to blame for this trouble. I would willingly die if it would spare your life. Your laws and ways are confusing to me. Yet, I know your honor is at stake here. God protect you, my love, for never have I known a man such as you."

Rebecca confronted Gray Eagle. Her inability to comprehensively converse with him angered and frustrated her. "Why can't you stop this? If they demand my life in payment for the other brave, then give it to them. It is not worth the sacrifice of Bright Arrow's. I am only a white slave, but he is a great warrior. He is your son. Stop him! Stop this fight! He must not die for me. I love him. If only I could make you understand, Gray Eagle . . ."

The intense love she felt for Bright Arrow was clear to each of them. She would honestly exchange her life for his! She truly loved him! She cried out to the dauntless chief, "Many of you have been kind and gentle with me. I know this. I have tried to show how grateful I am by obeying you and by holding my tongue and resentment. Do not allow him to fight for me again. I have seen the sadness I have brought into this tepee. Send me away now. Spare his life and return the joy and peace which I have innocently taken from each of you. I was lucky to be captured by him and to live in your tepee. But I am bad for him. I only cause pain and trouble here. Hand me over to them. You must!"

Gray Eagle actually smiled at Rebecca. Her selflessness touched him deeply. She was like Koda Joe, not that evil scout. He stroked her cheek ever so lightly. "Hiya," he stated in a calm tone. "Rebecca hiya ya. Rebecca Bright Arrow winyan."

Rebecca gaped at him. "You want me to stay here with him? I can remain his slave?" she asked skeptically, fearing to trust her ears.

Since she had spoken in English, he could not reply. But when she made these questions known in Oglala, he nodded. Elated and mystified, she spontaneously hugged him. "Thank you. But I still cannot be responsible for his death. I love him."

Shalee pulled her away from the two men. She smiled at her. "Hiya wohdake. Hehoka Ska ki-ci-e-conape. Rebecca koda. Rebecca yanka." Shalee nodded for the two men of her heart and life to depart. They smiled and left to face their unknown fates, each appealing to Wakantanka for guidance and survival.

Shalee repeated her soft command for Rebecca to sit down beside her, "Yanka, Rebecca Kenny. Wakantanka wayaketo. Kokipi sni.

Rebecca koda. Rebecca tipi," she declared, hoping Rebecca would comprehend her encouragement and offer of permanent truce.

The two women anxiously waited for the hopeful return of their men. An aura of consternation and trepidation filled the seemingly airless tepee. Each knew what this day could cost them. Rebecca prayed to God to spare the life of both men. Shalee prayed to the Great Spirit who was God with an Indian name.

To ease their tensions and to make time pass swifter, Shalee tried to communicate her joyous condition to Rebecca. Through a series of signs, drawings, and words, Rebecca finally grasped what this woman was telling her. "A baby! You're expecting a baby. How wonderful, Shalee. Such a special gift. I will do all I can to help you. You must not work so hard or risk injury. Do not worry, for I will take care of you and the chores. Another child . . ." she murmured wistfully, wondering what it would be like to carry the child of the man you loved, to gaze into its face and see both you and him represented there, to be joined forever in the body of another person.

"I wish I had a brother or a sister. My mother lost her first . . ." Rebecca nervously began, but was silenced by the threat of death which was sounding loudly outside this tepee, ever increasing its volume and speed.

The eerie drumming abruptly halted, and so

did her anxious chatter. The steady, vibrant voice of a man spoke up. No doubt it was the ceremonial chief telling of the challenge. Rebecca tensed and trembled. "Please don't let him die," she prayed softly.

When the noises of the deadly battle could no longer be ignored, both women rushed forward to peer through a slit in the flap. The fight was ominous, for the two men appeared evenly matched in strength and skill. Horrified, the two women helplessly witnessed this bloody duel, which could swing in either man's favor at any moment. Each lunge artfully parried was quickly followed by another, even bolder, one. The terrifying battle went on and on . . .

The still air was abruptly filled with the clattering of many horses' hooves. Another party of Cheyenne warriors rode into camp. Shalee stiffened. Had they come to war upon them? What should she do? Should she attempt to flee into the protective cover of the cool forest. What imminent danger did they represent to her, her family, the Oglala, her unborn child?

An angry shout was heard above all other sounds. Her terrified gaze flew to the lined, coppery visage of the Cheyenne chief. His face was not stoic. It was suffused with vivid rage. He called out sharply to White Elk, "Cease this disgrace upon yourself and your people! You dare to earn the rank of chief by claiming the life of Bright Arrow and Wanmdi Hota! Falling

Tree has told me of your rash plans. You will not bring war between the Oglala and Cheyenne with your greed and lust. You are no longer a Cheyenne! We are shamed by your unforgivable actions. Leave this camp and that of the Cheyenne. Forget this foolish deed. Forget your lust for Princess Shalee. Beg the Great Spirit for his forgiveness and to halt your madness."

The air was strangely motionless and silent as the old chief related these facts for all to hear. Gradually, angry murmurings against White Elk could be heard. Hostility permeated the windless area where the battle to death had ceased only moments earlier. "No! Bright Arrow must die! You are old, Silver Star. Too old to lead the Cheyenne against their enemies. I claim the rank of chief. Who will side with me?" he brazenly encouraged treason in the speechless warriors, those with him and with Silver Star.

White Elk raised his arms skyward, then loudly asserted, "Hear me, Cheyenne! Silver Star is old. He has grown soft and weak. He sits in his tepee while I plan and ride for him. We have no need of a chief with cloudy vision, a weakened body, and a dead spirit. His courage is gone. He is like a woman now. How say you, Cheyenne?"

A loud, ominous swish sang through the oppressive air. A heavy thud registered in the minds of everyone present. White Elk whirled and glared at the self-assured warrior sitting astride a ghostly white stallion beside Silver Star; Flaming Bow was wearing the wanapin of Silver Star, symbol of successor.

Flaming Bow called out to him, "You challenge for what I already possess, White Elk. Silver Star has chosen me the next chief. I desire peace with my brothers the Oglala. I have ridden with Bright Arrow many times. He is a man of honor and courage. You are not. This day, the Great Spirit will judge your treachery. All Cheyenne who side with White Elk step forward and share his fate. All who side with me, place your arrow within his traitorous body," came the new chief's verdict.

A look of sheer terror filled the wounded warrior's face. "You cannot do this, Flaming Bow," he cried out, a note of pleading in his voice. Searing pain was evident within his eyes. A stream of scarlet liquid eased down his cinnamon back and soaked into his tanned breeches. "I will lead the Cheyenne, not you!"

White Elk's fear and pleas instilled disgust and hardness within the hearts of even his own followers who had been craftily deceived into this perilous situation. Before he could speak again, his body was assaulted by countless Cheyenne arrows. He spun and fell beneath their forceful impact, and screamed as they pierced his vital organs.

Flaming Bow urged his albino horse forward. He paused before Bright Arrow. The Chief met the warrior's steady gaze and declared, "I have no battle with the son of Wanmdi Hota or the Oglala. Standing Bear and White Elk have paid for their deeds. I say we forget this matter. What do you say, Bright Arrow?" he inquired.

"I say the matter is settled. I say the Cheyenne have another great chief, one who is brave and noble, one who is wise and cunning. I say to Silver Star, there is no dishonor in growing old. This is a part of each warrior's life-circle. You have led your people well. It is not the Indian way to take away honor which has been earned or given to a man by the Great Spirit. You have earned the right to live out your days in happiness and safety. These are the words of Bright Arrow to his friends, Silver Star and Flaming Bow." A smile relaxed Flaming Bow's serious expression.

"As with your father, you will make a great and wise chief one day. It is good, Bright Arrow, my friend." His tone vibrated with intense concern, as he focused his eyes and words upon Gray Eagle. "Today, there are grave matters which concern both the Cheyenne and the Oglala. We must rest, then talk."

"You are welcome in our camp. Deer-Stalker will show you where to rest. Then we will eat and talk," Gray Eagle cordially replied.

A sinewy brave stepped forward to lead the

Cheyenne warriors to a tepee for visitors. Gray Eagle ordered water sent to them for washing and drinking. They headed back to their tepee. Upon entering, Shalee rushed forward to greet them. Rebecca timidly and wisely waited for Bright Arrow to approach her. When he did, she could not contain her joy and relief. This time, even Gray Eagle lacked any visible resentment toward her romantic overtures to his son.

When Flaming Bow and Silver Star came to join them for the late meal and to talk, he smiled mischievously and jovially teased, "I can see why Standing Bear and White Elk desired the woman of Gray Eagle, also the white captive. Both are very beautiful. The Great Spirit has smiled upon Wanmdi Hota."

Gray Eagle grinned cheerfully and replied, "Soon He will smile upon us again, for Shalee now carries another child." His pride and joy were apparent to all present. Shalee sent him a radiant smile which declared her love for him.

"May you both live long and happy lives. But I hear trouble brewing in the winds to the west, Wanmdi Hota. Many whites have come seeking the shiny rocks in our streams and hills. The white-eyes kill for this rock which reflects the light of Wi. They camp in many places. They slaughter the animals in the forests and upon the plains. Others have joined them to steal the skins of Wakantanka's creatures. The Bluecoats protect them in exchange for furs and shiny rocks. Many more Bluecoats come every day. Soon, they will overrun our lands. We must stop them!" Flaming Bow proclaimed forcefully.

Bright Arrow and Gray Eagle listened closely and carefully to the new chief's words. Gray Eagle's heart skipped a beat at the old chief's words. "I have told Flaming Bow and my young warriors of how Gray Eagle called the tribes together long ago to battle many white-eyes and Bluecoats. Many tales of your daring and cunning that great day still rest in my aging heart. You led the tribes to conquer all whites for many winters. Now, they have come again. They grow stronger with each new moon. Once more you must call the tribes together to battle them. As before, we must wipe them out to save our lands and peoples."

Flaming Bow glanced at Shalee and smiled. He innocently remarked upon the stirring tales which Silver Star had revealed to him. "This time, the daughter of Black Cloud is here and safe. My heart and hands grew eager with excitement and pride when I heard of how Gray Eagle bluffed the Bluecoats for her release. I must discover what great magic and wisdom you used upon your enemies at the old fort, where another now stands upon the face of our lands."

Bright Arrow stared at his father. What was Flaming Bow's meaning? He had never been told of this staggering feat of daring and victory.

293

"My father led a raid upon the old fort? How so? When?" Bright Arrow asked.

Flaming Bow looked at him in utter surprise. "You have not heard of how Wanmdi Hota called the seven tribes together and destroyed all whites and Bluecoats within our lands! Silver Star told me how the Bluecoats raided the Oglala camp and captured your mother. Wanmdi Hota banded all together, friend and enemy alike. He fearlessly attacked the fort. All were slain or captured."

Gray Eagle waited to see how much Flaming Bow would reveal about his past and that portentous event. It would be rude to interrupt the telling of such awesome coups. He silently listened to Flaming Bow's colorful tales. Thankfully, Shalee and Rebecca had left to draw water and to gather wood for the night. He prayed Shalee would not return and overhear this news. She might react in a revealing manner. He must explain these mysterious circumstances to her before Bright Arrow could question her about it.

Enjoying himself greatly, Flaming Bow dramatically went on, "Wanmdi Hota made them cower in fear and shame. The daughter of Black Cloud was released by the soldiers. Many thought it strange at that time, for no one knew she was the daughter of Black Cloud who had been stolen from his camp at two winters and raised by the white-eyes. The Great Spirit knew and recalled her feet to the land of her people and to the tepee of her father. Silver Star told me how your father went to the Si-ha Sapa camp and challenged for her hand in joining. No one taunted him for loving a white slave then, for she was in truth Si-ha Sapa. Perhaps it will be the same with your white slave," he joked, unaware of the tension in both Oglala warriors.

"You speak strange words, Flaming Bow. Why do you say my mother was once the white slave of my father? How could that be?" he debated.

Flaming Bow glanced at Gray Eagle, wondering at this curious secret. Gray Eagle frowned in displeasure. He stated, "That was a sad time for Shalee. We chose not to speak of it again."

Bright Arrow argued, "But he claims she was your slave! Explain this to me," he softly demanded, intrigued by this startling news.

Flaming Bow realized his error. He suggested, "Such matters should be spoken of in private, Bright Arrow. My tongue spoke before thinking or without the knowledge of this secret. Your father speaks true. It was a sad time for Princess Shalee. Do not recall it to her mind and heart. Speak of this later with your father," he advised, wishing he had not mentioned such a degrading and tormenting time in that lovely creature's life.

"You are wise and good, Flaming Bow," Gray Eagle said. "Later, my son, I will tell you what you wish to know. Do not hurt your mother by speaking of this matter before her. There are vital problems which concern us. Speak of them, Flaming Bow," he stated, firmly dismissing that perplexing story.

Bright Arrow politely remained silent and respectful before the others; yet, his mind was not upon the business at hand.

Did this explain the anguish and sadness which he frequently read within his mother's eyes? Was it possible? She had been raised as white! She had been captured and enslaved by his own father! He called to mind the events which Shalee had told him earlier. Evidently she had left out many incredible things! No wonder she had so fiercely resisted Rebecca's enslavement! She knew what such an existence was like! She had actually lived it! There was much to hear and to resolve, and he would do this . . .

The warriors proposed scouting parties to study the movements and strength of the soldiers and whites. They decided to meet again in ten days to discuss their newly gathered information and eventual plans. Gray Eagle said he would call together the chiefs of the seven tribes. Another joint venture against the whites might be planned to slow their continual encroachment and wanton destruction. But this time, he would let another warrior lead it. Since Bright Arrow's mind was ensnared by past and present troubles, perhaps Night Hawk or his son could lead this monumental raid.

Shalee and Rebecca returned. They served the men wine made from buffalo berries and bread pones spattered with tasty specks of dried fruit and roasted nuts. The hour grew late. The night birds began to sing their melodious songs. Cicadas promptly joined their buoyant tune. The Cheyenne warriors returned to their tepee to sleep. They would leave at dawn.

"Father," Bright Arrow called out. "Come. Let us walk and speak of many things," he remarked as calmly as he could.

Shalee looked up. Curious eyes met with Gray Eagle's unreadable ones. He smiled lovingly at her. "Rest, wife. You carry our child. We will return soon. There is much for warriors to say and to decide," he stated, hoping she would accept this excuse.

She smiled, fondling his hard chest. "Do not worry about me, husband. What harm could befall me when I live under the wing of a mighty eagle? You bring pride and joy to my life. The Great Spirit guards us all this day." She took his hand in hers and caressed her cheek with it, then kissed it. The message in her smoldering eyes was crystal clear.

Bright Arrow watched this tender, romantic exchange. It was obvious his mother loved Gray Eagle deeply. Didn't that mean Gray Eagle had done nothing wicked to her in the past? She came over to her son. "Did I not tell you that everything would be good again, my son? We are all safe and happy as the Great Spirit wishes."

"You love my father very much," he stated, needing to hear her concurrence.

"Yes, Bright Arrow. I have since the first moment our eyes met many years ago. I have loved only you as much." The glow in her eyes confirmed her words.

"This is good, Mother. Peace and love will live in our tepee forever."

The two men left. Shalee wished she could tell Rebecca so many things, but it would still be unwise. Some day, perhaps it would be different. The two women exchanged smiles and sat down to work on winter garments.

Bright Arrow and Gray Eagle walked along in silence, one planning his questions and the other deliberating his coming answers. The full moon lighted the clearing, enhancing the mood of solitude and graveness. The trees seemed to fuse into one massive shadow, acknowledging their individual presence by occasionally rustling their leaves. Fireflies playfully danced upon the breeze, their iridescent tails flickering like the sun upon a speck of gold. The mournful hoots of an owl touched their alert ears, their keen senses always sharp and clear. A startled racoon darted from the stream's edge, swaying the bunch grass with his hasty retreat. They halted, each briefly listening to the soothing sound of the brook as it rushed over a small cascade of rocks.

A safe distance from camp, Bright Arrow turned to face his father. "There is much I do not know, Father. How did you first see and know my mother?" he came directly to the point. "What do you hide of Rebecca's past?"

Gray Eagle sighed heavily, weighing how much he should tell his son. If others spoke of the past to him, many events could be revealed. Perhaps it was best to confess most of it, omitting only one deadly secret. "There was a time long ago when things were not good between your mother and me," he cautiously began. "I will start with the day we first saw each other and tell you of events which brought anguish, torment, shame, and deception into our lives. Perhaps it is past time you knew of such matters," he said in a resigned tone. "Perhaps you will then understand my feelings for your Rebecca."

Yet, he remained silent and rigid for a lengthy time. Through a break in the dense treeline, he could sight the shadowed mountains in the far distance, outlined against the dusky horizon. Tonight they seemed to jut from Mother Earth as an evil hand, ever rising as a threat of ensnarement.

Ever since Rebecca's arrival, an ominous song had drummed incessantly within Gray Eagle's head. Each day that perilous tune had increased its volume. He had become mesmerized by its powerful strands. He was powerless to control himself or the effects of the past. So many things depended upon how he resolved this dilemma. Where and when would these echoes of the past cease? Twice in his life he had issued a reprieve for Powchutu. Now, words echoed from beyond the grave, calmly singing the Death Chant. But for whom?

"It troubles you to recall such times?" Bright Arrow ventured.

"Yes, Bright Arrow; for I did many things to Shalee which were cruel and unjust. Many times I revealed weakness, fear, and dishonor where she was concerned. I did not wish you to learn of such things," he confessed in a strained tone.

"I do not understand. . . ," he stated, doubting his father could ever possess or reveal such traits.

"Remain silent until I finish. Then you can question what still confuses you. In a time before you were born when Mother Earth was happy and green, a white trapper shot my father. For many moons Running Wolf lay dying in the sacred mountains until the Great Spirit renewed his body. I had lived twenty-five winters. I was much like you: proud, daring, confident. I was alive with hatred for the whites who invaded our lands. I had never known the true love of any woman. In my anger, I recklessly sought out the foe who had shot Running Wolf. But this anger dulled my senses. I was taken prisoner by a small band of whites. They took me to a place where many trees were lashed together to make a wall against us. They mocked me, taunted me, beat me, and tried to kill me."

Hostility sparked brightly within his jet eyes at these recollections. "They placed a rope around my neck and led me about as they would a beast. They bound me to a post and lashed me across my chest. But I remained silent and proud. This angered them more, for they could not shame me. There was a young girl with them. She was beautiful and gentle. She was unlike the others. She did not understand this evil treatment and great hatred. She pleaded with her people to cease my torture. She argued with them. When they would not heed her pleas, she pulled a firestick upon them and forced them to stop. She was very angry and showed much courage. I could not believe my eyes and ears. I thought her mad. The others despised her for halting my torture and for speaking out against it. They spoke badly of her and treated her cruelly. Still, I refused to believe her special," he reluctantly admitted, clearly envisioning that day.

He inhaled before continuing this disturbing tale. "They locked me in a place made of many logs which hid the sky from my eyes and denied me fresh air. They refused me food and water. They voted for my death. The white girl came to me in the darkness to bring food and water. She put medicine upon my chest. As she helped me, I bit her hand. I was cold and cruel to her. A warrior's honor does not accept aid from an enemy. Later, White Arrow came and we escaped. Many moons later, I returned and destroyed what they called their fortress. Knowing their tongue, I had heard of a secret place where this white girl would hide in times of danger. I found it and captured her. As with Rebecca, I made her my slave. But my captive rebelled against my hold on her life and power over her body. Many times I was forced to punish her defiance. Once she rashly and bravely tried to escape, dishonoring me for my open trust in her. She was put to the lashing post, as is our custom. I chose to lash her myself in hopes of staying the pain and damage of the whip. It was useless. She nearly died. While she was lost to unconsciousness, the tribes met to speak of war against the Bluecoats and white settlers. I was chosen band leader for this joint raid. Before I could return to my camp, the Bluecoats attacked. They killed, maimed, and burned. They took our white captives away with them into the big, wooden fence."

As Gray Eagle paused, Bright Arrow injected, "What happened to your white girl? Did she die?" Was she somehow connected to his Rebecca? he fretted. Yet, obviously his mother did not know Gray Eagle had once taken a white captive into his heart and tepee . . .

"Be silent for a time more and you will hear all. Many warriors from all tribes rode to the fort. To humiliate them, I demanded the white girl's return. I said she would pay for their deeds. I said she would be tortured and slain before their eyes. Cowards as they were, they bound her and sent her back to me. But I did not kill her. I savored their anger and my deceit, as all we warriors did. She returned to my camp and tepee. The fort was destroyed and all slain. But somehow, the one with yellow hair who had attacked my camp escaped. I did not know this for many, many moons." Echoes of rage returned to ring loudly within his mind.

"But where is the white girl now?" Bright Arrow anxiously questioned, his interest piqued by this inconceivable story. His father and a white captive?

"Your patience is small this day, Bright Arrow," he playfully chided him. "A man cannot talk as swiftly as the river flows."

"Why is it so wrong for me to have a white slave when you possessed one?" he reasoned aloud.

"Hold your tongue and logic. All whites and Bluecoats were purged from our lands and forest. They did not send others here for many winters. They feared the mighty Oglala and his brothers. The girl was at my side for only two moons after that battle. Because she was white, I struggled to retain my honor as she lost hers. To prove she was only a slave to me, I was very cruel and cold to her. Yet, I loved her," he quietly admitted, astonishing his son.

"You loved a white-eyes! That cannot be! What of my mother!" he angrily exploded. This was impossible!

"If you cry out again, I will speak no more! The telling of this story is difficult. Hear all my words, then speak out. Black Cloud and Brave Bear of the Si-ha Sapa came to my camp that next sun. Black Cloud claimed my white slave was his daughter. He spoke of a time when she was two winters old. He said she had been stolen from his camp and raised by the whites. I did not believe him. He put his akito before my eyes. He then revealed a matching akito upon my white captive. It was clear to all present. My white slave was the chief's kidnapped, half-breed daughter. He claimed her and took her away from me and my tepee." Gray Eagle waited for this stunning news to settle in.

Bright Arrow stared at him, absorbing this information. "You are saying my mother was that white slave?"

"Yes, Bright Arrow. I pleaded with Black Cloud for her hand in joining. He refused. He wished her to join with Brave Bear. He was angered by my cruelties to her. Her fear of me was known to all. I challenged for her and won. We were joined. Later, when she learned of my secret love and my reasons for her past treatment, she forgave me. She had also loved and desired me since that first day at her fortress. All said it was the will of the Great Spirit for me to find her and to bring her home. All said it was right for us to join. As Shalee, my honor and face were spared. I have them and her, as it should be," he declared.

"This is why she resisted Rebecca's coming and going?" Bright Arrow speculated.

"Yes. I feared she saw herself in your white slave. I did not wish echoes of our past to haunt her. I did not want her to recall my evil against her when I thought her white. She suffered much shame and anguish in those times."

"This is what you argued about when you

struck her?"

"I did not wish you to learn of my evil deeds against her. I reasoned you might use our past to argue for Rebecca to remain," he said, knowing it did not excuse his behavior.

"I am now a man, Father. You could speak of this to me. Yet, there is another reason why you hated Rebecca. Tell me why," he softly insisted.

Dreading for Bright Arrow to learn such episodes from another, Gray Eagle wisely decided to relate other facts. "At the big fort, there was a half-breed scout named Powchutu. He befriended your mother and loved her. In those times, Shalee did not know I spoke her tongue. The scout had been kind to her. His friendship cost her much, for the whites despised the half-breed scout and deeply resented your mother's life with me. I spared his life that day. When Black Cloud took her away, Powchutu went to his camp with me to tell her many things. Shalee did not trust me, so he told her of Shalee and her real people. Her fear of me was still great. The moon of our joining, she escaped the Si-ha Sapa camp. I followed her and told her all that lived within my heart. We were to camp alone to make peace and find trust. I left her side for food and water. Powchutu secretly trailed me. Once more my instincts were dulled by relief and joy; he shot me and left me for dead. He desired my Shalee and determined to have her. When he went to her side, he told her I had left her in the desert to die. He said I hated her white blood. He said our joining was a trick to save face and to be rid of her. He took her far away, never saying he had shot me, never saying why I did not come after her. He was her friend. He was as her own brother. She had no reason to mistrust him or to believe my sudden vow of love and acceptance."

. He sat down to ease the tremblings within his shaky legs. Bright Arrow sat down beside him, not daring to break his concentration on the bittersweet past. "A past friend of Shalee's who had led her people here found her. She was ill and dying, for she had lost our first child. Powchutu had allowed white trappers to attack them and injure her. When she was well, Powchutu took her from the friend's dwelling and went to where many other whites lived. Within a few moons, Powchutu was killed by the Bluecoat with yellow hair who had somehow escaped the destruction at Fort Pierre. Yellow-hair then took Shalee prisoner."

"A white man held her captive?" Bright Arrow angrily exploded, distressed by the agony his dear mother had suffered. He was their second child?

"Yes. He threatened to tell others about her life with me if she did not join him. She had no money, as the whites call it. She was alone and afraid, so she joined him. I had dishonored him at the fort and many other times. He had been injured and could no longer take a woman to his mat. He hated me, and he hated her for not going to his mat at the fort. He wished revenge on both of us. He placed what the white man calls a bounty upon me, offering much money for my scalp and wanapin. I went to slay him, for he also paid much for such things of other great chiefs and warriors."

"My mother joined a white-eyes who traded in bloody souvenirs! She would die first!" Bright Arrow disputed such repulsive claims.

"She was very young, Bright Arrow. She did not know of his evil trade. Her heart was lost to me, and she believed I had betrayed her, had left her to die. Her choice was either join him or become a whore to survive. Which evil was greater?" he asked.

"This is strange and confusing, my father."

"I dressed as a white-eyes and sought him out. After slaying him, I found Shalee in his wooden tepee. I was furious, for I thought she also wished me dead. Powchutu had told me many lies. He said she had only accepted me for the safety of their unborn child which she supposedly carried. But the child was in truth mine!"

"What did mother say when you found her?"

"Nothing! For I was too proud and angry to

allow her to speak. I treated her as shamefully as when she was my white slave. The white friend I spoke of before followed after us to speak for her. We had met many times in the past; we were friends. He knew many things I did not, things even Shalee did not know. He came and talked to us. It was good, for Shalee was then carrying you. There was much to forget and to forgive. But our love and desire were strong. We did this, and we have been happy many winters. The friend who came to uncover Powchutu's treachery was called Joe Kenny.''

This name obviously meant nothing to Bright Arrow. Yet, he sensed that it should from the way Gray Eagle stressed the name and now looked at him. The enlightenment came when Gray Eagle added, "The girl in our tepee is called Rebecca Kenny.''

Baffled, Bright Arrow reasoned upon these new and disturbing facts. Rebecca's father had been his mother's friend and protector. Yet, Rebecca was too young to be the child of Joe and Shalee, to be his half-blooded sister. That deduction elated him, but inspired another mystery. Since his father knew these facts, why did he resent Rebecca and wish her gone?

"Rebecca is the daughter of your friend Joe Kenny?'' he asked.

"Yes,'' Gray Eagle laconically replied.

"How could you hate the daughter of a

friend?" he inquired.

"The white woman with whom Joe Kenny joined had loved another man before him. He had been slain by Yellow-hair. It was that man's child she carried. Rebecca does not know she is not the true daughter of my old friend," he hinted, testing Bright Arrow's intuitive skills, allowing him to gradually extract the full truth.

Dreadful qualms filled Bright Arrow. "Who is her true father?"

"Powchutu," he tersely replied, that one name exposing all.

It required only a brief time for Bright Arrow to digest the implications of this one crucial fact. "She does not know this truth you hold within you?" he stressed for clarity.

"No. Koda Joe told me before he left to join her. Your mother learned this and rebelled against sending her away. That is why we battled, over Powchutu's daughter and the secret I had kept hidden from her."

"You punish Rebecca for the evil deeds of her real father?" he questioned.

"Powchutu stole Shalee from my mat shortly after our joining day. He filled her head with many lies. He caused her great shame and anguish. He caused the death of our first child. He placed her within the hands of Yellow-hair. Rebecca carries his evil blood. How could I allow the daughter of Powchutu to have my only son? Does a wise man hand his life and honor over to his worst enemy?''

"She does not know about this evil!" he argued in her behalf.

"That changes nothing! She is white! She is his daughter! You are the son of Gray Eagle. You could become the next Oglala chief at any sun. A warrior faces constant death and danger. The whites could strike me down with the rising sun. Would warriors follow a chief who keeps an enemy within his heart and tepee?''

"You are wrong, Father. Rebecca is also a half-breed like my mother. She is innocent of his evil. A man must stand upon his own deeds and skills. We cannot take glory or blame for the acts and words of another. Is this not so?" he demanded.

Gray Eagle pondered his logic. "In many ways, you are right. Still, it changes nothing in the eyes of our people. To them, she is white. A half-breed is even more despicable," he reminded his son.

"But I am a half-breed, Father," Bright Arrow asserted.

"You are the son of Gray Eagle and Shalee. What little white blood you carry does not matter. Hers does . . . Many know how Powchutu stole Shalee. To reveal who she is would endanger her life. If she remains here too long, others might guess her dark secret. How can a warrior present a face which is stained with weakness to his enemies? We have said much and I grow weary. Let us speak no more of these troubling matters tonight. I also have things which I must say to your mother. Return to our tepee and send her to me."

Bright Arrow returned to their tepee and told his mother to go to the stream and speak with Gray Eagle. She left Rebecca and Bright Arrow in silence, wondering at his moodiness.

At the river, she questioned her husband about Bright Arrow's strange behavior. Gray Eagle related their conversation to her. Wide-eyed, she questioned, "You told him all these things? About me? About us? Our past?"

"There was a need for him to hear them from me, not another. I told him only of the things which others know. I did not speak of Matu's trick. He does not know you are white. Only White Arrow knows this truth and he will never speak of it to anyone. Even so, Bright Arrow still desires to keep Rebecca. What do you say?" he candidly asked.

"To me, she is the daughter of Joe and Mary. I cannot find hatred for her within my heart. She has suffered much. But I will not defy your decision. If you wish her gone, I only ask you to send her to someone who will not harm her. I fear what her stay could bring to light."

He smiled, for she had spoken the words he

longed to hear. "My love for you increases each moon. I sense a great threat in her remaining here, but she can stay . . . for now. We all agree she must never know her real name. All secrets must be carefully buried again."

"It will be as you say, my husband."

Arm in arm, they returned to their tepee.

Chapter Ten

For the next few weeks, an unchanging pattern dominated their lives. For the men, each day was spent in one of two ways. The braves hunted game and protected the encampment; the warriors raided whites and harried the soldiers. Each morning the dauntless warriors would leave camp, only to return at dusk. From the prizes they brought home, it was abundantly clear who had been that day's victor.

Countless trappers and greedy miners were furiously driven from the Indians' forests, hills, and plains. These particular men were frequently slain; any women or children with them were taken captive. Gray Eagle's pretension of generosity allowed most of these unfortunate captives to go to the other Indian villages. He declared that he did not wish his camp flooded with white-eyes whose blood

315

would mingle with theirs in despised half-breed children. As was the Indian custom, confiscated goods and furs were passed out amongst those in dire need of them, mostly Indian women who had lost their mates in fierce and deadly skirmishes with the whites.

This mode of operation seemed to please and to stimulate the warriors who were united against this new influx of white men. These raiding parties relentlessly ambushed small troops of soldiers from the newly established Fort Dakota, a strong fortress which was in sight of the previously demolished Fort Pierre. Perhaps it was this constant reminder of the awesome capabilities of the unconquerable Gray Eagle which imbued these soldiers with respect and fear. It was no secret how quickly and easily the mighty Eagle had swooped down and accomplished this drastic feat.

The Indians would forcefully strike at the careless cavalry units without warning. Gray Eagle ordered several bands of skillful warriors to cut off the fort's supply routes with frequent and costly assaults. Then many men and supplies found their way into the aim of an accurate, flaming arrow or as the target of a forcefully hurled lance.

The cavalry's counterattacks did very little to staunch this onminous surge of defiance. Within a few weeks, the soldiers were reeling from slashes of the sharp and lethal talons of the legendary, indomitable Eagle. Nothing they attempted seemed effective upon these determined warriors and their intrepid leader. In desperation, they practiced atrocities which made the Indians appear the ones who were civilized.

Feeling condoned, the Indians retaliated in like manner. The cruelties and sacrifices escalated on both sides in this unyielding war. Gray Eagle requested another meeting of the Warrior Society in the camp of the Cheyenne, wanting to keep his beloved white wife as far removed from this heart-rending action as possible. He suggested another crafty plan to further harass and to eventually disable the fort. In a stirring tone, he outlined his thoughts and plans. The warriors listened intently and agreed with his logic and wisdom.

Gray Eagle then assigned each side of the fort to four different tribes. Each group of warriors would be responsible for terrorizing all whites and soldiers in their designated area. It would be up to each band to make certain the cavalry did not use their secret doors in the fort's towering walls to receive supplies, additional men, or much needed weapons. The cavalry would not be permitted to use those hidden exits to gather wood for cooking or heating, to hunt fresh game in the nearby forest, to carry out raids upon their camps which were vulnerable with the warriors occupied here and in the surrounding area, or to draw water from the river which was four hundred yards from the fort's walls. Gray Eagle had shrewdly devastated the trough which ran from the river into the fort via a small, square opening at the base of the back wall. Surely this lack of water for the whites and their animals would take a heavy toll upon their resistance. Still, the Indians realized one critical point: if the fort was well-stocked, it could require great patience and persistence before this rigorous plan defeated their enemies. Anticipation of their triumph flooded the warriors with new zeal and valiance.

"If our tribes were joined as one, Gray Eagle," Chief Flaming Bow commented, "you would be our great leader. Perhaps in time, the Great Spirit will also give to me your same wisdom and cunning. We were wise to name you as the band leader for this last skirmish with our white foes."

Bright Arrow was consumed with happiness and genuine pride in his father. He listened closely to his father's words, hoping to learn all he could from this illustrious warrior before the day came when he must lead the Oglala.

Gray Eagle smiled. "Your words honor me, Flaming Bow. But I am no longer a young and powerful warrior. The final raid must be led by another warrior. Unless the Society says otherwise, I say the son of Chief Night Hawk should lead that important raid; he has earned this right with his courage and assistance."

The vote was taken; Gray Eagle's suggestion was approved by each warrior and chief present. Gray Eagle's next words disturbed the many warriors who inwardly knew they were accurate. "This war will settle our conflict for many moons. But more whites will come another day. Once before, we joined together to disband and to purge them from our lands. But more came. With the next winter, still more will press forward to take lands which are ours. The days of lasting peace have ended forever. The white man refuses honorable truce. He wishes to steal what is ours. Many warriors have been slain. The face of Mother Earth bears the scars of the white man's treachery. Others will come, and the war will begin once more. With this battle, we only earn a few moons of peace and happiness. But we must continue to push back each new flow, for to allow them to gather strength and size would be dangerous to us."

"Your words bring sadness and anger to my heart, Gray Eagle," Silver Star expressed in a strained voice. "But you speak wise and true. The survival of our people is in the hands of our new chief and our noble band leader. I am old and tired. I will remain in my camp to guard the women and children. Fighting belongs in the hands of younger and stronger warriors."

"There is no dishonor in growing old, Silver Star. This is the way of the Great Spirit. Soon, I will follow in these same steps, as will all men who live.''

The old chief beamed in renewed spirits. The talk continued until many trying matters were settled. Finally, each band of warriors headed for its own village.

Witnessing this new uprising, many white settlers moved out of the Eagle's domain. Other pioneers and evil trespassers remained in the realm of the fearless Sioux, sealing their fates with this obstinance and greed. Men who were obsessed with the lust for gold, silver, and valuable furs recklessly invaded sacred burial grounds—and died for their greed.

But the most obdurate group was the cavalry. They belligerently refused to heed the warnings in the air; they resolved they would not be defeated and humiliated by one mortal man. They reasoned if he could be slain, the others would lose their sense of unity . . . None seemed to realize if the famed Gray Eagle was somehow struck down in this noble battle, another chief would take his place, then another if necessary. To the Indians, Gray Eagle was a magnetic legend; but he was not viewed as an immortal god. Assuredly he was the greatest warrior to ever ride the plains; but he was only human, a human who was smiled upon by Wakantanka.

For the Indian women and their white captives, this was a busy time. Their days were spent with routine chores, in tightly suppressed anxiety. It would not do to reveal worry and stress. Such emotions would display a lack of confidence in their warriors. So, this pattern continued: the braves hunted and fished; the women did their tasks; the warriors battled their enemies.

July had shown her torrid face. The season for the great buffalo hunt to prepare for the harsh winter was nearing. Yet, this grueling warfare went on, increasing in violence each day. By now, it was evident the soldiers had been well-supplied before this daring siege. The Indians had no way of knowing the fort had just received a massive load of supplies, or that the commanding officer was also cunning and prudential, or that the fort's water supply had been sagaciously safe-guarded against such a devastating ploy as was now in effect. The Indians did not know about the other trough which was buried beneath a foot of dirt and overgrown with prairie grass. This shrewd commander was most conscious of the defeat of his predecessor; he had studied every foreseeable measure which the Indians might take against them and had planned against it. A V-shaped, wooden trough had been placed in a long, narrow trench; covered with another matching, inverted trough; nailed together; and then concealed with dirt. As time had passed, new grass had grown over this area and blotted it from sight.

Lieutenant Timothy Moore had also assured the fort and his men against coerced starvation. He had maintained a hefty supply of necessities, sending out hunting parties each day for fresh food, conserving his dried or salted meats and vegetables for a day such as this one. At the first sign of coercible isolation, he had placed his men on strict rations in an attempt to out-smart and to out-wait the Indians. From where it stood now, he could hold out for another month; with luck, two.

In the Sioux camp, another drama was gradually unfolding. With the casual acceptance of a white captive in the life and upon the mat of Bright Arrow, resentment was building up within several Indian maidens who had cast their eyes upon this valiant warrior and who had lost their heads and hearts over him. Each time these two people—the beautiful white girl and the stalwart Sioux warrior—were sighted together, this bitterness and hostility increased, especially within Desert Flower and Little Tears. Their rivalry for this famed warrior had been halted by the arrival of an intolerable opponent: a gorgeous white enemy. Sensing their loss more deeply with each passing moon he spent with this white creature, they inevitably joined forces against her.

Desert Flower and Little Tears pursued any path which might harass or belittle her before the others. They pressed, ridiculed, and tormented Rebecca at each available opportunity. They sought ways to make her appear disobedient. Quick to notice this emotional battle, Shalee made this cruel treatment and wicked deception impossible for most of the time. Knowing the stress upon the minds of the warriors, neither female said anything to Gray Eagle or to Bright Arrow.

As Shalee's slim body began to plump with child, Rebecca generously assumed the heavier chores. With the men away for most of each day, the two warriors were unaware of the immense help this white girl was to the Indian princess. Aware of her husband's feelings for this particular girl, Shalee did not expound upon her good qualities: the mistake of doing this same thing with Rebecca's father had once bred a great deal of trouble between Shalee and her husband. Yet, Shalee came to depend more and more upon Rebecca's kindness, attention, and strength. As a persistent spring flower which forces its head through the vanishing snows, their admiration and respect for each other grew each day.

One afternoon, Shalee was busy sewing new garments for this coming child. She determined her new son would have a special gown of carefully beaded leather to be first shown in. As she worked diligently and steadily upon the tiny garment, Rebecca left the tepee to gather wood to cook the evening meal. Deeply immersed in a fantasy about her lover, Rebecca did not take notice of the approach of Desert Flower and Little Tears, nor read their spiteful looks of malice.

"Ku-wa, Witkowin," Desert Flower offensively called her a whore, then ordered her to also gather her own supply of wood.

Rebecca stared at the baneful Indian maiden, then shook her head. "Rebecca Shalee kaskapi. Hiya." Having witnessed the amorous way these two girls eyed her master and the hostile manner in which they glared at her and treated her, Rebecca keenly surmised the motive for their fierce hatred. Still, she bravely refused the envious girl's commands, wisely declaring herself the captive of Shalee and not Bright Arrow.

Desert Flower boldly approached Rebecca and slapped her before the white girl could react. Furious, but wise, Rebecca did not retaliate, much as she wanted to do so. There was enough conflict with her presence in Bright Arrow's life without complicating it with charges of rebellion. She lifted her load of wood and turned to walk away.

Desert Flower's taunting laughter chafed her. Not knowing the meaning of the Indian girl's next words, Rebecca remained ignorant of being called a coward and other vile names. Desert Flower came after her and spun her around, causing her to drop the sling of wood. Before Rebecca could stop herself, she shoved the hateful girl backwards.

Desert Flower tumbled upon the hard ground. Blind fury washed over her. She jumped up and attacked Rebecca. Too stunned to respond quickly, Rebecca received many blows to her stomach, scratches upon her naked arms, stinging slaps to her face, and savage jerks upon her lengthy auburn curls. Inspired by this long-awaited moment of revenge, Little Tears promptly joined in.

The two girls took turns holding Rebecca's arms while the other one punched, pinched, and cursed the innocent captive. Rebecca struggled with all her might, but her diminutive frame lacked the strength to resist the power and determination of the larger foes. Just as Desert Flower drew a small knife from her sheath which was used to sever the stems of vegetables and spices, she sneered venomously, "I will carve your face so no man will ever look upon it again."

With a thundering shout, Bright Arrow flung himself into the supple, but sturdy, frame of Desert Flower. Knocking her to the ground, the small knife entered her left arm. She cried out in pain and surprise. Bright Arrow snatched her to her feet by a painful grip upon her braids. He ignored the blood flowing from her arm and the words spewing from her mouth. Within inches of her terrified face, he snarled, "If you ever touch her again, I will slay you where you stand,

Desert Flower! You bring shame to yourself and to your father! Go! Never come near me again!"

With that warning, he shoved her toward the path back to camp. She held her arm tightly to her side, then raced like the wind for her tepee. Bright Arrow whirled to confront the paralyzed Little Tears who had neither moved nor spoken. He assailed her in this same manner, then sent her running along behind the quickly disappearing Desert Flower.

He focused his attention upon the white girl who had helplessly sunk to the ground after her release by Little Tears. He hurried to her side and knelt. He protectively gathered her in his embrace. Eyes filled with unleashed anger, concern, and love travelled her face and body to assess the injuries revealed there. He spoke soft and soothing words to her. Although she could not understand his words of apology and comfort, she comprehended his expressions.

She snuggled into his strong arms and wept. His arms tightened around her and he grimaced at her anguish. He silently held her until she gained a small measure of control over her tears. "I did nothing wrong, Bright Arrow; I swear it. When she attacked me, I tried to ignore it and return to your tepee. She would not allow it. They began to beat me. I was too weak to stop them," she hastily gave her side of the situation.

Unable to reply to her words in English, he simply permitted her to understand his trust in her by his actions. He gently wiped away her tears and smiled into her tawny eyes. He lifted her light body and carried her back to his tepee. What did he care about the thoughts and eyes of others when his woman was injured?

Upon entering his parents' tepee, Shalee glanced up and paled. She quickly inquired about this confusing behavior. When Bright Arrow related the truth to her, she winced in disbelief and concern. Together they tended her injuries. Shalee warned her son of the dangerous jealousy in Desert Flower and Little Tears. They jointly decided it would be best to bring this offensive act to the attention of the girls' parents. No Indian had the right to punish or to order about the captive of another warrior. It was but an hour before both girls were severely reprimanded and punished.

Publicly shamed, greater resentment filled the girls and their friends. The youthful group resolved to make Rebecca pay for their humiliation and to cause Bright Arrow such mental anguish and shame he would gladly part with his offensive white captive who had stolen Desert Flower's rightful place.

The Oglala group of five braves and four girls put their destructive plan into motion. They frequently allowed Bright Arrow to "accidentally" overhear their fears and mockery over his blindness and weakness over his white slave. They hinted of an evil spell which she must have cast over him. They spoke openly of doubting his strength of mind and body since both were ensnared by an enemy. The conflict of forbidden love raged bitterly and savagely within him. He would never join with Desert Flower!

Yet, every time a path was opened for him to be rid of his torment, something altered his determined course. At times, he wished he had never cast eyes upon Rebecca! How long could he endure the taunts of his friends? Why didn't he sell her or send her away? He knew why . . .

With the pretense of repairing his weapons and making new arrows, Bright Arrow managed to remain in camp for those next two days. He made it a point to be casually strolling in the same area in which Rebecca worked. In the tepee, he also remained near her side.

To give the lovers as much privacy as possible, Shalee used this time to visit other Indian wives, to spend time sewing and working with them, and for necessary exercise if she was to maintain her good health.

In their solitude, the young lovers gravitated closer together. They spent many hours making love and enjoying the other's company. Bright Arrow worked with Rebecca, teaching her his language. Each hour, her Oglala vocabulary increased. Yet, it did not grow quickly enough to permit very much conversation.

On the second day, Bright Arrow followed

Rebecca to the stream where she was heading to wash clothes. He sat down to restring his new bow. He deftly and silently worked with the taut leather thong to secure it to the supple bow. When Gray Fox called him away to discuss a secret, he laid the bow aside and unsuspectingly strolled into the forest with the other brave.

In her concentration upon her chore at hand and on her warring emotions, Rebecca failed to note the cunning trick in progress behind her. The vile deed was completed without her knowledge . . .

Soon, Bright Arrow returned, his mind in a turmoil over the incredible words spoken by Gray Fox. Had Gray Fox misunderstood the words of the other braves? Did they resent Rebecca's position and presence so deeply they would actually vote against him as band-leader for as long as she remained with him? Could they be so consumed with hatred for her and disloyalty toward him? Could he endure such a loss of pride? Could he allow this difference of opinion to become a full-blown quarrel, to cause greater dissension, to force a choice between them and his captive? Was Rebecca worth that high price to keep her? He fumed as he realized his helplessness: an unfamiliar and haunting feeling. But how could he seek the truth when he had given Gray Fox his word of honor to hold his words between them? If others learned of Gray Fox's treachery, how could he continue to report the others' feelings as promised? Then, there was the question of Gray Fox's honor; he was as sly and cunning as his name implied.

Even more distressing were the accusations against Rebecca. Were the girls lying about her conduct? How powerful were the forces of jealousy and hatred? From a short distance, he furtively observed the white girl kneeling by the water's edge and washing his clothes. Had she actually flaunted her position as his woman before them? Did she provoke them by making faces at him and his parents when they were not looking? Did she truly glare at them in unsuppressed hatred when their backs were turned? Was she merely feigning love and obedience when around them, then openly revealing her hostility before the others to secretly and cunningly shame them? Did she think him so enchanted as to trust her every word? The charges were grave. But accurate? he fretted.

He slowly returned to his previous place upon the grass to further reason upon these disturbing claims. When he lifted his bow, the two severed edges swayed with the movement of his action. In disbelief and fury, he gaped at the ruined weapon. Who had dared this unforgivable treachery? Not even a female member of the same family was permitted to touch a warrior's weapons: it was believed powerful bad magic. There were no higher coups than to bravely steal the weapons, medicine pipe, or horse of an enemy.

He jumped up to question Rebecca as to what person had committed this horrible deed during his absence. He halted beside her, his stormy gaze touching upon the butt of a knife which was only partially concealed by the pile of clothes near her. He leaned over and snatched the knife from its hiding place. He shuddered with the rage swiftly building within his normally controlled body. He glared into the quizzical face of the white girl.

In utter confusion, Rebecca watched this inexplicable conduct. Just before verbally attacking her in English, he whirled to retrieve his now useless bow. He shook the bow with its dangling strands before her baffled gaze as he spewed forth a flurry of Oglala words which she could not comprehend.

In turn, Rebecca stared at the bow, the knife which he had withdrawn from beneath the clothes, and the look of accusation in his ebony eyes. In horror, the clues quickly fell into place to form a frightful picture. It was obvious to her that someone had cruelly set her up while both she and Bright Arrow had their attention elsewhere!

Shaking in alarm and dread, she shook her head in panic and denial of his apparent charge. "Hiya!" she blurted out, pointing to the knife and bow. She motioned to herself and shrieked,

"Rebecca hiya . . ." Unable to think of an Oglala word of denial, she rushed on with, "I didn't do that, Bright Arrow! I swear it! I would never even touch your weapons! Toka ku-wa. Rebecca hiya wayaketo," she declared, hoping the few words made some sense to him.

He glared at her, his burning gaze searing her. Did she think him so stupid as to be blinded by her beauty and deceitful innocence? So, her meager defense was an enemy had come and she hadn't seen or heard anything! Seeing the doubt in his stygian eyes, she began to cry.

She wretchedly vowed, "I love you, Bright Arrow. I would never do something like that. No doubt my enemies, your friends, have arranged this evil trick!" she snapped in unleashed anger and torment. "Why do they hate me so much? Believe what you will, but I never touched those weapons. I'd be a fool to keep the knife with me!" she said fiercely.

He dropped to his knees and seized her chin painfully, forcing her gaze to lock with his. His own probed hers with a glacial intensity and power which alarmed her. She murmured sadly as tears eased down her cheeks, "I didn't do it, Bright Arrow. Don't let them turn you against me. Please . . ."

He mentally cursed the lucid honesty and vivid anguish in her golden brown eyes and her strained tone of voice. He didn't know what to believe. Could he kill her if she were innocent?

Was he too enchanted to comprehend the truth? Would his friends go this far to tear her from his side? Even so, he could never bring himself to make such charges against them. Something drastic had to be done soon. Since he couldn't choose her over his own people and rank, there really was no choice to be made.

He stood up, then forcefully flung the bow across the narrow stream. He furiously tossed the offending knife as far downstream as his rage-taut body would permit. Without a word to her, he whirled and walked off.

Rebecca watched his hasty retreat in fear and distress, for she instinctively comprehended some vital decision about her fate had just been made. She returned to her task, tears of anguish and betrayal steadily dropping into the water.

On the third day, Bright Arrow rejoined the warriors to help them harass their enemies and to take his mind from his own troubles. His emotions in a vicious maelstrom, he needed time and distance to sort them out and to make his decision. This conflict could not go on; its toll was mounting every day. His eyes scanned the bruises still visible upon her face and arms from her confrontation with Little Tears and Desert Flower. Could he blame her for hating them and for wanting revenge? His reluctant decision imminent, he left without words, an embrace, or a kiss.

Rebecca watched her love ride off, painfully

aware things had been spoiled between them.
Her somber gaze touched upon two girls
nearby: Desert Flower and Chundra. Gleams of
triumph and vengeful pleasure could be read
upon their sneering faces. Rebecca stared at
them, wanting to scream, "You've finally won,
you witches!" She wanted to run to them and
beat them soundly. She did neither. She lifted
her head in feigned pride and serenity and
smiled at them. She slowly turned to re-enter the
tepee of Chief Gray Eagle.

Battling the white enemy gave Bright Arrow
the release he craved. But as viciously as the
Indians attacked, the soldiers responded.

The lengthy guard the Indians held upon the
impregnable fort sapped their energy and
dulled their senses. Each night as they camped
nearby, several soldiers would find some way to
leave the fort and to attack them in their sleep.
No matter if a guard was posted, the success of
these dauntless and crafty attacks continued.
The strength of this white enemy was made
known, for there appeared to be no effect from a
denial of food or water: facts which puzzled and
discontented many warriors.

Two of the tribes relinquished their assigned
tasks and returned to their villages to prepare
for winter. He-Who-Walks-Like-The-Wolf exploded one day, "Evil spirits feed and water

them! We have waited many moons for their defeat. The buffalo season has come. If we do not hunt them and prepare for winter, the white man will survive while we starve and freeze!"

His words sounded true, but were vexing. Gray Eagle warned of the closeness to victory. Yet, he could not persuade the stubborn warriors to remain at their posts. There was dissension in many other warriors who had grown weary at this apparent failure to out-maneuver their enemies. Gray Eagle was forced to admit this commanding officer was far more intelligent and admirable than the first one had been. Unable to retain the cohesiveness of this dissimilar group of tribes, he reluctantly can-celled the futile siege upon Fort Dakota: the action bringing a bitter taste to his mouth. The groups of sullen warriors headed toward their own camps to rest, to hunt, and to protect their villages and families. Another day, Gray Eagle swore, the white man would taste defeat at their hands!

The three remaining tribes returned their attention to the same types of harassment they had used before their brothers deserted them. At first, the soldiers boasted of victory, savoring their triumph, misinterpreting it. The white men attacked and savagely murdered bands of exhausted warriors. Mutilated bodies were sus-pended from tree limbs as vivid warnings to other braves. Villages were attacked during the night or while warriors were out hunting. One of those tribes who had yielded defeat at the fort against Gray Eagle's fervent warnings was nearly demolished. The death toll and wanton destruction mounted; the gruesome animosities rapidly increased. The hideous clash seemed endless, the sacrifices limitless and too frequent.

Each side became more and more determined to resolve this deadly duel in his favor. A new plan formulated in the crafty mind of Gray Eagle. It was a perilous suggestion for any man who volunteered for this daring mission. But Gray Eagle knew it was the only hope for the survival of his people . . .

Early that next morning, Gray Eagle sent Bright Arrow and three of his best warriors to the other villages to call for another war council, then the chief headed to his home. Within three days, chiefs and band leaders from the camp of the Cheyenne, Blackfoot, and Brule entered the Oglala village. When Bright Arrow, his warriors, and representatives from the Sisseton tribe did not arrive—pricklings of dire warning disquieted the Eagle's mind and heart.

By nightfall, it was apparent something was gravely amiss. Gray Eagle called together a small band of his prime warriors. They left in search of his son. They anxiously covered the territory between the Brule camp and the Sisseton village. Nothing. They slowly traced the trail from the Sisseton camp toward the

Oglala one.

Gray Eagle's heart lurched wildly when they eventually discovered the horrifying evidence of a bloody confrontation with the Bluecoats. Markings of an ambush and fierce battle could be read upon the face of Makakin. The missing bodies of Bright Arrow and Chief Night Hawk told a bleak story which the mighty warrior refused to accept so quickly and easily. If those two warriors had escaped this vengeful attack, they would have returned to the Oglala camp by now. Since they had not and their bodies had not been found with these corpses, only two alternatives were left: their lifeless bodies had been stolen for some odious purpose or they had been captured. Each possibility was terrifying. Taking the Oglala and Sisseton bodies with them, they pensively returned to their village.

As they soberly rode into camp, everyone turned out to view this new treachery. Shalee mutely listened, paled, then fainted. Surely her son was as good as dead. She feared to think of how the whites at the fort would eagerly torture him before slaying him. If they merely suspected his identity, that torture would bear greater brutality. She was brutally confronted with the precarious existence of an Indian. Suddenly it was not a battle between her people and Gray Eagle's; it was a lethal conflict between her people and the whites.

Gray Eagle lifted her limp body in his

powerful arms and carried her into their tepee. Alarmed, Rebecca mechanically and silently tagged behind him. Observing Bright Arrow's absence and Shalee's reaction to the bitter words of her husband, she could easily imagine what was wrong. Dread washed over her lithe frame. She was as helpless as her mute mother had been on such occasions; she could not even ask her terrified questions and be understood.

Gray Eagle gently laid his unconscious wife upon his mat and stroked her cheek. Anguish filled him, for she desperately needed his comfort and closeness; yet, their son needed his attentions far more.

Rebecca boldly seized his arm. "Bright Arrow?" she fearfully demanded. When he trained his tormented gaze upon her, she winced at the anguish revealed there. She also paled and wavered. "Please understand me," she pleaded in vivid alarm. "What happened to Bright Arrow?" At his continued blank stare and silence, she shook his arm and shrieked, "Bright Arrow! Is he . . ." She could not voice aloud that agonizing question.

Her outburst drew a reaction and response from the puissant chief, but not the one she had expected. She was stunned when Gray Eagle gazed into her ashen face and earnestly beseeched her in fluent English, "Take care of her, Rebecca. Protect her and my child. Let nothing and no one harm them while I am gone. I must speak with the war council. Bright Arrow was taken captive by the Bluecoats. We must find some way to rescue him. If he still lives . . .''

Before she could recover her wits, Gray Eagle was gone!

Chapter Eleven

In utter shock, Rebecca stared after him. He could speak English! And what about Bright Arrow and Shalee? But her anger at this deceit was instantly appeased by the terrifying memory of Bright Arrow's precarious situation. What if her people killed him? What if he was being brutally tortured this very moment? Recalling tales of hideous horror which she had overheard from other whites, she trembled at the fate of her love.

She hurried to place a wet cloth upon Shalee's colorless face. When the Princess's lids fluttered and her eyes opened, Rebecca tenderly coaxed, "Do not fear, Shalee. Gray Eagle and the other warriors will rescue him. Bright Arrow is brave and cunning. Perhaps he will find some way to escape the fort. He cannot die! He cannot," she fervently exclaimed, tears spilling forth.

Shalee winced in anguish. How could they ever get him out of that impregnable fort? How could her son possibly escape when the soldiers were certain to have him locked securely in a sturdy blockhouse? No matter how fiercely her husband had struggled to keep the ghastly truth from her, she knew how the soldiers had been dangling the bodies of dead warriors from trees. What if they hung Bright Arrow's body upon the fort gates as a punishment and warning to the Indians?

Rebecca's mind was running in that same direction. "Someone must get inside the fort walls to free him." The moment she said this aloud, an idea came to mind. "That's it, Shalee!" she confided in excitement. "I could pretend to let the soldiers find me wandering about after my people had been slain. Surely they would take me into the fort. I could win their trust. At night, I could sneak over to the blockhouse and free Bright Arrow. I know I could do it! They would never suspect a frightened white girl who had seen her people massacred. It's perfect," she complimented herself, glowing with relief and quivering with suspense.

Shalee was staring blankly at her. Rebecca assumed this baffled expression to mean Shalee could not understand or speak English. "I must go to Gray Eagle. He speaks English. He will hear my words. He must agree to this plan! If only he will trust me to carry it out," she wistfully murmured, doubting he would.

Shalee cautioned herself to patience. Was Rebecca serious? Pretending to know a little English, she slowly ventured. "Rebecca risk . . . life . . . Bright Arrow? Rebecca white. Bright Arrow Oglala."

Astounded, she gaped at Shalee. "You speak English, too? Why have you kept silent? All these weeks we've worked and lived together and nothing!"

"Secret. Rebecca white. Shalee Oglala," Shalee said.

"Can Bright Arrow also speak my tongue?" she was forced to ask. "After all this time, surely you realize you can trust me! I love him. I can understand your silence and mistrust, but it isn't necessary. I would never hurt him."

"Gray Eagle teach Bright Arrow wasichu tongue. No tell enemies. Bright Arrow hear evil plans with secret. If tell secret, wasichu no talk. Rebecca good. Rebecca stay here. Fort bad. Bluecoats bad."

"But I'm the only one who could trick them into taking me inside. I could free him! They'll kill him if I don't go! Please let me try," she implored.

"You wish escape Bright Arrow? You go fort. Stay? You tell Bright Arrow name! Bluecoats torture, kill," Shalee fenced, her heart racing madly.

"No! I would never do such a wicked thing. I love him!" she hotly denied.

"You white captive. You hate Oglala. You run away to fort. You avenge Rebecca," she continued.

"That isn't true, Shalee. I don't hate you. You have been very kind to me. I've seen what real Indian slavery is. But in this tepee, I've known acceptance and love. I would not betray you. Besides, what kind of life could I have there? I've seen how squaws are treated. They despise us more than your people do! I love Bright Arrow. I wish to remain with him, even as his captive."

"You love enemy? How so?" she asked, lacing her tone with skepticism.

"I honestly don't know. It sounds crazy, and maybe it is. But I do love him. I would risk my life to help him," she earnestly vowed. "There's so little time. Please . . ."

Shalee studied her luminous eyes for a time. She wondered what this girl would say if she knew her father had once been their friend. Could such information increase her loyalty to them? "You daughter of Joe Kenny. Joe Kenny old friend to Gray Eagle and Shalee. Sad to hear of death. Kenny good white man. You good like father?" she asked the shocked girl.

"You knew my father! How? When?" Rebecca instantly responded.

"Before you born. Kenny bring white-eyes here in wagons long ago. See trouble. Stop. He fight bad white-eyes at Gray Eagle side. He leave. Live in cabin. Trap furs. Marry girl with silent tongue. That how you learn signing?" she said, knowing the danger of revealing too much too quickly.

"You know about my mother, too?" Rebecca pressed, intrigued and astonished.

"Kenny speak of Mary on last visit here. Leave to marry. No see again. How die?" Shalee dodged the question.

"A fever two years ago. I was taken to live with my mother's kinsman . . . Jamie O'Hara," she replied, shuddering at the recall of her near fate at his insidious hands.

"O'Hara bad man. Mary no like. Treat bad, Kenny say," she stated to confirm their past relationship with her parents. "Mary no happy in Louis."

"You're right. He was a wicked man. I hated him!" she heatedly confessed.

"You say father name. I tell Gray Eagle. Joe Kenny koda. Gray Eagle . . . 'prised. That why he let you stay," she reluctantly lied out of necessity. She could never tell Rebecca why her husband had despised her, nor pardoned her!

"But why was he going to send me away?" she broached the subject which Shalee needed to avoid for countless reasons.

"You white. You capture eye of son. Son warrior. Son next chief. Not good warrior, chief to desire white squaw. Lose face. No take Oglala woman while have you. Not good. Other laugh. Make son look weak. Not good. Understand?" she entreated.

"Yes," Rebecca dejectedly answered in a tremulous voice. "But words cannot erase love. I know it is wrong and foolish, but I could not halt the feelings he stirred in me. I'm sorry," she apologized for interfering in his life and bringing them embarrassment. "Even so, I still love him and want him."

"I carry child. Gray Eagle say you stay here to help me. Gray Eagle not wish son to want you much. It bad to love enemy."

"Love? Is that what Gray Eagle fears? That Bright Arrow might come to love me, too?"

"Fear impossible. Love not. This bad. Cause trouble."

"What should I do? I would rather die than leave him."

"Shalee know. You save Bright Arrow, win much favor in Oglala eyes and hearts. Oglala repay courage and good deed."

"They would let me remain as his captive if I free him from the Bluecoats?" she anxiously questioned.

"Heart say yes; head say maybe," Shalee replied candidly.

"Why do you have green eyes?" Rebecca unexpectedly asked as she gazed into them. Shalee smiled, then laughed.

"Shalee daughter of Chief Black Cloud of Si-ha Sapa and white squaw. Black Cloud take white woman long before days of hatred and battles. Bright Arrow carry little white blood. Not good take white girl and give sons more white blood. Must join Oglala girl. Then sons carry more Oglala blood," she clarified.

"But how could I give him a son?" Rebecca asked.

Shalee laughed mirthfully. "You sleep with son. Baby come from such touching upon mats. Is not so?" she teased.

Rebecca paled. "I've never even considered it. What would happen to such a child?" she fearfully questioned, eyes wide with dread.

"Child stay here. Child not true Oglala. Child never follow Bright Arrow as chief. Child like mother, slave. No harm come to him. Shalee promise."

Rebecca sighed in relief. "You are indeed a special woman, Shalee. I trust you. Bright Arrow won't marry either of those two girls who attacked me, will he?" she anxiously and jealously asked, fearing to become a slave to either.

"Bright Arrow not fool. No marry Desert Flower or Little Tears. Both bad. Punished for hurting slave of other warrior."

"They were punished?" she asked in astonishment. Shalee nodded. "But what of Bright Arrow and my plan? Will Gray Eagle agree to it?" she returned their conversation to the most

347

pressing subject.

"When he come, you stay silent. I tell him of plan. Must tell no one of white tongue. Keep secret. Yes?" she gently demanded.

Rebecca smiled. "You show great faith in me. I will never reveal this secret. I will do as you say."

It was late when Gray Eagle came back to his tepee. He found Shalee nervously waiting for him. To be able to speak freely, she asked him to go for a walk. They strolled around in silence for a time, each lost in thoughts and worries of their own. Shalee halted her aimless roamings beside a tall tree. She gazed up at the full moon while she gathered her wits and courage. She could only pray Gray Eagle would not be overly upset with her for her actions.

"Gray Eagle," she hesitantly began. He came over to stand beside her. Without meeting his piercing gaze, she confessed her conversation with Rebecca.

"Why did you do this thing, Shalee?" he demanded. "She will betray us all," he concluded, dismay etching harsh lines upon his striking face.

"No, Gray Eagle. I do not believe she will. When I went to Fort Pierre long ago, my love for you would not permit such a betrayal. Her love for Bright Arrow will guard our secret. With all I feel inside, I think she can carry off this trick. There is no other way to get to him. Even if she lies, what further danger could there be?" she reasoned with her distressed husband.

"She could tell the Bluecoats we speak their tongue," he promptly replied.

"To do so would only prove we liked her and trusted her. That would look bad for her. Our son's life is at stake. We have no choice but to trust her to help him. She loves him, Gray Eagle. She also hopes to win our favor by doing this."

"You said nothing of Powchutu?" he abruptly quizzed, that haunting look returning briefly to furrow his brow.

"Nothing. It is best she live as Joe's daughter."

"What will the others say about this sudden trust in her?" he fretted.

"Would it not prove her love for him? Would it not justify his keeping her? You could tell only a few of your trusted warriors about this plan. Then, if it failed, nothing more would be said of it. But if it works, our son will return to us. You can say it was best that only a few knew of it."

"What if Rebecca is caught? They might also kill her," he said.

"She said she did not wish to live without our son. Once I knew and felt such warring emotions. It will give her the courage and strength to carry out this daring plan. Do you forget she offered her life in exchange for his at the challenge of White Elk? Perhaps the Great Spirit gives her this chance to prove she is not evil like her father. Perhaps He uses this event to earn our acceptance of her."

Gray Eagle pondered his wife's words. It was true the Great Spirit often worked in mysterious ways. Besides, there was no other way to rescue his son. "Let me sleep upon this idea. I will talk to Rebecca when the sun awakens. The Bluecoat leader is cunning and wise. He will not slay a noted warrior too quickly."

When they returned to their tepee, Rebecca was asleep. Her moist cheeks testified that she had cried herself into exhausted slumber. A medallion belonging to Bright Arrow was clutched tightly within her hand, and this sight stirred hope in Gray Eagle's heart.

Shortly before dawn, he watched Rebecca arise and sneak out of the tepee. He stealthily followed her. As if by mystical guidance, she sat down beneath the overhanging branches of the same spruce tree where he and Shalee had talked last night. She stared unseeingly at the shiny amulet in her grasp. She wept in fear and despair.

"I cannot even think of life after your death, my love. Such a very short time to have you . . . Why did our paths cross if only to have them separated so savagely and quickly? So much hatred, Bright Arrow, and so little time for love. Why must it be so? Please, God, give me the courage to save him," she fervently prayed. "Even if it costs my life, I must help him. I must see him once more. Do not allow it to end this way. Help me . . . Give me strength and courage and cunning. Please . . ." Rebecca murmured words which could be echoes of similar ones spoken countless moons ago . . .

Suddenly, Gray Eagle inquired, "You love him this much, Rebecca?"

Startled, she jumped and looked up at him. "Yes. I would trade my life for his. Send me to the fort. I will find some way to release him. I swear it."

"What if you are captured? What if Bright Arrow refuses to leave you behind and risks recapture to free you?"

"Once I have found a way to disarm the guard and open the door, I will hide from his sight. Later, I will find some way to escape. Will you allow me to return here?" she entreated.

"You are but a woman, almost a child. Such a dangerous mission would be foolish in your hands," he replied.

"That's why it will work! Who would suspect a woman, almost a child, of trying to help him? While they sleep, I can free him. There are doors in the fence which he can pass through in secret," she protested.

"What if he loses time by bringing you along?" he asked in a gentler tone.

"I will not permit it. He can travel more

quickly and easily without me. Each night, Oglala warriors could hide and wait nearby for his escape. It might take days before they trust me and no longer watch me so closely. I will only attempt desperate measures if it appears they will slay him before my plan can work. If there is time for words between us, I will demand he leave without me. To leave together would only endanger both our lives. I cannot move as secretly and agilely as he does. He will know and accept this. I will need to dress as a white girl, for they despise squaws more than you do. They must never suspect I have been captured before. They must think I have miraculously escaped an attack and they have bravely rescued me. Their great pride and hatred will assist me," she asserted.

"After the way I have treated you, do I dare trust you, Rebecca?" he asked candidly, his expression challenging.

She solemnly countered, "Do you dare not trust me? Did you not trust my father? No matter what you have done to me, I must do this for Bright Arrow and myself. Despite how you feel about me, you must also do this for Bright Arrow. I am his only hope for survival, just as he is for mine. Is your pride and hatred more important than your son's life?"

He walked away from her, halting with his broad back to her. She wondered what he was thinking and feeling. To realize the life of his only son was in the fragile hands of a white girl had to vex and shame him. She arose and went to stand behind him.

"Please, Gray Eagle, let me try to save him. If you so demand, I will not return to his side. All that matters is his life," she issued the words which made his decision for him.

"Perhaps my eyes and senses are clouded with love and worry for my son. I will agree to your plan, Rebecca. But if you deceive or betray him, I will kill you with my bare hands. If you help him escape, then I will send someone to watch for your escape; I will return you to my son. Even so, a slave is all you can ever be to him. Is this enough for you?" he sincerely challenged her.

Her eyes softened and glowed. "Yes, Gray Eagle. Even a small part of him is better than none. I will do nothing to dishonor him before the eyes of his people. One day he will also become a great chief."

"Then come. We must do this quickly before they take his life—or I change my mind."

They returned to his tepee and related their daring plan to an anxious Shalee. Gray Eagle left the two women to ready his warriors and their horses. As Shalee helped Rebecca prepare for this perilous deed, they chatted nervously. When the white captive was dressed to leave, the Indian princess affectionately hugged her and remarked, "You small and young to face such danger, Rebecca."

Rebecca smiled radiantly and asserted softly, "Not too young to save my love from certain death. Besides, I'll soon be eighteen," she said wistfully as Gray Eagle entered the tepee to fetch her.

Both Gray Eagle and Rebecca hugged Shalee and departed quickly before the sun sank too low in the July heavens of azure blue. Shalee watched them ride away, her turbulent thoughts on her endangered son.

Within two hours, Rebecca had been dressed in her old clothes and was on her way to an unknown destiny. As they lingered for several scouting parties to return to where they awaited news of the troops' movements and locations, Gray Eagle mussed her hair and dirtied her face. He grimaced as he pulled briars over her arms and legs to make her appearance credible. She bravely submitted to these precautions.

"It must appear you have been hiding and running from us for many days. Near the edge of this forest over there," he advised, pointing off to the east, "the Cheyenne attacked three wagons two suns ago. The Bluecoats have not seen this yet. When you say these were your people, they might believe you. Tell them you hid beneath bushes by the trail. White Arrow has marked the path to prove your words if they check out your story. Speak of a warrior who paints red and green dots upon his face. He is the leader of the Cheyenne who raided the wagons. You must act hungry, tired, and afraid," he cautioned Rebecca.

"I will do all you say. Where will the warriors wait for Bright Arrow?"

"There is a big tree near the fort. It grows tall at the side where Wi first shows his face. Send my son there. When you escape, you will also go there. I will tell you words to say if you come near Bright Arrow to let him know of these plans."

"But he will know all I say," she said.

He frowned at her, alerting her to her careless error. "Still, there are certain words which will tell him of our plans. You must forget we speak your tongue. These signals will alert him to my trust in you."

She flashed him a meek look, then listened intently to his instructions. "Mention an arrow-wood tree if you speak within his hearing. This will tell him where to meet us. Speak words about truce, travelling alone, pretend you see a hawk above you, and ask which bird you hear singing ghostly songs at night. This will tell him to listen for your coming during the night, to leave alone, and I am waiting nearby. It will also say you are our friend and we have truce. Perhaps you could speak of returning to the man you love. He is bright and alert; he will capture the right words from you."

"I will remember and do this. If I am

discovered after his escape and cannot return to him, tell him . . ." She turned away from Gray Eagle's piercing stare, blushing like the fiery sunset. Yesterday they had been bitter enemies; today, she was telling him her innermost feelings!

"Speak, Rebecca. I will give him your words," he coaxed. His tone said she could trust him. She did.

"Tell him I love him and wish him happiness and safety. Tell him not to worry about me. Make him understand I did what I had to do. If I am slain, do not allow him to endanger his life by avenging mine. I will not dishonor your trust in me, Gray Eagle."

"If you cannot free him in time, tell . . ."

"No!" she heatedly exclaimed. "Do not even suggest such a thing," she pleaded, tears filling her eyes.

"Tell him we will pray for his safety upon the Ghost Trail," he insisted. "Tell him we love him. Tell him I will avenge both his life and yours."

Her eyes glittered with tears. She smiled. "He is lucky to be the son of Shalee and Gray Eagle. Would that I had been born an Indian and could become a part of your family," she sadly whispered.

"Return to us, and you will remain in our tepee," he subtly promised.

"You are truly a great warrior. I am grateful

for your words and kindness. I can see how my father would admire and respect you. I wish he were here with us now. Life without him has been very hard and sad."

White Arrow joined them. "The Bluecoats come this way. We must leave her now," he stated in Oglala. He smiled at this small girl who was so much like Shalee. Once he had almost won Shalee from his best friend and lifelong companion when the noble warrior had been tempted to part with her to prevent his loss of face. If he were not already joined to Wandering Doe, he might be tempted to take this unique girl from Bright Arrow and relieve him of those same torments which his best friend had once endured. But he was content with his Oglala wife.

Gray Eagle told his friend, who had walked and ridden at his side since youth, to make ready to conceal themselves nearby. He faced Rebecca for perhaps the last time, "Be careful, Rebecca. May the Great Spirit guard your life. When it is safe, return to us." He tenderly caressed her cheek and hurried away.

Rebecca silently offered up a prayer for all of them. She refused to consider what might happen to her if Bright Arrow was already dead, or if she couldn't find some way to release him, or if she couldn't escape later, or if these men decided to taste her treats before taking her to the fort with them—if she made it that far . . .

A resonant voice called out softly from the thick underbrush, "Do not be afraid of them, Rebecca. We will not allow them to harm you. We will follow you to the fort and protect you that far," he stated as if reading her frightful thoughts.

"Then I have nothing more to fear," she confidently whispered, preparing herself to confront the soldiers from Fort Dakota in a few more minutes.

Chapter Twelve

Rebecca gingerly flung herself to the ground, assuming a prostrate position of someone who was too exhausted to flee or to even care anymore. Her shoulders drooped in despair and fatigue. Her face was partially concealed by a flowing mass of tousled auburn curls. Her arms were covered with dust and scratches to aid her image of sole survivor of a gruesome attack by wild Indians. She had not eaten or taken water since yesterday when this terrifying drama began. She appeared every inch the defenseless female in great distress and danger.

Upon sighting her, the sergeant hastily shouted his orders, "Company halt! Draw weapons!" Trying to conceal his apprehension, he called out, "You there on the ground, what ails you? Who are you?" To his men, he hastily advised, "Tighten your ranks, men. This could be a trap. Stay alert and ready.''

At the sound of his voice, a lovely, but dirty, face slowly glanced upward. Terrified eyes scanned the troop as if doubting their reality. "You're soldiers," she exclaimed weakly. "I thought . . . you were them . . . come back to kill me, too." She then began to sob and babble hysterically, her real fears making this quite easy for her. "Indians attacked us. Killed everyone . . . so much blood . . . All alone . . . Help me . . . We haveta hurry. They'll come back! They'll kill us!" she shrieked in frenzied terror.

Eyes sweeping the tree-line and ground, the sergeant cautiously urged his horse forward. She pulled herself to her feet as if she barely had enough strength left to accomplish this small feat. "Who attacked you? Where'd you come from?" His lazy eyes inched over her from chestnut head to bare feet.

"Back there somewhere," she sadly offered through dry lips. "I've been running . . . and hiding for two days. My father . . ." She began to weep uncontrollably. As if unable to support her slender frame in her weakened condition, she sank back to the ground upon her knees. She covered her face with dirty, scuffed hands. She wept. What if they didn't believe her? What if her love was dead? What if this was a cunning betrayal and Gray Eagle slaughtered each of them?

"How'd you get away from them Injuns?" he asked suspiciously. His wary gaze searched the dense growth of trees for any movement and the ground for any clue to undesirable company. Seeing nothing to evoke fear or skepticism, he asked, "What's your name, girl?"

"Rebecca. Rebecca Kenny," she stated despondently. "They told us it was safe here. They said the cavalry would protect us. Where were you when they attacked us and killed my family!" she charged.

"We can't be everywhere, girl! You say everyone else is dead?"

"Yes," she wretchedly said. "I'm so tired and sleepy. I was afraid to close my eyes. There's wild animals here," she craftily selected what she presumed was the natural thing to say.

"Come with us, miss. You'll be safe at the fort from them devilish redskins," he declared, devouring her entrancing features and curvaceous body.

"What about my family? You can't just leave them there unburied. I don't have any clothes or anything," she murmured in dismay. "I couldn't go back there, even for food or a gun."

"Don't you worry none. Ole Zack'll take real good care of you," he vowed huskily, chuckling softly. His groin tightened uncomfortably.

"But my family! The animals might . . ." She began to sob again.

"Sorry, miss, but we can't stay out here all

day. It ain't safe. Best git you back to the fort. You could use some food and rest," he coaxed, hoping to be amply repaid for his service and kindness. She was a beauty!

Rebecca astutely comprehended the lewd gleam which filled his eyes. She was definitely safe for now. Like Jake, this lecherous man also wanted some private property. He wasn't about to share her with his troop. Hopefully the people at the fort would protect her from this lecherous fiend. But if she snubbed him too obviously, he might not let her get that far! She demurely complied.

"You're right, sir." She waited for his instructions, feeling Gray Eagle's keen gaze upon her back. So far, everything was going as planned. Yet, the hardest part still loomed ahead.

"Here, ride with me. I'll help you up behind. Hold on tight. We can't have you falling off," he playfully jested, savoring the tantalizing warmth and sensuous feel of her body.

The ride back to the sturdy fort was repulsive, for Sergeant Zachary Smith would occasionally shift in his saddle to casually press his back into her tender breasts, lewdly wiggling his buttocks against her most private region. She pretended to naively ignore these actions and his stodgy body. She was sorely tempted to pinch the roll of fat which surrounded his flaccid waist, but did not. She tried to mentally block out the foul odor of his sweaty, unwashed body and his horrid breath.

Finally the lengthy ordeal was over. They approached the fort's lofty gates of slender saplings lashed tightly together. Sergeant Zachary Smith slid off his horse and tied the reins to the hitching post. His lathered horse, weary from bearing the weight of two riders, greedily drank from the trough beside the hitching post. He came back to assist her down. When his clammy hands seemed to linger too long upon her shoulders, she turned to gaze at the sights and scenes around her, forcing his arms to fall away. Not even a scrub tree had been left standing within the barren confines of this large fort.

"Where is the commanding officer's quarters? I must tell him about my family and the attack. I'll ask for his assistance and protection here. Perhaps he could send a message to my father's sister in St. Louis," she added with feigned childish hope. It was vital she fool them completely. As she spoke to him, she seemed to look listlessly about her.

"We don't need to bother Lieutenant Moore. He's got a lot on his mind with all this Injun trouble. You just follow me, miss, and I'll get you some food and a place to sleep. Ole Zack'll take real good care of you," he repeated his prior suggestion, then grinned in lecherous anticipation, hooking his thumbs under his suspenders.

"I think my father would wish me to see Officer Moore," she timidly announced, pulling her attention from her subtle inspection of the fort to deal with this annoying and persistent man.

Zack took her arm in a firm grip. "Ain't no need. I know how to take care of this matter. Come along, Miss Rebecca," he entreated, thinking his authoritative tone would settle the matter for him. It did not.

"You're hurting me, sir," she cried out in alarm, needing to attract assistance with this crude soldier.

"Ye hae ae problem 'ere, Sergeant?" a controlled voice asked, noting the unfamiliar girl with frightened tawny eyes and a dishevelled appearance.

"No, sir. We found this gurl wandering around out there. Says her people were attacked and killed. I was trying to take her for some food and rest," he sullenly explained, vainly attempting to govern the irritation and disdain in his raspy voice.

"Tae ye quarters, Sergeant!" he commanded. "Bring 'er tae my office. I'd lik' tae speak wi' 'er myself," he calmly ordered, denying Smith's lewd plans for her. A Scottish burr laced his mellow voice.

Rebecca curiously glanced from one man to the other as if confused as to which man and order to obey. She mutely waited for them to inform her. "Come along, miss. Lieutenant Moore wants to talk with you. So he says," Zack mumbled under his breath as they trotted off behind the giant man with flaming red hair and deep blue eyes who looked much younger than the burly Smith.

Once inside the commander's office, Rebecca gradually repeated the story which she had memorized. She cried in the appropriate places, feigned nausea in others, and terror in still others. When the tale was completed, she slumped wearily in her chair. "I have kin in St. Louis if you can contact them for me, sir."

"Nae, that'll be impossible anytime soon, Miss Kenny. Ye see, we hae quite ae problem wi' an Indian uprisin' right now. But dinna worry, lass. Ye're safe 'ere," he confidently stated to foster hope and relief in the delicate creature who sat before his dusty desk.

"But I have no clothes or money, sir," she wretchedly declared.

"My men will pay for chores. There's washin' an' cleanin' tae be done. Once ye've rested properly, ye kin do my chores first," he genially remarked, a strange twinkle in his blue eyes.

"Thank you, sir. You are most kind and thoughtful," she timidly stated, hoping she could be gone before he demanded more than servile behavior from her!

"Sta' 'ere. I'll see th' cook sends food o'er. I'd lik' ae word wi' ye, Smith." The two men left.

Rebecca was quickly peering out the grimy window. Her heart lurched with excitement and hope as she recalled the secluded location of the blockhouse at the front right corner of the fort. Patience, Rebecca, she cautioned herself.

Her curious gaze settled upon the two men. It was clear they were arguing over something. She wondered if it was about her. The fractious sergeant looked furious with the masterful lieutenant. Smith stalked off in the direction of what had to be the cookhouse. As Moore headed back her way, she hastily returned to her seat before his cluttered desk. She laid her folded arms upon his desk and rested her forehead upon them as one utterly exhausted and dejected.

When Moore entered his office, he thought for a moment she was asleep. He came to stand beside her. When he reached out to stroke her hair, she feared he might astutely realize it was clean and shiny beneath its tangled mess. She lifted her head and cast droopy eyes upon his flushed, passion-filled face.

"Do you have some water, sir? I'm very thirsty," she asked.

He shook his head to clear it of unbidden lust.

He went to a pitcher and filled a metal cup with tepid water. He handed it to her. She greedily consumed the entire cup, then moistened her dry lips. "Thank you again, sir."

"Na need tae keep thankin' me, lass. Ye bonny smile does it guid. How auld 're ye, Rebecca?" he unexpectedly inquired.

"Almost eighteen, sir. Why?" she asked inquisitively.

"Nae partic'lar reason. Jus' wondered how long it took ae lassie tae get sae beautiful," he boldly flattered her, then grinned mischievously.

She blushed a deep rose and demurely lowered her gaze. Not knowing what safe or proper statement to make in response, she remained silent. He chuckled merrily. "Such ae flow'r makes ae prize worth dying for," he vowed huskily.

"Sir?" she questioned naively, her eyes filled with provocative innocence.

"Excuse my forwardness, lass. Tis been ae guid time since I laid eyes 'pon anythin' lik' ye. Where were ye headin'?" he asked.

"I'm not certain, sir. Papa said somewhere near a fort where we'd be safe. I suppose he might have meant here," she hinted shyly.

The door opened and Zack returned with her food. Moore glared at him. "A'fore the morn, Sergeant, I suggest ye learn tae knock a'fore enterin' this private office," he stormily reprimanded the startled man.

Flustered and embarrassed, Smith nearly dropped her dish of food. She quickly glanced away, also disquieted by the harshness and subtle innuendo in Moore's voice. She shrewdly realized this man was most disarming, for he had just revealed a streak of hostility which had been previously concealed beneath that roguish charm and gentle manner. He would make a dangerous enemy!

Zack set her dish upon the desk and hastily excused himself. No doubt to curse this mysterious man whom she had vastly misjudged. She ate slowly and carefully, intentionally presenting manners and breeding which might hinder a siege upon her innocence. She would guilefully lead this man to think she was a gentle creature who must be courted before bedded! A man showed no respect or patience with a loose woman, but he might with a lady or someone special . . .

Moore observed her closely, delighting in what he witnessed and perceived. Unnerved, she glanced over at him and sweetly asked, "Is something wrong, sir?"

"Nae. Why?" he inquired, brow lifted inquisitively.

"You keep staring at me. It makes me uncomfortable," she confessed, blushing again.

He chuckled heartily. "Sorry, lass. Jus' canna help myself," he admitted, a raffish smile brightening his keen blue eyes.

"But it isn't polite to . . . ," she defensively began, then hesitated at the right spot to make an artful point. She then stammered dramatically, "I'm . . . sorry, sir. That was . . . rude of me. I guess I'm overly . . . tired and frightened. You've been very kind." Tears filled her expressive eyes, concealing the deceit within them.

"Tak' ye ease, Rebecca. I understand ye fears an' doubts. It's only lookin', lass. That's all," he earnestly stated. Yet, she could imagine him mentally adding, for now . . .

"You must think I'm terribly ungrateful. I don't mean to be. So much has happened in the past few days," she said with despair.

"I know, lass; I know . . . Tak' it easy. Nae one'll hurt ye 'ere. Come, ye kin rest in my quarters while I find ae suitable place for ye." Observing the look of sheer terror which flooded her golden brown gaze, he grinned and added, "Ye'er safe, Rebecca. I wad nae hurt ye, lass," he reassured her.

"But Papa wouldn't think it proper for me to sleep in a stranger's room, sir. Perhaps there's some family or a couple I can stay with," she modestly suggested, eyes wide with uncertainty.

"If ye canna trust the man in charge 'ere, lass,

then ye papa's taught ye tae be tae wary o' others. I gae ye my word, lass, nae harm'll come tae ye in my care," he gallantly vowed, knowing there was harm, and there was . . . harm. She was positively a skittish filly who'd take time and patience to break! But what was a little time and wooing when the prize would be well worth it? Maybe it was his season for taking a wife . . .

Rebecca alertly read the commander's change in mood and expression. He was quickly becoming more interested in her than in her feminine attributes! She had surely made a valuable conquest and won a powerful protector, deluding him completely! "Then I place my safety and honor in your capable hands, sir," she softly agreed.

He grinned lazily, also believing he had won a cunning victory. "Follow me, lass. I know ye be tired." He led her to his room and pointed to his inviting bunk. "I'll let na one disturb ye rest." He closed the door and left.

Rebecca walked over to the bunk and sat down. So far, so good, she sighed in relief. She was exhausted, both mentally and physically. Besides, there was nothing she could do just yet. Soon, she was napping peacefully.

Moore peeked in on her later. She was curled up in a snug ball, lost to all her problems. He leisurely surveyed her from head to toe, as much as he could see. He smiled to himself. She was such an intriguing mixture of sensual woman and innocent child. Without warning, his tour of duty didn't look so bad anymore. He left again. There was a certain brave of great importance whom he wished to study once more . . .

Later that afternoon, Rebecca awakened from her slumber. She reminded herself to behave as the mourning, terrified girl. Hearing the outer door squeak as it opened, she decided to make some points in her favor. She began to toss upon the bunk and to mumble. Sure enough, Moore noted her distress and came to her side just as she effectively cried out, "No! Don't kill them! Papa, watch out! Savages . . . no, no, no," she wailed in a pitiful tone.

Moore shook her and called her name, thinking her to be ensnared by a nightmare. She jumped and shrank against the wall, staring at him in terror. "'Tis me, lass. 'Twas only ae bad dream," he attempted to comfort her.

She instantly dissolved into tears, her slender shoulders slumped in dejection and grief. He pulled her into his comforting embrace and spoke to her as if calming a frightened child. She clung to his dark blue shirt and sobbed openly. She fiercely resisted the nagging of her guilty conscience, reminding herself that both Bright Arrow's and her lives were at stake now. How had she talked herself into this mess? It was far more difficult to carry off than she had imagined. More and more desperate lies and pretense were demanded, and this was trying for one so artless and sensitive. The worst part was that Timothy Moore actually seemed sincerely concerned about her, seemed honestly drawn to her. Using innocent people went against her grain. Yet, Bright Arrow would die a horrible death if she did not help him. Then, there was her enslavement to him. No white man would want her if this information became known . . . she was as helpless as a Mayfly caught in a spider's web!

Restoring some control to herself, she pushed away from Timothy's solace. She sniffed and cleared her constricted throat. "I'm sorry, sir. It's just . . . this situation is so terrible and new to me. Why is there such hatred between us? Why did they slaughter my people?"

"They be cold-blooded, heartless savages, Rebecca. They think they own ev'ry inch o' this land. They're determined tae shove us out. 'Tis too late, lass. The white man is 'ere tae stay, nae matter the cost."

"Is it worth the high price, sir? How many innocent lives will it take to pay for each acre we take from them? What about girls like me who lose their families? What about the brutality? I hate it here! I want to go home," she stated sadly, referring to the cabin where she had been born, the cabin which no longer existed.

"Tha' is nae possible, lass. Yer home an' family 're gone. Ye hae tae mak' ae new life an' find ae new family," he ventured.

"How? Where?" she innocently seized his dangling bait.

"'Ere wi' me, lass. I could use ae wife lik' ye," he proposed.

She stared at him. "But we've just met! You don't even know me, and I know nothing about you. How can you propose to a total stranger?"

"Time is e'er precious out 'ere, Rebecca. 'Tis best tae mak' use o' wha' we hae. Ye could gie me happiness. I could tak' care o' ye. 'Tis ae proper trade."

Flustered by his unexpected proposal, she nervously glanced off into space. From appearances, she seemed to be considering his remarks and offer. Her gaze came back to his. "Could I have a few days to think about it? Right now, I'm confused about everything. We've only just met. I . . ." she hesitated.

"Ay, lass. Wi' the Indians stir'in up such ae ruckus, we canna go about. I'll ask ye agin in ae week. Wha' sae ye?" His twinkling blue eyes watched her closely, too closely for her jittery nerves.

"That would give us time to get to know each other. I wouldn't want you to marry me out of pity or because I'm the only available female," she murmured softly, then blushed.

He chuckled. "A'where I'm concerned, ye be the only female alive. The wee moment I looked at ye, I knew ye were the lass for me. I lead ae dangerous life, Rebecca. I dinna hae time for ae slow courtin'," he excused his blunt rush.

She studied him for a time, deliberating his appeal to her. Enlightenment gradually settled in; he reminded her of her father, all except for that violent streak which he had briefly revealed to her and his flaming red hair. He was nice looking and kind. His appearance was neat; his voice compelling. He was the highest ranking officer here, so he could easily afford a wife. His quarters were clean and tidy, saying much about him. His blue eyes sparkled with vitality and warmth.

She smiled shyly. "On my journey out here, I met many men, Lieutenant Moore. But you seem so different from them. If not for my father's keen eye and protection, I daresay I would have been pestered by some of them. I did not like the way they looked at me or the things they suggested. But you," she shrewdly remarked, "you're not like them. You don't undress me with your eyes or try to touch me improperly. I like you, sir, and I will think seriously about your offer of marriage."

A pleased grin claimed his mouth. "Ye be amazin', Rebecca. 'Tis ye bad fortune wha' gae me my guid luc'. My han' wasna e'er gie'en tae ae lassie a'for.''

"Perhaps we will both profit from this terrible situation," she concurred with a bright smile.

"Wha' sae ye tae some fresh air? Ye look ae wee bit pale," he cordially offered.

"That sounds delightful, sir," she eagerly accepted, wanting to study the fort and to escape his vexing aura.

"Call me Timothy, Rebecca. If ye wad lik' tae freshen ye bonny face and hair, ye'll fin' water an' ae brush o're there," he stated, pointing to a washstand.

"Thank you . . . Timothy. I'll join you shortly."

He walked into his office, closing the door behind him. He congratulated himself for not joining her upon his bunk as he had been sorely tempted to do. Not that anyone could have stopped him from having his way with her, but she was too special and innocent to spoil so quickly. Besides, she would be his in less than a week. Once he turned on his charm and pressure, she would fall victim to him . . .

They leisurely strolled around outside. The setting sun played favorably upon her coppery locks and softened her golden eyes to a bewitching amber glow. He gave her an entertaining and enlightening tour of the fort, chatting and laughing in high spirits. Urging herself to appear naturally inquisitive and not overly suspicious, she memorized every facet and detail which came before her line of vision. The fort was laid out in an efficient pattern. It was clean, but barren. Not a tree had been left standing to ward off the summer sun which would soon be blazing down upon it as July steadily moved forward.

As Moore halted to converse with two of his sentries, she absently scanned her surroundings. They had stopped near the front gates which protected them from their fierce enemies, the awesome Sioux and their brothers. The center of the courtyard boasted one object: a flagpole with the standard and the flag of this fledgling nation called America. To her immediate left, there stood a squat building which was the doctor's quarters and the infirmary. In the far corner, a long and narrow building which emitted fragrant smells declared itself as the cookhouse and eating hall.

As her eyes roamed onward, she noted the stables where the horses, gear, stable-hands, and animals' rations were stored. Directly before her, she viewed a lengthy building which was used for the enlisted men. This two-story structure was the largest in the fort. Next, to her right at the back was the officers' quarters which also housed the commanding officer Lieutenant Moore. This one-story wooden structure had more room and was in better condition.

To her right on the front wall was situated the supply shed, also a two-story structure, for the storage of goods and weapons. Beside it in the corner sat the blockhouse, the imprisoning abode of her love. Except for the cookhouse and stockade, each structure was situated three feet from the lofty, protective wall of Fort Dakota. She hastily pulled her gaze from the blockhouse; she feared her look might give away her anguish and motive for being here.

The two soldiers left Moore's side. He returned his attention to the lovely creature next to him and began to boast about the valuable prisoner in the blockhouse.

"This brave is the son of Gray Eagle?" Rebecca asked disarmingly. "The men on our wagon train spoke of him and the Sioux. They said he is the most feared Indian alive. Is that true?"

"Ne'er ae doubt! I hae ne'er come up against ae more cunnin', dangerous enemy. He's lik' snow on ae sunny dae. First he's there, then he's naught. He's brilliant. He's cauld. He's guid at slippin' through the tightest fist. Then a' ye hae is the slimy evidence he was there at one time! But I'll get him someday. Once he's struck down, the others 'ill slink away an' behave themselves. They think he's immortal. He can get them tae dare anything. They'd follow him tae hell an' back if he ordered it. He's ae legend aroun' these parts. But once he's dead, they'll think twice afore challengin' the cavalry!" he snarled contemptuously.

"You believe the Indians would make peace with us if this Gray Eagle was slain?" she questioned curiously.

Perspiration beaded upon his forehead. His brow furrowed in serious thought. "I dou' it," he finally admitted. "But we'd stan' ae better chance o' vict'ry an' survival if he fell tae our bullets." His frank honesty brought a smile to her face.

"You seem to have many soldiers here. Why can't they ride to his camp and take him prisoner? Or perhaps capture him while he's raiding innocent people like us?"

"'Tis naught tha' easy, Rebecca. He's quick an' sharp. He's nae ae fool. The way I see it, he knows ev'ry move I mak' whilst it's still in my haed! I hae tried tae trap him, trick him, bait him, an' attack him. Nothing works. Maybe the Indians're right. Maybe he does possess some pow'rful black magic or ae charmed life. 'Is pow'r comes frae the devil, I daresae."

"Have you ever seen him or met him?" she asked, her eyes wide with wonder and suspense.

"Only frae ae distance through fieldglasses. I hae ne'er seen such ar'ergance an' confidence.

There's ae look 'n his eyes which could chill ye blood an' soul. Ae man wad be ae fool naught tae respec' him an' his pow'r," he declared to the young girl who knew all too well how that piercing ebony stare could unsettle a person!

"This brave you captured, how do you know it's his son?"

"Mos' Indians wi'out warpaint look much the same. But this lad is the spittin' image o' the Eagle himself. It's somethin' about their size, looks, an' color which stands out," he replied.

"I don't understand," she murmured, intrigued by his description which sounded envious.

"If they be naught Indians, ye could call 'em han'some. They hae bold, insolent features. They look a' muscle an' pow'r. Then, their skin's ae golden br'wn color; whereas, mos' Indians 're ae reddish shade or ae deep br'wn. I wad recognize them anywhere."

"You called him a lad. How old is he?" she quizzed.

"'Bout ye age. But in ev'ryway that counts, he's ae full grown warrior. Just as vicious an' hostile as his papa. He wad slit ye throat wi'out e'en thinkin' about it."

She feigned shock and dismay. "Thank goodness you have him locked up securely. Are you planning to trade him for white captives or execute him?" she inquired, hoping to keep her tone from revealing her emotional interest in the brave's fate.

"I hae nae decided yet. One thin' for sure, it wanna do tae kill ae lad of his impor'ance too quickly or too lightly. I'm kinda surprised his papa hasna come tae parlay for his release," he muttered suspiciously. "Devils they be, but they hae close knit families."

"What if this Gray Eagle doesn't know you have his son? Or he might think he's dead already. Possibly he doubts you know who this brave is. If so, then to come here would only reveal his identity," she reasoned.

"Ye could be right. I hae considered that idea myself. But he's ae smart one, an' I'd bet my stripes he knows we hae him. If he knows me as well as I know him, he thinks I'm waitin' tae see his reaction. He's probably out there now within sight o' us plannin' some darin' rescue. Nae put it past him. He'd challenge the Devil himself if he had somethin' that belonged tae him!" he stated.

"I'm afraid, Timothy. Why don't you make some deal with him if he's that dangerous and powerful? What if they attack us?" She feigned the appropriate fear and tremors which were certainly expected of her in this dire situation.

"Wha'er I said, lass, He's nae fool. He knows he canna tak' this fort. If he tried, the first casualty wad be his son," he remarked, confident in his own power.

He surprised and thrilled her by asking, "Sae, wad ye lik' tae tak' ae peek at 'im?"

She had wondered how she could get close enough to give Bright Arrow her secret messages without seeming overly eager or looking suspicious. Anxiety filled her eyes. What if Bright Arrow showed recognition of her? Yet, Timothy read this apprehension as fear of any Indian.

As she hesitated, he said, "Ye dinna hae tae, lass. I know ye fear an' pain 're still fresh."

"If you're certain he's locked up securely, then I would like a look at him. Then, I can tell my children I saw the son of Gray Eagle himself. I've seen regular Indians and fiendish warriors before, but never one as important as this one. Is he as famous as his father? What's his name?"

He chuckled at her girlish notions of evil villains and romantic heroes. For now, her curiosity was greater than her fear, or so he assumed. "He canna harm ye, lass. He's naught the Div'l 'imself in spite o' wha' I said. For certain, he's doing his damnest tae be ae match for 'is father. But who can blame 'em? In his place, I'd do the same. Name's Bright Ar'er. Rumor calls him the shinin' light tae guide his people. Says he's straight an' true lik' ae real ar'er, an' just as deadly. Come along. See for yeself if I should quake in my boots," he teased.

Just before they reached the blockhouse, she halted. Timothy reached out to take her hand. "Dinna worry, lass. He canna get tae ye. I'll be right beside ye."

She looked up at him and smiled. "With you beside me, I shouldn't fear anything or anyone, Timothy. It's just that I'm a little scared to look at another Indian after they attacked our wagon train and killed my people only a few days ago. If your men hadn't rescued me in that arrow-wood forest, that warrior with the red and green dots upon his face might have found me and . . ." She ceased her talk, not because of her insinuation but because she needed to recall the other clues for the alert ears of Bright Arrow who was standing behind the wooden bars only a few feet from them, his face impassive and his eyes fathomless.

"After travelling alone in that forest for two days, I was beginning to lose all hope of rescue. I was giving up when Sergeant Smith found me. I was so tired and hungry. I can almost hear those eerie birds that sing at night. Any other time, their singing might have been soothing and enjoyable. But I was too frightened. It was like evil spirits calling my name. But how could you understand? I bet you'd never known or felt fear in your entire life. I sometimes wish I were a man: strong, brave, and carefree."

"I'm sorely glad ye be naught ae man," he joked lightly. "Fear is nothin' tae be ashamed o', Rebecca. It teaches us caution, an' wisdom, an' patience."

"This Gray Eagle you spoke of, what would you do if he offered a truce in trade for his son? What if he offered to exchange himself for his son? Just think of the fame you would receive: Lieutenant Timothy Moore captures the legendary Gray Eagle himself!" she exclaimed in excitement. "You said you knew this Gray Eagle well. Would he trade his life for his son's? You said his death would deal the Indians a fatal blow. Why don't you suggest it? That way, you could have a truce, Gray Eagle, and great honor all wrapped up as tightly as a rabbit in a hawk's claw."

He chuckled mischievously. "It wad'na work, Rebecca."

"Why not? You said this Bright Arrow was as important as Gray Eagle. Besides, Gray Eagle must be getting old and his son is young. It only seems logical to save the younger warrior. If that were your son in there, would you let him die?"

"Nae way! E'en sae, I'd find another way tae save him."

"But you just said no one could get inside this fort or would dare attack it," she reminded him.

"He knows I wad nae kill Bright Ar'er without ae great deal o' thought. He'll use that

383

time tae come up wi' some cunnin' plan tae free him. Tell me, lass; if that was your son or husband, wad ye trade ye life for his?"

"I'm ashamed to admit that I might be too cowardly and selfish to do something so noble and dangerous. It could be a trick and then we'd both be captured and killed. Even so, I think I would risk anything for someone I loved, especially a child I had borne." She craftily added to prevent any hints of deception, "Could we go now? I'm very tired." She did look extremely weary.

"Sure, lass, an' ye can now tell our children that ye've met the notorious Bright Ar'er, son o' the infamous Gray Eagle," he stated wistfully.

"Our children?" she innocently echoed.

"I hae nae doubts ye'll agree tae marry me in one week. An' naturally we'll have lots of babies." He grinned roguishly.

"Babies?" she echoed fearfully.

"'Tis naught an unknown word tae ye, is it?" he teased.

"No. I just never thought about love and marriage or babies," she shyly confessed.

"Well, lass, ye hae one week tae think plenty. I wanna allow ye tae say nae," he whispered, half-serious, half-jesting. A wife, a home, and babies . . . Why not?

Her head jerked up and her eyes widened. "There go those night-birds again! They remind me of those dark hours when I was running and hiding in the forest." She shuddered.

"Time tae go inside. Ye be chilled." He took her hand and led her away, unaware of the jet eyes which drilled into his body, then softened as they shifted to the dainty girl who was hurrying to keep up with his lengthy strides.

Chapter Thirteen

Bright Arrow apprehensively paced the close confines of his prison. His thoughts warred with each other as he tried to figure out how Rebecca had entered the fort. He could not imagine his father trusting this white captive enough to allow her to come here and attempt to free him!

Yet, he had discerned her messages in her deceptively innocent words. A thought more inconceivable flashed across his mind. Her words could only mean that Gray Eagle had communicated with her in English! That also meant she now knew he understood and spoke English! He wondered why she did not feel betrayed and vengeful. In her place, he would! Such a risky mission was highly dangerous, even more so for such a young and inexperienced girl. Why had his father allowed her to come here? How could she possibly free him? He knew . . . she already had that smug Bluecoat beguiled by her beauty and innocence. But for his father to trust her this much?

Calling to mind certain words which she had spoken within his hearing, he smiled. She actually loved him enough to forgive his silent betrayal, to risk her own life to save his, and to challenge any danger to free him. But if the Bluecoats caught her trying to release him . . . her resulting fate was too awful to consider. It was too late; she was here. Her plan, or his father's, was already in motion. Without alerting others to his knowledge of the English tongue or to his closeness to her, he could not plead with her to drop this charade.

Speculating upon this unique woman he loved and desired, he wondered if she was cunning and daring enough to carry off such a far-fetched plan. Why had she clearly hinted at his leaving her here? How could he possibly ride off and leave his love behind to face the results of his escape?

Did she plan to escape herself later and return to him? Was there another side to this brazen scheme? Did his father have other plans in mind for her, for her eventual return to his side?

Dread washed over him. Had they made some deal: his rescue in exchange for her freedom? Did she want to remain here with her own people? But she loved him! She had proven this in countless ways. Did she wish to call a halt to their forbidden love which only tormented both of them? Was she here to free him in more than one way?

His muscles grew taut and strained. He clenched his jaw in suppressed rage. His father had no right to make such a deal: she was his captive! It couldn't be true. She loved him and had pleaded never to leave him. She could never return to the whites; they would never accept a used squaw. He paced the small confines of the nearly airless cell.

Rebecca had come to help him. That fact alone was staggering. If only he knew the terms of their agreement. If only he knew if she truly wanted to part with him. But even if that thought had not crossed her mind before, now that she was back with her own kind she might wish to remain here. Doubtlessly, freeing him was nearly impossible. If so, at least she was safe and free. Safe! he furiously scoffed. Safe in the grasping claws of another man!

Rebecca demurely sat across the table from the Scottish rogue who ruled the fort. Baffled by the stew she was eagerly consuming, she questioned Timothy about the vegetables. Timothy chuckled gleefully as he told her about the potato eyes which a farmer had brought with him and planted inside the fort wall outside the spiked wooden fence. The far-sighted Irishman had also planted carrots and a variety of other vegetables. The venison stew had been simmered for hours and was delicious. She relished each mouthful as she politely listened to his talk.

When Timothy offered her a small cup of Irish whiskey, she wisely refused it, saying, "Papa never allowed we womenfolk to partake of strong spirits, but thank you, sir." She presented him with a feigned look of sadness at the recall of her fictitious father, as would be expected of a girl who had so recently lost her family.

"Dinna look sae sad, lass," he encouraged. "Ye've naught tae fear. I know ye heart be filled wi' loneliness, but 'twill pass in time. Ye mus' think o' yeself now. Ye people be gone. Life goes on," he concluded solemnly, not wishing to appear unfeeling.

"I know, sir . . . Timothy. But it's so hard to adjust to sudden losses and changes. I can't help but worry what my life will be without my family. You're a man; men know nothing of being a helpless female. We're not allowed to exist as you do. If I were a strong man, I could help myself."

"If ye were ae strong man, ye'd be ae dead one. Ye wad hae fought them Injuns lik' the others and died along wit' them. Hae ye nae joy in being ae bonny lass?" he queried her earnestly.

She mused over his sincere and serious words in light of her shameful deception. "I honestly don't know. Perhaps in time I will." She sighed heavily as if totally exhausted. She was, but from the mental stress of this game.

"Ye be tired, lass. It's off tae bed wit' ye. We dinna hae tae linger o'er dinner sae long. Ye sleep in my room an' I'll bed down out 'ere. Ye hae nothing tae concern ye lovely head wit'. I'll protect ye frae now on," he gallantly promised, then flashed her an engaging grin.

She smiled warmly and bid him goodnight. She went into his room and lay down upon the hard, but inviting, bunk. She tossed for a while, then fell into slumber.

It was a while before the excited Timothy could fall asleep upon his bedroll in his office. His amorous thoughts lingered upon the beautiful girl occupying his bedroom. Having Rebecca Kenny dropped into his lap was a sheer stroke of luck! She was totally alone, helpless, and emotionally vulnerable . . . or so he believed.

Most of the following day was spent under the watchful eye and in the intriguing company of Timothy Moore. He made certain his rough men showed her the proper respect and courtesy. Each time she appeared sad or thoughtful, he would draw her from her pensive or somber mood with colorful tales of his past adventures.

He told her how he had received this commission and how he had studied the failures of the last commander to prevent committing his same mistakes. He spoke of the notorious Gray Eagle and his daring exploits. In awe and surprise, she learned of the recent unsuccessful siege upon this fort. She intently listened to his explanation of this bloody and endless warfare. Knowing both sides, her mind instantly debated each one.

Yet, Timothy won himself a measure of respect from her. It was clear he presented Gray Eagle with a worthy opponent: cunning, alert, steadfast, and daring. Tragically, there could only be one victor in their final skirmish. She was forced to admit that Timothy Moore was a most unusual and arresting male. He was ruggedly good-looking and extremely charming. In spite of her cautions to herself, she discovered herself laughing merrily at his stories and gaily quipping back before she could catch herself. She fretted over this vivacious and serene conduct in a girl who had just faced unmentionable horrors.

She needn't have worried at all. A smug Timothy viewed it as his doing. He continually congratulated himself on his great prowess and disarming manner. Despite her recent losses and heartache, she could not resist his wit and magnetism! He prided himself on being able to lure her from her self pity and misery. After all, she was very young and susceptible. To those of her age, death was like a bad dream, an illusion. The present moment was reality. Soon, she would no longer withdraw from him.

Each time they strolled around the fort, Rebecca would nonchalantly study its interior for any weakness. By mid-morning of the second day, she knew where each hidden gate was located; she knew where the men slept and worked; she knew their schedules and names. This familiarity had a certain disadvantage. Before she came here, they had all been anonymous enemies who were imprisoning her love. Now, they were names and faces. The only thought which compelled her to carry on this farce was the reality that no life would be taken during her rescue of Bright Arrow.

Bright Arrow . . . she had not been given any opportunity to get near him since that first day. Wanting her to forget her painful experience as quickly as possible, Timothy did not take her near the blockhouse again. Nor did he mention the illustrious brave who was held within it. Fearing suspicion, Rebecca wisely withheld all questions about him. Yet, each time she strolled upon the arm of Timothy Moore, she could feel the force of those ebony eyes upon them. How she longed to gaze into them! How she hungered for his kisses and caresses! Hopefully this nightmare would soon be over.

* * *

Rebecca was accurate; Bright Arrow witnessed every meeting she had outdoors with his fearless white foe. As he restlessly lay upon the thin, dirty blanket, he inwardly raged at what might be taking place between that lovestruck white man and his own beloved Rebecca, the woman who would do anything to secure his freedom and survival. How he yearned to break out of this restricting tepee, to slay his self-appointed enemies, and to rescue his woman. Could he bear the humiliation of being released by a mere white captive?

If he was to live to love and to fight another day, he would have to deny his pride and accept Rebecca's assistance. He desperately needed to be free of this imprisoning stockade. With only one small window and the July sun beating down without mercy during the long day, this place was tormenting. There was little room to exercise and to keep his lithe body in shape and to keep his reflexes sharp and alert. He had been given little edible food to maintain his strength and vigor. But why waste food and water on a dying man? These past four moons had sluggishly passed without sufficient food, water, sun, and fresh air; the heavy toll on his spirit, energy, and patience was rapidly increasing.

He had not been permitted outside the hewn walls of this timbered place since his arrival. What little air there was reeked of urine from past prisoners and this present captive. He craved fresh food, a walk in the cool forest, a dip in the refreshing stream, an intake of crisp air, a clean blanket, a vengeful retaliation, a night of love with his woman, a look at his camp and parents: freedom and all her wondrous faces.

He hung his head in shame, tasting his degrading defeat and display of weakness. Surely the Great Spirit would not allow him to die in this shameful manner; a warrior should die in battle, defending his lands and people. His last words should be ones of greatness. He should not start his walk upon the ghost-trail with the taunts of white enemies singing within his ears. His life should not end with ropes binding his body. How could he face the Great Spirit with this stain of dishonor?

He went to the small opening and inhaled several breaths of air, noting the guard on duty. His heart was heavy; his little one could not defeat a powerful man who watched over him sun and moon. It was futile; he was certain to die soon. Yet, dying did not frighten or distress him; it was the manner of his death which tore at his troubled mind. If only Moore would place him within a tight circle of armed enemies and allow him to die while battling his foes, even without a weapon of any kind. If only he could die honorably. But what did white-eyes know of honor!

He walked over to the left side of this keep and

picked up the nasty blanket. He shook it and spread it upon the hard ground. He lay down upon it. He could not sleep; his mind helplessly returned to the scene of his defeat. He closed his dark and stormy eyes to envision what had taken place a few moons past, to discover what he had done wrong, to learn why he was the white man's captive, to determine if this defeat could have been avoided . . .

The Oglala warriors had gone to the camp of the Brule and Cheyenne with a message of the new war council to be held in the Oglala camp. They had ridden to the Sisseton village to deliver this same invitation. Chief Night Hawk and three band leaders had mounted up to return with him and his two warriors.

As they had travelled along, the Sisseton warriors had been relating their recent battles with the Bluecoats. Bright Arrow had been in the lead with Deer-Stalker close behind him. They reached a point where the trail between the Sisseton and Oglala villages passed between two large groupings of boulders and lofty rock formations. There were only a few scrub trees, prickly bushes, scattered clumps of buffalo grass, and slender cottonwoods in view; nothing large enough to conceal a hidden enemy.

Since crafty Indians were known to secret themselves amongst such groupings of rocks, most Bluecoats and settlers did not venture near them.

Their band had been elated and relaxed, unaware of the peril before them. They had laughed and joked as they had dauntlessly entered the narrow trail which traversed the middle of this canyon. The moment they had exited at the other end, the Bluecoats had fallen upon them: armed men against unsuspecting, weaponless foes. The following moments were a blur to Bright Arrow, for things had happened quickly.

A large unit of Bluecoats had instantly surrounded them from both sides. With loud shouts, slashing sabers, roaring gunfire, and deep-rooted hatred, they had charged forward to slay his entire band. The Indian war cry had seared his ears from several directions at once. There had been only enough time for a few of them to draw knives and tomahawks to defend themselves. The battle had been lost from the first moment.

He shuddered at the recall of Deer-Stalker's body which had suffered jagged gashes from more than one strike from the Long-Knives' deadly sabers. Talking-Rock had received two gaping holes from destructive fire-sticks. One of the Sisseton warriors had a crushed skull from the forcefully delivered blows from the butts of those same fire-sticks. It had been a gruesome, bloody sight which had greeted his gaze as he had sat motionless in the midst of five well-armed foes, their weapons trained upon his rage-taut frame. His own knife had been knocked from his grasp during his previous battle.

He rubbed his still smarting hand with its bruised flesh. He was extremely lucky it wasn't broken. It needed some herbs upon the cuts; but these hateful white-eyes had neither cared for his injury nor offered him a bandage.

He had sat proud and erect upon his mottled Appaloosa. His face had remained impassive and contemptuous of his danger and enemies. Only his turbulent gaze had exposed his inner rage, which was tightly leashed. He had appeared to calmly await his own death. None had been offered him! A stalwart man in blue and yellow had approached him the moment the skirmish had been decided.

Bright Arrow's keen gaze had pierced this white man who had ordered the wanton slaughter of his warriors and his allies. This Bluecoat's carriage had revealed pride and confidence in his own prowess and position. His feet were clad in shiny black boots, then covered in dust. Many yellow slashes decorated his uniform's sleeves. A yellow bandanna was knotted loosely at his throat. Upon his hat was a circle which surrounded two crossed sabers, a likeness to the shiny weapon which swung from his narrow waist. Fieldglasses rested upon his chest from a strap around his neck. His hair was flaming red, hanging to his collar, coming from beneath his cocked hat to grow upon the sides of his face to where his strong jawline began. His face was smooth and clean-shaven in the white man's custom.

Lines of cruelty etched his face. His eyes were brittle blue, cold and unfeeling. As he reined in his mount, a look of surprise crossed his face, followed by irate disappointment. Bright Arrow had observed this mighty foe with great intensity and intrigue.

"The infamous Bright Ar'er," he had sneered in contempt and annoyance. "Frae ae distance, ye look lik' ye father. I hae hoped tae entrap the Eagle himself," he confessed, telling Bright Arrow this man had been lying in wait here to capture his father. His fieldglasses had deceived him!

"Nae matter," he concluded. "Ye be just as guid as ye father. 'Tis ae wonder wha' he'll trade fur ye . . . ," he pondered aloud, his mind considering this delightful situation. "Wad ae man exchange his life fur tha' o' his son?"

The lilting burr in this white man's voice was difficult for Bright Arrow to interpret. Yet, he understood enough to discern his plans. Two soldiers had wrestled with the Indian brave as they attempted to bind him with several ropes. Once bound, their leader had taken his reins and ordered his troop to move out and back to the fort.

It was that moment when Bright Arrow had

been given the chance to view their bloody triumph. Only he and Chief Night Hawk remained alive, but the older chief was wounded badly. He had not seen his elder friend since their arrival here, nor had he heard his name or state of health mentioned. Had he died or been killed? Maintaining his silence, Bright Arrow had not asked. He had continued to present an unaffected, stoic expression and dauntless air.

Moore had tried to question him several times. He had even called upon the fort's scout to interpret his words; Bright Arrow had responded to neither. His scornful gaze had swept both men before he had turned his broad back upon them. Moore had snapped, "Ye be an arr'gant devil! Just lik' ye papa! But ye be ae man, son, and ye'll die lik' one." Bright Arrow had wondered at the irrepressible tone of begrudging respect in Moore's voice. Was it possible that the white-eyes also respected a worthy adversary? This conclusion was new, perplexing!

Since Rebecca's surprise arrival, Moore had ignored him completely! His full concentration had been upon her. Rebecca had not been brought to view her intrepid enemy again; wisely, she had also ignored him. He jealously watched them each time they appeared outside his wooden tepee. He strained to hear her laughter and words. She was playing her game well, for she had Moore bewitched. What plagued his troubled mind was the events he could not witness and the words he could not overhear. How far would his Rebecca go to win Moore's confidence and affection? He could not even force himself to imagine the answer.

It was evident to Bright Arrow that Moore would never release him or trade him. During his incarceration, he had learned too many secrets. He had discovered the reason for their unsuccessful siege upon the fort: the hidden water supply, the hefty store of supplies, the number of men and weapons, and the concealed gates in the fort's walls. To exchange him for any number of white captives or the Eagle himself, would also exchange the vital information which Bright Arrow now possessed.

This very night, just before Wi had left to sleep, Moore had come to visit him. That conversation still rankled his warring emotions. It was too late for him, and his forbidden love was in the control of this powerful foe.

Moore had stood at the small window, staring at him for a long time in brooding silence. Bright Arrow had returned his piercing glare. Finally, he had spoken, "I canna free ye, lad, nae trade ye. Ye be ae man o' honor. Ye know I mus' kill ye. Ye fate 'twas sealed when ye 'ere born ae redskin. 'Twill do us both ae fav'r tae end it. Tae'morr'r, Bright Ar'er. I dinna risk waitin' nae more. I got tae turn my 'tention tae other matters. I got ae woman tae think o'. Pray tae ye

Great Spirit, lad, fur ye'll join 'em afore another moon.'' He had turned and slowly walked away . . .

It was settled; he would die with the coming sun; there was nothing and no one to save him. His mind and body were exhausted, but he could not sleep. The events from the first moment he had laid eyes upon Rebecca Kenny to the present crawled through his mind.

Rebecca nervously and silently paced Timothy Moore's bedroom. For the past two and a half days, she had patiently and apprehensively bided her time as she watched for the opportunity to release her Indian lover. No daylight hour or moment of nightly protective shadow had presented such a moment. Each time Timothy had lingered for conversation or a meeting in the cookhouse, soldiers had always been scattered around in the courtyard. In the midst of darkest night, she had also been denied any opportunity to sneak out; Timothy slept upon a bedroll in his office, between her and the door. She had frequently noted the sentry's rounds beyond the only bedroom window, preventing that path of assistance.

Each passing hour had instilled her with the reality that Bright Arrow's time was steadily and relentlessly running out. Not one meager chance to attempt his release! she fretted in fear and alarm. Things had not gone as expected or planned. She had not counted upon a love-struck commander! She had not considered a total lack of solitude at night! Everything had gone differently than imagined.

Instead of instantly going to work for Timothy and his men to earn her keep, she had been pampered and guarded like a valuable treasure! Most of her time had been spent in the commander's company or barricaded in his bedroom.

Rebecca cocked her ear toward the door crack. The soldiers chatted and joked for a few more minutes. Then to her horror, she heard Timothy casually announce he had decided to hang Bright Arrow from the large wahoo tree outside the fort's walls: hang him at sunrise tomorrow!

She quaked, nearly fainting from shock. Time had cruelly deserted her! Bright Arrow's release appeared impossible. Yet, an attempt must be made tonight or never. Never . . . the word's finality shocked her terrified brain.

"Never touch him again? Never see him again?" she whispered in anguish. How could she allow her love and life to end in this bitter and savage manner? Never! Never! Never! the awesome word drummed within her head and heart like an ominous chant until she covered her ears to shut out the tragic song. Tears of agony eased down her cheeks as echoes and images of shared ecstasy flooded her mind . . .

Chapter Fourteen

About midnight, Rebecca stared out the window which faced the back wall of the fort. Although there was very little moonlight with which to study her hazardous surroundings, the cramped area directly before her line of vision was deserted. She whispered a fervent prayer, summoned her lagging courage, and stretched out her trembling hands to open the back window. Anger and despair flooded her tense body; it was stuck. As she prayed for guidance and assistance, her panicky gaze found the pin-like peg which hindered her progress. In renewed hope and suspense, she struggled with the stubborn peg to pull it from its hole. Just as she was about to give up this seemingly futile battle, the peg moved and finally pulled free. She sighed in relief and offered up a prayer of gratitude.

Taking care not to make any noise, she set the peg down. To her surprise and delight, the window lifted without a sound. She peered outside. She scanned the direction of the enlisted men's barracks. Not a single soul could be sighted in the narrow area between the two-story complex and the lofty back wall. Thanks to the unusual chill in the night air, most windows along the back of that wooden structure were closed. She climbed out carefully to prevent any excessive noise, then lifted her blanket out behind her. She wrapped the dark blanket around her slender body to hide her clothing. Rebecca hastily glanced in both directions, hesitating briefly as the dangers and rewards of this daring episode rushed into her mind. Knowing what was at stake, she cast aside all thoughts to failure.

She inhaled deeply several times to slow her racing heart, then made her way to the corner of the building that housed Timothy's quarters. Calling upon every ounce of courage she possessed, she peered around the edge of the wooden structure. As with the enlisted men's quarters, not a lantern light or man could be sighted. She stared at the distance to the other end of this building; it seemed an eternity away.

She observed the seven windows which opened into the officers' rooms. What would happen if only one of them came to his window to catch a breath of fresh air? As she paused in self-doubt, her gaze touched upon the block-house at the far end of this structure: that ominous location which contained the reason for her life or death. Her wary gaze thoroughly scanned the rear of this building, yet no human sound invaded her senses.

To her, it all seemed too perfect. She waited at the corner of the building for a long time. Aware of the swift passage of time which could tragically defeat her, she readied herself to accept whatever perilous fate could result. She bent forward and quietly made her way to the other end of this timbered structure, not daring to halt or to glance up in soul-shaking fear of meeting the gaze of one of those officers.

She gingerly peered around the edge of the abode. Alarm washed over her body and rushed into her turbulent mind, for the rest of the distance to the blockhouse was across open space. She leaned against the hard surface of the wooden facade hardly daring to breathe. The back of the blockhouse was constructed against the front and side walls of the mighty fort, offering no secret space or darkness to conceal herself once she approached it.

Without any concern to the health or comfort of captives, the side of the imprisoning structure before her line of vision was windowless. In her horror, she promptly recalled there was only one window in the blockhouse: a small opening near the securely barred door which faced the adjacent supply shed. With this set-up, there was no way she could observe the entrance to the jail or assess its security measures.

Her heart lurched; there was a guard on duty. She nervously watched the man in the navy blue uniform with its yellow trim who had suddenly appeared from between the five feet of empty space which separated the blockhouse from the supply shed. She keenly observed the soldier who indifferently held his long weapon by the tip of the barrel. He sighed heavily as if utterly bored. He aimlessly paced back and forth as if making some critical decision. Unknown to the panicky girl, he most assuredly was. What now? she fretted.

As if suddenly sensing eyes upon him, the guard glanced around. She flattened her slender, shapely frame against the rough wall. But in fact, he was simply looking to see if anyone was about to note his rash departure. Time slipped into limbo as she awaited his impending decision which would affect many people. He was sleepy and had decided to go to the cookhouse for some black coffee. After all, he rashly concluded to himself, what could happen in only a few minutes? He casually strolled off in the opposite direction of the cookhouse, fortunately located in the shadowy corner on the other side of the front wall.

The careless guard nonchalantly strolled past the supply shed, the vacant area before the front gates where he roguishly waved to the sentry on duty high above him on the rampart, past the combination doctor's quarters and infirmary, and into the cookhouse. Rebecca watched him closely and intently. Either her prayers were being answered or something weird was going on! Was she being tricked into exposing herself? Did Timothy suspect her treachery? Was he allowing her to trap herself? No matter, this was the only chance she would have.

She hurried over to the front corner of the building and looked around into the empty courtyard, ecstatic no one was about. In the shadow of the two-story supply shed, she knew the sentry could not spot her. She quietly made her way between this building and the jail. Alertly looking about, she eased to the edge of this new challenge to make certain there was not another guard left behind. Sighting no one to stop her, she rushed over to the door which separated her from her beloved. She lifted the bar off the hooks and hastily opened it. Bright Arrow's arresting face appeared before her frightened eyes. "Hurry! He'll be back soon," she whispered to her Indian lover.

She put the bar back in place, hoping that would prevent a prompt discovery of their actions. He silently followed her over to the back of the tall wooden building. "There are soldiers asleep inside. We must be very quiet. Your father is waiting for you at the big tree.

There is a door in the fence," she whispered, pointing to it. "You must go quickly and silently before the guard returns. Be careful, Bright Arrow," she fearfully entreated, eyes caressing his face.

"You must come with me," he stated in clear English.

She sadly shook her head as she softly argued, "It's too risky. You can move faster without me. I would only slow you down. I'll join you soon. Your father will explain it to you. Go quickly. I must get back before discovery. I love you, Bright Arrow," she declared to her warrior.

He kissed her and held her tightly. "I cannot leave you here. You are my heart now. I love you, Rebecca. They will torture you for helping me escape."

Their eyes met and fused. Harsh laughter broke this romantic spell as the returning guard joked with the sentry. Fear travelled her lovely features. "You must go now. The soldiers will never suspect a mere girl of releasing the awesome Bright Arrow," she teased to lighten his worries, then continued seriously, "I will come to you later. I promise. I could never live without you. Please hurry before both our lives are endangered."

"There are many things I do not understand and must know. But I cannot linger to hear them. If you do not return to my arms and tepee, I will come back for you," he vowed, his mind in turmoil at these confusing events. Yet, he vividly recalled how taken the commanding officer was with his woman. She was right; who would suspect a tiny white girl of this brazen feat of daring and courage?

"You are also my heart. I have no life without you. Your father promised I could remain at your side once I escape," she softly informed her lover.

He kissed her, then reluctantly made his way to the door. He opened it quietly and was gone. With great care to silence, she hurried back to the window. It was extremely difficult, but she finally found her feet upon the wooden floor inside Timothy's bedroom. She gingerly pulled the window sash down and replaced the wooden peg. She hurriedly went to the bunk and lay down. It was done. He was free. She dreaded to think of trying to get through the tightened security which his escape would surely bring about in the morning. She closed her eyes and wept, fearing she had seen him for the last time, praying she had not.

"He loves me," she whispered happily. "At least he loves me ... Be happy and free, my love, for I know how special that is." It was a long time before peaceful slumber could ease her cares and fatigue.

Rebecca yawned and stretched contentedly. She rubbed her heavy eyes and sat up, resting her back against the rough wall. Her puzzled eyes fused with the stormy blue ones of Timothy Moore. He had placed a ladder-back chair near her bed and had straddled it. His arms were folded, resting upon its back; his cleft chin was propped upon his interlocking hands. He was glaring at her. One booted foot began to drum ominously upon the wooden floor. She glanced down at this curious motion, then back up at him. She was utterly perplexed by his odd behavior. For if her part in last night's treachery had been uncovered, he wouldn't have waited until mid-morning to seek out the guilty culprit.

"Well?" he demanded harshly. The intensity of his fury made his eyes appear two shades darker than their normal blue. "Did ye sleep well, my lovely angel?" he inquired, his voice terse and his eyes challenging.

She stared at him. "Timothy, is something wrong?" she softly questioned.

"Timothy, is something wrong?" he bitterly mocked her in a frigid tone. "Ye sit there all innocent-lik' wi' those doe eyes an' ask me what's wrong? I should'av know ye were tae guid tae be true! Ye filthy doxy! Ye cunning bitch! How dare ye mak' ae fool o' me! Tell me, Rebecca, whose whore be ye? Gray Eagle's or Bright Ar'er's?" he crudely demanded. His eyes blazed with hostility and hatred.

She whitened. "What did you say?" she asked in disbelief and shock.

"Dinna play that innocent, little lass routine on me! I should slit ye lying throat right now. Why dinna ye flee wi' him?" he snarled, his knuckles blanching white as he balled his hands into tight fists.

"Leave with whom? What are you talking about? What have I done to make you so angry?" she questioned. He knows! her terrified brain warned. What now? What justifiable reason could she offer for releasing him? What monstrous punishment would be meted out for this odious crime? She suddenly recognized the absurdity in Gray Eagle's crafty plan. She should have fled with her lover. There was no logical reason for her remaining behind! Logical, no; cunning, yes . . . In the darkness and solitude, why couldn't she have fled as quietly and quickly as Bright Arrow?

Timothy jumped up, knocking the chair to the floor. He furiously kicked it out of his path. He swaggered forward, slowly and menacingly. Her back to the wall, she could retreat no further. A hand snaked out and landed a stunning slap across her right cheek, sending her senses to whirling wildly and fearfully. "Nothing is more deadly than a crossed man," her father's warning echoed from the past.

A livid print was instantly visible. Slender, white welts gradually appeared in the midst of a fiery red background. Blood eased from the corner of her lip and rolled down her trembling chin. She was paralyzed by the brutality of his sudden attack and the awesome animosity which oozed from him. Her wide eyes mirrored her fear and alarm.

"Naught sae cunnin' an' brave anymore, are ye, harlot?" he scoffed venomously. "I asked whose whore ye be! Is it Gray Eagle or his son? I'll brook nae more lies," he stormed at the frightened girl.

"Neither," she replied in a tremulous voice. Her shaking hand went up to her stinging cheek. She touched the blood which flowed from her throbbing lip. She peered down at her crimson-tinged fingers. She paled and shuddered, unable to pull her gaze from them.

Timothy grabbed a handful of auburn hair and harshly yanked her head backwards, forcing her terrified gaze to lock with his belligerent one. She cried out in pain and alarm. Tears filled her panicked eyes. "For all ye cunnin' deceit, whore, ye overlooked one thing. My own eyes followed ye trail all the way tae an' froe the blockhouse. Ye see, me lovely traitor; tae avoid the dust, the yard is swept each night wi' ae brush-broom after my men turn in. Ye tracks were as clear as ae sunny dae!"

He seized her slender wrists and held her hands up before her ashen face. "Ye should hae washed the blood off ye hands an' my window peg. Tae, ye smeared the dust on the window sill climbin' in an' out. Yer crime is as naked as the

414

dae ye was born. I'm nae fool, whore. The only thing which puzzles me is why ye stayed behind. What's the plan tae get ye out safely?'' he demanded.

Trapped, she knew her fate was sealed. What a blind and stupid fool she had been! With one sly ploy, Gray Eagle's son was both free of his white captors and of his white captive! Tricked! Deceived! Betrayed!

Timothy yanked upon her hair again, forcing her to cry out in anguish. He laughed harshly. "That be naught compared tae wha' ye'll soon suffer, whore. Ye owe me an' my men plenty. We'll collect ye debts afore we toss ye body out tae him," he threatened.

She wasn't afraid to die, but to endure degradation first . . . She closed her eyes. Those telltale tracks denied any hope of using fresh air as an excuse for opening the window last night. Tears joined the trail of blood, dropping steadily to her dress. "Believe it or not, Timothy, but it couldn't be helped. I'm . . . sorry," she whispered softly.

"Sorry!" he thundered at her. "Ye dinna know wha' it is tae be sorry yet! The only regret ye hae is being discovered sae ye canna return tae his mats! Why, damn ye?" he exploded. "Ye be white, nae Injun!"

Assailed, she desperately lied to him, her eyes and expression revealing an honest despair and sadness. "Because he is holding my parents and little sister captive. That first day I came here, you asked if I would risk my life for someone I loved; as you can see, the answer is yes. I did free the Indian brave, and I would do it all again. I couldn't stand my family's torture anymore. It's far easier to die, Timothy, than to stand there helplessly watching and listening to your own family being . . ." Could she pull off this deception? she wondered in terror. Could she outwit Gray Eagle's lethal treachery or dispel Timothy's suspicions?

She swallowed and inhaled raggedly. "It doesn't matter now. He'll probably kill them anyway. Papa said an Indian was a man of his word, but I don't believe it's true. I think Papa was only trying to convince me to come here so at least one of us could escape torment and death. God, what am I doing here in this savage land?" she cried out in anguish. She had lost Bright Arrow, and now she would lose what little dignity she had left. Strange, but her defeat would ironically come at the hands of her own people and not his, just as the truculent chief had plotted.

Timothy glared at her. He abruptly released her hair. She covered her face with her hands and wept. He apprehensively paced the floor, contemplating her unexpected claims. Knowing of Gray Eagle's cunning mind and his awesome power, Timothy seriously wondered if Rebecca might now be telling the truth. Did this crafty ploy explain why Gray Eagle hadn't contacted the fort or made any attempt to attack them? Was he truly blackmailing this vulnerable girl into helping him? Her excellent acting in the preceding days spoke out against her.

"Wha' were Gray Eagle's plans, Rebecca?" he asked in a deceptively calm voice.

"I was only ordered to find some way to free Bright Arrow. I was to tell him, 'Ya wanhu. A'ta ku-wa.' There's a warrior in his camp who speaks pretty fair English. The words are supposed to mean his father was waiting near a certain tree and for him to go there after I released him. In exchange for my help, Gray Eagle promised us my family would be released and we must leave his lands. He said after Bright Arrow returned to his side, my family would be set free in exchange and sent here to get me," she lied most convincingly.

She looked up at him, her injury loudly accusing him of the same kind of savagery which he was fighting everyday. "I'm sorry for using you like that, Timothy. I didn't mean to humiliate you or to hurt you. I know it was a shameful and wicked thing to do to my own people, but especially to you. You've been so kind and gentle with me. I know you can never forgive me for betraying you in this cruel manner. Gray Eagle is far more cunning and deadly than even you imagine: he said you would never suspect a mere girl. I had to do it,

Timothy! My father told me that even if he lied and they were . . . didn't survive, at least I would be safe and free. Safe and free? Some joke, isn't it?" she scoffed bitterly. But that wasn't what ravaged her tender heart. She had been used just as vilely and deliberately as she had used Timothy.

He observed her rueful expressions and listened to her tremulous voice. Rebecca continued, "I tried to talk you into making a truce and trading him so I wouldn't have to help him. Why couldn't you have released him? How important could his death be to you? You claimed you knew Gray Eagle well. Yet, I fear you are vastly ignorant of the full measure of his power and daring."

She levelled her misty eyes upon Timothy's turbulent expression and asked gravely, "Will he keep his word? Will he release my family like he promised?"

"I'm afeared I dinna trust ye, Rebecca. Ye fooled me once, but ne'er again." Yet, he couldn't forget or explain the fact she had been left behind. A new idea struck him. "Zounds! He left ye behind tae open the gates for them tae sneak in an' kill us while we sleep! That's why ye still be 'ere!" he furiously concluded.

Aghast, she gaped at him. Even to free her lover, she would never have gone that far! "No! I would never do such a wicked thing, not even to save my own family! Sparing Bright Arrow's life to save my family is one thing, but to help the Indians massacre an entire fort? My God, Timothy, surely you can't honestly think I would do such a thing!''

''I dinna know wha' ye might or could do, Rebecca. Ye sweetly wormed ye way in 'ere an' into my life. Then ye release one of the mos' deadly warriors alive. Now, ye play the pitiful, innocent captive! An' all the while ye charmed an' wooed me, ye was plottin' agin' me!'' he snapped hatefully. ''Trust ye? Nae way, lass.'' Bitterness contorted his features.

''You'll have to when my father comes here tomorrow,'' she bravely and boldly announced. ''Then you'll see I speak the truth.''

''Nae one will be comin' 'ere, Rebecca,'' he denied her words. ''Nae one will get in or out. Ye be mine now, lass,'' he vowed.

She made one last attempt to deceptively vindicate herself, ''He won't release them? It was all for nothing?'' The tension and fear too much, she fainted.

Timothy seized her shoulders and shook her violently. ''It canna work, lass. I'm on tae ye grand actin' now.''

He gazed down into her ashen face with its fresh injury. He dropped her frame upon the bunk. After several pinches upon her cool arms without any response, he knew she wasn't pretending. He suddenly recalled her bad dream on that first day. She had cried out, ''Don't kill them." He carefully analyzed this precarious situation. What if she was telling the truth? Vexed by this enigma, he gritted his teeth until his jaw cramped.

He splashed cool water upon her colorless face, arousing her. He was looking at her in a strange manner. "Will you please wait for two days before killing me, Timothy? You can lock me in the stockade if you wish. Give my family time to get here and explain. Just two days, please . . ." she entreated wretchedly.

"If ye do hae a family in his camp, Rebecca, then I'm sorry for ye. He wanna let them go."

"But he promised! I risked my life to save his son's! What about their famed generosity and coups for courage and . . . and for keeping my end of the bargain?" she shouted at him.

"Indians dinna mak' deals wi' enemies," he announced, observing her intently from beneath slightly hooded eyes.

"Then why did he trust me to keep my word?" she argued.

"Ye tell me, lass," he somberly challenged, intrigued by this mystery before him.

She sighed wearily and vowed, "I honestly don't know. I guess because he realized how stupid and gullible I was. But Papa said . . . Papa said for me to obey him. Why, Timothy?" she sadly beseeched him.

"Why dinna ye tell me this sooner? I could hae helped," he smoothly stated, waiting for the moment she would entrap herself. "Ye Papa was wrong, lass."

"What could you have done? Ridden into his camp and rescued them?" she sneered angrily. "You know that was impossible! I was forced to help him."

"I could hae protected ye, an' kept him captive. I could hae traded him for ye family," he sought to trick her again.

She refused his tainted bait. "I asked if you would trade him for white captives, and you said no. Besides, you wouldn't have helped me once you'd heard the truth. I know how you men feel about white women who've . . ." She turned away from him, dramatically using her one remaining argument, acutely aware it would sway him in one direction.

He grabbed her by the shoulders and pulled her around to face him. She lowered her head in mock shame. He put his hand under her chin and lifted it, forcing her to look at him. She squeezed her eyes tightly shut. She quivered in her attempt to hold back her tears. Timothy and her newborn guilt had been unknown faces when she had planned this perilous charade.

"Wha' truth, Rebecca? White women who do wha?" he sternly demanded.

She opened her eyes and glared at him. Her fury at Gray Eagle and herself and her pain at Bright Arrow's loss ripped at her heart. "What do you think they do with white women,

Lieutenant Moore! Would you have helped an Indian . . . slave? Would you have asked one to marry you? Would you even want to touch her? To even look at her? No, Timothy. If I had told you everything, he would still be your captive and I would be treated like dirt. It was bad enough to free him, but to tell you about my life in their camp . . . I couldn't. The past few days are the first time in weeks that I've felt clean, safe, happy, and loved. Loved?" she sneered bitterly. "Who could love or desire an Indian squaw? Does that answer your questions, sir? Have I spilled enough blood and guts upon your floor? God, how I wish I were a man!" she fiercely exploded to release some of the tension within her.

"Who did ye belong tae, Rebecca?" he questioned cruelly and persistently.

She glared at him. She had foolishly allowed Gray Eagle to shove her from his son's life. But the thing which hurt most was the fact her lover had not recognized this cruel ploy and prevented it. Or had it been clear to him last night? Had this ruse offered him the perfect solution to his dilemma? Had her lover also betrayed and deserted her?

This feigned drama was mysteriously becoming real to her, for in many ways it was. "Would you prefer to know how many instead? For some curious reason, a savage doesn't give you his name while he's raping you. Maybe four. Maybe six. Was there any reason to count such degrading acts of violence? Just to clarify my devious methods, what would you have said and done if I had confessed everything?'' she challenged, gluing her defiant gaze to his sullen one.

Annoying guilt chewed at his gut. He resisted her pull upon his conscience. ''Ye dinna trust or lik' me enough tae find out,'' he parried, not ready to commit himself in either direction.

''You're wrong, Timothy. I knew exactly what you would think and feel about me. I've seen women who were rescued and returned to their own kind. Enforced whoredom is cruel enough, but coerced into that same position by your own people is utterly barbaric. What now, sir? Am I to be hung or shot?''

''Ye sound mighty sassy about dying. Ye talk tae eager tae get it done quickly. Is tha' it, Rebecca? Ye want it done quickly an' easily?'' he probed.

''You and I both know what has to be done. I only want it ended, Timothy. When you've lived in Hell for weeks on end, death begins to look awfully good. If my parents are dead, my life is over. The Indians despise me; my own people hate me and wish me dead. Why fight the inevitable?'' she murmured despondently.

''Ye dinna think your treachery an' betrayal deserve some punishment first?''

''In your eyes, I'm certain they do. You've

wanted me since I first got here. This is only an excuse to justify your doing the very same thing to me which they did. I knew there was never any chance for us to marry. Even if you had been serious, you would have guessed the truth the moment you took me. Would you mind explaining something to me?" Before he could say yes or no, she asked, "If an ex-slave isn't good enough to marry or to be accepted again, why is she good enough to sleep with? Isn't making love far more personal and degrading than befriending such a soiled woman?" she reasoned. "Why risk danger to rescue her?"

"Ye confuse sex wi' luv, Rebecca," he corrected her.

She thought about that a moment, then calmly agreed, "I suppose you're right. But it shouldn't be that way," she mumbled to herself.

She walked over to gaze out the window. She was very still and silent. He wondered what she was thinking and feeling. Even if she spoke the truth, what difference did it make now? Soon, his men would know of her humiliating treachery. He could almost hear their mocking laughter and ridicule at his own infatuation with her.

"Rebecca?" he called out from behind her. She did not move or reply. "Ye'll probably fin' this amusin', but I was serious about marriage."

"Perhaps before you knew the truth, Timothy. But you wouldn't have felt the same once you learned it. I haven't known you long enough to bare my sullied soul. If I had married you without telling you, you would have despised me afterwards. I wish things could have been different. I wish I could have known you before . . . before I had nothing left to offer you," she stated, needing to hurt him as he was hurting her, was going to hurt her even more.

"Damnit, Rebecca!" he suddenly thundered at her. "Why did ye allow those savages tae tak' ye!" His hands were tied, and Gray Eagle had accomplished it. How that intrepid warrior must be laughing at his stupidity! A tiny girl and his worst enemy had bested him!

She turned and levelled her misty gaze upon him. "How was I supposed to stop them, Timothy? I would rather have died. But they didn't kill me! Afterwards, what did it matter? Only avoiding horrible torture mattered anymore. Is that my real crime, Timothy; I survived? If I'm so stained and wicked, then kill me here and now! Just let it be over," she begged him.

"It isn't tha' simple, lass. By now, my men know who was responsible. How would it look tae them if I allowed ye tae go free? My 'onor an' command 're at stake," he sullenly informed her.

"Honor? What could I possibly know about honor?" she cried. "Unless it's what you men do in its name!"

"Wha' else can I do?" he demanded, waiting to hear her response. What had she expected in response to this treachery?

Sensing his guile and indecision, she wearily shrugged her shoulders and stated, "If I were the commander, I would execute a dangerous traitor publicly. That should adequately restore your honor and authority. You certainly can't trust me anymore, not that I don't blame you. You can't release me because then you would never know if I returned to an Indian lover or if they killed me for you. You have to consider your image and respect among your men. You could imprison me, but that would require a guard and free food. You claim the Indians probably killed my family by now, so I could never prove my motives for releasing Bright Arrow. It seems quite clear to me. I did release him. I did deceive you. Guilty as charged, sir. The penalty is death. When? As quickly as possible. How? Since you were the one I humiliated and betrayed, you should kill me. Bare hands or knife or gunshot? Does it really matter?" she challenged.

"Ye be takin' this mighty calmly, dinna ye think?"

"No, Timothy. But I've lived in fear for a long time. I've seen people die horrible deaths every day for weeks. Somehow its threat doesn't sting so harshly anymore. Death isn't so awful, only the length of time it requires. Do you know how long it takes a man to die from thousands of knife slashes? Have you ever seen a man watch his own heart cut out? Or seen a man's body accept twenty arrows at once? Or a girl of fourteen raped over and over until she's mindless or dead? What do you honestly know about Indian slavery! I did what I had to. Now, you must do the same. What horror or pain could you possibly inflict upon me that I have not already witnessed or endured?"

"I wish I knew if ye words 're true. If only I could trust ye, Rebecca . . ."

"You can't; I made that impossible," she candidly declared, dismaying him. "After all these weeks of pain, it'll finally be over . . ."

"If I let ye escape, wad ye go back tae the Sioux camp? Wad ye be safe there?"

"If you sent me out there, you would be killing me just as surely as if you shot me. You say you know the Indians, particularly Gray Eagle. Could any white woman be safe and happy in his camp? You asked if I was his whore. No, Timothy; he has never touched me. You also asked if I was Bright Arrow's whore. If his raping me makes me his whore, then yes. But I am not his squaw. As for their accepting me, no. They despise all whites, including defenseless women. Do you know what it took to let him go after what he's done to me?" She laughed coldly and asked, "Do you want to know what he said to me before he slipped out the door? He laughed in my face and called me a 'witkowin.' Do you know what that word means, Timothy? It means whore; I've heard it enough to know.''

"Ye slep' wi' Bright Ar'er?" he snarled, enraged.

"Slept? No." She waited for his next question.

"Ye know wha' I meant! Did he mak' luv tae ye?" he snapped.

"Love? No. You just explained the vast difference a moment ago. Sex is not love, remember?''

He pounded his fist into his open hand. "I should hae killed the bastard! Do ye think I could tak' his leavin's?'' he scoffed insensitively.

"No, Timothy. I knew you couldn't. No white man would. Why do you think I kept silent? Even love can't be that forgiving and unselfish. But if I had known Gray Eagle was lying, I would have killed Bright Arrow myself," she lied. "Gray Eagle would like nothing better than for you to hang me.''

"If ye mak' any attempt tae leave this room, I'll kill ye wi' the slowness of ae turtle. I hae some thinkin' tae do. I'll warn ye now, lass; ye bes' decide tae tell the truth." He whirled and left. The door clicked as it locked from the outside. He called through the door, "There's ae guard outside the window. Dinna force me tae

428

kill ye afore I hae time tae mak' the right decision.''

She sat down upon her bed. All appeared hopeless and spoiled now. All she could do was wait to die . . . Betrayed by my love, the heart-rending words echoed in her turbulent mind.

It was very late the next afternoon before anyone came to her stuffy room. She had been denied food and company. The water in the pitcher had been used up the previous morning. Thankfully the chamber pot did not reek from its daily disregard. She had cried until there were no more tears to call forth. The lantern would not light without oil and there were no candles available. So, she sat huddled upon her bunk: alone, hungry, thirsty, and numb. Yet, she savored the anguish and darkness, for they suited her mood. For what she had done, she deserved fatal punishment. The solitude, rejection, and denial of physical needs took its toll. She became listless and somber. She had been given too much time alone. The pains and sacrifices of the past two years fused into one massive agony, creating a void of total despair, gradually engulfing her in a protective world of unreality.

The door opened and in stepped Timothy Moore. She never even glanced in his direction. She continued to stare unseeingly at the floor. He came forward and stood before her line of vision. No reaction.

"Hae ye decided tae tell the whole truth yet? It's been two days."

Nothing. He squatted down, his face only inches from hers. Nothing. Her eyes were blank, as was her face. "I've decided tae accept ye story since I canna prove otherwise," he announced into the stillness. "Ye can remain 'ere an' work for me an' my men."

Nothing. "Wad ye lik' something tae eat? Perhaps ae hot bath?" he tempted the girl.

"Rebecca? Wha' 're ye tryin' tae pull now?" he stormed, hoping to startle her out of this remote mood. "Suit yeself. The door's unlocked. I'll hae some water an' food sent in." He left, leaving the door ajar.

Rebecca didn't even notice. She had forced herself into a world where there was no pain. It was so quiet and peaceful there. Reality didn't exist; physical pain didn't exist. Deeper and deeper she swam into this blissful, protective ocean of nothingness. Soon, her father would swim out to meet her and guide her safely to the other shore . . .

When Timothy came back hours later, the food was chilled and untouched. The bath had not been used; it, too, was cold. She hadn't moved. What was the matter with her?

He tried to lift her head, but her body was nearly rigid. Her flesh was clammy. He leaned over, sighing with relief when he detected a

faint heartbeat. Was she willing herself to die?
Was such a thing possible?

He shook her. He slapped her several times.
Nothing. Nothing except red prints upon her
ashen cheeks. She hadn't even winced or
reacted. Her eyes remained dull and glassy. She
couldn't be faking this curious state! Had she
endured the hell which she had described? Had
her pain become too much for her? During the
war, he had witnessed mindless shock before.

A knock sounded upon his office door. He left
her to go answer it. The scout Fire-Brand
entered, keenly observing the girl who sat upon
the lieutenant's bunk in a deep trance.

He spoke with assurance, "I have learned the
facts you seek. The girl spoke the truth. I came
to where warriors were camped. They laughed
and talked of the trick they had played upon her
and her family. One called Deer-Stalker spoke
of how they tortured her people until she agreed
to free Bright Arrow. They told her she could
earn her freedom and that of her family. They
were all slain before she was halfway to the fort.
They spoke of taking a knife from her one night
when she attempted to kill herself. They spoke
of how they cut pieces of flesh from her mother's
body each time she refused to pleasure them.
They spoke of a younger girl about twelve.
They told the one called Rebecca they would
ravish the child if she did not free Bright Arrow.
Another called Winter Owl talked of how Gray

Eagle himself pledged his word of honor she and her family could go free if they left the land of the Oglala. Once she agreed, they treated her kindly. Bright Arrow was with the warriors I sighted. He said he did not kill her, but left her to face the hatred and punishment of her own people. All laughed at his cunning and our foolishness."

"Sae, she was tellin' the truth after all? Nae wonder she agreed tae his plans. She should hae trusted me, Fire-Brand. I could hae helped her," he said sadly.

"How could she trust any man after what was done to her?" the scout commented. "She is young. That was much cruelty for the heart and mind of one such as she. It was a cunning trick, for no one guessed it. There is more. The warriors spoke of a joint meeting of the chiefs of all tribes. Deer-Stalker said each chief was to bring his two band leaders and meet with the others at the place where the giant river and the little join to become one. They are to speak of war. The vote will be taken."

"When, Fire-Brand? If we could surprise them an' wipe them out, each tribe wad be at loose ends. It wad tak' months tae regroup. By tha' time, we could hae more men an' supplies 'ere an' ready." His excitement was evident.

"But it would require most of the men to make a successful raid upon that camp! You cannot leave the fort with so few men to guard her!'' he reasoned.

''This is our big chance, Fire-Brand. We could end this new uprisin' wi' one deadly blow. Nae tribe wad attack while their chief was parlaying for joint warfare. When is this meeting tae tak' place?'' he softly demanded, suspense washing over him.

''In one moon,'' he calmly replied. ''But to leave the fort unguarded invites danger.''

''Tomor'er night! Guid, Fire-Brand. Ye call the officers together in the cookhouse. We hae some plannin' tae do. The fort'll be safe for one dae.''

Timothy returned to Rebecca's side. He did not notice the sly look upon the scout's face. Fire-Brand watched the girl for a moment. His coming report to Bright Arrow would not sit well with that fierce warrior. He would surely make the lieutenant pay dearly for abusing his woman! Moore was a fool. All it took was a few devious words to convince him of the girl's innocence . . . He wondered what Moore had done to her to take away her great courage and cunning. Bright Arrow was lucky; for she possessed the heart of a warrior, the gentleness of a doe, the cunning of a fox, and the beauty of a rare flower. It was not so incredible after all that the intrepid warrior wanted her back in his tepee, even though she was white. Still, she was the daughter of Koda Joe, a white friend to many Indian tribes.

Timothy could find no way to make Rebecca respond to him. The doctor came to check her and to sedate her with laudanum. The rigidness of her body lessened and color gradually returned to her cheeks. Her respiration grew stronger. "She'll be out a day or two. See she gets water and soup forced into 'er. I'll see 'er again when she comes around. Just shock, sir. I've seen it lots of times in cases like hers. The mind reaches a point where it can't accept anymore torment. It sort of hides from real life until it can rest and heal some of the anguish. She's mighty young to have been through so much. Might never be the same or could be just fine, if things are better when she wakes up."

"I'll be leavin' in the morning. I wan ye tae tak' care o' her for me. We know she let him go, but she had guid reason. Don't matter anyway. Looks lik' we'll ambush ae meetin' of all chiefs an' head warriors tomor'er night. This war's about o'er, Doc," he declared confidently. He sighed heavily to release pent-up tension.

"What about this girl?" the doctor speculated.

Timothy gazed down at her. He tenderly caressed her bruised cheek and stroked her tangled hair. "As soon as she's well enough, I'll marry 'er," he announced.

"You'll what!" Doc exclaimed in amazement. "But she's a squaw! You can't!"

"I'll admit she's slightly used goods, Doc. But

she's somethin' special. I hae ae long look at the real girl when she briefly forgot who an' wha' she is an' why she was sent 'ere. She hae ae smile which could light up the darkes' night. She's gentle an' smart. In ae way, she's still pure in mind an' body. She's everythin' I've wanted an' needed in ae woman. I'd be ae fool tae let wha' happened stand 'tween us. She wasn't tae blame an' we both know it.''

"Think she'll accept you?" Doc Weldon inquired.

"If for nae other reason than tae prevent ae life o' whoredom 'ere. In time she'll return my love an' know I did only wha' I was forced tae do in response tae her treachery.''

"What about the men? What'll they say?"

"I dinna gie ae fig!" Timothy exclaimed. "I'll gie 'em the facts. Besides, my tour o' duty is up 'ere in ae few months. We'll head back tae Tennessee an' start ae new life.''

"Isn't there another woman waiting for you back there?" he reminded him of the southern girl he had spoken of before.

"Yep! But she canna compare wi' Rebecca. I've found ae dream, Doc, an' I dinna intend tae wake up for ae long time.''

"In that case, I'll take real good care of her, sir,'' he promised, then chuckled heartily. "She is mighty pretty,'' Doc commented enviously just before both men left for the meeting.

Moore gradually related the facts which Fire-

435

Brand had reported to him, including the imminent war council and Rebecca's coerced part in Bright Arrow's escape. He promptly ordered no discussion about Rebecca, telling them she was in his hands from now on. Hearing colored facts and recalling Moore's attachment to her, this didn't seem so shocking to anyone except Smith. It was evident that Smith still craved her for himself; yet, he wisely yielded to Moore's greater size and rank.

The officers and scout talked of their plans to surprise the war council and kill everyone present. The eagerness to have this matter settled dulled their wits. This reckless and arrogant lot of men were excessively self-assured of their tactics and skills. Even being fully aware of the cunning of Gray Eagle, they never once speculated upon an attack upon this fort while most of the troops were out chasing an illusive camp! They never once considered they might be riding into an ambush. The lie was too convincing and compelling to ignore or to reason out. Snared by their hatred and conceit, they would fall right into the crafty scheme of Gray Eagle . . .

Just before midday, the troops were called together to head out. They had waited until the last minute to prevent being sighted by the chiefs at the war council. Sticking close to the forest, they could conceal themselves; yet, this tactic would slow their arrival until nightfall.

They were to surround the camp and attack at the sound of the first shot. Everyone was to be slain. Prisoners would invite an attack upon the fort by warriors determined to free their chiefs. With all chiefs and leaders slain, confusion and disunity would rule for a long time as others battled for the right to become the next chiefs and leaders. Then the soldiers would constantly harass and conquer the weakened, disputing tribes. The plans seemed faultless. One dauntless act could render this entire area powerless and in the white man's undisputed control. Or so they naively believed. . . .

But once again, they had underestimated the resolve and intelligence of Gray Eagle. Their so-called half-breed scout Fire-Brand was none other than the illustrious son of Night-Hawk, chief of the Sisseton tribe, member of the awesome Sioux Nation. Fire-Brand had slowly worked his way into their confidence by permitting the sacrifice of several braves and by leading raids upon his alleged enemies, the Indians. Proven trustworthy and competent, he could now lead these white foes into total defeat. This new fort which stood upon the face of Mother Earth in the midst of their lands would be destroyed this very night! Without its protection, the frightened settlers would hurry back to their own lands. Peace would soon rule their plains and forests again.

Fire-Brand raged against the sluggishness of

their plans. Eventually, he would have opened the gates in the darkness to permit his warriors to enter here and wipe out this bold threat against them. For in that careful delay to avoid suspicion and to insure success, his father had been slain and Bright Arrow captured. For all his anger and hatred, he had done nothing to bring suspicion upon himself which might deny revenge against them.

Rebecca had unwittingly saved Fire-Brand from discovery by releasing Bright Arrow. He had made it a point to overhear her explanation and to use it to gain her time and kindness until she could be rescued and returned to Bright Arrow's side. She had won Fire-Brand's respect with her courage, love, and daring. She had won his gratitude by allowing him this chance to avenge his father's slaughter.

If Bright Arrow cannot bring himself to keep you in his tepee, Fire-Brand thought, then I will make trade for you, Little One . . . If given the chance, your coups would shine as brightly as our own! Your Indian heart is more important than your white skin! Your blood will join with ours and you will become one of us, as with Koda Joe your father. You have earned this right, Little One. You have earned it . . .

The men mounted up, two abreast. The gates were opened wide and they rode eastward to face humiliation and danger. The gates closed, sealing the remaining whites in a world as lost to reality as Rebecca was.

From the forest to the west of the fort, hard black eyes observed this military action. A smug grin curled up the corners of his sensual lips. He mused, White-eyes are mindless. They ride away in search of a sweet dream which only the Indian will know and taste this day. To the puissant man at his side he declared, "You are wise, Father. See how they rush to destroy us. Fire-Brand says she was captured. If they have harmed her, I will slay them all. Rebecca is mine. Is this not so?" Bright Arrow softly asked.

Gray Eagle's resigned gaze met and locked with his son's. "This is so . . ." he gravely concurred, trying to suppress his annoyance at himself for the careless flaw in his plan. He should have told Rebecca to return with his son under such favorable conditions as were presented that portentous night. She and Bright Arrow must have been too distracted to realize there had been no reason for her to remain behind!

Chapter Fifteen

The three largest units from Fort Dakota
gingerly made their way through the dense
forest, clinging to the protective cover of the
trees and underbrush. The troops travelled
silently, each man preparing himself for what
was to come at nightfall and for maintaining
secrecy.

About mid-afternoon, Fire-Brand reined in
his horse to allow Moore to ride up beside him.
The scout's voice was low and guarded. He
suggested that he and Private Hansley move on
ahead to scout out the approaching area. He
told Moore he would send Hansley back with a
warning if necessary. Otherwise, they were to
join up at a large rock formation just before they
reached the Indians' rendezvous point.

"We would not wish to ride into an ambush
or alert hidden scouts. If we find any braves

posted along the way, we will dispose of them. You must keep the men and horses quiet. The warriors must not be alerted to our presence before we attack.''

Moore readily agreed with these precautions. Hansley was informed of their plans. He and Fire-Brand rode off into the trees. Hansley thought it strange when they veered off to the east of the trail, but said nothing. He assumed the scout knew what he was doing. They rode for a time, then Fire-Brand halted abruptly. He motioned for Hansley to come up beside him. He placed a finger to his lips for silence, disarming Hansley completely.

The sandy-haired man in his early twenties did as commanded. Fire-Brand mutely pointed at something to their left. Hansley shifted in his saddle to look that way, dreading to imagine what he might see there. A searing pain shot through his body. He glanced down at the knife buried in his chest. Horror flooded his sea-blue eyes. He gaped at the man at his side, the man who had ridden with him many times.

Fire-Brand's face was impassive. His jet eyes were indifferent to his malevolent deed. His aura was menacing and arrogant. His gaze went to the protruding knife and the stream of blood flowing down Hansley's chest. "Soon you will die, White Dog. All white-eyes will die. You take our lands. You defy our laws and soil our women. You steal animals and destroy things which are ours. Your Bluecoat friends ride into a trap. The fort will soon be attacked. All Bluecoats will die this very day. I am Fire-Brand, son of the Sisseton chief Night-Hawk which your people killed."

Hansley's anguish and terror were written upon his drawn face. He knew he was dying. He knew the fort and the troops were powerless against a planned assault. He wished he had the strength to pull his gun and kill this treacherous man. He shuddered and fell to the hard ground, the fall increasing his pain. The last thing he knew was Fire-Brand's chilling look . . .

Fire-Brand slipped off his horse's back. He concealed Hansley's body in the underbrush. He took the animal's reins and rode back toward the fort to join up with Gray Eagle's party. He laughed to himself. Moore's troops would have a bitter skirmish upon their hands at nightfall! They would be lucky if any of them survived! Three small units held no chance against the mighty warriors of four tribes who had united to share this victory!

Fire-Brand gave the pre-arranged signal: three hoots of a horned owl. An answer came immediately. He headed in that direction. By dusk, a large band of warriors from both tribes had stealthily surrounded the fort. At the distressing news about Rebecca's health, the waiting seemed endless for Bright Arrow.

Gray Eagle looked at Fire-Brand and nodded.

It was time. A tingling excitement suffused him. The scout mounted up again, sagging in his saddle. He galloped headlong toward the fort gate. "Stacy! You there, Sentry! Open up! It's me, Fire-Brand! The others are coming in! It was a trap! Lots of wounded!" he shouted lie after lie.

The gates swung open wide in anticipation of the troop's rapid arrival. "Keep a sharp eye out for 'em! I'll alert the others," he called out as he rode past the stunned guard. But instead, he made his way around the fort's walls, opening all other gates to allow his warriors to enter.

Before the remaining soldiers could be aroused and armed, the fort was overrun with Indians. Taken by surprise, it did not take long for them to attain their bloody victory. Fire-Brand called out to Bright Arrow, "The girl you seek lies in that place." He pointed out Moore's office, then hurried off to engage in this long-awaited bout of vengeance. The fruit of his labor would soon taste sweet!

Bright Arrow entered the darkened quarters. His apprehensive search revealed her limp body upon the narrow bunk. Fire-Brand had fortunately informed him of the sleeping medicine which they had given to her. He wrapped her in a blanket and carried her back to his waiting horse. He left the fort to wait for the others out of the line of danger.

His panicked eyes scanned her pale face and

the bruises there. At least she was alive! He held her possessively and snugly. It felt good to have her body against his. He had feared to never see or touch her again. He would never permit anyone to ever harm her.

Two hours later, others joined him. The few whites which still lived were now captives. The new fort lay in burning ruins, devastated just like the old one. The band of Sisseton warriors headed for home with Fire-Brand as their new chief. The band of Oglala warriors rode out as well. They rode all night, only stopping occasionally to rest their horses or to water them.

Rebecca did not awaken the entire trip. Bright Arrow's worried gaze frequently studied her ashen face and still body. Even his father's words of encouragement failed to lift his dismal spirits and to lessen his fears. She could not die! Not now!

Shalee came out to greet them, her wide eyes checking each man for wounds. Finding none, her attention went to Rebecca. "Is she hurt, Bright Arrow? Did they harm her?" she asked anxiously.

"Yes, Mother. But I will make her well again. Fire-Brand said they gave her medicine to make her sleep. When she awakens, she will see me first. She will know all is well."

He carried her into their tepee and laid her upon his mat. Shalee and Gray Eagle followed after him. Gray Eagle explained Rebecca's weakened condition and harsh treatment to Shalee. The Indian princess grimaced in anguish. She helped her son care for his white slave. They carefully and tenderly forced water and nourishing soup down her throat. They kept her warm.

There was a mysterious tension and curious excitement in Shalee which neither warrior could fathom. Each time this strange mood was questioned, Shalee would smile mischievously and promise to tell them later. First, she needed to speak privately with Rebecca Kenny to resolve her own suspicions and hopes. Too, there was a tormenting secret she must soon relate to her husband which might end these destructive echoes from his past, a dark secret which his dying father had confessed to her in his last days of failing health, a weighty secret which should have been revealed eighteen winters ago. Shalee winced at the pain and anguish that carefully guarded secret had wreaked upon all their lives. She alone held the key to release them from the past.

It was mid-morning the following day before Rebecca began to moan and to stir. Elation and suspense brightened the young warrior's eyes. He waited apprehensively for her to open hers. He leaned over her prone body and tenderly stroked her damp hair. He spoke softly to her, calling her from her land of protective darkness and rosy dreams.

Gray Eagle and Shalee sat upon their mat, knowing this first moment of blissful reunion belonged to them. Both had faced death and separation; both had endured pain and humiliation. This would be a time of healing and accepting for them. Gray Eagle's arm went around his wife. Too late he had caught the perilous mistake in their frantic plans. Even at great risk, Rebecca should have fled with his son. Gray Eagle pulled Shalee's body close to his. She snuggled against him and laid her dark chestnut head upon his bronze chest. He kissed the top of her head and rested his cheek there. "Soon the past will die, my love," she whispered.

Rebecca's eyes struggled to open. Her body felt strangely light, oddly detached. Her mind was hazy and sluggish. Her mouth was dry. She fought to regain her senses and to clear her vision. She stared at him in disbelief. Was she dreaming? Was she dead? Her hand reached up to touch him, to ascertain these facts.

Her weak voice questioned, "Bright Arrow?"

He beamed, white teeth revealed in a striking smile, eyes glowing with liquid black fire. He caught her shaky hand before it could fall back to her chest. He kissed it over and over. "I feared you had left me forever. You have slept many days. I have not left your side since I took you from the fort. You are safe, Rebecca. Bright

Arrow will allow no man to harm you again. You are my woman. I came for you just as you came for me."

"You came back for me? Why?" she murmured in utter perplexity.

"For the same reason you came for me," he replied softly, his ebony eyes revealing love and concern.

"That isn't possible. Your father would never allow it. You're Indian," she reasoned against thinking her prayers and dreams had been answered.

"You are white. Yet, you love me. Is that impossible?" he chided.

"That's different," she argued faintly, fearing the chief's reaction to her daring rescue and return. Her dazed mind had difficulty accepting or reasoning out this incredible news.

"How so?" he teased, ignorant of her fears and suspicions.

"Your father and your people would never permit it," she weakly debated.

"My father says you are mine. The Oglala say you are mine. I say you are mine. Do you say otherwise? Many Oglala helped me rescue you from the fort," he delivered this shocking news to the wide-eyed girl.

"They said I could stay here?" she asked in astonishment. "They helped to free me? Even your father?"

"Yes. To offer your life for mine was a great

deed. It took much love and courage. When you are well, Wi will mingle our bloods. You will become as an Indian. You will be my woman."

"Because I saved your life?" she exclaimed.

"Yes."

"But I did it because I love you, not to win their favor and acceptance. I could not let you die." Her sleepy eyes caressed his handsome face.

"They know this. Many helped with your rescue. The scout at the fort was the son of the Sisseton chief who was killed when they captured me. He came to us and told of your capture. He led the attack against the fort."

She did not dare ask about the fate of the fort. She was here with the man she loved. She would become as one of them. She would live out her days with Bright Arrow and his people. Unaware of the presence of his parents, she smiled faintly and said, "I am blessed to be owned by you, Bright Arrow. One day you will be the great warrior and chief which your father is. In spite of all, I like him very much. He trusted me, Bright Arrow," she said in a tone of amazement. "He is wise and brave. I will be happy here. Your mother is so kind and beautiful. I will be good to them. I will obey you and your laws. I will give you no reason to be sorry for your love and trust."

Her lids drooped. He noted her fatigue and weakness. "Sleep, Rebecca. There will be time for talk later. I love you. I will protect you forever."

She smiled. "I love you, too," she murmured, then closed her eyes.

"Come, my son," the older warrior called out. "Let us go and walk together. Your life now reflects my past one as the stream mirrors my image when I look into her shiny face. We must speak of ways to stop your steps from following mine. There are many words we must speak to each other."

The two men arose and departed, each casting another look at the woman he loved and desired above all others. Rebecca's eyes remained closed as if already asleep. Shalee returned the heated look from her beloved husband who had shared so much love and pain with her.

Shalee moved to stand over Rebecca. She tenderly and hopefully gazed down at the youthful white girl, knowing how weak and exhausted she must be, dreading to have this new ray of hope dashed by her coming words, and needing to solve this haunting riddle which had plagued her mind since Rebecca's recent departure. If this was the time for ending nightmares and inspiring new dreams, she must act quickly.

She knelt beside the white girl and softly entreated her to wakefulness, "Rebecca? I must speak with you."

Rebecca's heavy lids fluttered and her amber

eyes opened slowly. "Did you say something, Shalee?" she faintly questioned.

Shalee bravely met her probing gaze and replied clearly, "Yes, Rebecca. You must answer two questions for me."

Rebecca stared at her entreating gaze and then at her soft lips. "You speak perfect English; I do not understand."

Comprehending there was only one way to win her trust and to explain her talent, she toughened her heart and asserted the one lie which must remain a secret for all time. "When I was two winters old, whites kidnapped me from my father's camp and took me far away from my people. My mother was Black Cloud's white squaw. Because of my skin color and green eyes, the whites believed me also white. I was raised as the daughter of a white couple. Long ago we came to the land of the Sioux. I met Gray Eagle and fell in love with him. When my real identity was brought to light, we were allowed to join in marriage. Because of the hostility between the white man and the Indian, my white blood has been ignored."

She watched Rebecca closely as she related this astonishing tale. "I first met Gray Eagle as his white enemy. For a time, I lived as his white captive before my real identity was brought to light. This is why I can feel the shame and agony which you now experience. Gray Eagle also recalls what it was like to face the shame and weakness of loving an enemy. He wished to spare our son those same torments. Do you understand what I am telling you, Rebecca?''

"Yes, Shalee. But you are an Indian princess, and I am all white. To protect the honor and happiness of your son is only natural. I wish it were not so, but I cannot change who and what I am.''

"Gray Eagle does not wish for Bright Arrow's taking of you to remind others that I also carry white blood. When the Cheyenne warrior came to challenge Bright Arrow, he taunted them before our people, for both had chosen a white woman over one of their own kind. This could cause much resentment. A chief cannot allow his name and leadership to be blackened by such a defeat.''

"I would do nothing to disgrace him or to hurt him,'' Rebecca vowed honestly.

"We often shame and hurt those we love without meaning to, Rebecca. How old are you?'' the Indian princess questioned in a curious tone.

"Seventeen. Why?'' she wondered aloud at this unexpected query.

"When were you born?'' Shalee went on, ignoring the girl's curiosity.

"In August of '78. Why?'' Rebecca questioned again, sensing this talk was important to the Indian princess for some odd reason.

"I had thought you older than my son. He

was born in February of '78. When Joe last visited us, he spoke of the child Mary was expecting. That was in June of '77. I am confused. You said you had no other family." Shalee prayed Rebecca would reveal the answers which she desperately needed to hear.

"My mother lost her first child during that summer. She became pregnant with me in November. Was that the last time you saw my father?"

"Yes. I was saddened to hear of his death and that of your mother. Joe was our friend. His daughter will also be our friend. Do not fear, Rebecca, you will be safe and happy here with us. Perhaps in time, others will forget you are white. I pray you and Bright Arrow will come to share the same strong love which is between me and my husband. You must rest now."

"Shalee, may I ask one question?" she inquired, but rushed on before she could reply, "Who is this Powchutu? Why does his name spark such anger?"

Shalee sighed heavily. "Once long ago, he was like a brother to me. But I was the woman he loved and desired. He was obsessed with winning me from Gray Eagle. He did many wicked and painful things to us. He became a vengeful and powerful enemy. He kidnapped me from Gray Eagle's side and took me far away. There was an accident and I lost the child I was carrying. I almost died. We have longed for another child, but I seemed unable to bear another one. While I was ill, it was your father who rescued me and returned me here to Gray Eagle. To hear Powchutu's name only brings back those terrible times of anguish. For a time, Gray Eagle believed I loved Powchutu and had chosen him. Peace and love were a long and difficult time in coming to us. Now, Powchutu's spirit returns to haunt us once more. Please do not ever speak his name again. To do so will only anger Gray Eagle and cause him to resent you. Powchutu is dead; let his evil soul remain buried for all our sakes.''

"I will do as you say. I promise never to mention his name again. In time, I pray your husband will come to respect and to like me as I do him.''

Shalee smiled affectionately. "Sleep now. All will be well again soon." For once, guilt did not fill her heart.

Shalee left to seek her husband with the information which she hoped would settle their past life, once and for all time. When she came to where her two men were standing, she smiled and embraced each of them. Bright Arrow left them to return to his tepee to watch over his love.

Shalee studied her husband closely. He seemed relaxed, and yet subtly apprehensive. He looked serene, and yet slightly worried. "This matter still troubles you deeply, my husband?" she ventured, dreading to broach the subject which plagued him.

"There is but one matter which haunts me, my love. I pray that time will heal its wounds and will halt its pull upon me."

"Perhaps what I must say to you will sever the strings which bind you so fiercely to the past. In my fear and panic, I ignored several things which Rebecca had said to me. I do not wish to displease you or to hurt you, my love, but I questioned her to learn the truth about this vital matter."

At his annoyed look, she quickly rushed on to expose her crucial information. "Rebecca is not the daughter of Powchutu. As with our first child, Mary lost her first one before it could be born. In all truth, my husband, Rebecca is Joe's daughter. She is his child in name and in blood. She was born during the last buffalo season; she is not yet eighteen winters old. There is no way she could be Powchutu's child, for he died before both the spring and winter buffalo hunts in the year before our son was born. As we spoke, she told me of the day she was born and of the loss of Mary's first child. She is Joe Kenny's daughter, my love," she stressed once more, making sure he was grasping the depth of her news.

"You spoke of Powchutu with Rebecca?" Gray Eagle asked in disbelief.

"Only to say he was a past enemy and to never speak his name again. Rebecca is young and sensitive. We must never tell her of the love between her mother and him. Perhaps it was never meant for the child of Powchutu to be born to face the evil which his father left behind. Our son loves and desires the daughter of our past friend, not our treacherous enemy. We must accept her as our new friend. Do we not owe her father this much, my love? In time, I pray others will accept her and her place within his life."

Gray Eagle contemplated this startling news. "She is in truth the daughter of Koda Joe? Perhaps you were right when you said the Great Spirit would reveal her purpose here. Can it be He shows me the scout's evil is gone forever? Did He lead her here to us for love and protection in exchange for the good deeds of her real father? Just as Koda Joe saved your life, she has saved the life of our son. If only she were Indian . . ." he murmured regretfully.

"Sadly she is not, my love, and she never will be. Until Indian hearts soften toward her, she must remain as his white captive. Who can say what will come with the new sun? The Great Spirit may find some way to make her Indian," she jested.

"Is there more you wish to tell me?" he asked, pulling her into his possessive embrace.

She laid her face against his hard, smooth chest and sighed in contentment. She moved her hands up and down his stalwart frame. Powchutu was dead; Joe and Mary were gone forever. Rebecca was here and safe; their son was at their side. The whites and Bluecoats had once more been halted for a time. A new child was growing within her body, their child, a child of love which would be a mixture of love and acceptance from both worlds. What purpose could that dark secret serve? How could she tell her husband the dying words of his own father? How could she tell this invincible warrior, this noble chief of the Sioux, this man who was the very air she breathed, that his worst enemy— that traitorous half-breed scout who had nearly destroyed their lives and happiness—was his half brother? How could she tell her lover that the man he had despised and battled many times was his own father's son, his own brother?

She unwillingly recalled the many times those years ago she had emotionally responded to the similarities in their looks, personalities, and traits. How she wished Running Wolf had never revealed this agonizing truth to her. How she wished Running Wolf had unselfishly proclaimed Powchutu as his son, for his mother was also Indian. What tragic irony; he had never been born a despicable half-breed! In truth, Powchutu was the son of a great Sioux chief and an Indian maiden from another tribe, a maiden who had been sold to a French trapper while carrying Running Wolf's son. Perhaps the envy and bitterness which drove him to such desperate and tormenting lengths would never have existed. How could she tell her love that the man who had lived and died as his bitter enemy carried his own blood? She could not. This secret must join the others which had briefly echoed from the distant past and now lay silent.

She hugged her lover fiercely and declared, "The past is dead, my love, only our bright future lives. Soon we will lose one son to his new love, only to gain another child when the snows refresh our lands. What shall we call our new son?" she asked her husband.

"What if this son is a daughter?" he jested in return, hope and joy flooding his powerful body, refreshing his spirit, cleansing his heart of the past.

She laughed merrily. "Perhaps our next child will be a daughter, but this one is another son. Until he seeks his vision and new name, we shall call him Wanmdi Taopi."

He grinned roguishly. "What do you need with a Little Eagle when you already possess a mighty Eagle?" he teased her, pleased with her choice. "It will be as you wish, wife. Come, let us see to our son and Joe's daughter."

She radiated the happiness and relief which flowed within her. "I love you with all my heart, Gray Eagle. If I have you forever, it still would not be long enough."

Before they could head back to their tepee, Bright Arrow returned to speak with them. He was grinning in satisfaction and pleasure. "In time, our people will come to accept Rebecca; this I know with all my heart. She brings such love and joy to my life. I could not give her up. We must never tell her about her real father, for it would hurt her deeply."

Gray Eagle and Shalee exchanged smiles and mysterious looks. When questioned about this odd behavior, they related the truth about Rebecca's father. "She is the child of your friend Joe Kenny?" he asked in disbelief.

"Yes, my son. The evil spirit of Powchutu now rests forever. The Great Spirit sent her to us for love and protection. He also wished to end this bitterness which had lived within my heart for many winters. We will never speak his name again in the tepee of Gray Eagle."

"She is happy here, Father. I will protect her from all harm. Yesterday's sun has gone forever. I will ask no more questions. The past must sleep once more."

Gray Eagle smiled at his son who was very much a man now. "This is good, Bright Arrow. At your side, the others will one day forget she is white. The moon will surely come when you two can join in honor. The Great Spirit was wise in sending her to us. She did not call the past to life; she dispelled its evil spirits forever. One day, the daughter of Joe Kenny will become Oglala."

Both Shalee and Bright Arrow glowed with love and respect for this powerful man. The war was over; the perilous echoes had ceased. Gray Eagle said, "Come, wife. We will speak of happy things. Our son can guard his woman."

Shalee fondly embraced her firstborn son, then took the hand of her husband to stroll in the cool forest.

In serene silence, they walked until they came to a private place. He halted and gazed all around him. "For a time, peace will rule our lands and hearts once more. I have much to live for, my lovely Grass Eyes. Perhaps it is time I learn to speak words of truce with the white man. They are many; more will come. They cannot be halted forever. There must be truce between us. Many have died and more will die unless the hatred is prevented with peace. I pray the Great Spirit will guide me on this new and dangerous path."

Boundless love consumed Shalee. "You are wise, my husband. If there is to be peace and survival, someone must take the first step in friendship. My heart sings at your wisdom and generosity. I do not wish to see my husband or my sons killed by the white man. We must strive for peace, if they will permit it. My heart is heavy with the fear they will not. Greedy men do not peacefully share what they can wholly take by force. I will pray for this peace we need."

He held her tightly against his towering body. "The echoes have quieted to a soft and mellow song. Its deadly chant no longer calls out warnings to me. From that first moment Rebecca came to us, you were right. She belongs in our tepee and with our son. There is no hatred or bitterness within me now. Powchutu no longer haunts me. I feel as though a heavy rock has been lifted from my body. Only joy flows within me, joy and love for you and our son."

She had made the correct decision in remaining silent about Powchutu's identity. She would never know why Running Wolf had denied his other son, but it was too late for either of them. She smiled. "I love you. Each day that love grows stronger and richer. We will never speak of the past again. Alisha Williams can rest peacefully in another time and place. At last, I am only Shalee, wife of Gray Eagle and mother of Bright Arrow. I am Oglala in spirit and heart."

He laughed devilishly and teased, completely relaxed for the first time in weeks, "Have you forgotten the child which grows within you? There is another to love and protect now."

She laughed merrily and hugged him again. "How could I forget a child of such great love who makes his presence known each day? We have waited and prayed so long for another child. I hope it is a boy to follow his father and his older brother. Everyone is safe and happy again. We are very lucky, my valiant husband." She placed her hand over the bronze one which was caressing her stomach.

She giggled like a young girl and mischievously ventured, "I think perhaps Bright Arrow and Rebecca should plan a tepee of their own. I find my need for you grows greater every day, as does my body with our child. I wish you all to myself before this new son demands our time and energy."

He chuckled. His grin tugged at her racing heart. "Before too many moons pass, I will speak to him about this selfish demand of yours. He must learn that white women are shy upon the mats before others. He will soon see this and wish his own tepee."

"You!" she playfully squealed at him, then laughed. She seductively taunted, "What would the indomitable Gray Eagle, the legendary warrior of the Plains, know of white women and their secret passions? He is joined to Shalee, a very jealous and possessive Si-ha Sapa princess."

Their eyes met, forest green with midnight black, and fused with smoldering passion. He tightened his embrace around her. His sensual lips came down upon hers in a blaze of ageless love and renewed commitment. As they sank to the lush grass to fuse their bodies as their hearts, the only echoes of yesterday which rang out were the melodious words: a child, a child, another child . . .